VAMPIRE CABBIE

VAMPIRE CABBIE

FRED SCHEPARTZ

MOBIUS
BOOKS

A publication of Mobius Books

Mobius Books
505 Christianson Ave.
Madison, WI 53714

Copyright © 2007 by Fred Schepartz

Cover Art by Jordan Castillo Price

Killdozer lyrics reprinted with permission from Killdozer

Madison Capitol photo by Cathy Stanley-Erickson

ISBN 978-0615617381

First Mobius Books printing: April, 2012

Acknowledgements

First and foremost, I'd like to thank the geniuses at Adobe who invented the PDF file, without which none of this would be possible.

I would also like to thank the Watershed Writers' Group for helping me pound this novel into shape and saving me from myself: Kandis Eliott, Steve Rogers, Meg Turville-Heitz, Cris Goodwin and the late Kathleen Massie-Ferch; Tanker and his after-bars, Harry and Don, the guardians of the Celebrity Drunk Table and all the bartenders at the Crystal Corner, all of you guys helped keep me sane following the marathon writing and editing sessions and the years of frustration waiting to see the book find the light of day (as it were); my brothers and sisters at Union Cab Cooperative of Madison, Wisconsin, I couldn't have done this without you; my fellow vampire cabbies anywhere and everywhere, you know who you are; my parents, Saul and Marlyn Schepartz, who never stopped believing in me; and finally, to Georgia, my wife, for her love, support and inspiration.

And as this novel gets reissued, I'd like to thank Renee at Literary Road for believing in me in the first place; all you readers out there who let me know how much you love my work; and Jeannie Bergmann and Jordan Castillo Price, without whom this reissue would not be possible.

Lastly, extra special thanks to the Madison Vampire Coven.

The Vampire Commentaries
PART ONE

March, 2012

My longtime friend and one-time trainer, Kern, is a big fan of the San Francisco acid rock band the Grateful Dead. Myself, I have yet to fully comprehend this notion of rock and roll, but I would venture to guess that it is my judgment against the judgment of millions. As for the Grateful Dead, every time I hear them, I cannot help but think that it does indeed take copious quantities of mind-altering drugs for them to be found palatable. But that is just my opinion. I would suppose it is a matter of taste.

Kern's favorite Grateful Dead song—and on this point, he is quite adamant, that the superlative refers to favorite "song" not favorite "jam"—is "Truckin'," which has the recurring phrase, "What a long, strange trip it's been."

Indeed, it has been quite the long and strange trip for me as well.

As the Americans would say, I have decided to come out of the closet.

My name is Aloisius Farkas. I am a vampire. And I have been driving a taxicab in the fair city of Madison, Wisconsin for a quarter of a century. Perhaps you have ridden in my cab. If you did, you likely enjoyed a safe and pleasant cab ride. You found the driver affable and even charming. If you rode with me recently, you might have noticed some graying around the temples and determined that I was perhaps in my late 40s or early 50s. In point of fact, I am much older than that. Considerably older.

I was a relatively young man when my mortal life was taken away from me. That was 1000 years ago. Over the centuries, I have seen my fortunes rise, and I have seen my fortunes fall. I am currently experiencing that latter.

For one such as I, a quarter century is but a wink of the eye, and yet, it really has been one long and strange trip. The following memoir, originally written in 1995 and originally published in 2007, is but the prologue of one of the stranger chapters of my long existence.

But I digress.

I said I would come out of the closet, and indeed I will!

I want to be absolutely crystal clear: despite the boilerplate disclaimer a few pages back, this is not a work of fiction. This, in fact, is a memoir. The name on the front of the book corresponds to a real person. He is the person who charms the interviewers and enthralls fans at readings and makes appearances at science fiction conventions.

That person is my front. He did not write this *novel*. I wrote this *memoir*. These are my stories, my words, but for obvious reasons, I could not approach publishing houses with this work, let alone parade around, waving copies of the book with my name on it, telling one and all that I am vampire! Hear me roar! Self-preservation for those such as myself is tied to secrecy, and I hold my self-preservation very, very dear.

So how did *Vampire Cabbie* come to be? After a few years, once I had settled into my new occupation and my new lifestyle, I found myself rather bored. To amuse myself, I started writing short stories about things that happened to me while living this strange life and working at this wonderfully bizarre occupation.

Unfortunately, I made an egregious error and brought some of the pages to work with me. A fellow driver noticed, and before I could conceal them, he had already digested the better part of a page. I glanced upward at him and saw him staring as if he were looking right through me, side-stepping my layers of illusion and defenses, seeing deep into my being.

He knew.

"You all call me 'The Count,'" I said weakly. "I just thought it might be amusing to imagine what it might be like to actually *be* 'The Count.'"

He did believe me.

We danced around each other for weeks, danced around the truth and the lie. Finally, as the saying goes, we both put our cards on the table.

"I don't really care," he said blandly. "It's freaky that you're a vampire, but it doesn't freak me out. Hell, it's kinda cool, and you must not be a cold-blooded killer because you would've killed me the moment you knew I suspected something."

And so it began. It turns out that he was quite an affable young man, as well as an aspiring writer. Thus we were able to help each other out. I provided the story, and my front helped pound it into shape. And together we lived through a horribly disappointing dozen years while we tried and tried and tried to get the book published. I am still unsure as to whether to be amused or annoyed at some of the rejection letter.

"The Count is not in the least a believable character."

"The premise, while amusing, is utterly ridiculous."

"Intelligently written." (Surely the kiss of death.)

"Glad to hear you're working on your next novel."

But then the day came when The Front found the right audience. A small press—a very small press—loved the book and eagerly published it. They have recently closed their doors, hence the reissue herein. In the wake of the publication, he became my public face, my alter ego, perhaps even the Jekyll to my Hyde. And I do have to say that he has served me quite well in this role, and despite what I write here, he shall continue to do so, for surely, you, dear reader, dismiss this commentary as mere literary conceit.

However, I would be remiss and utterly unfair if I failed to mention that The Front is indeed a real write. He is currently shopping his latest novel, *Guitar God,* which he describes as a "Jewish, suburban, rock and roll fantasy with a 1970s soundtrack." I have taken the opportunity to read the work. It is long, but it is a contemporary epic, spanning nearly 20 years. There is much story to tell, and as they say, the story moves right along.

As for this story, I have to say that despite the disappointment at how long it took for the book to get published, the timing in some manner of speaking was utterly Kizmet. Mere months following the publication, the American stock market crashed in much the same manner as in 1987, which, of course, led to me seeking employment and getting hired as a cab driver at Coop Cab.

Additionally, the book serves as a loving reminder of the Madison that greeted me when I arrived in late 1987. Sad to say, that Madison no longer exists. Many of the landmarks, as well as the wonderful personalities, portrayed in the book simply are gone. Red light districts have been replaced by absurdly expensive high-rise condominiums. Pretentious cocktail lounges where wealthy college students pay ten dollars for a martini have supplanted those hardscrabble establishments where working men would drink shots with their cans of Pabst. And I am aghast at how primitive our dispatch system was at the time when this book takes place. I can scarcely fathom how we managed, let alone thrived. This pre-digital technology was utterly Cro Magnon compared to what we have now. And I shall avoid the temptation to rant about the difference between a Dodge Diplomat and a Toyota Prius. Shall we say, it's like comparing an Iron Horse to the last of the sadly retired Space Shuttles.

Again, the last quarter-century has been a long, strange trip. There are many more stories to tell, but those will have to wait. What I do offer you in the meantime are these Vampire Commentaries. Look for them on Facebook. Please "Like" the Vampire Cabbie Facebook page. I will try to offer new Vampire Commentaries on a regular basis. I promise to share my insights and my observations, along with perhaps some inside information, the story inside the story, as it were.

Yes, vampires do use social media. And sometimes it gets us into trouble. But that is another story for another day.

Chapter 1
RUINED

Fall, 1987

I shall spare your pitiful life. In exchange, you may be my audience; my confessor, even. I might tell you that the story begins in Paris. Or perhaps it may be more accurate to say that the story really begins in the Black Forest of Germany. Or maybe the story begins simultaneously in both places.

****

In a Parisian discotheque, a driving, synthesized beat pounded repeatedly against my skull, a beam of sheer force, thick and blunt. The edges of the rhythm smoothed, transforming into the rapidly beating heart of a deer fleeing through a dark forest from a predator sensed but unseen, closing then overtaking, easily bringing down its prey, then plunging sharp fangs into its muscular throat.

I played with, but did not drink the glass of Pernod before me on the faux marble table. My eyes narrowed. Through clouds of blue smoke, the tightly crowded dancers became tree trunks, the flashing lights transformed into splinters of moonlight. I was gone in a moment from this rather unsavory Parisian district to the unspoiled confines of the Black Forest, where I had spent a whole month in feral bliss, devoid of civilization, of words, of even clothing, not pretending to blend in with humanity, but wallowing in the fullest extent of my predatory nature. Arising at nightfall, I had run free through the woods, stalking game, gorging myself on hot, wild blood, then burrowing in the ground before first light, only to rise again the next evening. I even allowed myself to be stalked by a black bear, who followed my scent and the trail of carrion for nearly a week before finally attacking. However, at the last moment,

I turned and countered, barely managing to muster the leverage to send the bear toppling to the forest floor. My fangs sank into his neck, and that great creature's essence streamed into my mouth. I drank, but left him with life; this done out of respect from one predator to another.

A man approached my table.

"*Monsieur*," he said in a gravelly voice.

My eyes focused wide on a gold razor blade the man had dropped on the table, my skin chafing suddenly against my silk shirt, the Armani suit I wore feeling quite constricting. I plucked the blade from the table, inspected it and, with a nod, handed it back to him, giving him a quick study. The sallow flesh under his quickly shifting eyes drooped. He was unshaven. His heart beat rapidly. Yet he looked quite smart in a double-breasted blazer. He turned and walked to the water closet. I followed momentarily. At each step the soles of my Guccis loudly unstuck themselves from the chipped tile floor as I slipped between women blooming like fragrant flowers, some in black leather, some in high heels and tight dresses with the shortest possible hemlines, gyrating around unwashed, unshaven men in black leather or well-tailored blazers.

The WC reeked of urine and vomit. The man sat on a sink, his back to the mirror. He scratched his stubbly chin and withdrew a plastic bag from the hip pocket of his blazer. It was full of folded paper packets.

I stood before him and peered into the bag, the back of his head and shoulders visible in the mirror in front of me, my own frame a barely discernible outline. As his fingers reached inside the bag, our eyes met. Black dots danced before my eyes, growing into large discs that began to pulsate and dissolve into a pair of bubbling red masses.

Quickly, my fangs sank into his neck as I shoved his sagging form onto the sink, his legs dangling above the floor. I drank hastily, taking about a pint before leaving the man draped over his porcelain perch, images from his immediate memory filling my crimson-tinted sight: a back alley, a flash of steel, the crisp line of red, then nothing, as shutters slammed shut, sparing me the rest of the man's thoughts. Too long in the wilds, I had forgotten to screen myself from the thoughts and feelings of my victims. Before departing, I returned his bag of goods to his blazer pocket.

"*Merci*," I said, leaving quickly. An appointment awaited. After a month incommunicado, surely there would be business requiring my attention.

****

For late November, the night was crisp and pleasant, allowing for an enjoyable evening at a sidewalk café. I sat alone in the warm night air without anyone thinking it odd. A French newspaper lay on the table in front of me, shadows from the flickering candlelight dancing on the newsprint. I took a furtive glance at the paper, taking care not to appear to be reading in the darkness though the words would certainly be quite visible to my eyes in little or no light. Besides, my associates were due to arrive any moment.

Rapid footsteps pounded against the flagstone, then fingers tapped none too lightly against my shoulder.

"Monsieur Farkas! Thank God I found you." It was Jacques LeMeux, my European commodity dealer, the commodities generally being art, rare coins and various antiquities of a rather eccentric nature. The normally reserved Frenchman was out of breath and sweating profusely.

"Please have a seat, monsieur," I said, snapping my fingers. A waiter instantly appeared, a rather tall and willowy fellow with long chestnut hair, who I was certain, if he had been another animal in a previous life, had surely been an Afghan hound. "Pernod, *s'il vous plaît.*"

"*Merci,*" LeMeux said. He sat back, arms crossed tightly against his chest.

"Is something wrong, Monsieur LeMeux?" I asked gently. After a thousand years, one can easily read distress in another's bearing.

LeMeux leaned forward again. "Monsieur Johnson will be here shortly. He will provide a full explanation." The waiter returned and placed the Pernod in front of LeMeux. My French agent promptly drank half the contents in one gulp.

Something *was* amiss; LeMeux was quite gregarious fellow and would normally exhibit more composure than this twitchy fellow sitting before me. "Monsieur LeMeux, I am asking you: is anything amiss? Did something happen during my absence?"

LeMeux downed the rest of his Pernod. His heart beat rapidly, and beads of perspiration dotted his forehead. "Please, Monsieur Farkas.

Monsieur Johnson will be here shortly. He will provide a full explanation."

Very well, then. Something had happened, and Bob Johnson, my aide-de-camp, would arrive shortly to explain. Disaster? Over the centuries, if I have learned nothing else, I have learned that disaster is a relative term. How many "disasters" had I endured? How serious could this one be?

Quite serious, perhaps. Johnson had tried to get me to carry a beeper or a portable phone on my long "vacations." But where was the practicality or purpose in that? Surely my affairs could stand a certain degree of my absence, and my confidence in Johnson's administrative abilities could not possibly have been higher. Let him worry; that was why he was paid the princely wages he received.

Johnson finally arrived, indeed looking worried; in fact, looking grim. "Ah, Robert, good to see you," I said. "Please have a seat. Would you care for a beer?"

"Please," he said blandly. The florid, big-boned American took a seat, fidgeting nervously.

I snapped my fingers, and the waiter reappeared. "A bottle of Beck's and another Pernod, *s'il vous plait.*" The waiter nodded, a frown most prominent. I smiled at his reaction to my order of a *German* beer, knowing full well that it might be more palatable to drink from the penis of a rutting goat than from a bottle of French beer. Germans brew beer; the French create wine.

"What is it you Americans say, Robert?" I said. "Back in the saddle? Apparently, I have been too long absent. Prepare my Learjet. Notify the staff at the New York office that I will be there very shortly. Surely there is much to be done."

"You don't have a Learjet anymore," Bob replied sharply. "If you're flying to New York, you're going to have to fly commercial."

LeMeux nodded in agreement. "We searched everywhere for you. Like Monsieur Johnson has told you many times, you should wear a beeper when going on holiday."

"Look," Bob said, "you know I'm not one to mince words."

"Yes," I replied, "you have been in my employ for a long time and, as you Americans say, I do know you are not one to mince words. So what is it that has happened?"

"While you were away, the American stock market crashed. I mean, a *major* crash, and … and … you're ruined."

I laughed in disbelief. "*Ruined*? What do you mean, ruined? What were my assets most recently valued at? One hundred million dollars American? One hundred million dollars does not simply disappear."

Bob stared down at the marble table top. This was perhaps the only time I remembered him not looking me in the eye. He always looked me in the eye. He was one of the few employees who could do so and not flinch.

The waiter returned and loudly slammed the bottle of beer and a glass in front of Bob. He took a long sip from the bottle and wiped his mouth on the sleeve of his jacket. "When you systematically liquefy your assets, they *can* disappear very quickly under the right circumstances. I warned you about the market."

"It had been quite profitable before my absence."

"Yes, and you wanted to make a *killing*." Bob took another long sip of beer. "It started on a Friday. The market dropped about two hundred points. The following Monday, it fell another six hundred."

Silence overtook me as the reality of the situation came clear. "The American economy has not entirely collapsed, has it?"

"No. Actually, it's bounced back fairly well. It'll take awhile, but the market should recover nicely."

"Then, so should we, correct? Surely Jenkins hedged against this sort of thing."

The mention of Jenkins caused both men to straighten in their chairs as if they had received substantial electric shocks. Bob toyed with his beer bottle. LeMeux downed his entire Pernod in one gulp.

"Your former financial manager has disappeared," Bob said.

"Motherless spawn of Satan! Robert, just what the devil has happened?" Heads turned; I had momentarily forgotten how loudly my voice can boom.

"I tried to reach him," Bob replied. "When the market crashed, I was in Europe. You'd told me to sell some of your real-estate holdings so you could buy more stock."

"Yes, I remember." Bitterness tinged my words. Jenkins had advised me that the market would continue to rise for at least another two years and had suggested selling my European holdings, which would be dropping dramatically in value, thus allowing me to buy them back later and make a handsome profit in the process.

"That fool. He didn't tell me what he was doing." Bob sounded angry. LeMeux searched forlornly for the waiter. "I'd been telling him he was being too optimistic, but he wouldn't listen." He paused and took another sip, then emptied the bottle and waved it at the waiter. "Jenkins thought he was getting a bargain, when it turned out he was buying at what would be an all-time high-water mark for the Dow. But he was so sure of himself that he made a huge—and I mean *huge*—purchase on margin—"

"He did *what?!*" Again, heads turned. I lowered my voice to an angry whisper. "He did what?"

"Jenkins took out a loan against your entire portfolio a week before the crash."

I buried my head in my hands and cursed silently in a long-dead language. "And then the brokerage house called in the loan, and we had to make up the margin, correct?"

"Yes," Bob replied. "We had to liquidate almost all your assets just to cover the margin call. But then, apparently, Jenkins panicked. He sold off what was left of your portfolio."

"Sold! The cretin should have been buying."

"Yes, he should have been, but like I said, he panicked." The waiter returned and slammed another bottle of Beck's in front of Bob, while gently placing a fresh Pernod in front of LeMeux, who immediately downed about half in one gulp.

"I hopped the earliest possible flight," Bob continued, "but there was no sign of Jenkins by the time I made it back to New York. He was gone, without a trace."

"And I presume that he, as you say, cleaned me out?"

"I'm afraid so. He liquidated what was left of your portfolio, then drained your Swiss accounts. Then just flat out disappeared."

"Motherless spawn of Satan," I spat. "We will find Jenkins. *I* will find Jenkins, and when I do—"

"Monsieur LeMeux," Bob interrupted, "can you please excuse us?"

LeMeux rose, looking relieved. "I am truly sorry about this regrettable state of affairs, Monsieur Farkas. If there is anything I may do to help, please feel free to let me know."

"Thank you, Jacques." I rose and clasped his hand. "I want you to know that I appreciate your service." I turned to Bob. "There is still some money, is there not?" He nodded, then produced a checkbook, hastily wrote a check and handed it to LeMeux.

"Thank you, Robert," I said, returning to my seat after LeMeux left. "I do forget myself sometimes." I leaned forward and lowered my voice to a whisper. "But when I find Jenkins—"

"You'll do what?"

"I will peel his flesh from his cowardly bones. Slowly! I will rip out his heart and squeeze the blood into my open mouth. While he watches!"

Bob shook his head sadly, but he appeared not the least bit shocked; as a very close and trusted advisor, he did in fact possess knowledge of most of my secrets. "Al, Jenkins is the least of your problems right now."

"How much am I worth at this time?"

"Cash reserves, about fifteen grand American. There's still a few objects which could be sold. They couldn't really get you enough to live on for any length of time, but—"

"No," I said sharply. "Those antiquities will not be sold in a panic, not when we cannot get an optimal price for them. They are my reserves, to be sold only in the most dire of circumstances."

Bob finally stared piercingly into my eyes. "These are not dire circumstances?"

During the mid-17th century, I had lived in Germany. I was quite well-off, the lord of a rather substantial manor. One lovely summer evening, while riding through the Black Forest, I encountered a quintet of high-waymen who ordered me to yield all my valuables. Instead, I dismounted and quickly bested the brigands, then galloped off into the night. The next night, I was confronted by the local burgermeister, accompanied by the five highwaymen, their faces badly bruised.

Despite the coming of the Age of Enlightenment, the burgermeister wanted to try me as a witch. If not for the timely intervention of a few human friends, I would have been burned at the stake. As it was, I escaped with little more than the clothes on my back, my prospects for the immediate future dependent upon shallow pockets and a few letters sent to friends and acquaintances throughout Europe explaining my desperate, nearly destitute situation.

I eventually received an invitation to study independently at Oxford. Following a few years of diligent work, I earned a degree, then conducted patronized research in England for the next several years, finally "retiring," wealthy once again.

In the interim, however, only the sale of a ruby-and-emerald-encrusted golden necklace belonging to the Byzantine Emperor Basil had kept me from complete destitution, thus allowing me to remain within civilization. In comparison, this latest situation was hardly dire, yet it had been centuries since I had been anything but wealthy. "Robert," I asked, "what options have I?"

Bob sipped his beer and shrugged his shoulders, running a hand through his silver hair. "Most millionaires, when something like this happens, they gotta go out and find a job. For those who started with nothing, it's no problem. Others, well—" His voice trailed off. "Of course, you're not just anybody who's lost a fortune. I'm sure there's ways for you to get your money back that aren't available to others."

"What exactly are you suggesting?" My voice sounded suspicious.

A crooked smile crossed Bob's face. "You could go up to Donald Trump, look him in the eye and tell him to loan you a million dollars seed money so you can start over. Hell, you could just tell him to give it to you. And, of course, he wouldn't have any choice."

I shook my head vigorously. "That is not an option. As a suggestion, that is dishonorable and completely disagreeable—and rather disappointing. What else might you suggest?"

Bob placed the beer bottle on the table and pressed a pair of steepled fingers against his lips. "Why not go back into the woods, Al? You seem to enjoy yourself there, and it doesn't cost you a thing."

Indeed. When too long among the civilized minions, I pine for the wordless solitude where my feral side may run free, yet when in the wilds for too long, I miss the comforts of well-tailored clothes and silk sheets. I miss humanity.

"Robert, quite regrettably, I have become too attached to my material possessions. And—I like to travel. I like people."

Johnson flashed a slightly embarrassed smile, obviously a bit amused by the irony of my last remark. "Then you have to get a job. You *need* money. Money means security because you never know when you might have to suddenly disappear. You need capital, and the only way you're going to get it is to work and save money. Lots of money."

"Agreed." Indeed. It was not like I have never had to do this before. "Do you have any ideas of where I might secure employment?"

Bob smiled slightly. "Didn't you tell me something about some sort of science degree from Cambridge? Of course, there's no telling how long ago that might have been."

"Actually, it was Oxford, sixteen-seventy," I said with a laugh.

"Well, I imagine you've at least made an attempt to keep up with all the advances over the centuries," Bob said, frowning.

I nodded.

He laughed nervously. "Well, I got you a job. I guess I didn't really lie about your qualifications. I said you had a PhD, but didn't say when you got it."

"Excellent work," I replied, feeling extreme warmth for this man who had served me so faithfully for the last fifteen years. I realized how truly fortunate I was that he had not chosen to abandon me when there was little benefit for him personally.

"Well, I don't know if you're interested, but it's at a major American university. There's this professor who's got a long-term, continually running experiment that needs to be supervised twenty-four hours a day."

"And I would be there supervising during the 'graveyard' shift, as you might say. Does he not have graduate students for this task?"

Bob shook his head. "It's too much to ask of even a grad student to babysit a lab experiment at three in the morning, seven days a week. So, what do you think? Interested?"

"Maybe," I replied. "I find myself forced to earn a living, and my employment options are somewhat limited."

Bob smiled. "The experiment is funded by a long-term grant, so the job would be secure. The hours are nine at night until five in the morning, five days a week. All you'd have to do is keep an eye on the equipment to make sure it doesn't explode. Most of the time, you'd be free to read, work on your own experiments, or do whatever. The professor said he could pay twenty thousand a year."

"This experiment must be very important to him." I groaned. The work sounded steady, but dreadfully boring. And it was *work*—something I simply had not had to endure for such a long time. "This sounds like a possibly viable option. What other choices do you have for me?"

Bob bowed his head, for a long time staring down at the table. "Al, I'm really sorry," he said finally. "I was able to get you this job by calling in a couple of favors. Professor Hanson owes me from way back, but really is happy about having such a qualified full-time person, and he said he could probably afford to pay more later."

"Was this all you could find?" Bob nodded, so subtly that it was barely noticeable. "I appreciate your efforts," I said, reaching a hand across the table and patting him lightly on the forearm, "but surely there must be many occupations in which I am quite capable of serving."

Bob shook his head vigorously. "You *are* qualified to do many things, Al. Many things! My God, you're one of the most exceptional people I've ever met, a true Renaissance man, but the world doesn't value Renaissance men anymore. We live in a world dominated by specialists. Ever hear the term, 'jack of all trades, master of none'?"

I nodded, knowing full well that my able assistant had never spoken truer words. My resume—if I had one—would appear rather spotty. And how could I explain all those gaps in my work record? In a world that demands explanations for a month of unemployment, how could I explain a century? "I also imagine my 'special needs' must have made your task more difficult as well."

"You've always had a talent for understatement, Al," Bob replied, a relaxed smile finally spreading across his face. "This particular job, you'd be working at night and alone, away from scrutinizing eyes."

"I enthusiastically applaud your effort," I said, smiling broadly. "Call your Professor Hanson and inform him that I will accept his generous offer of employment. So tell me, where is this university?"

"Midwest America," Bob replied. "The University of Wisconsin, in

Madison, Wisconsin."

"Very well then." I reached for LeMeux's discarded glass, raised it in the air and clinked it against Bob's upraised beer bottle. "A toast then. To Madison, Wisconsin: my new home for who knows how long."

Bob drank deeply from his beer, slouching back into his chair. He looked relaxed for the first time that entire evening. In fact, he looked quite tired.

"Of course," I said, "let us not forget about Jenkins. I will have my revenge, as well as the full return of what was taken from me."

Bob sat upright once again, and the relaxed smile fell from his face. "Jenkins is the least of your worries."

"I will have him, Robert. Mark my words. He will not escape my wrath."

"Your wrath is going to have to wait a little while, Al." Bob sipped his beer and leaned back in his chair. "The reality of the situation is this: he ran off with about twenty million dollars. That's more than enough money to allow someone to disappear and not be found. You just don't have the resources to find him."

Always a man of blunt honesty. "I am sure you are correct. Still, I will not forget about Jenkins."

"Neither will I." Bob snapped his fingers as the waiter passed near our table.

Chapter 2

A SLIGHT CHANGE OF PLANS

In his fifteen years of service, Bob Johnson's chestnut hair had turned silver. The flesh covering his ample frame had grown thicker. Had circumstances been different, I would have been able to watch his humanity come crashing down upon him, stooping him forward, breaking his limbs, as his organs, one by one, ceased to function. I would have had the singular privilege of watching him die.

However, circumstances were such that, after following him to Madison, where he would have made certain arrangements as per my instructions, it would come time to discharge him.

Bob caught the first available flight to the States. By the time a flight suiting my peculiar needs allowed me to join him, Bob had already found me a place to live, paid one year's rent in advance and purchased an inexpensive automobile for my use.

Though ships have always rendered me quite queasy, air travel has never been a bother. Of the alchemist's four basic elements, my closet affinity has always been with air and earth. Air is rather close to my true nature, certainly in a figurative sense. Earth binds me and my kind and has always been a force for birth and healing. Fire and water, however, are destructive elements, ripping and tearing us asunder.

Even transatlantic flights may be completed with few complications, so long as the flight leaves in darkness and arrives before the dawn—not a difficult matter considering the seven-hour time difference, thus allowing me to actually sit within the cabin as opposed to being sealed within a lead canister (a most distasteful prospect indeed).

A favorite tome accompanied me on the flight: *The Twelve Caesars*, the superb Robert Graves translation of the immensely entertaining history by Suetonius. Entertaining, yes, but an intentional choice for informational purposes; for the better part of this century, the parallels between imperial Rome and these United States of America have struck me as quite uncanny. Though much of my time over the last century had been spent in America, my experience with the provinces was quite limited. New York, Los Angeles, Paris, London, Rome, Berlin, Prague, Budapest—these were my cities. Madison, Wisconsin? Would the citizenry be ignorant peasants? Would cows sleep within houses with their human owners?

However, despite my fondness for Mr. Graves's flowing prose and the highly personalized accounts provided by Suetonius, the volume spent most of the flight in my lap unread as I sat musing about my predicament, eyes closed, unable to concentrate on the pages.

Was I to suffer the slings and arrows of despondency, spending most of my nights in a sterile laboratory monitoring someone else's experiment when my preference would be to attend the opera or the symphony in a city possessing some semblance of culture?

A darkened forest fills my sight. Musk drifts into my nostrils, the rich aroma washing over my entire being. A large, strong heart beats loudly. Torrents of steaming blood fill my mouth too fast to be gulped down my throat. Twin rivulets dribble down the sides of my jaw.

Daylight comes, and my bed is hard and earthen, full of twigs and stones.

Daylight comes, and my bed is a soft feather mattress, with a down quilt and silk sheets.

Choices must always be made: to live within the world of the humans or attempt concealment behind the shadows cast by their edifices. Except even the shadows have been obscured by the harsh, scrutinizing glare of ubiquitous humanity. In order to survive, I must hide in plain sight, just like Poe's purloined letter.

Paris, London, Berlin, Prague, Budapest, New York, Los Angeles—even Chicago. The plane landed at Chicago's hectic O'Hare airport, where we switched planes for the short flight to Madison.

My sole experience with the American hinterlands had been Chicago, a city possessing a rare mix of cosmopolitan flair and provincial ignorance. But Madison, Wisconsin? Every day, as many people arrive and depart from O'Hare as live in Madison.

After a forty-five-minute flight, the plane touched down in Madison, with a few—very few—city lights heralding our arrival.

Perhaps Madison was more civilized than I had imagined. There were no cows wandering around the small airport. And cabs waited just outside the baggage claim area, which pleased me, for Bob had left word that he would be unable to meet me upon my arrival.

Once my lone suitcase arrived, the conveyor belt sagging from its weight, a yellow cab awaited to offer me a ride to my new residence. As I approached, the driver remained seated, staring straight ahead, seemingly oblivious to a passenger desiring service, even after I had opened a door and inquired as to his availability. He grunted and pressed the truck-release lever, merely watching as his passenger hefted his bulky suitcase into the trunk.

"Fifteen forty-one Gilson," I told the driver, who grunted in acknowledgment. Bob, in his telegram, had said it was a basement apartment, on Madison's south side, with small windows that faced north. He also said it was not very expensive and that the landlord had reduced the price slightly when the first year's rent had been offered in advance. Hopefully, the abode would prove tolerable.

"I have never been here to Madison," I said. "Tell me about it. What kind of city is it?"

"Like any other," the driver blandly replied, "only less so."

Perhaps the driver should have laughed after a remark that one might interpret as witty, but he was silent and did not manifest even a slight smile.

The airport access road wound outward about a mile before we reached a main thoroughfare dotted with small clapboard houses of no discernible form or design. Shortly, the nauseating smell of cooked meat wafted into my nostrils. A factory loomed on the right.

"There is a meat-packing plant here?" I asked my friendly driver.

"That's Oscar Mayer."

"They employ many people?"

"Yeah, but not as many as the State or the University."

"How big is Madison?"

"A hundred-and-seventy thousand."

The road spread, now dotted with various small industrial plants. "Not very pretty, this part of town?"

"No."

"But I can see trees. Are there many parks? Does Madison have much green space?"

"Some."

My, quite the gregarious fellow. It seemed apparent that my driver did not consider it within his job description to be a fountain of information for a curious stranger in this city, let alone be polite. The thought occurred to me that I could do his job better than he.

The road curved and narrowed, the landscape quickly shifting from industrial to residential. "These certainly are lovely old houses. How old are they?"

"Early nineteen-hundreds."

"Is this the oldest part of town?"

"Yeah."

"These appear to be quite magnificent houses. Are they really as lovely as they appear?"

"No."

The architecture was quite eclectic; solid brick houses next to Georgians, complete with alabaster pillars, next to wooden Victorian homes. "This once must have been a rather fashionable area of town. Single families no longer live in these lovely structures?"

"No."

"Then who does?"

"Students. It's the student ghetto."

Indeed, a subtle change seemed apparent as we progressed. Even in the darkness, I could see peeling paint, unkempt lawns and a general lack of artistry in the landscaping. But above the squalor, a brilliant, glowing white dome illuminated the darkness.

"Is that the State Capitol?" I asked.

"Yes." His tone remained dull and monotone.

"It seems to be modeled after the Capitol in Washington."

"It is."

Just ahead, we stopped at a traffic light where I saw the first apparent signs of population; several pedestrians crossed in front of the cab while we waited for the light to change. This seemed to be some sort of commercial district, well populated with foot traffic, but oddly, no cars passed. The light turned green, and the cab sped forward, narrowly avoiding a trio of young women who had dashed across the intersection just as the light changed, causing my driver to sound his horn. One of the women stopped, turned and raised her middle finger, then strolled leisurely across the remainder of the intersection.

"Fuckin' bitch," the driver growled.

"What street is this?" I asked.

"State Street."

"It looks quite commercial, but why is there no auto traffic?"

"It's a mall."

"I beg your pardon."

The driver sighed loudly. "I said, it's a mall. A few years ago, they widened the sidewalks and closed the street to traffic. Only cop cars, cabs and buses allowed."

The road curved, and a series of tall buildings came into view, including a pair of concrete horrors of modern architecture. "Is this the campus here?"

"Yeah."

"Are you a student?"

"No." He sighed once again.

"This is your job, driving a taxi? You make a living doing this?"

He sighed again, louder than before. "What the hell does it look like?"

I presumed that meant yes, and it also meant that he wearied of my interrogation. By the blisters of Satan! It clearly was not my intention to offend this lout, but if he did not care for his job, certainly he could keep his frustration to himself and not take it out on his passenger.

At first glance, it struck me that cab-driving in this town ought to be interesting. Being the state capitol and the home of an internationally renowned university, it seemed apparent that Madison must boast a wide diversity within its population and must often be visited by a goodly variety of people.

As the driver drove with a seemingly permanent scowl on his face, I wondered if I myself might find driving a taxicab enjoyable. Certainly, it was obvious that I could do it better than this gentleman. My passengers would enjoy scintillating conversations with me as their driver as they rode quickly but safely to their destination.

Though not experienced for a few centuries, the notion of work was fresh enough in my memory for me to at least partially understand my driver's sentiment. After all, I did not find myself relishing the prospect facing me—yet from my perspective a positive outlook could make palatable virtually any situation, any job. However, did I not possess the luxury of knowing that in ten short years, my shackles would be broken? And while ten years, regardless of the tedium, is nothing to me, obviously it is a significant portion of a mortal's lifetime.

Finally, we arrived at the destination. After I paid the fare and a modest—and I do mean modest—gratuity (my passengers would tip *me* better), the driver got out of the cab and lifted my suitcase from the trunk. He was tall and stocky, with an overhanging stomach, surely from overconsumption of beer. Just before I turned from him, our eyes met, and suddenly I did not see the driver's brown eyes, but brown leaves coated with fresh blood, the tiny droplets growing and pulsating with the rhythm of a rapidly beating heart.

Without a thought, I projected my consciousness into his as my fangs dropped from within their housings. Without concern as to how bitter this fellow's blood might taste, I grabbed him by the shoulders and plunged my fangs into his neck, quickly drinking the requisite amount. After withdrawing, the driver stood motionless for a moment, then took a step, stumbled slightly, steadied himself against the cab, got back inside and drove off into the night. I stood outside the house, watching and waiting to see if anyone had noticed what had just transpired, watching and waiting for neighbors to emerge from home and hearth, wielding torches and pitchforks, accompanied by the local gendarmes, but no such reaction was forthcoming.

****

Bob had done well in the acquisition of living quarters, satisfying all my specifications to the letter. The basement apartment had just two small windows that would let in only a bare minimum of light—none, once covered with black paper. The main room was square, not too small, and had a fairly high ceiling for a basement apartment. The walls offered much space for paintings and books—but sadly, my art collection was gone, and my books were in storage except for a few boxes of my favorites, which would, I hoped, arrive shortly, along with my music collection.

Other than the main room, there was a water closet with a bath and a small kitchen. Ever resourceful, Bob saved me money, realizing that I generally dine outside my abode.

Still, despite the pragmatic concerns, it was obvious that the apartment would quickly prove claustrophobic—but what alternative did I have? Like it or not, this would be my abode for who knew how long, and that was that. Thus, I did not venture forth that first night, though I yearned to seek the darkness outside. Having arrived fairly late by most mortal standards and not knowing exactly what sort of late-night propriety the town possessed, it seemed most prudent to acclimate myself gradually to my new home.

When the sun set the second night, the darkness beckoned, and I could not stand another minute inside the apartment. I was to meet Bob in a couple of hours, but chose to take the time to acquaint myself with Madison. Bob had wisely left the key to my car on the kitchen counter.

The nondescript gray Toyota Corolla Bob had described would serve me well, both in terms of reliability and gas mileage. However, upon first sight of the vehicle parked outside the apartment, my thoughts drifted back to my beloved Bentley, which had only recently been sold. With a philosophical shrug, I started the Toyota and took a get-acquainted drive before meeting Bob.

Madison was shaped like a woman squeezed into a too-tight whale-bone corset, with upper and lower extremities that narrowed tightly into an isthmus between two moderately-sized lakes, the Capitol visible from virtually everywhere near the downtown area, towering above all other buildings. Later, I discovered that a city ordinance does, in fact, make it illegal for any building to be above a certain height and thus obscure the citizenry's view of their Capitol.

I liked what I saw during that initial drive. The city appeared tidy and well maintained, the wildly eclectic architecture attractive, except in the badly dilapidated student areas. The campus was lovely, especially the lakeshore section. A road that ran the length of the campus traversed an elevated section affording a stunning view of the lake and a stunning, finger-like peninsula called Picnic Point.

Bob was staying at the Concourse Hotel, just off the Capitol square, an odd term because, though the Capitol and its sprawling lawn is bordered by four streets which meet at right angles, the road surrounding the Capitol actually runs in a circle. (Further irony: Another quartet of streets, on the outside of the Capitol Square, is known as the Outer Ring.)

"Can I get you something?" the bartender at the Concourse asked. I had just arrived—five minutes late—but Bob was not yet there. Thanking the bartender, but declining his polite offer, I took a seat in a corner near a window that faced the Outer Ring and waited, enjoying the opulence of my immediate surroundings: the chair was solid rosewood, upholstered with satin; the table before me matched the wood of the chair, its surface polished to a highly reflective sheen, and this little corner was set off with floor-to-ceiling brass posts that possessed not a single smudge nor fingerprint.

After the bartender had asked me three times, I allowed the fleshy young fellow to mix me a scotch-and-soda, but the drink sat untouched on the table in front of me. Bob still had not arrived, which seemed queer; if punctuality was to be considered a virtue, Johnson was angelic indeed.

He finally arrived nearly an hour late, face flushed, brow knitted. Seeing him, I promptly ordered another scotch-and-soda, for he looked in need of a cocktail.

"Al," he began, out of breath, before even taking a seat, "I'm sorry I'm late—"

"Please, Robert, take a seat." The bartender brought over the cocktail and took my money, as Bob sat and took a healthy sip.

Bob took a furtive glance at the bartender as he walked back to the bar. "Something terrible happened." His voice was hushed.

I exhaled loudly. Too loudly.

Bob met my gaze, then looked away. He did seem quite agitated. "God,

I'm sorry about this, about everything. I never should've told you to come out here. It was just a waste of money, and you don't have much left."

"Please relax, Robert," I replied calmly. "Tell me. What has happened? Is my position still available?"

Johnson's eyes glistened in the dim light, as if he were near tears, a state far from the cool, confident composure he usually exhibited. "There's no job," he said, his voice shaking.

I nodded as calmly as possible and motioned for him to continue.

"Professor Hanson is dead." Bob took a big gulp of his cocktail. "The only option I had available for you, and it's gone. Dammit! There's other possibilities out there, but this probably isn't the best place for you to be, and what the hell are you supposed to do now? I don't think your landlord is just going to give you your money back, after signing a lease for one year. Dammit, Al, I'm sorry."

As the saying goes, Bob was always the one to keep his head when everybody else around him was losing theirs, myself included. Now, it was I keeping him calm. This was rather inauspicious. "Please, Robert—Bob, relax. Professor Hanson is dead? What has happened?"

Bob picked up his glass, then put it back down again. "Turns out the old goat was screwing one of his students. By all accounts, this young woman was quite brilliant, but for some reason she took a job in a massage parlor. Before long, they were meeting professionally on a regular basis, outside the massage parlor. Now, Hanson had no idea that the police believed the woman was involved in the death of a Madison man last winter, who was found in a snowbank on the south side of town. The man had been a customer at the massage parlor. Rumors had it that the man had been seeing one of the women at the massage parlor and had been quite generous with gifts of cash and jewelry, until his money ran out. The police had been trying unsuccessfully to link the woman to this killing."

"Robert, is there a point to this story? I may be immortal, but I don't have all night."

"Sorry, Al. It's a bit complicated. Anyway, Hanson also did not know that his mistress was also sleeping with a Milwaukee police officer, who was married to a fellow Milwaukee police officer. The wife suspected something and started following her husband. Then she started following

Hanson's mistress. She was determined to catch them in the act, and she did, sort of. She burst in on the young woman while she was entertaining. Apparently, he must have looked quite similar to her husband—from behind, at least. She pulled out her service revolver and started shooting. Before she knew it, two people were dead, the student and her male companion, who wasn't the woman's husband."

"No, it was Hanson. Now, that's just charming." I stared bleakly out of the window at the night that lay on the other side of the glass, blackness swirling into a jumble of images of trees and leaves and bears and deer and riding into Oxford on horseback, the ancient sandstone bell tower in the center of the campus rising majestically through the darkness before me.

From the corner of my eye, Bob's lips seemed to move, but few words seemed to reach my ears. "Talk to the landlord ... beg ... maybe get half the money back ... not much to work with ... a few months in advance ... hard to find cheap rent in the bigger cities ... have to work extra hard to find something before the money runs out ... maybe you might rethink just what you will and won't do."

A swath of yellow sliced through the darkness. Then another and another. "Cabs," I said.

"Yeah, cabs," Bob replied. "This town isn't so small that they don't have cabs. They'll probably park right out there." He pointed toward the window. On the other side of the glass, a sign read "No Parking. Taxi Stand." "Anyway, just give me a couple days. I'm sure I can think of something."

Inspiration seemed to come in a lightning flash of yellow. "There is no need. Perhaps I have found a possible solution."

"Really?" Bob's eyes bulged slightly from within their sockets. He grabbed his glass and drained the remaining contents. "Let's hear it. I'm glad you're so calm about this. Maybe between the two of us we can figure something out."

I pointed toward the window at the cab that had just parked in front of the hotel, just as Bob had predicted. "Why not get a job driving a cab?"

Bob laughed loudly. "Please, Al; you can't be serious."

"Oh, but I am. I can certainly assure you of that."

He scrutinized me closely. "Jesus Christ, you are."

"Let us examine the facts. First, I am virtually stranded here in Madison."

Bob nodded intently. "Correct. With a signed lease and rent paid in advance, we would have no legal leg to stand on. Maybe we could sublet, but then you'd get your money back in small portions once a month, and probably below face value."

I nodded. "Second, there is the matter of a résumé and the lack thereof. Simply put, I need to be able to get a job where the qualifications are, shall we say, lax."

"Agreed." He scratched his chin. "I've seen you drive in places a lot hairier than this. That's no problem. Any blemishes on your driving record?"

I thought for a moment. "I was last cited by the police in 1961. That was in Nice."

Bob nodded. "The only problem is, you'd have to know the city fairly well to make any money, let alone get hired."

I shook my head vigorously. "This city is not very large. I seriously doubt that will present much difficulty."

"Don't take it too lightly, Al."

My laughter echoed through the sparsely populated lounge. A couple glanced in our direction before returning to their own conversation. "Please, Robert, these are mere details. I do not care to be bothered by small details."

"Important details."

"I will conquer such details with the force of my will."

Bob shrugged his shoulders. "I don't doubt that you will. I've seen what kind of memory you have. You certainly can take advantage of that. Christ, if the brain really can be thought of as a muscle which needs exercise, I shudder to think what kind of shape your brain would be in if you didn't use it as much as you do."

"Senile vampires do not survive long before being slaughtered like rabid dogs."

Bob rubbed his hands together, trying hard to ignore that last remark. "Okay, assuming concerns one and two are taken care of, that leaves number three. You have certain special needs as far as working goes. How do you feel driving a cab would address those?"

I felt myself smile, perhaps for the first time since arriving. "This is quite the Socratic dialogue, is it not?"

My aide-de-camp returned my smile with one of his own. "Just making sure you know what you're getting into here. I want to make sure you've thought this through."

"But I have not. The idea came to me only a moment ago." My smile stretched wider; if nothing else, it was certainly fortunate to have someone like Johnson who was trustworthy enough to hold this conversation. "I am certain I would be able to work at night, which obviously is a concern. Also, even if I would be around people all the time, no one will be in my cab for long. No one will work side-by-side with me. I can come and go like mist, and my co-workers will never know much more about me than my name."

Bob muttered to himself, ticking off points one, two and three. "That covers the basic concerns, but I'm still not satisfied." He turned and waved at the ever-attentive bartender, who promptly brought over another scotch and soda.

"What continues to trouble you?"

After taking a short sip, Bob clasped his chin between his thumb and forefinger, perhaps drawing up another list of concerns. "Part of my problem, I guess, is only having known you for fifteen years. I'm sure there's plenty of Al Farkases I don't know, but the one I *do* know—well, I have a hard time imagining him driving a taxi. You're used to giving orders. I'm not sure how you'll do taking orders from someone else."

I found myself pulling at the taut skin on my chin with my thumb and forefinger. He was correct about that, but how hideous could it be, serving the public? Surely cab passengers do not generally make totally unreasonable requests. "I can adjust."

Bob cocked his head to one side. "I certainly hope so. You know, they say on-the-job stress is directly related to how much control a person has over their work. The less control, the more stress. I mean, Christ, kissing ass to spoiled college students? Dealing with all these damn one-way streets? Hell, there's a street right near here I noticed earlier today. It's only eight blocks long, but three of those blocks are one-way—and in different directions. Now, I know you won't be dropping dead from a heart attack, but I hate to think of a person such as yourself going a little nuts from stress."

"It would be too hideous an image to describe." I paused a moment, then smiled at the hyperbole of that last statement. "Your point is well taken, but the options are few. I have to do *something*, so why not cab driving?"

"Why not?" Bob parroted. He glanced at the cab parked on the other side of the glass, drew pen and paper from his blazer, and wrote down the cab company's phone number. "I'll call them tomorrow and let you know about their hiring procedure."

I shook my head vigorously. "This is my penance, not yours. I'll make the call." I reached across the table and tried to grab the piece of paper, but Bob pulled it away. "I am serious, Robert. Give me the paper."

Very seldom one to disobey a direct order, he tore the piece of paper from his pocket-sized binder, folded it in half and placed it within my hand.

"What do you mean, 'penance?'"

"This whole ridiculous situation is my fault—"

"No, Al, it's my fault. I should have watched Jenkins more closely. I should—"

I reached across the table and patted Bob lightly on his arm. How fortunate to have in my employ one whose competence was matched only by his loyalty. "No, Robert, it is I who am to blame. I did not delegate responsibility. I abdicated it. Even with quality people such as yourself, the circumstances as I allowed them begged for a disaster to happen. Perhaps there is a bit of Judeo-Christian in me still, but I must work as a wage earner, not merely because I need to earn a wage, but because I need to teach myself a lesson. I need to relearn the most basic lesson one learns in this world, that one must tend one's own garden. Better than anyone, I should have known that. Certainly that has been the key component in my survival over the years. To have forgotten that and still be intact is the absolute height of good fortune, but all good fortune comes with a price, and I think this is mine."

"Ain't no such thing as a free lunch." Bob drew my checkbook from his breast pocket, placed it gently on the table and pushed it toward me. "Guess I should hand this over, then."

The moment we both expected had arrived; yet, having worked so closely together for fifteen years, it seemed hard to believe our association would end so abruptly. I pushed the checkbook toward him. "I do have one last job for you."

"Name it." He smiled broadly.

"Leave a thousand dollars in my account and write yourself a check for the rest."

"Too generous, Al." His voice was firm.

"I am quite serious. With my rent paid a year in advance, I think a thousand dollars should prove sufficient for my short-term needs. And, certainly, you do have severance pay coming. You deserve every farthing. Your work has been exemplary. I just regret that I cannot pay you more."

Without another word, Bob wrote himself the check and gave me the checkbook. For a long moment, we just stared at each other in awkward silence. Finally, I said, "Perhaps, in a few months, we might find Jenkins, get my money back and I can rehire you."

Bob nonchalantly shrugged his shoulders. "Maybe. Twenty mil makes it pretty easy to disappear. I'll see what I can do, but resources are limited."

"Any effort is appreciated. So what do you think you will do?"

"There's this old friend who runs a finance house. They've got a large group of mutual funds. About a year ago, he offered me a job as fund manager for their European fund. I'll give him a call and see if the offer still stands."

"Ah!" I slapped the table top. "An excellent prospect. You will keep me abreast of any interesting investment opportunities."

"Of course. If I can still get the job."

Bob had one more cocktail before we bade our final farewell. I left the lounge knowing it might be a long time before the world of satin and solid rosewood would be mine once again. Perhaps Jenkins would be found and my fortune restored. Perhaps I would work for ten years and save enough money to fight the good fight financially.

A cold gust of wind hit me as I exited the hotel. A yellow cab sat idling in the cab stand, the driver reading a newspaper. A block ahead, the traffic light flashed yellow. Below, blinking letters of white and reflected yellow read "State Street." The gusting winds carried voices wafting to my ears from the pedestrian mall, imploring me to come and join them.

Chapter 3
HIRED

Sunlight. You mortals seem to always wonder about that. Hollywood again—but this is one facet of our existence whose accuracy is not butchered by they of the silver screen.

Bob once asked me if the application of sunscreen would allow me to endure sunlight. I replied that sunlight affects vampires in a more spiritual way, and therefore, sunscreen would have no discernible effect. However, over the years, I have become less vulnerable, my body seemingly becoming 'harder' and more impervious to such things; when forced to flee Spain during the Inquisition and having no choice but to leave before nightfall, my flesh actually blistered beneath my clothing. Now it merely stings. Even after 1,000 years, sunrise still will kill me as surely as a stake, but once the sun passes its apex in the sky, its power seems to weaken, allowing me to be exposed to its rays.

Thus, I did not despair when they told me that I would have to apply in person between nine and five. Dark glasses, a wide-brimmed fedora and my black leather jacket with the collar turned upward provided ample protection from the waning sun, which, it being late November, hung very low in the sky, even in mid-afternoon.

When I was ushered upstairs to see the operations manager, a nervous, skinny little fellow named Kevin, I was confident of my prospects. Fully prepared, I handed Kevin my New York driver's license and a copy of my driving record, which the State of New York had kindly faxed that afternoon. The operations manager inspected the materials and, with a nod of the head, ushered me into a large room dominated by a mammoth, Arthurian round table. He handed me an application and a test to measure geographic proficiency. I smiled broadly at Kevin. Anticipating such a test, I had studied a map of the city.

Then the struggle began; first, with the employment application. Education? Well, I did receive that degree from Oxford. Otherwise, I am self-taught. It is quite astonishing what one can learn in a thousand years.

Employment history? How does one explain being independently wealthy for the past three hundred years?

Eventually I decided against mentioning the Oxford degree, instead merely recording the name of a private school for boys in Germany I knew of. As for employment history, I cited my position as president of Farkas Imports for the last fifteen years, and stretched the truth by stating that I had taken over the family business. Actually, I had started the business myself, utilizing rare and unusual objects collected over the centuries, a practice many vampires have engaged in (and we *are* a family of sorts).

The geographic test presented greater problems. First, an eight-and-one-half-by-eleven-inch photocopy of a Madison map proved quite difficult to read. Second, the street names were missing.

The test covered two pages. On one page, I was required to identify main thoroughfares. My geographic study, along with a superior memory, made this task relatively easy.

Part two, however, presented more difficulty, requiring identification of certain landmarks, such as shopping malls, the State Capitol and various public schools. Without sufficient frames of reference, I had to simply guess.

When the test was complete, I found Kevin at his desk, or what I assumed was a desk; the object he sat behind was covered by mounds of paper. The operations manager glanced at the application, then the geographical test. His response was most shocking.

"Sorry, Al," he said. "Looks like you didn't quite pass the map test. Sure came damn close."

That ridiculous test would prevent me from being employed, while that lout who had picked me up at the airport was able to insult his passengers with impunity? "I *almost* passed?" Incredulous, I simply did not know what else to say.

"Yeah." Kevin picked up the application and studied it further. "I see you just moved here. You did pretty well, considering. Three more right answers and you would've passed. Hell, that's better than some students

I've seen who've lived here the better part of four years. They come here looking for jobs 'cause they got their degree, but don't know what to do with themselves, what with the job market for bachelor degrees gone and taken a shit. Yeah, they walk in here, barely get half the answers on the map test and wonder why we don't wanna hire 'em. But what are we supposed to do when the only streets they know are Langdon and State? Hell, there's more to Madison than frat parties and campus bars."

"In my life, I have lived in many places and have learned how to master a city's geography in a short period of time. It is merely survival."

Kevin leaned back in his chair. "Hey, just spend some time checking the city out. Come back in a week. You're allowed to take the test again. If you want to."

I smiled broadly at the operations manager. "I will do just that. I am grateful for the opportunity. This is really where I want to work."

"That so?"

"Yes. I had moved here for another job, but it was unavailable when I arrived. One of your drivers gave me a ride from the airport. He was so courteous and professional, it just seemed to me that this company would be a good place to work." Yes, a lie—but within all lies, is there not a grain of truth?

"Well, it is." Kevin smiled, and I noticed a bright twinkle in his eyes. As the Americans say, I had pushed the correct button. "Hey, being a worker-owned-and-operated cooperative makes a big difference in an industry known for its corruption and exploitation. Co-op Cab is probably one of the best cab companies to work for in the whole country."

Co-op Cab. Of course, a cooperative! No wonder this Kevin fellow was so sloppily dressed. No wonder they allow that lout to work. The commoners take over, winning the right to languish in their own mediocrity, just like the collective farms of Eastern Europe. "I have never worked for a cooperative," I said.

"Well, they can be a real challenge. Hell, a real pain in the ass sometimes, but they're worthwhile." Kevin made a show of shuffling through a pile of papers on his desk, and I knew I was occupying too much of his time.

"I will study the city's geography," I said, rising from my seat. "Then I will return and pass your test."

"You betcha." Kevin stood and shook my hand warmly. "Look forward to seeing you again, Al. Nice meeting you."

"My pleasure. I will return in one week." I pulled my hand away, turned and left, wondering exactly what kind of challenges a cooperative could possibly present, and wondering how I, Count Farkas, always Lord and Master, might respond to a place where the serfs are also the masters of the estate.

****

I redoubled my efforts, attacking the available geographic resources with ferocity, poring over city and campus maps, utilizing mnemonic techniques learned long ago to memorize locations of each and every "point of interest" as designated by a tourist map, then weaving the Toyota in a tight tapestry of closely overlapping circles, grateful that Bob had selected a vehicle that burned petrol so efficiently. I drove to the West Towne, South Towne and East Towne malls (oddly, there was no North Towne). By the four winds of Hades, what determinations will future archaeologists make when they unearth the ruins of this society only to find shopping malls?

I would pass that map test.

In the interim, my books and recordings arrived—old friends able to provide solace to a lonely soul. Molière, Shakespeare, Camus, Dante, Bizet, Mozart, Brahms, Bach, Beethoven, Miles Davis, Charlie Parker and Art Pepper. Alas, why cannot today spawn such giants?

With the arrival of the weekend, it seemed time to once again explore State Street, the bridge connecting the twin pinnacles of Madison's power and influence: the Capitol at one end and the University campus at the other.

On street level, between these icy spires of elitism, the common revelers reside. At the east end, the Capitol erupts, piercing the night with its brilliance. Bascom Hill marks the other end, defining the center of the campus—the epicenter—for upon the top of this glacial blister sits one of the oldest buildings on campus, which houses the university's chancellor. A professor would later tell me there is a secret tunnel that runs underneath Bascom Hill, leading to an elevator that opens within the chancellor's office. However, only tenured professors know about the tunnel and elevator, or so he had said, though this puffery was most assuredly a jest.

My previous foray being on a Tuesday, the street had been relatively quiet and certainly had not betrayed the carnival atmosphere of this Saturday night: the bars overflowing, the broad sidewalks dotted with jugglers and troubadours, Christmas wreaths hanging from each and every light post.

Although late in November, the night was clear and still, the sky a tapestry of twinkling flowers. It was chilly, but not as cold as winter in Wisconsin would become, though I am no expert on relative temperature; my wardrobe decisions are based on fashion, not utility. This early in the winter, my thin black leather jacket did not cause me to stand out among legions of heavily bundled, shivering people dreaming of warm hearths. The other street inhabitants were dressed in much the same manner as I, hardy folk that they were, well accustomed to the raw clime.

A world-renowned university creates a somewhat cosmopolitan atmosphere. Strolling very slowly, letting people course past me, the proof reached my ears. A pair of Chinese couples nearly bumped into me, speaking rapidly among themselves, switching back and forth from Mandarin to Cantonese. A Caucasian male spoke with a tiny Japanese woman, his command of her language astounding; he certainly made himself well enough understood to cause her to giggle several times, with her hand covering her mouth. Through the window of a crowded bar, I saw an eclectic collection of brown and black faces, perhaps from as many as two dozen countries in Asia, Africa, the Middle East, Latin America and the Caribbean.

Eclectic indeed. Much to my surprise, this six-block street offered quite a range of haute cuisine, Greek and Italian perhaps the least exotic, contrasted with Afghani, Moroccan, Thai, Bolivian and even Nepali, which I did not recall ever before having seen outside Kathmandu.

Still, this international variety stood out mostly as a stark contrast to the vast crowds of European descent, including many, many Nordic blondes (who seemed to be the most-lightly clothed). A crowd of young women stood outside a drinking establishment called "Stillwaters"; none wore a coat or even the thinnest of jackets.

Ahead, a strapping young university student approached, then turned into an alley (his cardinal-red sweatshirt identified his institutional affiliation). I peered into the alley and watched him. The alley was actually a driveway running between a pair of parking garages.

My spine tingled. I had not fed in about five days; if it was not yet actually time, it would soon be.

With barely a conscious thought, I willed my body to transform from solid matter to mist, chuckling in silent recall at the memory of my first attempt at this feat: fearfully exhilarated, wondering if my body would be able to regain its cohesion, wondering if my arms would not end up where my legs were supposed to be. Having been under François's tutelage for nearly two centuries, he had finally seen fit to teach me how. When I had rematerialized, intact and fully clothed, it still seemed unbelievable.

I willed myself to reappear just ahead of the fellow's path, around a corner, out of sight. At the proper moment, I emerged ten feet in front of him, my eyes instantly meeting his. My consciousness thrust gently into his, and for a short moment before lowering my mental filters, naked coeds danced before my eyes. My will was imposed firmly upon him, but without pain or fear—long ago, before ever having encountered François, I fed on terror as much as blood, but I have long since ended that distasteful practice. Blood is *not* always enough, but there are emotions far tastier than terror from which a vampire may feed. Besides, it is quite rude to unnecessarily terrify someone who has been kind enough to yield some of their essence.

Instead, I merely took my requisite pint (which tasted of barley, hops and yeast), then let the lad set off on his merry way, where he surely would replace the fluids he had just lost. He resumed his ambling gait, then stumbled and fell. I hid around a corner and watched him lie on the pavement for a few minutes, his breathing labored. He attempted to push himself up, but failed, his face slapping against the asphalt.

He sat up and pressed his face between his knees. From around the corner, three men spotted him and ran to his aid—friends apparently. They helped him to his feet and lent support as they marched off into the night.

"Pretty hammered!" I heard one yell.

I licked blood off my lips, puzzled at this fellow's reaction. He had definitely been drinking, but not that much. I had only taken a pint, no more, and almost certainly a little less. He looked large and healthy. Perhaps he had recently donated blood.

With or without his knowledge or consent.

****

Monday, on a nicely overcast afternoon, I returned to the cab office and did indeed pass the test. Kevin seemed happy with the result and announced that interviews were to be held Wednesday. I felt quite encouraged, assuming that Kevin would conduct the interview. However, my assumption proved incorrect when the operations manager made a reference to "the Hiring Committee."

"I thought *you* might be conducting the interview," I replied sheepishly.

"Hey," Kevin said, "this is a co-op. We have committees for everything. But don't worry—they don't bite."

No, I certainly did not think that they did, but, as I quickly discovered, they did have teeth. On the appointed day, the waning afternoon sun shone brightly, causing me excruciating pain; I almost turned back halfway through my drive to the co-op office, but instead just gritted my teeth and used long-practiced mental discipline to block out the pain. After a short wait, they ushered me into the room where my geographic competence had been tested and sat me down at the round table. The four Hiring Committee members faced me from the other end of the table—four mortals staring at me, scrutinizing me, surely trying to peer deep into my being. I attempted to reassure myself that they would not suspect anything odd about me, that their scrutiny was based solely on the desire to hire the best possible applicants. Certainly this notion was easily intellectualized, but my kind has never liked close scrutiny, has never liked bright lights, though I knew the florescent lights that illuminated this room make everyone ghastly pale. That is why I prefer to wear tans and light browns, as well as muted pastels. These colors tend to offset the effect of my deathly pale flesh. The notion that vampires wear black is nothing but drivel.

The oldest member of the committee, a casually dressed, bird-like woman of approximately 40 years, finally broke the silence. "Thanks for coming, Al," she began. "We'll try to make this as painless as possible, but I will let you know that the hiring committee takes its responsibility very seriously. I'm Maureen Hellenbrand, general manager of Co-op Cab."

A female manager! How American.

"This is Kern," she continued, pointing to her right. "He drives nights and is an on-the-road trainer."

"Howdy," Kern said, with the kind of grin an American might call "goofy." He was long-limbed and stocky, with long, thin hair and a scraggly beard that seemed to be bushy just to be certain of covering his whole face, including what would have been bare spots had his beard been properly trimmed.

"I'm Carey Antonelli," a rather grim, rather masculine, rather large woman said. "I also drive nights."

"And I'm Dale Simmons," said a neatly dressed man with a proper, closely cropped beard. "I work in the waybill office."

"Bean counter," Kern interjected, fondling the red star pinned to his blue denim jacket. Dale smiled. Maureen glared at Kern. Obviously, Dale was the fussy, fastidious accounting type, unless this cooperative had diversified into agriculture.

Maureen launched the first salvo. "Please tell us: why do you want to be a cab driver?"

Let the games begin, I thought. "I need a job. I simply need to make money."

"But you were president of your own company," Carey replied quickly. "Why go from that to being a lowly cab driver?"

"My company went out of business. Again, I need a job. And I think I would enjoy the independent aspect of cab driving, so accustomed I am to being my own boss, as it were."

"Ah," Dale said, smiling slyly and stroking his beard like a chess grandmaster whose opponent had unwittingly just left his queen unguarded. "But surely no cab driver is an island unto him or herself. We don't want free agents. We need people who work and play well with others. You would need to be able to work as a team player with your dispatcher, your fellow drivers, and, of course, the staff in the waybill office."

"Of course," I replied, fearing that I had already represented myself in a detrimental manner. What was it they wanted to hear? "I have always enjoyed working with others, sharing ideas, having others share their ideas with me. All of us working together to solve whatever problems there are that require solution."

"How long do you plan on sticking around?" Kern asked gently.

"As you can determine from my employment application, I have just recently moved here in Madison. I find this town quite lovely. And, thus far, all my interactions with the people at Co-op Cab have been quite positive. Certainly, if hired, I think I would stay for a good amount of time."

The committee members nodded their heads, seemingly in unison. "Now, you know we're a cooperative," Maureen said. "Have you ever been employed at a worker-owned-and-operated cooperative?"

"And are you now or have you ever been a member of a cooperative?" Carey added.

Are you now or have you ever been in league with Satan? Is that not what the Grand Inquisitor had asked so many years ago? "My apologies. I would have to answer no to both questions. However, the cooperative model seems ... intriguing. I would certainly look forward to learning more about it." Yes, a lie, but I did need this job.

"I should hope so," Dale said, his words vaguely tinted with sarcasm. "How would you feel about working at a place where sometimes it becomes necessary for you to do certain things where you don't get paid, but because they benefit the whole, they benefit you?"

"And there's two other cab companies in town that you could've applied at," Carey said. Maureen craned her neck forward. Kern leaned back, stretching his long legs in front of him. "Why come here?"

Julianne had been my lover, had given herself to me fully and freely. Her whole self. Her body, her essence, her soul. A particularly nefarious strain of the grippe had swept across Spain. She was dying until I intervened. But then her brother betrayed us both to the Inquisition. When the Inquisitor questioned me, I could not find the correct answers. Apparently, neither could Julianne.

"I am not sure exactly to what you refer," I answered, blinking back to the present, knowing I had applied for a position at this particular cab company simply because I had no knowledge of the other two. "Certainly, I would expect to get paid a full day's wage for a full day's work. However, if, within the cooperative structure, there is anything I can do to benefit the common good, well, I most certainly would be willing to help in whatever capacity I could. As for why Co-op Cab—" What had Kevin said? "It would seem that Co-op Cab, being a cooperative, is probably one of the best cab companies to work for in the whole country, especially given the corruption and exploitation of the taxi industry."

"Good answer, Al," Kern said with a laugh. He sneered at Dale and Carey. Carey crossed her arms in front of her ample chest. Dale sat back in his chair and rubbed his beard, a sly smile still on his face, prepared for the next salvo. "You got my vote. What office are you running for, anyway?" He paused, laughed again, and smiled at me. "Co-ops can be frustrating places, Al. Having owned your own business, you're probably used to having your way. Often, in a co-op, things happen where nobody gets their way. We make progress, but sometimes it's real slow because we try to be as democratic as possible, through majority if not consensus."

"Democracy is good," I replied, immediately regretting the simplistic nature of that remark. "If people want to run their places of work, then they should have the opportunity to do so." Yes, yet another lie—but once the first lie is told, the rest get shockingly easy.

Heads nodded. I think they liked that answer, but did I believe it myself? What *was* I getting myself into?

Maureen broke the short silence. "At Co-op Cab, we take pride in being a full-service cab company. No New-York-style cabbies here. We're courteous and polite, we open doors, and we don't drive like maniacs. Many of our passengers are elderly or disabled. These customers require greater care and take more time than other customers. As a driver, you would be paid commission, not by the hour, and if you get too many elderly or disabled passengers, you might not make as much money. How do you feel about that?"

"They are paying customers and therefore must be treated with the same degree of respect as all other customers." Surely, this was what they wanted to hear; that is, unless they were trying to determine if I was trying to tell them what they wanted to hear. "If customers receive poor service, they will call another cab company, and that would be a bad situation. I would treat all customers with the high degree of respect that I myself would expect to receive."

"You're near two calls," Carey abruptly interjected. "Remember, you only make money when your meter's running. One call is going from one end of town to the other. You know this, but you get the other, and it's some little old lady going about two blocks, and she moves real slow. How do you feel about that?"

"Regardless of how I feel, I would keep my feelings to myself. This woman has done us the honor of calling our company and therefore should be treated accordingly. Besides, that is merely one call. Time, after all, is the great equalizer."

Dale and Maureen nodded. Kern smiled. Carey scowled. "You're assigned a call," Kern said. "You get there as fast as you can, but the person's been waiting a real long time. They're pissed off, and they're being abusive to you, even if this isn't your fault. How would you deal with that?"

The Grand Inquisitor had been correct to brand me as in league with Satan and sentence me to the rack, for who but one in league with Satan could escape his shackles and disappear into thin air? Poor, sweet Julianne was unable to perform such magic.

"First," I began, "I would not take any of it personally. Human nature often dictates that people will lash out at the most convenient target, regardless of whether or not that person, place, or thing had anything to do with their predicament. Therefore, I would exert great effort to not allow this person to get under my skin, as it were.

"Second, I would do whatever possible to soothe this person, which of course, I would be best equipped to do if I maintain my composure. This person might be a frequent customer, and we would not want to lose their business. Or maybe it is their first time calling us. I would want to do whatever I could to let them know that this situation was an aberration."

"Then, you'd lie," Kern said, laughing loudly.

"Ignore him," Maureen said, her eyes never leaving mine.

"Hey, there's times in the afternoon when calls rot," Kern countered.

"We're working on it," Maureen replied, shooting Kern an angry glance, then turning back toward me, waiting for my answer. Was this not my interview?

Rot. Julianne's sweet soul gone, her body rotting in a mass grave, for I was unable to rescue her, having arrived too late to stop them. Her screams echoed in my skull as I searched for her, knowing her torturers relished her anguished cries, marveling at how many turns she could take before even her spine finally snapped like so much kindling.

"Perhaps," I finally answered, "there are certain times of the day when the volume of business may result in less than optimal service. That being the case, I would attempt to explain it to the customer. Whenever possible, I would explain reasons why we were so late and offer viable suggestions as to how the customer might help rectify the situation."

"As you can tell," Maureen said, nodding at my response, "cab driving can be pretty stressful. How do you deal with stress?"

Ah ha! Did some applicants state that stress presented no problems, an obvious and transparent lie that would surely not go unnoticed by the committee? But what could *I* say? That I ran naked through the woods, stalking deer, bear and other large prey, relishing the hunt before drinking the steaming blood of my quarry, whenever I felt excess tension? "Stress is a part of life," I said. "One must accept that stress exists. One must yield to stress to overcome it."

"Lao Tsu!" Kern clapped his hands loudly.

"I appreciate your time, Al," Maureen said. "Only one question left." She glanced at the others. "Okay, who wants to ask it *this* time?" Dale rolled his eyes. Carey rubbed her temples and stared at the ceiling. Kern leaned forward, rubbing his hands vigorously together.

"I'll ask it. I'll ask it," Kern said, squirming excitedly in his chair.

"Go ahead," Maureen replied.

"Okay, Al. If they made a movie of your life, who would you want to play you?"

Motherless spawn of Satan! What kind of question was that? My mind drew an irritated blank, then suddenly I heard my own voice blurt out: "Frank Langella."

Kern laughed out loud, as did the others, even Carey. "Why?" Kern asked.

I was embarrassed and alarmed, then remembered there are no

shadows in which to hide, only plain sight. "I admired his work in the 1979 version of *Dracula*. He brought an unprecedented sensitive sensuality to the role."

"There is no right answer to that question," Maureen said. "It's just something we ask, just because we've always asked it."

"Without tradition," Dale added, "we would be like a fiddler on the roof."

Maureen ignored Dale's remark. "Again, Al, thanks for your time. We'll be in touch."

I rose and shook hands with all the committee members. The way Kern smiled, I firmly believed he would support me. The others were inscrutable, but, studying Carey's scowling countenance, I wondered if this had merely been an exercise in folly. Had others performed tasks on my behalf for so long that it would be impossible for me to secure even the most menial of employment?

Immediately following the interview, I braved the sunlight again, returned to my apartment and crawled into bed, awaiting the kindness of nightfall while considering the interview and wondering if the future would be a soft mattress and silk sheets or hard, sun-baked earth full of twigs, pebbles and rocks. Except that my mattress was now a thin futon, lying atop an unforgiving oak floor, and my sheets were not silk, but itchy linen. Still, even this rather austere comfort was greater than that within the earth.

****

A few days of uncertainty later, the phone rang, awakening me from a deep slumber. It was my first phone call after Bob had arranged for installation.

"I'm calling to offer you a job at Co-op Cab Cooperative," Kevin said.

"Excellent!" I replied, with as much excitement as I could muster at the ungodly hour of one in the afternoon. "I am pleased, Kevin. I accept your generous offer of employment."

"Great," he said. "Glad to have you aboard. On your application, you said you wanna work nights?"

"That is correct. I am very much a night person. Also, I have a condition … my eyes are very sensitive to sunlight. I can drive during later day hours, but it is quite painful. I was hoping to drive late nights."

"We can accommodate you, Al. I'm always looking for late drivers."

"This is almost too good to be true." Instantly, I regretted my remark.

Kevin laughed. "Just what I like to see. Enthusiasm. When can you start?"

"Ah, immediately."

"Well, first, there's training. Can you make Monday at one?"

"Yes," I replied, hoping Monday would be overcast. Maybe there would be a solar eclipse.

"Good. You'll start with in-house training. That session lasts about three hours. Then, we'll see about hooking you up with an on-the-road trainer."

By all the false gods of heaven! How much training would I need? How much training does it take to pick up passengers and take them to their destinations? "I will get on the road sometime, will I not?"

Kevin laughed heartily. "Sure, Al. Our training is pretty extensive, but there's no such thing as too much training. Our rookie drivers are a zillion times better prepared than their counterparts at any of the other companies in town. Don't worry, the trainers'll keep you pretty busy—at least, busy enough to keep from getting bored."

I certainly hoped so.

Chapter 4

TRAINING

After the weekend, the day of training arrived. Having always been a paragon of punctuality, I found myself waiting, in the same star chamber where my interview had taken place, ten minutes prior to the appointed hour, and was joined a few minutes later by a young woman of strong distinction in her appearance, who, with her long, dark hair and eyes, swarthy complexion and sharp, angular features, reminded me of the many gypsies I had known over the centuries; sadly, one in particular about whom I did not wish to think.

"Oh, hi," she said, seemingly surprised by my presence.

"Hello," I replied, finding myself staring at her, my eyes tracing the sweeping diagonal of her jaw. "Are you to be the one who trains me?"

She laughed. "No, I'm here for training too. I'm Nicole."

"Pleased to make your acquaintance," I said, rising and extending a hand. She shook my hand firmly, like a man. Another place, another time, and I would have kissed her hand like a true gentleman, but alas, this *is* a different time—and a very different place. "I am Al. Al Farkas."

"Nice to meet you." We both sat. An awkward silence filled the room, myself unsure what to say next. Round of hips and bosom, firm and strong in the arms and legs, this young woman looked enough like Anya to be her granddaughter—but that, of course, was impossible.

"Seems they got a long day of training set up for us," Nicole said finally.

"Yes. Kevin informed me that Co-op Cab has the most vigorous training program of any cab company in the city."

"Yeah, he told me the same thing."

"I cannot help but wonder how much training we actually need. How difficult can it be to drive a cab?"

Nicole shook her head. "Don't know. But, the times I've been in a cab,

I've tried to listen to the radio, and I can't make heads or tails of it."

Shuffling footsteps drew our attention to the doorway as two young men entered the conference room and loudly plopped themselves into chairs. Resplendent as they were in torn, faded denim trousers, the tails of their flannel shirts trailing over their thighs, I reasoned that they were college students, their general slovenly appearance reminiscent of the legions of American students I had seen backpacking across Europe, trekking from one youth hostel to another. "Training?" one asked.

"Yeah," Nicole replied. "I'm Nicole. This is Al."

"Good afternoon," I said.

"Hey," the first said. "I'm Gino, and this is Quinn."

"*¿Que pasa?*" Quinn asked, obviously not actually seeking an answer.

Following the introductions, there was silence until Dale from the Hiring Committee appeared, cradling armfuls of materials, as dapper as before in a crisp Pierre Cardin dress shirt, charcoal-gray wool slacks, a smart-looking sleeveless v-neck angora sweater and brown Guccis, identical to a pair I had recently owned. His ensemble must have required deep pockets, and that gave me cause for encouragement regarding my own financial prospects as a cab driver.

"Hello all," Dale began. "I'm not going to bother with introductions since I've already met all of you. And I'll assume you've gotten acquainted over the last few minutes."

Dale gently placed the materials on the table, including four black binder notebooks, which he slid to each of us. "There's a training notebook here for each of you," he said. "You can keep these. Each notebook includes various fact sheets, several of which I'll be referring to during this session. Also, you'll find a Madison map, a street directory and our company manual. These are very valuable resources, so don't lose them."

Dale congratulated us on being hired, then urged that we pay close attention in order to more easily pass probation. Indeed, one would think this job would require more talent than that provided by a team of organ-grinder monkeys.

"Straight from the top," Dale continued, "I want to stress that this *is* a cooperative, which means this is a different kind of a workplace because *we* own it. I cannot stress how important it is for you to understand what it means to work at a worker-owned-and-operated cooperative. As a means of illustration, I'll tell you a story."

He might as well have used the word *indoctrination*. Has that not been the polite word for it, in much the same way that "reeducation camp" was the polite term for concentration camp?

Dale droned on and on about the history of Co-op Cab, which actually had some fascinating aspects. Its predecessor had been the more-standard sole proprietorship. Disgruntled employees (along with, no doubt, several rabble-rousers) formed a labor union that ended up putting that company out of business. Subsequently, the out-of-work drivers formed their own company. Thus, the serfs bought the estate, making each and every one of them lord and master. Or so they claimed. As Orwell said, "Everyone is equal, but some are more equal than others."

As the indoctrination continued, I caught myself staring surreptitiously at Nicole, Anya's features becoming superimposed on my fellow trainee's face as the present faded from my sight.

Though I certainly had traveled a great deal during much of the early 1930s, Prague had been my home. Yes, in retrospect, considering what was happening in Germany at that time, it would seem the height of foolishness to have stayed in the Czech capital, but there were commodities to sell, and one tends for one reason or another to procrastinate.

Anya and I had become acquainted in Budapest in 1935 while I was there conducting business. Though it had been a chance meeting during an intermission of a Chekov play, it turned out that I had actually known her family for a number of generations.

1935 was a bad time to fall in love in that part of the world.

Dale's voice, speaking the words "patronage dividend," pulled me back to the present. In profit-making years, a patronage dividend was distributed to the membership on a proportional basis dependent on how many hours a member worked relative to the total number of hours worked. Each member received a certain percentage of their share of the profit, the rest going back into the co-op as equity.

Finally, Dale announced the conclusion of the first section of training and allowed us to take a ten-minute break. Gino and Quinn disappeared almost instantly, but Nicole lingered. I felt her gaze, but remained seated, opening the notebook and making a show of studying the pages held therein, feigning a conviction that the information contained on those pages was actually important.

The notebook did contain some useful information, including price lists for package deliveries and various maps, as well as names and addresses of bars and hotels. After all, there was a definite purpose here, and distractions had to be kept to a minimum. For my kind, intimate relationships with humans always present problems and must be approached with a high degree of circumspection, especially when dealing with American women, who are so much freer and independent than their European counterparts.

Also, the mere sight of Nicole shot daggers of pain deep into the core of my being. Fortunately, she left after a few long moments.

About ten minutes later, Nicole, Gino and Quinn returned, quickly followed by Dale, who immediately placed a large piece of posterboard covered with Mylar on a tripod stand at the front of the conference room.

"Procedures," he said, with a wide flourish. "There's a lot to cover, so I'll just jump right in." He brandished a large marker and pointed it at the image of the cab radios used by Co-op Cab. Much to my surprise, the system was actually computerized.

"Much of what follows will be covered by your on-the-road trainers," Dale continued, "but redundancy is good." He touched the image of one of the buttons on the cab radio with the marker, and again I saw Anya's face.

She had moved to Prague, and together we had lived in a charming garret in the theater district. We both had been following events in Germany with great interest and had decided to leave, but various obstacles delayed our departure. The sale of a 16th-century Russian icon failed to come to fruition, the buyer having been waylaid at the border. Traveling money was desperately needed, so we waited for another buyer, who did in fact arrive in Prague in time to make the sale, but the transfer of his funds was bundled up in too much red tape.

German tanks crossed the Czech border. Soldiers patrolling the streets made it unsafe to leave our garret, but our exodus could be delayed no longer, for the Germans had already commenced house-to-house searches for Jews, Gypsies, and other undesirables.

Our survival was punctuated by the ticking of the clock on the wall of our garret, where we spent our last night together, holding each other close, hearing coarse German shouts as the hours slowly passed before my agents would come for us.

We had managed to book passage aboard a train, but it would not depart until the next afternoon. Before daybreak, Anya would have to seal me inside a crate within which I would have to travel, at least until nightfall. Yes; again, the first rays of morning sun are deadly, and when the sun rises, even when safely sequestered, I become virtually catatonic.

I shall never forget the sight of Anya peering into the crate before she nailed the lid shut. She smiled bravely, leaned down and kissed me, her lips like rose petals. I wanted to pull her into the crate with me to hold her, keep her safe, but one of us had to remain on the outside to make sure we both safely boarded the train. When she closed the lid, I caught one last glimpse of her, the brave smile cracking at the last moment, revealing what I already knew, that she was frightened, which, to tell the truth, was no different from what I was feeling.

The word "bid" broke through my musing. Dale's pointer touched the button to the far left on the bottom row of buttons.

"This is the most important button on your radio," Dale said. "Your bid button is the one that makes you money. The other buttons are empty, acknowledged, destination, or 10-7—which means 'on break.'"

When the bid button was pressed, the number of one's cab on the dispatcher's computer screen lit up. This did not indicate a monetary bid, but merely a driver's desire to be considered for one of the available calls "on the board." Dale said calls were given to the closest cab; that is, unless the dispatcher determined that there was need to shift the entire fleet in the direction of a glut of calls.

A lengthy dissertation followed concerning how to bid, when to bid, why to bid. How, when and why to bid with packages. How to use the question buttons and the difference between a "HiQ" and "LowQ." Dale even discussed the simple matter of how to handle the cab radio, certainly an exercise in the obvious; I had had quite a bit of radio experience during World War II working with the French Underground.

It all seemed rather simple, actually, and after Dale concluded his

highly repetitive explanation, the expressions worn on the faces of the
other trainees seemed to relax. Like the others, I found it a Herculean
task to maintain my attention, even though my mental discipline was
superior to that of these children.

Dale placed a new piece of posterboard on the tripod. "This is a waybill,"
he said. "Waybill being the standard industry term for the paperwork
cabbies use to keep track of what they do during a shift."

I rolled my eyes. Before I knew it, I was once again staring at Nicole.

*Fists pounding on wood broke through my slumber. I heard a crash and
Anya's agitated voice. Then she screamed.*

I could not even lift my arms.

*I lay paralyzed, only able to listen to Anya's screams, to the sound of
a body loudly striking the floor and walls, the sound of tearing fabric, of
smashed furniture.*

*By the time I could lift my arms and break open the crate, the garret
was silent. Anya lay on the floor on the other side of the garret, her clothes
tattered rags, her body a mass of bruises and abrasions, her lovely flesh
ripped and torn asunder, her throat cut.*

*Bending down to close her lifeless eyes, my gaze shifted back toward the
crate from which I had just risen. On the floor next to the crate was her
white lace tablecloth, a bouquet of roses, the shattered remains of a vase
and a puddle of water, quickly spreading across the polished oak floor.*

*She had disguised the crate as a dining table, just to be especially sure the
Germans would not inspect the contents for booty, covering the crate with an
heirloom passed from mother to eldest daughter for two dozen generations.*

*No conscious thoughts directed my actions for the next several hours.
Suddenly, I was no longer in the garret, having rematerialized in front of
a quartet of German soldiers.*

*Then I was kneeling on a soldier's chest, ripping open his shirt, tearing
flesh all the way down to bone, cracking open his sternum and sinking
my fangs directly into his heart as his fellow soldiers watched in horrified
paralysis.*

*I have no way of knowing how many German soldiers died that night,
but accounts of my exploits were published in newspapers as far away as
England, where the citizenry reading the more plebeian newspapers were*

entertained by accounts of "The Prague Mangler."

Suddenly, I realized Nicole was staring at me. Or rather, she was staring at me staring at her. I quickly averted my gaze.

Dale explained how to take readings from the taxi meter and where on the waybill to record that information. It seemed he realized that perhaps all this information was obvious; a certain sarcastic tone was apparent in his voice as he explained trips and units.

He then walked us through a mythical shift and showed us how to balance our waybills at shift's end. Though his tone was sarcastic, his countenance seemed to attach a high degree of importance to the general topic of paperwork. Perhaps it was the "bean-counter" aspect of his being which caused him to do this.

Mercifully, Dale allowed us to take another ten-minute break. When we returned, he turned off the lights and showed a defensive driving film.

"This covers the basics," Dale said. "We have an in-house defensive driving course that you will all be required to complete before passing probation. It's about eight hours over a two-day period."

My fellow trainees groaned loudly. I heard myself groan as well. Dale smiled, making a show of shaking his head sadly. "Now, we *do* want you all to drive safely." More sarcasm in tone, but obviously not intention. "Remember, an accident can and will ruin your day."

When the training session ended, I departed as quickly as possible. Upon reaching the bottom of the stairs, my sensitive ears heard Nicole speak to the empty room, thinking no one could hear her: "Where'd he disappear to so quickly?"

****

Three nights later, I sat waiting for my on-the-road trainer, in the "driver's room," a cozy chamber full of chipped formica tables with adding machines on each, and dented steel chairs in the vicinity of each table. The walls, once white, were a dingy gray. A stack of lockers stood against one wall, on top of which was an amazing collection of coffee cups, glasses, silverware and seat cushions. A small refrigerator and microwave oven were stacked in a corner next to a coffeemaker. Newspapers were strewn everywhere.

A pair of drivers, both heavy-set, sat at a table, balancing their waybills. They ignored me as I sat, idly thumbing through my training notebook. My trainer was late. Finally, a tall, gangly fellow walked in, whom I recognized; it was Kern from the Hiring Committee.

"The Count!" he exclaimed. "The Count. I get to train the Count. Hey, Bob, John, you gotta meet this guy. He's the Count."

They turned and stared at me, disinterest quite visible in their eyes. "Why do you call him 'the Count,' Kern?" one asked as he folded his waybill and slipped it inside a manila envelope along with charge slips, call slips and cash.

There are no shadows. Vampires must hide in plain sight.

"Why do you think they call me the Count?" I replied, speaking in my best Bela Lugosi voice, staring at the driver with faux menace. Kern laughed loudly.

"Yeah, when we asked him the movie star question, this guy answered Frank Langella. What'd you say, Count, that he 'brought unprecedented sensitive sensuality to the role of Dracula'? The committee got a good laugh outta that."

Wonderful. Still a mere trainee, and I already had a diminutive variation of my name. However, despite the vulgarity, it seemed in my best interest to let them have their amusement.

"That so?" John or Bob asked.

"That is correct," I said. "Actually, my name is Al. Al Farkas."

"I'm Bob, this is John." I shook hands with both.

"Whatever Kern tells you," John said, "do the opposite. If you want to know how to do things right, just ask me."

"Don't listen to them, Count," Kern said with a smile. He brushed his long, thinning hair out of his eyes. "Get trained by me, you're learning from the best."

Bob and John howled with laughter. "You so good, Kern, why you still driving nights?" Bob asked, heavy sarcasm in his voice.

"I make money at night," Kern replied. "Don't need to get spoon-fed to make my money, not like you day-jerks."

"You make your money competing with rookies," John said. "You wouldn't make dick on days, competing with real cabbies."

A few more barbs were passed back and forth, then Kern finally decided to commence my training.

"I've already punched in," Kern began, "for both of us." He swept his long arms in a slow circle. "This is the driver's room. Our home. But this isn't like in *Taxi*, that TV show. You shouldn't be spending much time here. Drivers who spend too much time in this room aren't making money. You make money only one way: being in your cab, ready to take a call."

Kern gave me a short tour of the driver's room, pointing out the bulletin boards. One bore announcements of committee meetings and meeting minutes, another displayed general information about the cooperative, as well as a lurid photograph of a crumpled cab with the caption, "Accidents will ruin your day."

"This is Democracy Wall," Kern said, pointing to a third bulletin board full of typed and hand-written letters. "You got a beef with anyone or anything, feel free to put it here."

I attempted to read one of the missives, something about drivers who leave their cabs unattended by the gas pump, blocking access for anyone wishing to refuel their vehicle. The author seemed rather miffed, though it was hard to tell, the childish scrawl barely legible.

Kern pulled me by the arm and dragged me toward a steel cabinet. "In here's all the different forms you'll need. Waybills, charge slips, leave-of-absence request forms, vehicle maintenance request forms." He made a big show of taking a deep breath. "And accident report forms. But you won't ever be needing to fill one of those out, right?"

Kern seemed to await a response to what surely was a rhetorical question. "Right," I said finally.

"Okay," Kern said. He strode toward the dispatch office. "You get a cab from either the dispatcher or one of the phone answerers. If they don't have a cab yet, you're put on the waiting list."

A dispatcher sat in front of a glowing green monitor. He stared intently at the half-dozen slips of paper that lay on the table before him, chin cupped in his hands. "Nothing works," he said. I was unsure whether he was talking to a driver or to himself.

I followed Kern around to the other side of the table where the phone answerer sat drumming her fingers on the tabletop next to the phone.

"Ready for a sled?" the wispy young woman asked.

"A sled for two," Kern replied. "Nothing too nice. Got a trainee tonight." He turned toward me. "Rookie drivers usually don't get to drive the nice cabs. But, hey, all cabs are good cabs. Yellow's my favorite color."

"Yeah, Kern," the woman said in a perfunctory tone, rolling her eyes, "and all calls are good calls."

"Al," Kern said, "this is Sharon, phone answerer *and* dispatcher extraordinaire. Sharon, this is Al. The Count."

"Why do you call him the Count?"

We repeated Kern's game; it seemed the height of rudeness to not play. Besides, would a nickname not make me seem more "human" in the eyes of my fellow workers?

He plucked a key from the desk. "Sixty-six. You're going to like this one."

"Better not take that one," Sharon protested. "Frank Nelson is working tonight, and he's got a real jones for that sled. Don't know why; it's a real piece of shit."

Kern rolled his eyes, dropped the key on the desk and picked up one in its place. "Seventy," he said.

Sharon nodded and rapidly punched the keyboard in front of her. "Seventy," she said, "another good cab for a trainee. Okay, you guys are logged and ready to go."

"Thank you," I said, then followed Kern into the parking lot as he went in search of our cab.

"Always a problem, working later night shifts. Makes it hard to find your cab in the dark."

Harder for mere mortals, I thought, having already spotted the cab in the back corner of the lot. "Over there," I said, pointing toward the cab. Kern grunted with consternation.

He folded his tall frame behind the steering wheel and moved the bench seat nearly all the way back—he was a good head taller than

I (and to think I was once considered tall!)— then immediately started the cab and turned on the heat. "This time of year, you gotta get the heat cranked right away. Cab's colder than shit when you first get in." He shivered. "We'll be using my waybill— officially, that is—but I want you to keep track on your own, as if this was really your shift."

Kern showed me how to take beginning readings from the digital counter on the meter which kept a permanent record of total trips and units. The mileage reading came from the car's odometer.

"First thing you should do," Kern said, as we drove to the petrol pump, "is inspect the outside of your cab." We parked at the pump, and I followed Kern as he walked around the cab. "She's in good shape. No fresh dings or dents left by someone else for us to be blamed for."

There were plenty of imperfections on the body of this behemoth. "How can you tell if a dent is fresh?"

Kern chuckled. "Fresh dents don't got rust on 'em." He pointed at the petrol pump. "Now, this is our refueling, inspection and cleaning station. There's mirrors to check your lights. It's well lit here, so you can inspect your cab. We got wiper fluid, which you wanna make sure you got plenty of this time of year. Also, we got solvents for special cleaning in case someone pukes, pisses or shits in your cab."

"Charming," I said, suddenly thinking about the cab's rear-view mirror and trying to quickly conjure a contingency plan. My passengers would be able to look at the mirror and not see their driver!

"Now, we're ready to rock and roll," Kern said, after we had checked our supply of charge slips in the glove compartment, made sure headlights, tail lights, brake lights, backing lights, hazard lights and all turn signals were operational, washed the windows and filled the windshield wiper fluid reservoir.

"Remember, don't leave the lot without bidding on a call, unless there's nothing to bid on."

"How can I tell?"

"Listen to the radio."

I cocked my ear, but there was nothing but silence. "We are clearly bored," the dispatcher finally said, the transmission clear, but crackling, a loud squawk nearly bursting my eardrums when he closed the channel.

"What does that mean?" I asked.

"Clearly bored. That's slang for a clear board, meaning there's no calls. Let's roll. Put on your seat belt."

I complied, and Kern drove out of the parking lot, turned a corner, then turned onto a thoroughfare with three lanes on each side, separated by a large median: East Washington Avenue. Ahead, at the summit of a gentle rise, the Capitol glowed brightly. It was a majestic sight.

"Not much going on," Kern said. "Let's go check out some med labs. Chances are you won't be doing many deliveries driving late nights, but most of the nighttime deliveries are lab deliveries."

Kern maintained a steady speed as the cab climbed East Washington, weaving around the occasional car. He began to explain the process of bidding for calls. "All of your radio transmissions must be concise," he said. "We use a lotta slang. Check the slang glossary in your manual. For instance, when bidding, you don't have to say East Washington Avenue or West Washington Avenue. You can just say, 'the Ave.'"

"How will the dispatcher know if it is East or West Washington?"

"They'll know by your cross street. For instance, that street we just passed, Patterson? We'd call that, 'Pat and the Ave.' Same thing with some of these other streets. West and East Johnson is John. East Gorham is Egor."

Kern caught me shaking my head. "Don't worry," he said. "You'll pick it up before too long. The key is eliminating unnecessary words. You don't have to say 'street' or 'road' or 'avenue.' The name of the street will be enough. And you don't have to say 'going to.' 'To' is enough by itself."

We circled the Capitol and turned onto West Washington. Kern pointed a couple blocks ahead. "The first med lab on our tour. The Meth. That's the Methodist Hospital." Kern reached down and pressed the 10-7 button. The dispatcher quickly responded, and my trainer explained that we were commencing a tour of medical laboratories.

After he showed me the Methodist Hospital laboratory and pharmacy, we were almost out the door on our way back to the cab when a security guard came running toward us, a plastic bag in his hand. "Got one for you," he said with a smile.

Kern flashed a toothy grin, accepting the bag which held a vial containing yellow liquid, along with a pink piece of paper. This, he explained, was a voucher that should be handed in with the waybill at the end of the shift.

"Cool!" Kern exclaimed, once back inside the cab. He pointed at a flashing red light illuminating the lower right corner of the radio. "See that? The dispatcher's been looking for us. Most likely because he wanted to assign us to pick up this package. But we're one step ahead of him. Now, when you return to your cab after being out of it, always check to see if that light is flashing. If it is, it means the dispatcher hit your call button, and you should immediately hit your HiQ button." I reached down and punched the HiQ button. Kern smiled at my initiative and lifted the microphone from its cradle.

"Seventy," the dispatcher said.

"Right here," Kern replied. "If it's about the package to GML, we already got it."

"Ten-four," the dispatcher replied.

"But hey," Kern said, "we got a trainee here. How 'bout you nuke us again?"

"My pleasure," the dispatcher replied. A few seconds later, a loud series of beeps filled the cab.

"Thanks," Kern told the dispatcher. He replaced the microphone. "Dispatchers will also use the call button to get your attention if you're not paying attention to the radio when they're looking for you. You don't want them to have to nuke you during rush hour. They get pissed if you do that too often, and if you get that kind of bad rep, the dispatchers might not see your bid light as quickly as more attentive drivers. But hey, don't lose any sleep over it. A co-op is willing to work with people. Hell, I remember back at Yellow Cab, if you didn't answer up right after a dispatcher called your number, they'd pass right over you."

I put on my seatbelt and watched as Kern did the same. Instead of moving toward our destination, he turned on the interior light. "Before we leave, we need to figure out the rate from here to GML."

I shook my head.

Kern snorted loudly, then explained how to calculate a rate from the delivery-zone map. His tone was patient, but he seemed to bristle slightly when I was unable to find GML on the map. Once he explained that there was a list of accounts, including addresses and the zones where they reside, it was easy to determine the proper rate. I retrieved a charge slip from the glove compartment and began filling it out. "How did you know it was going to the General Medical Lab?"

"This delivery always goes to GML. Besides, that's what it says on the voucher. Of course when you're assigned the call, the dispatcher will give you all that information, but if you need to filter out some information, you can feel free to not hear the destination 'cuz ninety-nine times out of a hundred, it'll be on the package. It's the origin that's important."

I completed the charge slip and handed it to Kern for inspection. He nodded thoughtfully, then crossed the name Farkas from the top of the charge slip and replaced it with his own.

"Already thinking like you're the one in charge here," Kern said. "I like that." He shifted into gear, and we were on our way.

It was good that we went to GML because it seemed doubtful I could have found the lab on my own. At night, one has to park in a garage across the street and cross an enclosed sky-walk to get to the lab.

After departing GML, Kern took me to a half-dozen other laboratories, concluding with the Red Cross, where I was once again the butt of one his half-witted attempts at humor.

"I saved the best for last, Count," he said, as we drove past the sign with the large red cross. "We deliver a lot of blood, but remember, they don't like it when drivers deliver boxes full of empty packets."

You may laugh at the irony of this, but be assured that underneath *my* feigned laughter lay no thoughts of how nice it would be to enter a blood bank with impunity. Did I not have a job to do? Was I not doing this for money? Kern had mentioned that sometimes we deliver food to customers. If a human driver could complete such a delivery without eating the food, why would I not be able to deliver a box of blood without ingesting the contents of those nice little packages? Besides, chilled blood is as distasteful to me as chilled red wine is to a human connoisseur.

"Time to learn how to make money," Kern said, after we left the Red Cross. He had me punch the empty button. As he had said, we were now "10-8," ready to take calls. "Hear that?"

"I am sorry. Apparently, I missed that last transmission."

"Okay, just listen."

A moment later, I heard the dispatcher's voice crackle over the radio: "Odana and Grand Canyon."

"Ever use a radio before?" Kern asked, as he lifted the microphone from its cradle. I nodded. "Great." He punched the bid button and handed me the microphone. "Remember, you need to know what you're going to say before you say it. And we're in cab seventy. I'll make it easy for you." He promptly pulled the cab over to the side of the road.

The dispatcher called our number before I could read the street signs before us. I opened the channel and paused a moment before finally stating our location.

"Seventy," the dispatcher replied immediately, "the Radisson. Comes up."

I looked at Kern. "What is our assignment?"

"Seventy," the dispatcher said, "did you copy?"

"I got it," Kern said. "Just say ten-four."

And so I did, excited that we had finally gotten a call. But where was the Radisson? I knew it was a hotel, but its location and how to get there was a mystery.

"Update the radio," Kern said. "And you didn't have to say 'at the intersection of Blackhawk Road and University Avenue.' Just Blackhawk and U."

I pressed the acknowledge button, then paused and consulted the radio zone map, but it was all gibberish. I hastily flipped through the training manual, found the listing of hotels, acquired the address of the Radisson, then matched it with the city map, again consulted the radio zone map and finally pressed the northwest button.

"How do we get to the Radisson?" Kern asked once I had finished shuffling through my papers. He snorted as I reopened the map.

"It's at Grand Canyon and Odana," I said after quick study. "We can get there from Mineral Point Road."

"How do we get to Mineral Point Road?"

"That is a good question, Kern."

"Well, check this out. Cab driver's shortcut." He took a sharp right and drove like a madman down a stretch of particularly bumpy road and past a cemetery. "This is Franklin. Franklin runs straight from University to Speedway. Speedway turns into Mineral Point. Pretty cool, huh? No stop signs. No lights. A key to cab driving. Gotta keep moving. Remember, moving wheels mean big deals."

Big deals for whom? Was he not getting his usual commission plus an extra hourly wage for training? I was not completely certain it was all for my benefit. But I had successfully turned words into money. By the false bliss of heaven, I *could* do this. If someone like Kern could do it, if all these children I had seen around the cab company could do it, certainly I could as well.

Shortly, we arrived at the hotel. As we pulled up to the front entrance, Kern continued his dissertation.

"It's what I call 'the fine art of loading calls.' It changes depending on time of day, whether the pick-up is a house, an apartment, a hotel, a bar or a restaurant. It's always easiest when they're right out there waiting, but you can never count on that."

Except there they were, waiting right in the lobby. I immediately pressed the destination button.

"Very good," Kern said with a laugh. "Of course, these guys, for once being ready to go when we got here, they're not making my job easier."

The two men, quickly chilled by the night air, practically sprinted to the cab.

"Howdy," Kern said. "Where to tonight?"

"State Street," one said.

Kern shifted into gear, maneuvered out of the parking lot and turned on the meter. "Which end of State?" he asked. "Down by the campus? At Lake Street?"

"Just get us close to the bars."

"No problem," Kern replied. "Oh, by the way, we're training tonight." The men grunted, then began speaking among themselves. I consulted the radio zone map again. I could find State Street and was pretty sure it was in the downtown zone, but wanting to be absolutely sure, I consulted the city map. Kern shook his head.

"We're moving, so we should be listening to the radio closely," he rebuked. "Now, we're a ways from the downtown, so we shouldn't bid until we get much closer because there'll be plenty of cabs already in that neck of the woods that'll beat us on pretty much anything. If, on the other hand, we were going *from* the downtown *to* the Radisson, I would say bid on anything west."

"What if I hear an intersection called, but I am uncertain where it is?"

"When in doubt, bid. The dispatcher might make fun of you over the air, but fuck 'em. And remember, if you get a call every time you hit the bid button, you're not bidding enough."

It was becoming clear that Kern was quite the mercenary fellow—but who better to learn from?

"Are you paying attention to our route?" Kern asked.

"I am trying." Mineral Point had become Speedway, curving around that lovely cemetery before turning into Regent Street at a queer five-way intersection where three different streets converged. "From here we would take Regent all the way to Park? Where we dropped off that specimen at GML?"

"Not bad," Kern replied, "but it'd be better to take Regent to Monroe, cut over by the stadium, then turn north onto Randall and east onto Johnson. Going downtown to deep west is pretty easy. Just three basic routes. Regent to Speedway to the Point. Monroe to Odana. Or straight out University, though you might want to take the Old Middleton cut-off. Remind me to show you that one."

My head spun with the names of all these streets. Fortunately, Kern quieted as the dispatcher called a cluster of intersections, some of which I actually did recognize as downtown and campus. Extensive mnemonics *would* be necessary.

"Would now be a good time to bid?" I asked. We were much closer to the destination. Kern handed me the microphone. "State and Lake," I said aloud to no one in particular, just an exercise, then I pressed the bid button and watched for street signs. Momentarily, the dispatcher took our perfectly executed bid.

"Seventy," the dispatcher said a moment later, "get the Six-oh-two for Peggy."

I acknowledged the call and held my peace until we dropped off our passengers. The fare was nine dollars. They smiled and handed Kern a ten and two ones, then wished me luck.

"Where's our next call?" Kern asked.

I had written it on a piece of scratch paper. "The six-oh-two," I parroted, "whatever that is. Wherever that is."

"It's a bar, the 602 Club at six-oh-two University Avenue, also known as 'The House of Sparkling Glasses.' Great place. Year after year gets voted best dive bar, but that's a lotta bullshit. Just 'cause it's not all glitzy and full of students, they think it's a hole, but it's the most intellectual bar in town."

My kind of place, I thought. "And where is it?"

"Frances and U, right at the corner."

I promptly searched my city map for that intersection. Kern sighed loudly. I knew what he was thinking, but if it was necessary to look up every point of origin and every destination, so be it.

"The fine art of loading calls, part two," he said. "When you pull up to a bar or restaurant, give it about a minute, just to see if they're watching. If not, we go inside and dig the person out."

A minute passed, and I followed Kern inside. The small bar was crowded and dark, made darker by the forest-green walls. Bordello-red upholstery on the chairs, stools and booths glowed luridly in the dim light. Dust-coated artwork covered the walls, giving the place a definite Bohemian feel to it. Kern edged his way through the crowd. The bartender seemed to know him.

"Hey, Kern," the bartender said, brandishing a glass goblet. "Schooner?"

"Nah, I'm working. Unfortunately. Somebody call for a cab?"

"Yeah." He turned to his right toward a woman who was quietly smoking a cigarette. "Peggy! Cab's here."

The woman turned toward Kern. "I'm right outside," Kern said, then he turned and fought his way back through the crowd toward the cab.

"The fine art of loading calls, part two, sub A," Kern resumed once back in the cab. "Some drivers go into a bar and start yelling at the top of their lungs. You can do that if you want. I think it looks bad. Also, some drivers will stand over the passenger until they leave, then escort them to the cab. Again, you can do that if you want, but I'd just as soon do it this way so the person doesn't feel so rushed. You probably get a better tip this way."

Shortly, the woman emerged, and we took her to the near south side. Once at the destination, he took the woman's money and made change. The dispatcher recited a few intersections, and I heard the name "Fish." Fish Hatchery? I hit the bid button, and by the time Peggy had left the cab, we had another call.

"Very good, Al," Kern said. I had not thought he was paying any attention to what I was doing. "Now, do you know where Martin Street is?"

"No, but I can find it quickly on the map."

Kern shook his head. "Forget about that for now. You seem to have the radio down pretty good. I think it's time for you to drive."

"Drive? Now?"

"Sure, why not? I can see you know how to handle the radio. I can also see you don't know where anything is, but there's nothing I can do about that. Now, I wanna see you behind the wheel."

"Whatever you think best." The moment of truth had arrived; something had to be done about that infernal rear-view mirror. I dallied for a short moment, snapping on my seatbelt, moving up the bench seat, which caused Kern to groan and wish for a newer vehicle with bucket seats.

"I hate short trainees," he said as his knees pressed against the glove compartment, bending him into the fetal position. "Okay, for now, I just want you to drive. I'll tell you exactly where to go, and I'll handle the radio. I want you to concentrate on nothing but driving."

Momentary panic thundered into my being. Kern would not allow me to stall much longer, but then I noticed a small lever at the base of the mirror. Pulling the lever forward caused the mirror to tilt upward, giving me a view of the cab's ceiling, yet the back window was visible.

"Anti-glare position," Kern said.

"Ah, excellent," I replied, shifting into gear and feeling the car drift forward. I turned right, coasted toward Fish Hatchery and, once there was absolutely no traffic coming from either direction, gingerly pressed the accelerator. The vehicle responded, but not with the aplomb of my beloved Bentley and certainly not anything like my last Jaguar. It struck me as inconceivable that anyone could lose control of one of these relatively tame creatures.

"Martin's coming up on our right in about a half mile," Kern said, "right before the Starvin' Marvin's. That's a convenience store, locally owned by the Marvin family. They make great sandwiches, a nice thing to know if you get hungry."

The brightly lit convenience store glowed in the distance, but it seemed unlikely I would buy sandwiches there. At the appropriate street sign, I flipped the right directional indicator, slowed, braked and made the turn. Kern nodded his head after each small action.

"Here's the fun part," Kern said. "Finding an address on a dark street. How's your night vision?"

"Not bad," I said, proud to have drifted into the vernacular and doubly proud when I found the address with greater ease than Kern would have expected. He grunted, then grudgingly complimented me as we watched, only to see no one emerge from the apartment building.

"The fine art of loading calls, part three. If it's daytime and you pull up in front of a house, if you don't see somebody coming out right away, you might blow your horn. You can do that at a small apartment building, too. But we don't honk after dark. So, we hit the HiQ button, and when the dispatcher answers, we ask for a phone call. Also, it's a good idea to say the address to double-check that you're at the right place."

I reached for the HiQ button, but Kern stopped me.

"Wait at least a minute before asking for the phone call. If the person comes out right after you ask for the phone call, make sure you tell the dispatcher."

"Another HiQ?"

"No, just break right in."

A minute passed, and I requested the phone call. The passenger emerged shortly thereafter. His destination was Baird Street. I reached for the street directory, but Kern stopped me.

"I'll show you the way," he said. "For now, I just want to see you drive."

This was just as well. Kern's labyrinthine path toward the destination was far from readily apparent on the map, a classic demonstration that part of what makes Madison a complicated place to drive is the dearth of streets meeting at right angles.

"That will be two dollars and fifty cents," I said at the end of the ride. The passenger tried to hand me some bills, but Kern intercepted them.

"We're training," Kern said. "I'm the bag man."

The man smiled. "Keep the change, but make sure he gets the tip."

"No problem," Kern said. After the passenger left, my trainer pointed at the street sign that stood before us. "I want you to look up this street in your street directory."

Kern wore a knowing smile when I turned to him, perplexed after finding the street in the directory. "I don't know any of these streets that are used as points of reference."

"I didn't think you would. The street directory is useful because it's quicker than reading your map, but it doesn't do you any good if you don't know the referenced streets. The map gives you a clearer picture, but it's cumbersome and doesn't really tell you the best routes. What might look like a real good shortcut may not be."

"May I assume that there is no replacement for knowing the city like the proverbial back of one's hand?"

Kern nodded. "Feel free to ask your passengers for help if you don't know where something is. Generally, they'll be perfectly happy to give you directions. Hell, it's in their best interest. If someone's gonna be a jerk about it, fuck 'em. To keep from looking like too much of a moron, you can say something like, 'do you have a favorite route?' That usually works pretty well. But also, play up that you're new. That works pretty well for sympathy tips. Besides, no matter how well you know the city, always remember that you do have to go the way the passenger wants. After all, the customer is always right."

"I have heard that saying before."

"Well don't forget it, Count. The customer is always right, that is, unless they're a raving psychotic."

I shifted into gear and eased forward, retracing our previous route. Kern pointed out a strip of bars, saying calls were frequent from those establishments. He pointed to his right as we passed the intersection of West Washington and Park, saying it's called "the five points" in cab slang. We reached Park and Regent, which brought an earlier association that was somehow helpful in painting an internal geometry; Regent also crosses West Washington. This whole area is one big triangle.

"We call this Spaghetti Corners," Kern said. "Before urban renewal, this was a Italian neighborhood, Sicilian mostly, but the city tore it all down. Prejudice mainly. The 'Tenderloin' may not have been the prettiest place in the world, but it *was* a real, honest-to-God ethnic neighborhood."

"Where did these people go?" Hulking medical buildings loomed on either side, shrouding in long shadows the lone remaining businesses, Josie's restaurant and a Fraboni's deli.

"The suburbs. Wherever they could afford to go. Supposedly, during that particular urban renewal period, the Italians were paid considerably less for their homes than their Northern European counterparts. Anyway, that's just a little Madison history from someone who's lived here his whole life. So what should we do now?"

The radio was silent. I would have thought that with the cold weather, there would be more people calling for cabs. "I do not know."

"Finding a cab stand wouldn't be a bad, but I have a better idea. Can you find your way to the airport?"

"I think I know where that is. Shall we go there?"

"Ahead, warp factor seven, Mister Sulu." Kern laughed. "Y'know, there's an amazing mental process that goes on when you get assigned a call. It's kind of like having a little *Starship Enterprise* inside your head."

I have watched the television show to which he was referring on occasion and found it mildly entertaining— though it seems astounding that these humans are so fascinated with outer space, where none of them will ever go, while there are so many mysteries on this planet that they take for granted every day of their lives.

"You get a call, and it's like there's a little Captain Kirk who orders a little Mister Chekov to plot a course. Then, once the course is plotted and laid in, a little Mister Sulu takes you where you want to go."

"Fascinating," I replied. Kern laughed at that. He seemed at ease, hopefully due to my performance. It did occur to me that Kern might have the power to say he did not think I would be suitable for the task of driving a cab. My radio acumen was satisfactory, and my driving was more than satisfactory. Obviously, my knowledge of the city was limited, but had I not passed their geographic test? How much would they expect?

"I'll say one thing," Kern said, practically reading my mind. "You drive well. Don't think I haven't been watching. Of course, some trainees I'm almost scared to watch, but you drive very sanely. You use your turn signals. You seem comfortable behind the wheel, and you're never in too much of a hurry. That's good. Very good."

"I have been driving quite a long time."

"Too bad you've been driving in Madison only a short time."

"You are concerned?"

"Yeah. If you knew the city, I'd have to say you'd make a great cab driver, but you don't, and it worries me. We'll talk about that later. For now, just get us to the airport in one piece."

"Aye, aye, Captain."

At the airport, Kern pointed out the taxi-loading area. Only six cabs were allowed in the stand. Additional cabs had to sit in the adjacent overflow area or risk getting ticketed by airport security.

"They love writing us cabbies tickets," he said. "It's bullshit. They need us, but they treat us like shit. You know, the guy who runs the airport was one time actually quoted as saying that cabs at the airport are like fleas on a dog."

The ready stand was full, and a few cabs sat in the overflow area, but there appeared to be no one inside waiting for baggage. I wondered if we would stay, and speculated what value the cooperative would garner from paying Kern an hourly wage just so the two of us could sit at the airport, but my trainer had altruism on his mind.

"Slow time," Kern said. "Let's head back uptown. I'm not much of a trainer if I let us just sit here and shoot the shit for an hour, waiting to load."

We left the airport and ran about a half-dozen calls before Kern announced that our training session was complete. His announcement felt abrupt. Had he decided my training was adequate? Or had he felt that no amount of training could make up for a total lack of geographic knowledge? As we drove back to the office, I glanced furtively at his face, trying to read an expression that was totally enigmatic.

Kern showed me how to refuel the cab and take the ending readings. We parked the vehicle and gathered up all our belongings, then returned the cab key to the dispatcher.

Kern sat me down in front of an electronic adding machine and walked me through the process of balancing a waybill at shift's end. He counted his money and handed me a five-dollar note—my share of the tips. After we completed the paperwork, he seemed impressed, then plucked an evaluation form from his rucksack and began filling it out, explaining each point as I watched.

"Driving, I'll give you a five." Categories were each judged on a numeric scale from one to five, five being the best. "Radio skills, another five. You were shaky at first, but got it down pretty good. Paperwork, a definite five, but when you're anal-retentive, paperwork comes pretty easy. Customer relations, another five. That Old World charm should work pretty well, especially with the women." He winked at me.

The last category was "knowledge of the city." I held my breath as Kern wrote a two on the form. At the bottom, a line read, "should this trainee be hired?" Kern paused, tapping his pen back and forth between the box that said "yes" and the one that said "no."

"Your knowledge of the city is not good, not good at all, and I am very concerned about that, Al. Now, there is something you have to understand. Just because the Hiring Committee decided to hire you, that doesn't guarantee you've got a job here. All new drivers are on probation when they start. They have to pass probation before they become members of the cooperative. As of right now, you don't have any of the rights a member has. You could get fired tomorrow and have no right to appeal."

I held my peace, held my breath, waiting for Kern to complete what the Americans would call his pregnant pause.

"Also, I want you to know, as a trainer, I can recommend that we not hire somebody. Management is free to ignore me if they want, but the few times I've said, 'don't hire this person,' they *have* listened to me."

Another pregnant pause. What was Kern implying? I wished he would just say whatever it was he wanted to say. How typical of these commoners. They crave power, and when they finally get it, all they can think of is how to use it against their betters.

"With seasoning, I see absolutely no reason why you can't eventually become one hell of a cabbie. You're smart, you do everything else well. Your knowledge of the city will come in time. I am therefore recommending that we hire you. And, considering that you've mastered everything else, and that you're simply going to have to get to know the city on your own, I'm concluding your training, as of now."

"That is wonderful!" I grabbed Kern's hand and shook it vigorously. "When may I start?"

"You'll have to talk to Kevin about a schedule. Give him a call tomorrow. He'll set you up. Just remember, take it slow. No one's gonna expect too much from you right away. As long as you don't crack up any cabs."

"I will remember that."

"Also remember, we *will* be watching you, Al. Granted, I'm telling you to take it slow. I'm telling you we never expect too much from rookies right at the beginning, but do not forget, you are on probation, which means you can be terminated at any time. It also means that if you're not cutting the mustard, your probation may be extended past the standard guidelines."

"I understand." My tone quickly shifted from enthusiastic to solemn.

"Bottom line, everybody's gotta pull their weight. We have the interests of the entire membership to keep in mind. You're allowed to work through problems, to make mistakes, but only up to a point. We need drivers who make money. We don't need drivers who cost us money just to have them on the road. Capeesh?"

I nodded soberly. "Yes. I understand." Quite fully.

Chapter 5
WORKING FOR A LIVING

The most atypical aspect of my first night as a cab driver was that the weather was downright balmy for early December—death to a business dependent on inclement weather. However, this was a determination made only in retrospect. The basis for normal weather was not within my lexicon, though it did indeed become quite aesthetically pleasing when the first snowflakes began to fall.

But, that first night, the unseasonably warm temperatures proved quite an inauspicious beginning. No matter; had Kern not said to take it slow in the beginning?

He also had said, "We'll be watching you."

I shall never forget my first cab (though, with luck, maybe the memory will fade over the next several centuries). She was not a pretty sight; the exterior was covered with dents and mottled with rust—the phone answerer who had given me the keys described the cab as, "rusty but trusty." Indeed! The upholstery was torn and stained, and the driver's seat bore a huge indentation from too many obese drivers. As I settled behind the wheel, a spring pressed into my buttock. I sank down a few inches, making it difficult to see over the cab's hood. Though the night was warm, it took several tries to successfully start the vehicle before it finally muttered to life, belching a cloud of black smoke. And the cab did not ride any better than it looked. The acceleration was sluggish, and the shock absorbers were virtually non-existent, causing me to wonder if human drivers of this cab would pass blood when urinating.

What had Kern said? All cabs are good cabs? But some cabs *are* better than others, and over time I did get to drive much nicer vehicles than this. Unfortunately, rookie drivers often find themselves driving the worst cabs in the fleet, partially because, when they select, they lack the knowledge of what cabs to seek and what cabs to avoid. Also, rookie drivers often end up driving what no one else will drive, not wanting to appear too choosy, thus giving themselves the reputation of a prima donna.

Nor shall I ever forget my first call. The cab had been inspected inside and out, all variety of lights checked, mirrors adjusted, windows washed, windshield wiper fluid reservoir filled, charge slips all in good supply, seat belt clasped in place, the microphone in hand and there were calls on the board. I hit the bid button and waited for the dispatcher to respond.

"Fifty," the dispatcher said after what felt like an incredibly long time.

And now for my very first bid. I trembled with excitement. "Back lot."

"Head up, Fifty," the dispatcher replied. Either the business was uptown or the dispatcher suggested an improvement of my existential outlook.

"Ten-four," I replied, then shifted into gear and moved with controlled alacrity toward the calls. The dispatcher called off the board, and again I hit the bid button.

"Fifty," he said after calling a few other cab numbers.

I keyed the microphone and spoke, watching for the next intersection. "East Washington and … Patterson."

"Fifty, reading the streets signs, the Paradise."

"Say again?" That was what Kern had said I should say if I did not understand a dispatcher's transmission.

"The Paradise Lounge."

"Where and what is that?"

"Mister Farkas, the Paradise is a bar. Just off the Square, at Carroll and Main. Do you copy, Mister Farkas?"

"Ten-four," I said, momentarily annoyed that he had seen fit to use my name twice in one transmission and was using a rather impudent tone.

Still, excitement filled me, because this was my first call on my first scheduled shift, my first chance to actively participate in the rebuilding of my fortune. My first chance to re-learn how to fend for myself. Kevin, the operations manager, was kind enough to honor my request to work during the best money-making shifts, while allowing for my "special needs," providing a schedule of 6 PM to 4 AM, Tuesday through Thursday, and what they call "circle shifts," 8 PM to 6 AM, Friday and Saturday.

Having consulted my street directory, I proceeded toward where my call should have been only to find an impediment in an angry red sign reading "DO NOT ENTER" where I had hoped to turn. After circling the Capitol Square again, I found the other end of the block—and yet another truculent sign bearing an arrow pointing to the right with a line through it, the lettering underneath reading, "Except bikes, buses, cars and police-authorized vehicles."

The traffic light at my intersection turned green, but I did not move. What in the name of all the false gods of heaven was meant by that sign?

The light turned yellow, then red. When it turned green once again, I threw caution to the wind and made the turn, noticing a restaurant, Crandall's, a bar, with big letters just above the front door, The Shamrock, a glass door, with steps leading upward, The Rising Sun, which I suspected might be some sort of house of ill-repute. Next to that establishment was a plain wooden door, which bore no lettering that I could see, and the door after that was another bar, with a large, green neon sign in the front picture window. Clancy's. I promptly hit my HiQ.

"Where is the Paradise?"

"Carroll and Main." The dispatcher responded to other questions before even waiting to hear my acknowledgment. I hit the HiQ again.

"Yes, Mister Farkas. What can I do for you?"

"I am at Carroll and Main, right around the corner from the Inn on the Park. Where exactly is the Paradise?"

"Right in front of your nose, Fifty. The door immediately west of the Rising Sun. And, Mister Farkas, try to make your transmission more concise."

"Ten-four." Had I not been reasonably concise? This dispatcher seemed not a nice fellow, but I shoved that thought to the back of my mind, then backed up a few feet and parked just west of the plain wooden door, with no window, no neon, no brightly painted signs. My gaze moved upward. Near the top of the building hung a plain black-and-white sign, so dingy that the lettering seemed to blend in with the background. "Paradise Lounge." This *was* the correct place.

The fine art of loading calls. That is what Kern called it. He said we go inside bars and restaurants to "dig out passengers."

No one waited in front of the bar. No one emerged. After about a minute, I went inside. The bar was dark as a cave, the wood paneling absorbing almost all the light. The air reeked of cigarette smoke and stale beer. Though the darkness was certainly comforting, the bar itself was a bustling beehive of humanity, and that is something that has always seemed queer about these mortals—their incessant need to crowd amongst each other and then perhaps complain about the crowding, causing them to depart to yet another crowded bar.

"Someone call for a cab?" I quietly asked the bartender.

He was a cadaverous fellow with deeply set eyes and greasy hair, almost vampiric in appearance—almost. Most vampires, other than the feral ones, take more pride in their appearance. "Yeah. Granny! Cab's here."

"Granny" looked up from her perch at the end of the bar, a drink in front of her.

"I am right outside, ma'am." She nodded at me, and I turned to leave. Shortly, she emerged, her clothes hanging loosely over an emaciated body. When she neared the cab, I got out and opened the back door for her. She smiled at the gesture. Do cab drivers not exercise common courtesy, let alone chivalry? A lady is a lady, after all!

"Good evening. Where may I take you?"

"Twenty-five forty-six East Johnson."

"Do you have a favorite route?" I asked. Then, remembering Kern's advice, I added, "You are my very first passenger."

"Oh. Well, I'm just kitty-corner from Steven's Restaurant. Know where that is?"

"My apologies, ma'am; I do not."

"Well, just take the outer loop around to East Washington, go to sixth and hang a left. Uh, yeah, it's after six, so you can do that. Hang a left on sixth, turn right on Johnson, and I'm right at the end of the block. On the left-hand side."

"Right away, ma'am."

Kern's words—*be nice, and make conversation*—echoed inside my skull. "I trust you have had an enjoyable evening?" I asked.

"Oh, yeah. Not bad. Just a couple cocktails. Been going to the Paradise near a quarter century. Used to go there after work when I worked at Rennie's. Remember Rennie's?"

"No. I am new to town."

"Oh. Rennebohm's used to have drug stores all over town. Now they're all Walgreen's. That statue on top of the Capitol? Joke used to be that was Mrs. Rennebohm pointing to where the next store would be. Had one right on the Square, at the top of State Street. Me and the other girls, we'd work the lunch counter, knock off about three or four, then go to the Paradise for cocktails. They closed the last Rennies 'bout five years ago."

"Did you seek employment elsewhere?"

"Naw, I was already over sixty. Figured I'd retire. It's okay, but I miss the girls, and I miss the Paradise. Don't get downtown much, living on the East Side. 'Sides, can't afford going out for cocktails any more than one or two times a month."

I passed the numbered streets marked our penetration into Madison's East Side. First, Second and so on, until a left-turn arrow with a line through it marked Sixth Street. I cursed in a long-dead language, then at the last moment saw the fine print, "4 PM to 6 PM," and Granny was absolutely correct: it was after six.

"That is three dollars and fifty cents," I said, once parked in Granny's driveway.

She handed me a five-dollar bill. I laid the crumpled note on my thigh, then handed her a dollar, but she stopped me before I could dig out the remaining 50 cents change.

"You're a very nice young man," she said, handing me back the dollar and reaching for the door handle.

I jumped out of the cab and opened the door for her and watched her until she was safely inside her house, then turned the volume up on the radio and listened.

Feel free to work at your own pace, at least in the beginning.

In order to pay Granny the proper attention, I had lowered the radio's volume, relegating the dispatcher's crackling transmissions to mere background noise.

"West near the U Hospital. West on the Lakeshore. Frances and U. Friendly Corners. Union Corners."

When in doubt, bid.

"Shifty," the dispatcher said. "Shifty, your bid." His voice had grown quite impatient. "Mister Farkas, do you care to bid, or are you just hitting your bid button to exercise your index finger?"

Shifty—he was using slang of an unfamiliar nature and then berating me for not understanding. What a disagreeable fellow! I looked up at the street signs. "Johnson and North."

"Anybody beat North and John for the Town Dump?" A moment later, "Fifty, get the Town Dump for Evan."

"Excuse me?" I asked, feeling puzzled. The Town Dump? Who would be there at this time of night? A city sanitation specialist?

"The Town Pump, Mister Farkas. It's a bar. At Union Corners."

"Where exactly?"

The dispatcher sighed. "Union Corners is the intersection of East Wash, Milwaukee and North, so called because it's one block west of Union Street and because the Union House bar is right there. The Town Pump is at the northeast corner. Do you copy, Mister Farkas?"

"Ten-four." I opened the map to determine the precise location.

"Update your radio, Mister Farkas," the dispatcher said, moments after his previous transmission. Hastily, I punched the acknowledge button, then consulted the radio zone map, just to make sure to update into the proper geographic zone. That completed, I proceeded onward to my next call and proudly managed to find the Town Pump on the first attempt.

The sight of a large yellow vehicle with a light on top prompted no movement from the patrons of this particular establishment. After the requisite minute, I went inside, only to quickly discover why the dispatcher had called this charming little bistro "the Town Dump."

The white walls had long gone yellow from the cigarette smoke and were dotted with the crushed remains of insects. The stench of stale and fresh vomit hung luridly in the air. The barrel-chested bartender wore a large, black patch that covered nearly half of his pockmarked face.

"Somebody call for a cab," I said, lowering my tone a couple of octaves and adding a pinch of gravel to my voice. The patrons, an odoriferous collection of scraggly beards and unwashed clothes, turned and stared. My nostrils pinched shut, trying to beat back the assault of unappetizing throats covered with sour-tasting flesh, yet this saloon bore a fond familiarity, being the kind of place common in the forgotten areas of bigger cities, often near the docks, where one can take sustenance with utmost prudence.

An old man staggered forward. He was sinewy, his face weather-beaten, as if he had slept for forty years in a sand storm. "Yeah, I'm comin," he growled.

"See ya, Evan," the bartender said, showing teeth that, much to my surprise, were intact and not rotted. "You take good care of Evan, ya hear?" I nodded, then held the door for my passenger.

"Where may I take you?" I asked, once inside the cab.

"Paddy's Pub. At the East Side Shop."

"Do you have a favorite route?"

"Well, back up a few feet onto North Street, then turn left at the light."

"I am afraid I cannot do that legally, sir." Or at all. A line of cars sat at the intersection, just around the corner from the bar, making the prescribed maneuver impossible.

"Then just go around the goddamned block. *I* don't give a fuck." Quickly agitated, he spoke not with flow, but with single, clipped sentences, the beginning of each one punctuated by a sound not unlike a freshly spun top, with several grains of sand imbedded within the works.

"Right away, sir."

"*Over* here to your right." We had traveled a mere quarter-mile. "*Right* in here. *Right* over there."

The fare was $1.75. He handed me a pair of sweaty, crumpled dollar bills.

"*Keep* the fucking change. *You* probably need it more than I do."

"Thank you, sir." Yes, indeed. Thank you very much. Time to call my broker and order ten thousand shares of my favorite blue-chip stock.

With a Neaderthal-like grunt, he was out of the cab and very quickly inside Paddy's Pub. I updated the radio and made the proper notations on my waybill, then consulted the list of official cab stands and was in for a pleasant surprise; the East Side Shop was an official stand. I hit my stand button, plucked Suetonius from the dashboard and resumed my reread of *The Twelve Caesars* while waiting for my next call. After all, Kern did say the cab stands were there to keep drivers from wasting too much petrol by driving aimlessly all over the city in search of fares.

According to my book, upon hearing that the Roman Senate had declared him a public enemy and that soldiers were near, Nero had decided to take his own life. He pressed a dagger to his throat, but could not complete the task that he knew would preserve the little that remained of his honor. A slave was about to help Nero come to an honorable end when the dispatcher interrupted.

Thirty minutes and 40 pages had passed. "Fifty, where are you?" The sweet-as-vinegar voice of the previous dispatcher had been replaced by the excited, high-pitched yodel belonging to none other than Dexter. I had met him during my training. He was the full-time graveyard dispatcher and had served in that capacity for a number of years. Or, as he had said, "When the company moved into this building, I came with the place."

Dexter was a tall mass of protruding bones. His face was ruddy to the point of being lurid, and his prominent Adam's apple would rapidly bob up and down when excited.

I'd been told Dexter's knowledge of the city was downright arcane.

"East Side Shop," I replied.

"Well, you been sitting there awhile, Fifty. The business is uptown. Do you wanna come up for a call or sit and wait for your inheritance?"

"All calls are good calls, are they not?"

Dexter laughed. "Fifty, come up to the Willy Bear."

"Where is that?"

"It's the old 'Jack of Diamonds.' At Few and Willy. Twelve-ten Willy."

"Ten-four." There was no Willy Street in the directory, but I presumed that "Willy" was slang for Williamson, which runs northeast from East Wilson and South Blair to the Yahara River, making it another one of the four thoroughfares that cover the length of the Isthmus. And if I did have a problem finding the Willy Bear, at least this new voice over the radio would provide instructions without editorial comment; while the previous dispatcher croaked like an angry toad, Dexter chirped like a happy cricket.

The Willy Bear proved quite easy to find. And the passenger was waiting outside the bar! And she moved quickly to the cab! And, when the fare ran $2.50, she handed me a five-dollar bill and told me to keep the change!

Ah, sweet mystery of life, at last I have found you.

****

The evening's commerce eventually settled into a mildly lucrative rhythm, providing a tolerably balanced mixture of satisfaction and confusion. All in all, the shift proved uneventful, the meter totaling $74.00, with another $15.00 in tips. No millionaire gave me a hundred-dollar bill for a five-dollar fare and said "Keep the change"; however, no one saw fit to vomit in my cab.

As I would discover, most of our business centered around the downtown/campus area, though a few longer, cross-town fares managed to present themselves, providing a greater meter, though leaving me far away from the downtown. Fortunately, all the peripheral areas were only a few miles from the downtown, a situation more preferable than, let us say, Paris, where a ride to the city's edge might be lucrative, but the return to the Champs-Elysées would take an eternity.

As Kern had suggested, I did work at my own pace, running a call, then proceeding to the nearest cab stand to be optimally prepared to receive the next assignment. After all, if, as Kern had said, time is money and a vampire has nothing but time, then would I not be a rich man indeed?

Perhaps not today or tomorrow, but my situation allowed for a high degree of patience, thanks to the fact that my rent and auto insurance for the next year had been paid in advance. Heat and electricity bills would still come due every month, but surely the figures would be nominal. Food, of course, was free and, thus far, plentiful. As the Americans say, most of my earnings this first year would be gravy.

Such was my evaluation of this maiden voyage on the good ship Co-op Cab as this first shift neared conclusion. And then the opportunity to run one more call presented itself, thus ending the shift on a positive note.

"Fifty," Dexter said, "get the Irish Pub at three-seventeen State, just east of Gorham. That's the old Merlyn's. For Sheena, the bartender. Comes east toward your office."

"Ten-four," I replied. Dexter had quickly gotten accustomed to my lack of geographic cognizance, but was nothing less than cooperative and helpful, freely giving instructions, thus allowing me to more easily unearth the locations of all the bars to where he had dispatched me. Motherless spawn of Satan! How many bars *were* there in this city?

Again, his instructions proved useful, allowing the greatest ease in seeking my quarry, and Sheena was watching through the front window, keys in hand, immediately able to secure the bar as soon as I pulled up.

"Eight-sixteen Spaight," she said, adding, "please."

"Right away. Do you have a favorite route?"

"Sure. Just turn here on Johnson. Take it to Patterson, turn right and take it right to Spaight." Her soft contralto seemed to smile. Lilac perfume tickled my nose, but underneath that artificial scent lay the true richness of her flesh. I opened my nostrils, letting her bouquet wash over my inner being. Deep inside me, something stirred, something to subdue because yes, there was a purpose here—to make money.

"I trust you have had a nice evening?" I asked.

"Yeah. Busy as hell. I'm beat. Can't wait to crawl into bed. I feel like I just wanna sleep forever."

"I understand. It has been an interesting night for me as well."

"Were you guys busy?"

"To tell the truth, I am not certain. This was my first night driving a taxi."

"Ohhh. How'd it go?"

"Not too badly. I am new to this town and do not have the easiest time finding where my calls are, but I am not entirely displeased."

Sheena laughed lightly, like soft rain. "I've thought about driving cab. Sometimes, when I'm getting real sick of bartending, I think about it. One advantage I could see is, while you might have an asshole in your cab for only five or ten minutes, I might have that asshole in my bar the whole damn night."

I laughed. "Do you see any sort of similarity between these two vocations?"

"A bit. You guys help us out a lot. When someone's been getting in our hair, we can just call a cab, and you make 'em disappear." She snapped her fingers. "Like, poof! Gone. And a lotta bartenders take cabs a lot. I mean, I have a car, but I don't feel like driving after hustling drinks for eight hours. Besides, I feel a lot safer having you come right to the door. I'd just as soon not walk in the dark to where my car is parked."

"Do you see many cab drivers on the other side of the bar when you are at work?"

"Hell, yeah. You guys are great customers. Always tip well. Goes hand in hand. Cabbies tip bartenders well. Bartenders tip cabbies well."

The turn onto Spaight revealed a sudden, breathtaking view. Ahead lay Lake Monona, its blackness flickering brightly under a gibbous moon, the downtown Madison skyline defining the northern shore.

The fare was $2.75. I flicked on the interior light and turned to collect the fare from Sheena, noticing her pleasingly rounded figure, her warm smile and her eyes, which were the color of nurturing earth.

She handed me a five-dollar bill and told me to keep the change. I watched her glide to her house, watched her open the door and step safely inside. Watched her disappear up the stairs. Watched as an upstairs light flicked on then off. Watched as she disrobed in the darkness, then disappeared, presumably into the sweet embrace of her bed, which she had said beckoned her so invitingly. Briefly, I considered parking the cab, but decided just to proceed back to the office.

"First night, huh, Al?" Dexter asked when I stepped into the dispatch office after refueling and parking my cab. He took my cab key, hung it on the appropriate hook and handed me my call slips.

"Yes, it was. Was my performance satisfactory?"

Dexter smiled and gave me a slightly quizzical look. "Not from around here, are you?"

"I have not long been living in Madison."

"Didn't think so." He took a deep drag from a cigarette. The expelled smoke enveloped the small dispatch office in a blue haze. "Well, you're not the best rookie I've ever seen, but you're not the worst. You'll do fine. Once you get to know where things are. Just remember, if you're having a problem finding someplace, feel free to ask. I'd always prefer that you ask instead of spending a half-hour driving in circles."

"I appreciate it. I much prefer your attitude to that of your predecessor. He was most uncooperative."

Dexter pinched his face in disgust. "Fucking twerp! Guy's a jerk. Gets a couple dispatch shifts, and he thinks he's God's fucking gift. Hell, he's only worked here a couple years. I remember when he started. Couldn't find his own cock in the dark to save his life. Go ahead and ask him whatever questions you need answered. If he keeps acting like a cocksucker, complain to Kevin or Maureen. They'll set him straight."

"Thank you."

"*De nada.*"

****

Thus, with satisfaction, that first shift ended. On the way home, driving on Williamson Street, I suddenly recognized that Spaight was two blocks away, and Sheena's scent seemed to fill my nostrils once again.

Drive onward, fool. Yes, pleasure was there for the taking, but I chose not to do so, common sense wisely governing my actions. Taking is most often what we do, simply because it is usually awkward to ask. However, accepting what is given is always superior to merely taking.

****

What remained of that first two-week pay period proceeded much in the same manner as that very first shift, with various peaks and valleys relative to the first night's revenue. The compensation was not great, but I despaired not, feeling relatively satisfied with my progress.

It was with great anticipation that I collected my first paycheck. Heavens! When had I last earned a *paycheck*?

The amount of money was not large, but when would it ever be, compared with those astronomical sums to which I had been previously accustomed? I found myself not displeased by the amount of money which could be deposited at my leisure in an automatic teller machine—that bore the inscription, "Tyme is Money," thus sparing me the trouble of finding a bank that remained open after dark.

My enthusiasm was dashed by a memorandum attached to the paycheck:

To: Al Farkas

From: Maureen Hellenbrand, General Manager

Re: Payroll fortification

I wish to call your attention to the fact that your paycheck has been fortified to raise your hourly wage to federally mandated minimum wage. As I'm sure you know, cab drivers are paid commission. However, according to federal law, all drivers must earn no less than minimum wage. Therefore, due to your low earnings for this pay period, your paycheck has been fortified.

This being your first pay period, it is understandable that your earnings might be low. I do want to let you know that if this situation persists, you may be required to undergo more training, and if you still are unable to significantly raise your revenue, you may find your probation extended. If your paychecks consistently need to be fortified, you may not pass probation.

Feel free to seek help if you have questions about any of the procedures or techniques necessary to do your job adequately. And also, feel free to see me with any questions or concerns regarding the above described situation.

We hired you because we believed you could do the job. Hopefully, you will prove that our faith in your abilities was not misguided. Good luck.

Damn the earth under my feet! Federally mandated minimum wage? What in the name of the false gods was that? The notion of a minimum wage seemed inconceivable. The last time my actions had earned money was when the sale of a Gauguin provided a net profit of almost four million dollars. How could I be concerned with pebbles when I had been accustomed to lifting boulders?

I was so stunned that Kern's approach escaped my attention.

"Hey, Count." He slapped the paper as I read it. "A fortune, ain't it? Don't spend it all in one place."

Quickly, the piece of paper was folded and secreted within the back pocket of my blue denim trousers. (Yes, I had resorted to wearing such attire. It seemed that to blend in, it would be prudent to dress as these slovenly young people do.)

"Perhaps not a fortune." That was all I could bear to say; there would be no force in Hades that would open myself to any abuse from the likes of this fellow. Hastily, I turned on my heel and strode to my cab.

And it was not a bad shift, having booked $80, with $15 in tips. At her shift's end, Nicole sat across from me, struggling to get the numbers on her waybill to balance. She looked up at me, eyes shimmering.

My stomach sank. *I do not want this. I do not need this. I do not want to even think about anything to do with this.*

She smiled warmly, her perfect white teeth almost sparkling. "Al, how's it going. Haven't seen you since training."

"Busy," was my terse reply.

"You have a nice shift? Damn!" She looked down at the tangled mess of charge slips and slapped the adding machine.

"It was adequate. Yourself?" Though not really interested, it seemed the polite thing to ask.

"Not too bad." She rummaged through the crumpled piles of currency. How can people be so sloppy with their money? My cash always was always very neatly folded and sorted by denomination. "Not bad for a Tuesday."

Suddenly, I *was* curious. "How much did you book, if you do not mind me asking?"

She shrugged. "I don't mind. Like I said, it was okay. Coulda been better, coulda been worse. Not quite one-twenty, but the other night I pulled in one-sixty, with nearly forty on the side."

One-fifteen had been my best effort thus far.

Suddenly, warning bells started ringing inside my skull. My revenue *should* have been higher. Somehow, there was a flaw in my work, though the thought still rankled me about the concept of minimum wage, as if just under is inadequate, while just over would be perfectly fine. How simplistically arbitrary!

Maybe Kern was to blame. Maybe he did a poor job in training me. "Nicole," I asked, "out of curiosity, who was it who trained you?"

"Kern." She nodded. "He was very thorough. I'm happy I got him. I've heard bad things about one or two of the other trainers, but I think Kern did a good job. Why?"

"No reason." Yes, yet another lie, but I did not want to discuss my failings with these children. My waybill was complete, and all I desired was to get home, listen to some Rossini and try to determine if this scrabbling for spare change was really what was most desirable at this time and under these circumstances.

As I rose to depart, Nicole's gaze locked upon me. "I was wondering…." She folded her waybill and tucked it into an envelope. "Doing anything? Wanna go get a drink or something?"

A drink. What irony. "I am sorry, but I think not." Too harsh. She looked hurt. "Please forgive me." I softened my voice. "I am just preoccupied, but I do not think I would be interested in a drink at this time."

She shrugged, her self-esteem still seemingly intact. "Okay, maybe some other time." Nicole smiled warmly, obviously taking seriously the notion of "some other time." Being polite can be such a burden.

Chapter 6
MARKED

You may cease that infernal tittering. Yes, this situation was most humiliating and having to seek help from Kern only exacerbated my shame.

I attempted to ignore the predicament, but that lasted about a week. Sitting in the cab stand at the Concourse Hotel, someone opened one of the back doors of my cab. Unfortunately, it was not a fare. It was Kern, as always, flashing that ridiculous grin.

"How's it going, Count?" His legs stretched across the entire back seat.

"Adequate."

"Just adequate? Thought you'd be making the big bucks my now."

I stared straight ahead. "I have simply chosen to follow your advice and work at my own pace until feeling comfortable. That is what you recommended, is it not?"

"Time to shift gears."

I turned. He sat up, his smile gone. "What do you want, Kern?"

"Just here to help."

Translation: whip one of the cooperative's workhorses to get more money out of it. "I do not require any help."

He shook his head. "Not the way I hear it, Count. Been talking to Maureen. You're not even making minimum wage. I saw your revenue per hour. You're making three bucks an hour. That eats shit."

A hot, red flash washed over me. Three dollars, six dollars. What was the difference? "I thought this variety of thing was confidential," I said, attempting to hide my rancor.

"It is, normally." He sighed loudly. "Look, as a trainer, I try to follow up on the people I train. I asked how you were doing. Maureen told me she had to write a warning letter about having your paycheck fortified."

Suddenly, his grin returned. "Hey, we can't be having that sort of thing. Makes *me* look bad."

Aha! Makes him look bad, and then perhaps they take away from him the lucrative privilege of training. "I do not require your assistance," I repeated.

"You're wrong there, Al. Hey, you don't need to take this personally. Hell, you're working under a tremendous handicap here, not knowing the city and all. We'll carry you a little while, but you're gonna be under the microscope, so the sooner you start pulling your own weight, the better your chances of passing probation."

"Why are you so anxious to help me?" A good question, or so it seemed. The centuries had long taught me to be suspicious of anyone offering assistance for no apparent price or reason.

"As I said, you're my trainee, and therefore, you're my responsibility."

"Does that mean you get in trouble if I do not become an adequate driver?"

"Nope. Look, I want you to do well. I want all my trainees to do well. I want all of us to do well. It says in the statement of purpose right in our articles of incorporation that we will 'provide a humane working atmosphere and jobs at a living wage.' That's where I'm coming from."

For the first time, Kern struck me as sincere. "Very well," I said after a long, silent moment. "I will consent to whatever you think best."

"Then, you'll let me ride with you tomorrow night?"

"Yes," I answered, resigned to never be free of his vulgar presence.

"Good. I'll be home tomorrow night. Gimme a call when you get a cab."

"And what do you expect in return for your generosity?"

"You become a good cabbie, it's good for the whole co-op. Just buy me a beer sometime. Or maybe two."

Aha! I knew there had to be some form of ulterior motive at work.

****

"That's your first mistake."

"To what are you referring, Kern?" As planned, I had collected him at his home after getting a cab. We had just run our first call, and he had already seen fit to take umbrage at my performance.

"You're empty, right?"

"Correct. There are calls in close proximity. We shall accept our next assignment shortly."

"But you could've already been dispatched a call before dropping off your previous passenger. Now, with no call in front of you, you gotta drive around aimlessly, wasting time, and time is a valuable commodity. Like I've said a zillion times, time is money."

"But did you not say that I should work at my own pace, take my time and not 'bid on the run', as you say, until I felt comfortable?"

"Jesus Christ, Al, I didn't figure you taking me so literally. I meant maybe you might do that for the first shift or two. But you've been on your own for a good two weeks. Time to put on the long pants."

"I beg your pardon?"

"Just get yourself another call, but this time, I want you to bid while running the call. I want you to make sure you have an assignment *before* you drop off your next passenger. Shit, no wonder you're not making any money."

"You will help me?"

"No, I won't. You gotta learn to do this for yourself. Look, you *can* do this. It's simple, really, but you have to be able to bid on the run if you're ever gonna make money. Just take it easy. Pull over to the side of the road if you have to, to copy the call. Or tell the dispatcher you'll hit your HiQ when you're ready to copy. Okay?"

I nodded my head. "Very well, Kern."

"Be ready," Kern said, after we had loaded the next call. "Listen carefully. The dispatcher's about to call the board."

"West near the U Hospital, west on the lakeshore, Breese and Hoyt, Randall and Spring, Lake and Dayton, Lake and Langdon, top of Wisconsin, Crystal Corners, Friendly Corners."

"Do it," Kern said.

I pressed the bid button, lifted the microphone from its cradle and watched for the nearest intersection.

"Seventy-five," the dispatcher said.

"Charter and John to one-hundred West Gilman." 121 W. Gilman actually, but Kern had said to just say what hundred block if I was unable to recite the exact intersection.

"Seventy-five, get the Edgewater."

"The Edgewater. Ten-four."

"See, wasn't that easy?" Kern laughed loudly.

"Yes. Quite easy."

"And now you can proceed immediately to your next call, getting maximum efficiency out of your time. You see, you're going to Carroll and Gilman, and the call was at Langdon and Wisconsin. That's only two blocks away. Of course, if you're downtown and there's calls downtown, you should always bid, even if you're not sure which call you might be up for. And sometimes, it'll be real busy, and you should just bid as soon as you load, even before you hear the dispatcher call off the board because, if you know there's tons of calls and they're everywhere, you know the dispatcher's going to need you to run *some* call, so just bid, and you'll get a call. That's what's called 'bidding blind.'"

"I was wrong to have ever doubted you, Kern."

"You're right about that, Count. So, do you know where the Edgewater is, even though I just told you?"

"I am not certain."

"No problemo. Just look it up after you drop off your current passenger."

****

"Seventy-five, where now?"

"Randall and John," I replied.

"The call's at five-eleven West John," the dispatcher said. "Eighty, where now?"

"Pick it up," Kern said.

"I beg your pardon?"

"Do you know where five-eleven West Johnson is?"

"Yes. It is right before Bassett, is it not?"

"Then, pedal to the metal, dammit. You're in a race. Christ, you drive like my grandmother."

"Did you not tell me to drive safely?"

"I did, but you gotta pick it up a bit. You can drive a *little* faster than the speed limit. Hell, cops won't pull you over if you're within ten. Lotta times Madison cops give us cabbies the benefit of the doubt. Floor it."

"Seventy-five, where now?"

"Park and Johnson."

"Eighty, where now?"

"Goddammit!" Kern spat. The traffic light at the next intersection was red, but would turn green momentarily, having turned yellow the other way, but then a Co-op cab made a left turn onto Johnson, the number eighty visible on the side of the cab. Kern loudly slapped his hands against his thighs. "Dammit, Count, don't you have any killer instinct at all?"

"I beg your pardon?"

"You're in a race, dammit. My grandmother would've beaten you, and she's eighty fucking years old."

"Again, as I told you, I am merely trying to drive carefully."

Kern slapped himself in the side of his head. "You can drive fast *and* carefully. Look, you're in competition out here. When the dispatcher calls a race, you've got to pick up the pace a bit. You've got to say, 'this is my call and ain't no one gonna take it from me.'"

"But is this not a cooperative? We are not out to slit each other's throats, are we? Or are we?"

"Usually, no. We try to keep racing to a minimum. As opposed to Capitol Cab where they race for nearly every call. A few years ago, two Cap Cabs were racing for a call, and they collided on West Wash. The cops who showed up couldn't stop laughing."

"So that means we are a cooperative most of the time, but not all the time?"

"No, I didn't say that. Like I said, we try to keep racing to a minimum, but sometimes, it's just a dead heat. The dispatcher will keep checking with the drivers until someone has a clear advantage. If no one does, they call a race. Just remember, any time you're being considered for a call and you know other cabs are being considered for the same call, pick up the pace a bit. Don't drive like a total maniac. Don't do anything illegal, like run red lights, or go the wrong way on a one-way street, or drive on State Street, but pick it up—because you know the other cabs will. Capeesh?"

"Yes, I understand. Killer instinct. I think I know what that is."

"I don't know about that. God, you're so fucking genteel, Count. You need to drive with more joy, more passion. Maybe some music might help. This cab got FM?"

"Yes, but there is nothing palatable to listen to at this hour."

Kern turned on the radio. "We'll see about that. Ah, here we go." He began humming along with the hideous, high-pitched screeching wail blasting from the radio. Why could he not listen when I had said there was nothing palatable on the airwaves? No classical, no jazz, just that wretched rock-and-roll, that children's music born from twelve-bar blues with three-chord progressions—possibly the lowest form of music ever known to humanity. Or even worse was country, which I found just too pathetic for words and sadly enough seemed to be growing in popularity. Was the collective IQ of this nation dropping lower than it already was?

"The Allman Brothers," Kern gushed. "'Jessica.' Man, the best cruising music ever. These guys are speed, man, just pure, ethereal speed. And that's what killed them, too. Duane—fucking god on the slide—drove his motorcycle into a peach truck after 'Eat A Peach' came out. Barry Oakley drove his motorcycle into oblivion exactly a year later, in almost the exact same place."

"Ah, but their music lives on."

"Damn right."

I was being sarcastic, but Kern was too daft to notice.

"So, what do we do now?" he asked. The board was clear.

"Find the nearest stand? We are merely a few blocks away from the Concourse Hotel. Is that not a good stand at this time of night?"

"It is, but I've got something else in mind. Let's go to the airport."

His manner was quite puzzling. "Just simply drive to the airport?" What was the term? Dead-head? Is it not a waste of fuel to drive clear to the other side of town for the mere possibility of loading a fare? Somehow, it seemed that Kern was not instructing me in the same kind of cooperative manner as when he had officially trained me.

"Sure, Count. Board's pretty quiet right now. It's about nine, there's a few planes due to land any time now. Sometimes, the airport can really make you a lot of money. Didn't you check out the airport schedule?"

I nodded, but honestly, the airport simply did not seem as high a priority as other aspects of the job that needed to be mastered, such as, as the Americans say, knowing my ass from my elbow.

"It's a hot time. Let's go. And pick up the pace a little bit. You can drive faster than the speed limit. Time is money. Let's go. Don't want all the fares to be gone by the time we get there."

The cab lurched forward as I depressed the accelerator, paying close heed to not exceed 35 miles per hour, which was ten over the legal limit. Kern would have me risk this job just to live up to what he thinks a cab driver should be? No gentleman, he.

"The airport's made me a lot of money over the years," he babbled. "Not without paying my dues. Had to learn. You betcha. That comes from sitting for a couple hours before loading someone going to the rent-a-car stand. Then, you go back and wait another couple hours, or just give up the ghost and leave. But then the time comes when you pull up and get a split-load, and it's all worthwhile."

"Split-load?"

"Yeah, didn't I tell you about split-loading, Count? At the airport, the bus stations. Man, it's the Holy Grail. It's better than sex! You load up your cab, charge people individually at a discounted rate, turn in what's on the meter and the rest goes in your pocket. It's fucking legal *and* doesn't violate any work-rules, as long as you follow proper pricing procedures and as long as everyone consents to sharing."

After crossing the Yahara River, which marked the end of the Isthmus, the road veered sharply north before splitting and turning into Packers Avenue, so named because it is where Oscar Mayer is located. The noxious stench of cooked meat floated into my nostrils as I spotted cabs moving south, all with passengers. Kern also noticed.

"Pick up the pace, Count." Kern's voice had changed from gently cajoling to authoritative. He tapped me on the shoulder and pointed toward the cabs in the southbound lanes. "Look at that. Count 'em. One. Two. Three. Four. There's action at the airport. Let's move."

A certain excitement crept into his voice as we reached the airport access road. "Okay, listen carefully. I got a feeling there may be a big crowd when we get there—"

"How would you know?"

"Instinct. Intuition. I just know, that's all. Anyway, listen carefully.

If there's a crowd of people, do not make eye contact with anybody. If someone tries to hail you before we get to the loading area, do not acknowledge them."

Something sounded improper about that. "But are we not going there for a fare?"

"Yes, but if there's a possible split, we don't wanna blow it by agreeing to take someone before we know where they're going. If they're going downtown, south or west, fine. But if they're going north or east, we're screwed."

I tried to protest, but Kern stopped me.

"You wanna make money, this is a great way to make money, and don't forget, it's all perfectly legal. It would be illegal to refuse service, so that's why we don't consent to take someone until we know where they're going. If we establish that everyone wants a cab, we can pick and choose, but if one person approaches us, we have to take them. Capeesh?"

"Not exactly."

"Don't matter. Just follow my lead."

On the way into the airport, two more cabs passed on the outbound, both full of passengers, their trunks overflowing with luggage, the lids tied down with straps. Kern rubbed his hands together vigorously, a lusty laugh coming deep from within his gut.

The scene at the taxi loading area reminded me of Constantanople when under siege by the Turks. The sudden appearance of an ox cart that might take them to safety had sent people into an excited frenzy, all begging the driver for a ride though he barely had room for himself. Even before the cab came to a stop, people streamed toward us, waving their arms. Following Kern's instructions, I stared straight ahead, fighting hard to ignore the thirty or so people all desiring transportation.

With a loud, throaty laugh, Kern jumped from the cab. "Who needs a cab?" he shouted. The crowd of thirty all raised their hands and shouted in affirmation. He laughed again and turned to me. "Pop the trunk, Count." He grinned broadly, then again faced the crowd. "We can't take you all, but we'll try our best. Okay, who's by themselves and needs a cab?" Several people raised their hands and stepped forward. "Who's going west?" Two people raised their hands. "Where you going?"

"The Radisson Hotel," a man in a gray suit said with a thick drawl.

"The Best Western Inntowner," a young woman said.

Kern nodded. "Count, load their luggage into the trunk. Anyone downtown? Campus?" Several hands raised. Kern surveyed them as to their destinations then selected a pair of college students, one man, one woman, both going to separate destinations on Langdon Street.

Momentarily, a not insignificant pile of luggage sat next to the cab. I commenced the task of loading the parcels into the trunk, but had run out of space with half the luggage still sitting on the pavement.

"Having a problem, Count?" Kern asked, after telling the people to be left behind that other cabs would be arriving soon.

"Another thing for you to teach me," I replied, pointing at the overflowing trunk and the pile of luggage still sitting on the pavement.

"Just watch and learn." Kern removed all the luggage, then placed the smaller items along the ledges that surrounded the well inside the trunk. He lifted the three full-sized suitcases and stood them up in the well with the bottom edges sitting against the lip of the trunk, stacked the remaining garment bags atop the suitcases, attached a bungee cord to the lid, pulled it shut and hooked the other end to the bottom of the license plate. Just to make sure the load was secure, Kern yanked at one of the suitcases, then plucked the bungee cord as if it was a violin string.

"Bungee cords," he said with a grin, "they've made me a lot of money over the years."

Kern had finally impressed me, but what kind of situation had he created here? And what on Earth was I supposed to charge these people? And where would we put them all?

"Don't worry," Kern said in reply to my concerns, seeming to read my thoughts. "Tell them that because they're sharing, they get charged individually, but at a discounted rate. Tell them they're being charged limousine rates, which are the lowest rates allowed by law. And it's five apiece for the students, seven to the Inntowner and ten to the Radisson."

As I was about to get back behind the wheel, I glanced at the crowd that stared longingly at my cab. In Constantinople, the mob had killed the ox-cart driver, in the process, tipping over the wagon. A wheel had broken, rendering the wagon useless. The ox bolted and broke a leg when the mob chased it into a ditch.

"Can you send more cabs?" a haggard-looking old woman pleaded, a pile of luggage at her feet.

"Of course," Kern replied. "Okay, we need two in the front, two in the back." He looked at me. "This cab has a bench seat, so you can legally take five passengers, but you gotta have two up front." Kern directed the two men to sit in front with me, while he sat in back between the two women.

"Oh, and Count," Kern said as we left the airport, "hit your LoQ and tell the dispatcher there's action at the airport. Always let the dispatcher know if there's action at the airport. Just make sure you wait until after you leave. You don't want to attract too much attention to the situation until *after* you've got your split."

****

Kern spent most of the ride conversing with the two women. Even without his attention, all the transactions were completed smoothly. The meter ran $15.00, but the cash collected totaled $33.00: $27 in flat-rate limo fares and six dollars in tips. Holy Grail indeed!

Afterward, Kern had me take him home. I tried to share some of my good fortune with him, but he would have none of that.

"Just go out there and make some money," Kern said, "now that you know how. And don't make me have to retrain you again."

Still, one question remained.

"Why was this manner of training so dramatically different from our previous session? Are you trying to tell me that being a good cooperative member and making money are states of conflict and contradiction?"

"Hell, no, Count. Like I said, the co-op wants you to make money. If you don't make money, the co-op doesn't either. It's just that during train-ing, we gotta cover the basics, and we gotta make sure everyone drives safe. Again, I'm not telling you to not drive safe, but you could drive just a smidgen faster. See, again, the co-op wants you to make money, but I can't exactly tell you all the finer points of making money while in my official capacity as a trainer.

"That's why I don't train on Sundays. That's the big day at the airport and the bus stations. Hell, makes it hard to demonstrate how to be a good cooperative member if I ignore the board and dead-head to the airport all the time. Besides, other veterans get pissed if I let out too many secrets to a rookie. After all, we need rookies to run calls that allow us airport rats to do what we like best."

"And what's that?"

"What you just did. Now, get outta my hair, Count. Buy me a few beers sometime. You owe me."

****

At first, Kern had just seemed ridiculous, then selfish, then finally he revealed himself to be a combination of all the possibilities, almost a microcosm of the cooperative itself and all its seemingly diametric contradictions, simply demonstrating that a cooperative is a rather peculiar organism, attempting to balance the interests of the many with those of the one.

Kern's message, however, eventually became clear; the best thing a driver can do for him or herself and the cooperative is to make money. And, thanks to Kern, that was exactly what I began to do. He had been correct in his assessment of my performance, and with his help those bimonthly paychecks began to increase steadily, albeit with certain peaks and valleys.

In my first three months, thanks to Kern's advanced instruction and bitterly cold weather in January and February, I managed to save about two thousand dollars, which then went into a reliable mutual fund. Long-term Madison residents commented that it was the harshest winter experienced in a long time, with the wind chill dropping as low as fifty degrees Fahrenheit below zero—and it seemed that once the snow began falling in December, it did not cease until late February.

However, another factor had asserted itself, contributing to the cab company's overall boom. Following what many called "the annual January thaw," the naked body of a university coed was found on the west end of campus, near the University Hospital, amid the remains of what had been a massive snow bank. Though the crime generated much sensational publicity, details were sketchy. It was publicly reported that her body was badly mutilated and covered with queer cuts, rips and tears. Rumors circulated like wildfire that the body had been drained of blood. That notion struck me as preposterous, merely the puerile imaginings of these vulgar Americans who seem to feel a need for that sort of grisly event.

I did not take the matter seriously. Instead, I just worked hard, as we all did, to provide service for all those people too scared to walk—for awhile at least, until the matter seemed to have been forgotten.

After three months, my probation finally neared completion. It had been a truly profound education in procedures, geography and defensive driving, especially considering the nasty weather conditions Wisconsin offered during winter, be it wet roads, wet roads covered with damp leaves, sleet, snow, or one of the greatest dangers of all: glare ice, also known as black ice, which manifested itself as winter loosened its icy grip. When the daytime temperatures climbed above freezing, the icy tongue of night would coat the streets with this invisible menace.

My first encounter with that fiend shall prove unforgettable. The invisible demon had transformed the roads into a dangerous creature to be respected and feared, and this creature's influence was felt all over town, making even the simplest maneuvers in a parking lot an adventure too exciting for my taste.

In a level parking lot, I was unable to get the cab moving without quickly shifting back and forth from drive to reverse, thus creating a rocking motion that eventually garnered enough momentum to inch forward.. Stop signs and traffic lights were all ordeals; even increasing stopping distance by a factor of ten could not prevent the cab from sliding into crosswalks and intersections.

After a few hours of this farce, I had a party of students going to the Field House. Although a traffic light near the stadium had turned yellow, I proceeded through the intersection without attempting to brake. The creature had made it very clear that it did not want me to use my brakes in any but the most gentle and gradual manner.

A block later, I glanced at the rear view mirror and saw the flashing lights. I immediately pulled over, hoping the vehicle would pass, hoping it was a City of Madison officer in a good mood; Kern *had* said the Madison police usually give cabbies the benefit of the doubt.

As the Americans say, no such luck. In the rear-view mirror, I watched the squad car pull over behind my cab. Then I watched the officer approach, noting that his uniform was not navy blue, but sky blue, marking him as University Police.

"Do you know why I pulled you over?" he asked, his voice a lisping, whining tenor. His face was round and fleshy, his nose flat, eyes dull.

"For running a yellow light?" I replied meekly.

"The light was red," he snapped.

"The light was yellow when I entered the intersection," I countered. "I am sorry, officer, but I was concerned that there might be ice in the intersection."

The officer removed the flashlight from his belt, turned and shined the beam at the intersection. The asphalt's sheen was inconclusive, its blackness glowing flatly under the streetlights.

"I don't see any ice," he said.

I held my breath and counted to ten. I knew it was especially important for me to cooperate with the officer, though I would certainly state my case, respectfully, of course. "There is glare ice all over town," I said finally. "I was simply attempting to exercise caution. It matters not whether there is ice in the intersection, only whether I think there might be."

"Hey, I don't care if there *is* ice in the intersection. I'm gonna write you a ticket. You gotta to stop when the light turns red. I was right behind you. I didn't see any brake lights. You didn't even try to stop."

"Christ, what an asshole," I heard one of my passengers say. The officer shined his flashlight into the cab.

"You mean," another passenger said, "you'd expect him to risk losing control of the cab just so he can stop for your precious traffic light?"

Thank you, I thought.

"These passengers?" the officer asked.

"Yes," I replied haughtily. "I am taking them to the Field House, which is just around the corner from here. If you would allow me to do just that, I promise I will be much more careful. I can assure you I have no outstanding warrants."

The officer gave me a scrutinizing look while fondling the various implements of torture hanging from his belt. "Gimme your driver's license," he said.

Reaching for my wallet, my eyes never leaving his, I thought of the cost of a traffic ticket and considered the importance of this petty little constable in the greater scheme of things. If reincarnation truly exists, I had previously encountered this gentleman when fleeing Germany after the incident in the Black Forest with the highwaymen who had attempted to rob me. He had said my traveling papers did not permit me to ride my horse, just transport it. This constable came too close to arranging a rendezvous between me and a burning at the stake.

"Just a moment," I said smiling. The officer frowned, his expression impatient.

I stared deeply into his eyes, watching them grow larger. My mind opened, projected. Sometimes the minds of others feel like granite, sometimes like steel, sometimes like a well-clenched fist. I almost laughed out loud; it was as if I had plunged my hand into a bowl of lukewarm oatmeal.

The frown dropped off his drooping face. Without a word, the officer turned, walked to his vehicle and drove away.

"Geez," a passenger said. "He's gone? What the hell?"

"I've never seen anything like that before," another passenger said.

I shifted into gear and moved forward slowly. "Sometimes you get lucky," I said, "and catch them in a good mood."

Apparently, Kern's lessons were well-learned. I had adjusted to harsh and hazardous weather conditions. My paychecks no longer needed to be fortified. About a week following the incident with the constable, half a shift had passed when I realized that I had not yet referred to my map or street directory.

And then came the opportunity to prove my mettle in a race. Grateful for dry streets, I was near the east edge of the campus. Ahead was another Co-op Cab, which displeased me because that cab would beat me out of most calls in the area.

"Lake and Dayton," the dispatcher said. Obviously, that had to be Witte Hall, a dormitory just a couple blocks away, most likely the other cab's call. But not necessarily.

The other cab crossed the next street just as the light turned yellow. As the Americans would say, I gunned the engine, and squealed through a left turn just before the light turned red—that constable be damned to hell!—then floored it toward the next intersection, the light snapping green just as I reached the crosswalk. The dispatcher took my bid, then took the other cab's bid. The race was on!

I felt myself grin as my cab flew through the intersection, the rear of Witte Hall on the right, the main entrance on the opposite side of the building. Kern would tell me to stomp on it, and that is exactly what I did.

Stop sign, right turn. Squealed a right turn at the next intersection and pulled up to the main entrance of the dormitory just as the other cab got the green light.

My grin would do Kern justice. Not only had I arrived first, but my cab was on the correct side of the street.

The other cab crossed the intersection, then stopped when even with my vehicle. Even in the darkness, it was easy to see that the driver was glaring angrily at me. Then, his expression changed from anger to close scrutiny, as if he were looking right through me.

Then his expression turned to fear.

And suddenly I recognized the driver. It was the fellow who had given me a ride from the airport when I had first arrived in Madison.

****

Shift's end—and it was a good shift, but now that it was over, my paramount desire was to wash my hands; as always, at the end of a shift, they were filthy. One thing I dislike about cab driving is how dirty my hands become after being wrapped around that filthy steering wheel for eight, ten, or even twelve hours at a time. Not that I have ever minded dirt, of course, if the dirt in question is earth. However, it is not sweet soil that besmirches the steering wheels of those cabs, but the sweat and oil from countless hands which makes the steering wheel sticky, the better to attract carbon from the exhaust and unmentionable grit and grime from the road.

I have always found hand-washing relaxing, not to mention pleasurable, feeling the blood-warm water flow over my flesh. However, the experience was always a cause for concern in the washroom at Co-op Cab.

A mirror covered the wall directly above the sink.

As much as I enjoyed hand washing, I tried not to linger, washing vigorously with my head down—mirrors have never frightened me, but it is rather unnerving to see one's clothes standing up by themselves.

Footfalls approached the washroom. I hastily shut off the water, shook my hands vigorously and wiped them on my Levi's. Just as I pulled the door open, someone pushed from the other side.

His stocky presence towered over me. Fresh scars, lurid and red, covered his face and hands. I tried to walk past, but taking me by surprise, he grabbed my arm and spun me around. The door swung shut and we stood staring at each other.

"What the fuck do you think you're doing?" he said, his fingers tightening around my biceps.

Be diplomatic, I thought. And get out of that bathroom as quickly as possible. I was extremely aware of the mirror just a few feet away, though it lay not in this man's line of sight.

"I am sorry," I replied. "I do not know what it is you are talking about."

"Bullshit!" he replied. "You *do* know what it is I'm talking about. That call at Witte! How the fuck could you beat me on that call? You were behind me. I saw you. You were behind me!"

"But I turned onto Frances while you stayed on University." I tried to keep my voice calm. "I got the light at Frances and Johnson. I merely got lucky."

"How the hell could you have magically appeared at Witte? And on the right side of the street!"

"As I just said, I hit the green light. It was nothing more than good fortune."

"Maybe I should write you up," he said.

"On what grounds?" Though it best served my interests to remain calm, I was beginning to get angry; this lout would not bully me. "There were no one-way streets to use as a short-cut. There were no fire lanes or driveways with signs saying 'no thru traffic.' I did not ram the cab through the back entrance and then come out the other side. It was a race, and I beat you, simply because I hit the traffic lights at the precise time."

My explanations did not soothe this fellow, but his rancor mattered not, for it was time to end this charade. I would simply break through his puny grasp, shove him aside and go finish my paperwork.

Then he happened to turn toward the mirror, and I knew what he saw. Next to his image was a mere vague outline of a human-shaped form and a black, leather jacket, somehow magically suspended in the air.

"What the fuck are you?" he gasped.

"A fellow cab driver," I snapped, then slapped his hand away and stormed out of the bathroom to complete my paperwork and go home, as always. I took a spot before an adding machine in a far corner, making curt greetings to Kern and a rather hefty fellow named Truck. The two sat opposite each other, chattering energetically.

I ignored the two, pouring over my waybill, working as quickly as possible. The work almost complete, Kern's high-pitched yodel drew my attention.

"Well, look what the cat done drug in," Kern said. "Frank Nelson! How the hell are you?"

Reflex action drew my attention toward the doorway where stood my belligerent fellow driver, now identified as Frank Nelson, his bulk obscuring most of the opening, his countenance every bit as cheerful as a block of granite. "Kern, Truck," he grunted.

"Long time, buddy," Truck said with a warm smile. Frank's expression remained intensely blank, eyes staring straight ahead.

"Hey, Frank," Kern said, jerking his thumb toward me, "you know the Count?"

"Yeah," Frank said, finally smiling. "I know 'im." He finally turned, his gaze boring into me as if to see right through me.

Chapter 7

TESTIMONY OF THE OSTRICH

*C*hrist! *Time to disappear, I'd say. What the hell happened? I thought your victims don't remember 'cause you hypnotize them or something.*

Let me explain. Normally, they do not remember, but sometimes recall is possible. For instance, one hundred years ago, there was a London prostitute upon whom I had dined who had a sudden attack of recall. This breakthrough occurred when she spied me riding in an open-air carriage one warm evening after I had spent an enjoyable outing at the symphony with a pair of acquaintances. As the carriage passed the corner where she attempted to peddle her wares, she saw me, and immediately her face went through several rapid contortions of puzzlement, fear, more confusion, then finally recognition. The woman ran in front of the carriage, forcing the driver to come to a sudden stop.

"Guv'nor!" she screeched. "Show yourself! I know you. You can't hide."

We simply ignored her, for the moment. My acquaintances, Igor Petrenko and Claude LeBlanc, both antique dealers with whom I had done much business, looked at each other and shrugged their shoulders, then smiled knowingly at me.

"Count Farkas," Petrenko said, "I had no idea. Consorting with a woman of this type. I never would have expected this from you."

LeBlanc laughed. "Our dear Count has always been full of surprises. You know this woman?"

I made a show of flashing a relaxed smile. "It would seem, if I do not, I shall soon."

The prostitute moved to the side of the carriage, studied us, then pointed accusingly at me. "You! You're the one." She turned to my associates. "This one's a pervert, he is. He bit me on the neck. Left teethmarks. They stayed around for a week."

A whip cracked in the night. The woman squealed. As the carriage lurched forward, I tossed a few coins at her feet. I never saw this prostitute again and quite frankly, never worried about the incident. Even though the amnesiac effect of my "attack" had apparently worn off—which can happen, though rarely—it was obvious that she was unable to comprehend what had happened to her.

Therefore, there seemed little need to pay much heed to Frank's reaction. If he remembered what had happened, he certainly would not believe that he had encountered a "mythical" creature such as myself. More likely, Frank would attribute the memory to overconsumption of alcohol or some of those hallucinatory drugs young people seem so compelled to ingest these days.

Not that this situation could not present hazards, but it seemed hiding in plain sight was still the best option. Surely this fellow would not believe he had been attacked by a vampire. Perhaps he would merely think me a homosexual who, as the Americans say, had made a pass at him.

The folly of vanity, you say? Perhaps you are correct on that point.

For the time being, I would wait and see if further developments transpired. My greatest concern at that time was making money, and again, my destiny was on the road.

Frank Nelson triggered a rush of memory regarding the prostitute, though I had not thought about her for quite some time. It was a passenger who aided this process, pointing out the tart's contemporary counterparts, just a few blocks east of the Capitol in a rather sleepy residential area up the street from a coal-burning plant.

"Look at that," he said, pointing at a pair of women standing on the corner, smoking cigarettes and pulling their long coats close to them to guard against the mid-March cold. "Christ, people pay them? *They'd* have to pay *me*."

Indeed. It did seem obvious that these women would have little appeal to all but the most desperate mortals. Even in the darkness, the unsavory nature of these women's personas was easily apparent. One woman was a Negro, emaciated to the point of skeletal. The other was blonde and plump, her flesh puffy and sallow. Unsavory indeed; but not necessarily without their uses. But I jump ahead of myself.

Though Kern had told me March was traditionally a busy month due to continuing inclement weather and because every weekend featured some high school athletic tournament, on that particular Tuesday, it seemed most of my shift was spent idling in cab stands. Tacitus accompanied me through this tedium. Having completed *The Twelve Caesars*, it seemed time to reread *Annals of Imperial Rome*, though sadly, Tacitus, with his highly bureaucratic approach, simply could not provide the entertainment of the more personal histories of Suetonius.

Another cab parked in front of me at the Concourse Hotel taxi stand. The driver emerged and walked toward my vehicle. Praise to those who might deliver me from my boredom. It was Kern, whose presence, much to my surprise, was becoming less intolerable.

"Hey, Count," Kern said, as he climbed inside and stretched his long legs across the back seat of my cab.

"Good ee-vening," I replied in my best "count" voice, drawing a hearty laugh from Kern. "I am grateful of your presence. This is quite a slow night."

"Tell me about it. And the airport really bit the big one tonight." He exhaled loudly. "And nobody's been murdered lately, so people ain't scared to walk anymore."

"I imagine there is an inverse relationship between warm temperatures and our level of business. May I presume that business is appreciably slower during the summer?"

"Yeah, but that don't necessarily mean you'll be making much less money. There's fewer calls, but there's fewer cabs, so it evens out. There's lots of out-of-towners coming in for classes and conferences. For a whole month, there's the big graduate school for bankers. That's a thousand bankers per two-week session, all coming here to party. Unfortunately, they don't party like they used to."

Dexter's crackling voice broke the radio silence. "Count, where are you?"

I lifted the microphone from its cradle. "Concourse."

"Count, you have a personal at the Six-oh-two Club for Nicole. She works here."

"Ten-four." Indeed—but why ask for me?

"You dog!" Kern said, mock anger and real envy in his voice.

"I beg your pardon?"

"Hey, man, surface. Don't be drowning in the bottom of the pool." Kern shook his head back and forth slowly. "She's the prettiest woman in the fleet. And straight too. Not many of those floating around."

"Ah, well," I replied, "it would seem that if you have got it, you have got it."

"Sure, Count. Whatever you say. Must be that old-world charm thing." Kern winked, then slid from the cab.

Nicole had been watching from the large picture window at the front of the bar. She emerged just as I pulled up. She sat in the front seat, her scent most apparent, the beat of her heart loud and strong.

"Hi, Al. Glad they were able to send you." Her voice was relaxed, though her words were ever so slightly slurred.

"Thank you for requesting me. It has been a terribly boring night thus far. Where may I take you?"

"Home." She sounded tired. "Three-twenty-one North Hamilton. Right at Ham and Gorham. Sorry it's such a short fare."

"Ah, but all calls are good calls, and you, as a fellow driver, will surely tip me well."

"Depends on how well you service me."

I let her last remark pass. She was probably being facetious. The image of Kern and the old woman who had asked him if he wanted to earn an extra dollar came to mind. "So you live right by James Madison Park? It must be nice to live in proximity to such a nice beach."

Nicole laughed. "Haven't lived here too long, have you Al? The lakes are awful for swimming, all choked with weeds and algae. And at night, there's too many bums. Besides, I'm not a beach person. I like the night, just like you do."

"The night does have a beauty all its own," I replied.

"It does." She reached for the book on my dashboard. "Tacitus? Didn't know you were into Roman history."

I nodded. "Certainly. I greatly appreciate the parallels between Rome and the United States. And the Romans themselves are fascinating."

"Sure, but you'd never know, reading Tacitus." She tossed the book carelessly onto the dashboard. "He's accurate, and he grounds his histories well in terms of who was consul, who were tribunes at what particular time. I had to read him for a class. God, talk about dry."

A growl escaped my throat. "Indeed. If Tacitus were not already dead, I think I might be tempted to kill him."

Nicole laughed lightly like the wind. "You *do* have such a unique way of putting things. I've got this book that might interest you. It's a five-hundred-year-old edition of Seutonius's *The Twelve Caesars*. It's a beautiful, leather-bound volume. In Latin."

"I am impressed."

"Well, you should be." Saucy laughter escaped her lips. "My father gave it to me. He was a classics professor. I'd love to show it to you sometime."

"I would like that," I said, and immediately regretted it.

After a short ride, we arrived at her house, a white Georgian mansion surely chopped into several flats. Nicole reached into the glove compartment and pulled out a charge slip. I handed her my clipboard and pen and turned on the interior light. As she filled out the charge slip, her scent wafted into my nostrils, a chorus of beer, vodka, sweat and cigarette smoke, not so much competing, but somehow combining to form a whole that was more appetizing than one would expect—for above it all rose the faint, sweet aroma of her flesh. I took a deep breath and closed my ears to the pounding of her heart.

As she handed me the clipboard, her fingers lightly brushed the back of my hand, causing the hairs to stand on end. She faced me, eyes wide and so very, very brown.

"You know, Al...." Her voice trailed off. Her heart began to beat faster. "I'd love to show you my father's book. How 'bout you come over this weekend if you're not doing anything. I'm a pretty good cook. I'll cook you dinner, and you can look at my father's book."

Motherless spawn of Satan! This American woman had just asked me out on a date. And to think that Henry James's Daisy Miller was considered forward!

"Nicole," I began. "I must say I am very flattered by your attention. Very flattered indeed. But I just cannot reciprocate." Indeed, my purpose was to make money and not get distracted by the first attractive woman who showed an interest in me. Besides, the mere sight of her caused a flood of unwanted images—of Anya, her lifeless eyes staring upward, her exquisite body mutilated.

"Ohmygod, you're gay! Maggie told me you were. She said you make her gaydar go off like crazy, but I didn't believe her."

This provoked laughter on my part. Her best friend, housemate and fellow Co-op cabbie could not have been more incorrect, in fact, could not even venture to provide any reasonable speculation about my sexual orientation. It did occur to me to play along with this charade, but that might provoke attention from those of the male gender—and I would again find myself in the same situation.

"No, I can assure you that I most definitely am not a homosexual."

"You're not interested. I'm just being a pest." Her voice trailed off. She turned away from me and reached for the door handle.

It would have been quite easy—and infinitely more prudent—to let her think anything she wanted, but the pain in her voice was obvious, and it touched me. These mortals do find rejection hurtful, most likely because they have so little time in which to find a mate.

"You remind me of someone," I said finally, wanting to ease her hurt feelings and realizing that, in fact, she did interest me perhaps just a little.

She touched my arm. "Some bitch who dumped you? Hell, I'm sorry."

I shook my head. "No. She's dead. Not to go into too much detail, but she died saving my life."

Nicole pulled her arm away and pressed both hands to her chest. "Fuck! Shit, I'm such an idiot. I'm really, really sorry."

"Nicole, it is not your fault. You had no way of knowing. Please, do not feel badly."

"Well, I guess I better let you get back to work, huh? Look, you wanna talk about it, I'm a pretty good listener. You know where to find me." Without another word, she was gone, but the sweet scent of her flesh lingered in the cab for a long time, mocking me, paralyzing me.

I remained parked outside Nicole's residence for a few minutes before finally departing, my lips shouting a curse in a long-dead language. No distractions! Dalliance was not my purpose.

Yet I could feel something awakening inside the very core of my being, a unique kind of hunger. And this lack of self-control on my part angered me. I had shut down that part of me. Surely, I could choose the time when again it would no longer be denied to me.

Later on that same shift, driving down East Main, I again saw the harlots, smoking their cigarettes, waiting for customers, and it did occur to me that they might indeed have a certain utility. Yes, utility was an appropriate term, for it seemed that, albeit extravagant tools, they could be tools nonetheless, for me to assuage my hunger in an impersonal way that would minimize my distractions and keep my appetite under control.

An hour after sunset, on a night free from my temporary servitude, I parked my Toyota a few blocks away and used the locomotion of my own two feet to seek out these ladies. The Negress was nowhere in sight. The blonde stood on the same street corner, smoking a cigarette, the smoke intermingling with her own breath, visible at each exhale. Upon closer scrutiny, her faux-fur coat looked ratty and of little defense against the cold. The temperature was fairly mild, unless one had to stand in it for hours at a time. I made a show of pulling my leather jacket close to my body, though even the most severe cold merely causes a slight stinging sensation, like the beams of the sun when it is low on the horizon.

"Need to be warmed up, honey?" she said in a hoarse, unalluring contralto as I approached. I turned and looked directly at her. Her face was covered with makeup, but still looked very pale. Close scrutiny revealed dark roots in her blonde hair. Thick lines circumscribed several circles around her plump neck. She opened her coat enough to show ample cleavage.

"It is rather cold, is it not?" I replied.

"I know where we can go to get nice and warm."

"Where?"

She pointed toward a ramshackle house just around the corner.

"How much is this hospitality worth in this day and age of high inflation?" I asked.

She laughed lightly at my "foreign" manner, which suited me just fine. Let her think I was a foreign visitor, feeling just a bit lonely, just as long as she did not see fit to overcharge me.

"Fifty bucks," she replied, "but it'll be worth a lot more. You'll see."

"Excellent. Lead the way, my dear." As I followed, a vague sense of alarm poked dull daggers into my being, but I merely attributed it to the realization that this action was illegal, this being the puritanical American Midwest and not someplace more practical, like Amsterdam or Vienna.

Her flat was as shabby as the exterior would have led one to believe, and it reeked of more organic materials than I cared to consider. Still, my purpose was not to critique this woman's aesthetic proclivity toward interior design, and thus I phased out the sights and smells of this abode.

"Come with me," she said. The tart tossed her coat aside, took my hand and lead me into the bedroom. "God, we gotta warm up those cold hands." Her dress was bright red, strapless and extended just below her hips. Stockings covered trunk-like legs, supported teeteringly by black stiletto heels. As a gentleman, I wanted to massage her feet, but realized that she was not the one who was paying for services to be rendered.

I lifted 50 dollars from my wallet, which she immediately snatched from my fingers. She reached inside my leather jacket and tried to unbutton my shirt. I twisted away and sat on the bed. "Take off your dress," I said. The lady let the dress fall to the floor and stood before me in red brassiere, black panties, stockings, garters and high heels.

"What would you like me to do for you?" she asked.

"Remove the rest of your clothing and come sit beside me." She complied, giving me a view of her ample flesh, which was the color of dead fish floating atop poisoned water, almost making me wish I had not ordered her to disrobe.

She joined me on the bed and again attempted to unbutton my shirt. I gently pushed her hand away.

"What *do* you want me to do for you?" she asked again, her tone more insistent.

"I want you to pleasure yourself."

"You want me to whack myself off?"

I groaned inwardly. "Yes. I want you to pleasure yourself fully and completely."

"That's it?"

"That is all I require, but I do mean *fully and completely*."

She nodded, then lay back on the bed, her hand lowered to the cleft between her legs. I moved close, reached a hand around her shoulders and stroked her stomach and pillow-like breasts with my other hand, feeling her skin, which was surprisingly soft and smooth.

Though her perfume was garish, the skin underneath smelled sweet, and the scent of her womanhood was strong. Beneath it all, her heart beat loudly and with increasing frequency as she worked harder and harder toward the designated goal. Her breathing grew deeper and more rapid, and she let forth the occasional moan and grunt.

"Please take your time, my dear," I said. "There is no need to rush."

The woman nodded, her breathing increasingly rapid and shallow.

I continued to stroke her back, but once she settled into a rapid rhythm of finger strokes and short, quick breaths, I stopped fondling her breasts and laid a hand on her stomach until she began to pant rapidly, before letting out a loud, guttural shriek.

Her body shook, and I gently tugged her chin toward me, met her gaze and touched her consciousness. Her expression went blank.

I plunged my fangs into her neck, their razor touch penetrating her soft flesh. Hot blood squirted down my throat.

The room faded from my sight, replaced by hard, static blankness, the blankness of one with no soul who had deceived a gullible consumer.

After licking the twin rivulets of blood dribbling down her throat, I departed, her bitter taste burning through my being. Far from being sated, I was more ravenous than ever before, and angry with myself, knowing that in an effort to control my hunger, I had only succeeded in opening Pandora's Box.

****

I quickly discovered that these cab drivers are a superstitious lot. Though making money depends on a certain amount of luck, skill is paramount; yet so many of my fellow drivers, Kern included, seemed to hold in reverence supreme beings called the "Cab Gods." If, when running deep east to deep west, they got a call nearby, going another long distance, the Cab Gods had smiled. In less fortunate times, as they said in their vulgar manner, they had been "fucked by the Cab Gods." And Eastern belief seemed to play a certain role, albeit in a childish sense of instant Karma;

according to many, the Cab Gods' whims were somewhat related to the actions of the drivers.

But who was I to argue? Certainly, it was the Cab Gods who had smiled upon us again in late-March, providing an unexpected storm, dropping eight inches of that crystalline white gold on Madison's streets, as if the bounty of this winter had not been enough. The driving was difficult for two days, but by Saturday night, the streets were clear and dry, yet the snow remained, providing people with incentive to leave the task of driving to the professionals who do it best.

On Saturday, the Cab Gods provided me with a lucrative shift, creating the kind of distraction necessary to take my mind off Frank Nelson and my burgeoning hunger. I had pleased our patron deities by showing up two hours prior to the eight-o'clock start time for my shift.

The Cab Gods rewarded my diligence immediately, seeing that my calls criss-crossed the far reaches of the city and always taking care that another excellent call would be available upon discharging my passengers.

Even when the string of calls snapped and I was downtown with not much to occupy my disturbed mind, the Cab Gods provided me with a flower hidden in cow dung, seeing fit to send me a flag who desired to go all the way to East Towne Mall and back.

Still, despite my efforts, no amount of largesse from the Cab Gods could distract me, nor could the lovely staccato rhythm of rapidly spinning wheels striking the pavement as the cab sped to yet another call. The hunger was real and action was mandatory.

Despite my better judgment screaming in protest, I telephoned Nicole and invited her to come to dinner at my apartment—better the familiar surroundings of my own abode. Her voice sounded enthusiastic when she accepted. We set the appointment for Sunday, my next available, unfettered evening.

Though I do not eat, my culinary expertise is not totally lacking. In fact, there has been many an occasion when I prepared a sumptuous repast for friends—but never beef or pork; the aroma of cooked mammal flesh has always made me nauseous. Chicken, however, is not a problem. Thus, I would prepare chicken paprika, a dish from my homeland of plump chicken breasts cooked slowly in tomato juice and vinegar with onions and a great deal of paprika. When the chicken is almost entirely cooked, sour cream is added, creating a thick, rich sauce. Certainly, Nicole would relish such a dish, though I never could; the paprika pepper was not introduced to Hungary until long after my desire for food had ceased.

While the chicken simmered, I inspected the apartment. A crisp, white tablecloth covered the small, folding table. The apartment was uncluttered and dust free. My futon was folded against the wall, forming a makeshift couch. My books were neatly arranged on their respective shelves. My record albums, though in a dated medium, were neat and orderly, organized in alphabetical order and divided into classical and jazz.

Satisfied, I cued up *The Magic Flute*, sat on the futon and paged through *The Wall Street Journal*, absorbing myself in an analysis of the burgeoning Pacific Rim markets. Soon, my apartment was thick with the aroma of cooked chicken and paprika, and hazy, lace-covered images superimposed themselves over my sight. A home of rocks, grass and mud. Two simple herders living together, working side by side to scratch out a meager existence that seemed neither meager nor simple. Just a young man and a young woman satisfied with their lot, satisfied with each other. Dinner would be a stew, with meat if available, served on earthen plates fired from clay dug from behind the house. The young man dug up more clay whenever plates broke, forming shapeless lumps into smooth pottery. The young woman lovingly filled the plates with whatever sustenance was available.

Visions of that life are fleeting, as easy to hold as quicksilver. So long ago, the memory is intact, but shrouded, coming clear only every so often as flashes, as snapshots, before fading, known, but not seen, except for that one image always available, ever haunting me.

Burning flesh washed away the lace curtains of recollection. The chicken was burning. I put away the newspaper and inspected the chicken. One side was slightly charred and required turning. Otherwise, the chicken was fine, cooked through and through, swimming in an ample amount of sauce. I lowered the flame slightly, then set a high flame under a saucepan full of water. Nicole was due shortly, so it was time to start boiling water for the noodles. A smaller saucepan held broccoli within a steel steamer suspended over water.

I opened a bottle of Bordeaux to allow enough time for this full-bodied red wine to breath. And yes, red wine with chicken was a bit unorthodox, but a faint-hearted white would find itself overpowered by the paprika; the Bordeaux would blend nicely with the spice and tomato sauce.

I splashed some wine over the chicken, then returned to my newspaper to await Nicole's arrival, which would signal time to commence steaming the broccoli and adding sour cream to the chicken.

Shortly, there was a knock on the door. According to the clock on the nightstand next to my futon, Nicole was exactly 13 minutes late. When I opened the door, she stood before me, a vision of beauty, holding a single red rose, garnished with a few sprigs of baby's breath.

"I couldn't come empty-handed," she said, handing me the flower. "Usually, I'd bring a bottle of wine, but you said you'd already taken care of that."

She looked lovely, dressed in jeans and a simple cotton peasant-blouse that showed off her curves nicely. Her long black hair was pulled away from her face on one side, held in place by a barrette that also held a small sprig of baby's breath. "Yes, if I had told you what kind of wine to bring, that would have spoiled the surprise I have cooked up for you. Please, come in."

"Thanks," she said, crossing the threshold and closing the door behind her. She glanced quickly at her surroundings. "I see you like the light and airy look."

Drawn shades covered the few small windows in the basement apartment, hiding the black plastic underneath. And the faux walnut paneling did little to make the apartment appear any less dark than it already was. Perhaps candles would have made my abode appear less grim, but I did not want to come on too strongly. This was just dinner,—just a friendly, innocent dinner.

"Well, as a creature of the night, I am not a big fan of the 'light and airy look.'"

"I can tell." She laughed. "Me neither. I've always hated getting up before noon."

"Please, have a seat." I pointed at the table as I strode toward the kitchen. "Preparation of the meal is almost complete. Would you care for a glass of wine?" She nodded, and I poured a glass of wine, then searched for something within which her floral offering might be housed. No vases available, I hastily emptied a bottle of mineral water, filled it with water from the tap, then dropped the rose inside.

"Thanks." Nicole said upon my return, accepting the glass of wine and admiring the new centerpiece on the table. "Now, that's an improvement. Lovely table, but it just needed something extra." She flared her lovely, elliptical nostrils as I took a seat opposite her. "Something sure smells good. What'd you make?"

"It is a surprise. You shall find out soon enough. I hope it will be to your liking."

Nicole swirled the wine in her glass, sniffed the bouquet then took a sip. She smiled broadly. "Very nice. Bordeaux, right?"

"Why, yes." I felt myself smile. Could this American actually possess some Continental culture?

Nicole took another sip and sighed, a big smile on her face. She slouched back in her chair. "My parents were big wine drinkers. I love Bordeaux." She flared her nostrils once more. "Doesn't smell like beef. Chicken? Chicken in some sort of red sauce? It'd have to be. I couldn't imagine you serving a full-bodied red with chicken unless the sauce called for it."

"You are most perceptive." I smiled, knowing full well that though she was able to deduce the form of the dish, she could not determine its essence, and the surprise would still be intact.

She swirled the ruby contents of her glass, then put the vessel on the table. "Hope it'll be ready soon. I'm starved."

"Very soon. I did not wish to thrust the food at you as soon as you arrived."

"That's real nice of you, Al. Say, why don't you pour yourself a glass. I've got something I want to show you." She reached into her valise of a purse and removed a parcel concealed within a brown paper grocery sack.

"I do not drink, but please feel free to enjoy."

She nodded silently, then removed an engraved steel box from the paper sack. She unfastened a clasp on the box, removed a thick, leather-bound tome and laid it on the table. "Then drink this."

"Your father's book!" My eyes felt as if they were bulging out of their sockets. I am not easily impressed, but obviously this volume was an unusual item and quite valuable; it most likely was half my age.

"I knew you would enjoy seeing it. By the way, have you thrown away Tacitus yet?"

My hand reached for the book and stroked the soft, worn leather cover. "No, he still torments me. May I inspect your book?" She nodded, and I lifted the book from the table, handling this priceless volume with great care. It was a wonderful specimen. The post-Gutenberg lettering was still lovely, hand-set Latin, full of flower and flourish. The inside cover bore the set-type number of this limited edition of *The Twelve Caesars*.

"You do read Latin, don't you?" Nicole asked.

"Yes, I do." To my ears, my voice sounded very far away. Something odd stirred inside me. This gesture of bringing me this museum piece was quite touching, but there was something else, a vague recollection. Inspecting the front and back inside covers revealed no signatures denoting previous ownership. Turning to the first chapter, about the life and death of Julius Caesar, I found that the capital gamma at the beginning of the chapter was upside down. I smiled, knowing this was a very rare book indeed; the mistake was corrected after the first print run. Why might I know this? This same edition, perhaps this same volume, was once mine.

"What is it?" Nicole seemed to notice my reaction.

"I am familiar with this edition." I pointed out the mistake, but stopped just short of full disclosure. I closed the book and replaced it within its box. Dinner was probably ready to be served.

While stirring the chicken, draining the noodles and broccoli and arranging the food decoratively on a plate for my guest, I thought of the book, relishing the opportunity to page through it; though bawdy, the Graves translation is relatively sanitized compared with the original, hair-raising Latin version.

"Very pretty!" Nicole exclaimed at the plate placed before her. She refilled her glass and spread the cloth napkin on her lap, then her eyes darted back and forth across the table. "Where's your plate?" she asked finally.

A small detail. A small contingency that somehow had taken me by surprise, even though this is the inevitable question I always find myself having to answer.

"I may eat later," I answered, somewhat stretching the truth. "I have this condition. Though I relish food, I find it difficult to dine at the same time as others. Watching others eat while I try to eat can make me a bit queasy."

Nicole had just lifted a forkful of noodles soaked in sauce. Her wrist suddenly relaxed, and the noodles slid off her fork, back on to her plate. "That's pretty weird, Al. Doesn't it bother you to watch me eat?"

I smiled nobly. "Not at all. Believe me, watching you enjoy this meal gives me as much pleasure as if I ate it myself. More, even."

Satisfied, she cut into the chicken and lifted a sauce-dripping piece to her mouth. She chewed and closed her eyes in obvious pleasure. "Delicious." She washed down the first bite with a sip of wine. "Wonderful, Al. But it's too bad. There's so many nice restaurants here in town. Must make eating out impossible."

"It does, but there is always take-out, I suppose. I have, however, on occasion, taken a meal in the dark corner of a quiet restaurant."

"Well, there's a few places like that, once-trendy bistros that people forgot about because the next trendy place opened up." She cut a piece of broccoli and swirled it in the sauce. "This *is* wonderful. What is it?"

"Chicken paprika, a recipe from my homeland."

"Ah, I knew you were Hungarian. Either that or Finnish." She enjoyed another bite. "I love paprika. And this paprika is real fresh."

She enthusiastically devoured the contents of her plate while I kept her wine glass full. Nicole took her time, clearly savoring each bite, her movements surprisingly graceful, considering the vulgarity of the act— vulgar from my perspective, that is.

When she had cleared her plate, I realized my great faux pas. There was no dessert! As I began to chastise myself for such a foolish oversight, Nicole said that she usually did not care for dessert. Relieved, I cleared the table and quickly washed the dishes.

Nicole was sitting on the futon when I emerged from the kitchen, Art Pepper playing softly on the stereo, obviously carefully selected from my jazz section. Her taste impressed me.

"Thanks for dinner," Nicole said when I had joined her on the futon.

She patted, then stroked my forearm softly. "It was delicious."

"Your company honors me greatly. A splendid repast is the least I can do." I pointed at the steel box. "Tell me about your father."

Nicole took a sip of wine and held the shimmering glass in front of her eyes. "My father," she began. "Like I said, he was a classics professor here at the UW. He died when I was in my early teens." Her voice trailed off.

"At least you got to know him."

"Yeah," her voice bore a slight tinge of bitterness. "People always tell me that, that I was lucky he was alive long enough for me to get to know him, for me to be able to remember him, but a lot of times I almost wish I didn't get to know him. If he had died when I was just a little girl, then I wouldn't know what I was missing, not having a father. That must sound terrible."

I patted her hand gently. "No, not necessarily. You may feel that way sometimes, sometimes not. It is quite natural."

"Yeah. Besides, my memories are mostly of him sitting in his study, reading Latin or Greek from some musty old book. Rome was his specialty, but I think he really hated the Romans. He was always talking about how stupid they were, how derivative their culture was. How no Roman ever had an original thought in their entire history."

"Why dedicate his whole life to the study of a people he did not care for?"

"Good question." She downed the remaining contents of her glass and reached for the bottle, her soft breasts brushing against my thigh. "To tell the truth, I think Rome killed him."

"An interesting hypothesis." I watched her place the bottle on the floor between her feet.

"I think he felt trapped, felt very unsatisfied. There he was, a tenured professor, with a nice house, a very nice wife and *such* a sweet little girl, but none of that made him happy. He didn't really have any other interests outside his work, and he didn't really like his work."

"But it sounds as if he found antiquity quite fascinating, even if he did not care for the subjects of his study."

"My mom told me Dad would've liked to have done his research on Greece, not Rome, but where he got his doctorate it was either Rome or nothing. And it was the only grad school he could get into *and* get funding, so he didn't have any choice."

"As a professor, he should have been able to do any research he wanted."

"True, but I think Dad chose to wallow in the trap. Maybe he'd been feeling sorry for himself for so long, he didn't know any other way."

I studied the fine lines of her jaw, the aquiline nose, her high, sculptured cheek bones. So much like Anya, but different, so totally different once I was able to get to know her as her own person and not the ghost of another. "You seem to possess tremendous insight."

"You think so?"

"Certainly."

She again touched my forearm. Her hand lingered, stroking the thick, black hair on my arms, making the hairs on the back of my neck stand on end. In a deep, distant place, there was a tingle.

"May I ask you something else?" I said quietly.

"Sure." She folded her legs in front of her and turned her body toward me. "Ask me anything."

"As I have stated previously, I am most flattered by your attention, but I am puzzled that you would be interested in me when there are so many younger men available. I look around, and there are so many strapping young lads. Why am I the one who arouses your interest?"

Nicole laughed heartily. "Al, you're not that old. Mid-thirties, maybe late-thirties. I don't think you're old at all."

I smiled broadly. "You might be surprised if you truly knew my age."

She scrutinized me closely and completely. "Well, if you're *that* old, you're pretty well-preserved."

"Ah ha!" I laughed. "Yes, well-preserved. That is it."

Nicole touched my hair with the palm of her hand. "Very well-preserved. You're hair feels so soft. I'd say silken, but—it's more like it's smooth, like a marble statue."

I reached up and touched the hand stroking my hair. Our fingers intertwined, then dropped slowly to the space between us on the futon, lingering together until I gently pulled my hand away.

"I do not seem that old to you?"

"Well, first of all, you're not so old that you're not good-looking. You remind me of some of those very pale, *very* handsome British actors, like a young Lawrence Oliver, with even more charm."

Kern's "old-world charm" but it was just supposed to work for tips. He had not said it would work elsewhere.

"You *are* older, Al, no question about that; but that means you're just mature, a lot more mature than these *boys*. I'm not really interested in them. I mean, a few years makes a big difference."

"You have had experience with less mature people?"

"Damn right, and I'm tired of it." Her head bowed for a moment, then rose. "You seem like a gentle, kind person. You're intelligent and easy to talk to. You seem to understand things, and you're funny, too. Plus, you're a good cook, a neat housekeeper and you don't have any roommates. What else would a girl want?"

Funny? That is not an adjective I have often heard another person use to describe me. Perhaps, as the Americans say, funny-strange, as opposed to funny-ha-ha.

Nicole slapped me on the thigh. "Well, I showed you mine, now show me yours."

"I beg your pardon."

"This woman you said I remind you of. What was her name?"

Quid pro quo. It *would* have been unreasonable to get something for nothing. Nicole's parents were children when Anya was murdered, yet for one such as myself, it was merely yesterday. Scarcely a night passes when I do not feel the phantom sensation of her hand touching mine.

"Her name was Anya."

"Did you love her?"

I nodded silently.

"She meant a lot to you, didn't she?"

"Yes, she did." I stared at the wood-paneled wall across the room, the grain fading and dissolving from the here and now before Nicole's voice pulled me back.

"How'd you guys meet?"

My voice sounded wistful. "I was in Prague, conducting business."

"Nice city. Been there a couple times."

"You are fortunate. One night, I was attending a play by Anton Chekov. During an intermission, a friend introduced us. I think that from the first time we looked upon each other, we knew we were destined to be close. It was not so much that we were kindred spirits. Oddly, our meeting was a strange coincidence. We knew not of each other, yet I was actually quite close to her family. She was a gypsy, and my family had had close relationships with gypsies many times over the years."

"I'm part gypsy," Nicole interjected.

"Yes, I can see it in your eyes, black like the soft, velvety night."

Nicole cooed softly, then laughed, beckoning me to continue.

"It was summer, and we went on outings together. I had to do a bit of traveling, and she accompanied me. It was not long before a bond formed between the two of us."

"It must have been very special."

"It was. So much of my life has been spent alone, and when someone emerges that I can enjoy such a bond with, it is quite exquisite."

"So what happened to her?"

I paused, the here and now dissolving before my very eyes, but Nicole pulled me back again, lightly touching my shoulder, her fingers ever so softly stroking the fabric of my shirt.

"She died protecting me," I began gingerly. Nicole nodded, prodding me to reveal more, to reveal all. "We were hiding from soldiers. Actually, I was incapacitated, and she was keeping watch until it was time for our train to leave to take us safely out of Prague. She could have fled to save herself, but she did not. Anya stayed with me, even when the storm troopers broke the door down. From where I was concealed, I could hear them beat her, rape her. Then, there was silence, and I was powerless to do anything to help her."

"My God," Nicole gasped, clamping a hand on my wrist. "God, how horrible. You must feel terrible. No wonder you were a bit freaked out. How can somebody ever recover from something like that?"

"Time heals." Indeed, time does heal, though some humans do not live sufficiently long enough for that to happen. Still, at least they are not haunted by memories for the next several centuries.

Nicole shook her head, her raven tresses falling forward, covering her face. She lifted her head and crossed her legs. "Wait a second. Storm troopers? In Czechoslovakia? I thought they didn't really have much of a standing army."

"You are correct." I paused for a moment, gathering my gumption. "They were not Czech. The soldiers were German."

"Ah, East German soldiers. But what were they doing in Czechoslovakia? Oh, must've been 1968. There must've been East German soldiers along with the Soviets when the Prague Spring was brought to its knees. I think I remember reading that the Soviets went in there with Warsaw Pact troops. Jeez, you were there? Wow. But, Al, even as terrible as that was, that's a pretty long time to be carrying that kind of baggage." She reached over and stroked my cheek. "You gotta let go of the past sometime."

Indeed, but while short-lived mortals have the luxury of letting go of their past, eternity gives me the opportunity to wallow in it. "It was a little longer ago than 1968," I said, after pausing a bit, summoning the courage for full disclosure. Yes, full disclosure! I spoke quickly before common sense could stop my reckless tongue! "Those Germans were not of the Warsaw Pact. They were Nazis."

Nicole's back stiffened abruptly. "Nazis! Come on. You can't be serious. You can't be that old. No way. You're pulling my leg."

"I can assure you, this is no jest. They *were* Nazis."

She slid away from me, her back rigid, but her voice still soft. "Why are you doing this? I don't understand. Are you having an approach-avoidance problem? I mean, it's probably my fault. I've been practically throwing myself at you when you're obviously not in the kind of space where you can get close to somebody."

"But I am ready. You are correct. It is time for me to let go of the past."

"Then, why push me away when I get close? Why are you making up stories?"

"I am *not*—" I stopped myself, deciding to try a different tact. "You *do* have gypsy blood coursing through your veins? How much?"

Nicole's expression turned from concern to bewilderment. She inched a little closer. "My maternal grandmother was a hundred percent gypsy. Why?"

"Do you or did you know your grandmother at all?"

"Did. She died fifteen years ago."

"Do you remember her telling any stories about strange creatures her people had encountered over the centuries?"

"Yeah." She stretched that single syllable in an auditory gesture of feigned patience. "Just children's stories, bedtime stories about were-wolves and vampires and strange creatures who were human, but had to eat raw meat."

I reached for her hand, taking it in mine, not squeezing it, just holding the soft, precious thing. "You know, back in the old country, I may have known your grandmother. In fact, I may even have known your great- or great-great-grandmother."

She yanked her hand away, abruptly stood and marched toward the door. "Okay, that's it. I've had enough." Her tone was annoyed, but still relatively calm in the placating way an overindulgent parent might speak to a petulant child. "I'm outta here. Thanks for a pleasant evening. Don't call me."

Nicole slammed the door behind her, leaving me to sit bewildered on my futon. Something metallic shimmered. She had left her father's book behind.

Chapter 8
THE CONSEQUENCES OF TRUTH

*T*hinking *with your cock?*

What manner of vulgarity is that? Such a queer expression, and quite inaccurate for one such as myself, if I correctly infer your meaning.

Well, perhaps in an odd sense, you may not be totally incorrect, though the degree to which you are correct is in a largely abstract manner. My judgment was in fact skewed in this matter, and considering the alleged dedication to purpose, I had made quite a royal mess of things. Common sense should have stopped my tongue from causing any further damage.

Briefly, I considered flight. With a few thousand dollars at my disposal, transport to anywhere on the planet could be arranged. Maybe Tibet. François was living there, the last I had heard. He had made the decision to leave humanity; perhaps it was time I did the same.

No, I would not take such rash action. Nicole merely believed me insane. Frank, most likely, did not know what to believe. Surely, no one would believe *him*, even if he was able to articulate what he suspected about my nature.

The business with Frank was simply the kind of accident that happens to my kind on occasion. However, I cannot say what form of temporary insanity caused me to reveal myself to Nicole before knowing her well enough to consider her completely trustworthy. Wait and see what comes—this was the only viable option. No sense in taking flight, not yet.

The only certainty was my responsibility to the job. Despite the situation, they still expected me to come in and drive a cab, even if I were a mere shell, heart and soul too distracted to even be considered present.

Tuesday, I drove aimlessly, with little monetary gain to show for my efforts. When there were no calls in front of me, I would drive toward the intersections recited by the dispatcher, but never in time to be awarded a call. I would commence toward the nearest cab stand until the next intersection was called, then I would turn around and drive toward that call, only to be beaten.

Perhaps if I had spent more time in a cab stand instead of constantly changing directions, the reward would have been greater.

Nicole was on the road that night. I wanted to talk to her to get a sense of whether she *did* believe me insane and, if she did not, whether or not she would betray me.

A chilling realization set in, that even if she did not believe me, if she repeated what I had said, and if Frank told anyone what he suspected, someone might put two and two together.

Realizing the futility of playing the board, I drove to the airport, knowing the wait might be substantial, but eventually a customer would be there for me.

Two cabs ahead, a door opened, and a large bulk emerged and lumbered toward my vehicle. It was Truck, aptly named for his big-boned frame bundled with vast rolls of fat covering rather thick muscles. His hair was long, black and stringy, his beard overgrown and quite unkempt. He wore a black leather jacket covered with thick, shiny zippers, heavy chains hanging from both epaulets.

He stopped by my door, his beard fluttering in the soft breeze. I rolled down my window.

"Hey Count, " he said, a gentle smile on his face.

"Good evening," I replied blandly, annoyed at the interruption of my solitude.

"You okay?" His smile faded, replaced by an expression of furrowed-brow concern.

"Adequate," was my terse reply.

"Well, I was wondering, because earlier you and I were racing for a call—"

"We were?" Indeed, my preoccupation was apparently quite overwhelming.

"Well, yeah." He removed his glasses and rubbed his eyes. "You had me dead to rights, but when I got to the call, the passenger was waiting out front, and you were nowhere to be seen."

"Then, apparently, you just simply beat me."

He shook his head. "No, man. I've seen you in action. No way in hell I was beating you to that call. Hell, you're one of Kern's trainees. When Kern trains somebody, they win races."

The fellow was sincerely concerned, though my mind was racing with various paranoid possibilities as to his real motive for speaking to me such. "I have been preoccupied, that is all."

"Yeah, that's what I figured." Truck reached through the window and slapped me lightly on the shoulder. "Hey, just keep your head in the game. You got something on your mind, don't let it get you into trouble. And if you're that distracted, feel free to come off the road. You tell dispatch you just can't drive, they don't have a problem with you checking it in early."

I thanked Truck. He bid adieu and returned to his cab. Shortly thereafter, headlights drew my attention to the rear-view mirror. A cab pulled up behind me, its driver long of raven hair, angular of face. What is it the Americans say? Let sleeping dogs lie? It seemed a good policy, except I still possessed her father's book, far too valuable a relic to keep when it belonged to someone else. Civility certainly mandated that something be said to her regarding this.

Nicole was not happy to see me. Upon seeing me approach, she leaned back in her seat, arms crossed in front of her chest. She opened the window but a crack.

"Yes, Al?" Her tone was guarded and condescending, the way one speaks to a child.

I backed up slightly and raised my hands, palms facing her. "I am not here to harass you in any way."

"Better not be."

"I merely wish to inform you that I still have your father's book. It is safe and awaiting your retrieval. If you so desire, I can drop it off at your house."

Perhaps, the mention of her father's book might have softened her demeanor. Perhaps not. "I desire no such thing," she snapped. "I'll come by and pick it up." She closed her window hastily and buried herself in a book.

At least her emotion was anger and not fear, allowing for a certain degree of solace. Obviously, she merely thought me insane. One *does* accept camouflage, regardless of whatever bizarre form it might take.

Eventually, a trio of planes landed. Flights had been delayed, but now the Cab Gods had blessed us. Every cab at the airport was able to load. Unfortunately, by this time, too many cabs had pulled in behind me, thus making it impossible to get a split-load, but at least there was activity with which to occupy myself.

It seemed that the Cab Gods chose to intervene personally to assuage my troubled mind. My passenger was a businessman going all the way to the Radisson Hotel, clear across town from the airport. Just before reaching the destination, a call materialized at a restaurant across the street from the hotel. It was mine and went to Middleton, a suburb directly adjacent to Madison's west side. A call in Middleton popped up. It went back toward the Radisson.

"Platte and Odana," Dexter's crackling voice said over the cab radio.

The Cab Gods had indeed taken pity upon me. "Gammon and the Point to Gammon and Odana," I said when Dexter called my number.

"A mere formality," Dexter chirped. "Count, the Ginza. Comes up."

It was a quartet of young women going to the Towers, a private, upscale dormitory populated mainly by children of affluent East Coast families. The Ginza, a Japanese restaurant very popular with Towers residents, was a mere stone's throw from where my previous call had taken me.

The women were waiting out front, loudly proclaiming their surprise at the quickness of my arrival as they got into the cab. Once the ride commenced, they ignored me. Their perfume stank like insect repellent, they chewed and cracked their gum loudly and scarcely a moment passed when all four women did not speak simultaneously in awful Long Island accents. Their conversation was the pinnacle of inanity. Still, they tipped me two dollars, and just before they left the cab, I got my next assignment, the Cab Gods seeing fit to send more manna from the heavens to improve my disposition. I began to wonder what form of sacrifice our patron deities would find most preferable. Perhaps, a pedestrian. Or maybe someone on a bicycle. Or, best of all, maybe one of those infernal motor scooters.

The next call was a mere four blocks away, at Genna's Lounge, a dark bar warmed by a preponderance of brightly lacquered mahogany. My passenger, watching through the large picture window, emerged as soon as I pulled up. His destination was the Crystal Corner Bar, on the near east side, right on Williamson Street. The fellow said nothing else until he broke his silence with a loud shriek when we were on East Johnson.

"Geez!" he shouted from the back seat. "That guy did a Juan Peron. Did you see that?"

"I beg your pardon?"

"Juan Peron, guy who used to be president of Argentina. The driver did a Juan Peron. You see, there's this road somewhere in Latin America. At a certain point, the road forks. Well, one day, Fidel Castro is riding down that road. The car comes to the fork, and his driver doesn't know what to do. 'Fidel, Fidel,' the driver says, 'we are coming to a fork in the road. What do I do? Turn right or turn left?' Fidel says, 'To the left, comrade. Always go to the left.' Later, Somoza is on the road. The chauffeur says, 'General, the road ahead is forking. Do I turn right or left?' Somoza says, 'Go to the right. Always go to the right.'"

"Willy and Rogers," Dexter's voice interrupted. More bounty, it seemed.

I lifted the microphone from its cradle, sorry to have to interrupt this fellow's story. "Excuse me, sir," I said, then keyed the mike when Dexter called my number. "Pat and John to the Crystal Corner."

"Count, fifteen thirty-four Willy. You'll be picking up an eight-year-old boy, taking him to nine-ten Spruce. It's a six-dollar flat, cash up front."

"Ten-four," I replied.

"Sounds strange," my passenger interjected. "Isn't it kinda late for a kid that young?"

My thoughts exactly. "It is. His parents are divorced. The lad's mother lives on Spruce Street. I am picking the boy up at his aunt's house. His mother was no doubt entertaining gentleman friends this evening."

"Hmm," the passenger said sadly. "Some people I just don't get. They have kids, they oughta take a little more responsibility."

"You are correct. But you were telling me a joke. Will you continue or just leave me hanging on a precipice of suspense?"

The fellow laughed. "Okay. Anyway, so later this same day, Juan Peron is riding down that road. They reach the fork, and the chauffeur stops the limo. 'Mister President,' the driver says, 'we have reached a fork in the road. What do we do?' Peron is silent. 'Mister President?' the driver asks again. 'What should I do? Should I turn right or left?' Peron thinks about it some more, then finally says, 'signal that you are going to make a left hand turn, then turn sharply to the right.'"

I chuckled loudly. "So, that is a 'Juan Peron.' I will have to remember that." Many other drivers tell jokes to their passengers, and apparently, it grants them better tips.

"Glad you liked it. I heard that from Steve Stern when I took his Intro to Latin America class."

Shortly, we arrived at the destination, and a smile had fought its way back to my face. "All right," the passenger said. "Paul Black and the Flip Kings are playing a special show tonight. That boy can play slide guitar like no one. Opened for Stevie Ray Vaughn and nearly blew him away."

The fellow paid the fare, along with a two-dollar tip, finally freeing me to pick up my next fare. No one emerged from the house until Dexter called them on the telephone. The boy's aunt shunted him out to the cab, her sharp voice slicing through the night. She wore a bathrobe and a disinterested expression as she handed me exactly six crumpled one-dollar bills.

The boy climbed into the front seat and struggled loudly to close the heavy door. Upon meeting success, he dutifully buckled his seatbelt across his puny frame.

"Hey, mister," the young lad said after a bit, "can you turn on your inside light?"

For any driver, it would be a hazard to drive in the dark with the dome light on. "Why?" I asked, as politely as possible.

"I wanna do mah homework." His voice was earnest, but not cloying.

"You were unable to do it before?"

He shook his head vigorously. "I was, but mah aunt got tired of me axing her for help, so she tol' me just watch tee-vee and quit buggin' her."

I turned on the dome light and watched furtively from the corner of my eye as the boy struggled over problems of mathematics. He seemed to have special difficulty adding six and eleven.

"Hey, mister," he said, the slightest tint of frustration in his voice, "can you help me with mah homework?"

"You have run out of fingers, have you not?"

"Yeah." He sounded sheepish to have had his dirty little secret exposed.

"I will show you a very special trick." The boy sat up very straight in his seat. "Adding six and eleven is no different than adding six and one."

"Don't dis me, man. That too easy."

"I am surely not 'dissing' you. You see, eleven is ten plus one, correct?"

"Yeah."

"Now, what is six plus one?"

"Seven," he chirped quickly.

"Seven plus ten?" He started using his fingers. "Do not use your fingers."

"Sorry, mister, but how'm I gonna figure it out?"

"How high can you count?"

"I can count to a hundred." He sounded quite proud of this achievement.

"Very good. Therefore, you should know that if you put a one to the left of a seven, that is seventeen and the correct answer to the problem you are trying to solve."

His jaw dropped. "Ohhhh! That's real easy."

"It is quite easy when you know how. Just remember that there is no reason to be intimidated by larger numbers because they are no different to deal with than smaller numbers. And do not use your fingers. Math is a skill that merely takes time to learn. It is a building block leading to bigger, better and more important things, but if you use your fingers, you will never really learn."

He nodded as he quickly completed the problems. Once he had put his assignment away, I flicked off the dome light.

"You sure talk funny, mister," the lad said, once complete was his homework.

"I might say the same about you." A smile spread across my face. The lad seemed bright. His hands were large, which told me he could grow into a big, strong fellow. But would he have a chance in this life, or would he end up like the other human refuse I have seen in big cities for as long as my memory has served?

The boy shook his head. "I don't talk funny. You talk funny."

"Where I come from, it would be you who talks funny."

"But you talk like 'the Count."

Most likely because I am a count. "I beg your pardon?"

"Y'know. The Count. On *Sesame Street*. The Count." His voice changed to a bad, high-pitched Bela Lugosi. "'I love to count. Ah! Ah!'"

Ah, yes, the famous children's show on public television. So now my people are being spoofed on a children's television show. How could we become more ubiquitous? Still, becoming a caricature surely helps to camouflage our true nature; relevant, considering my current circumstances—this boy would not be scared of vampires; he would merely think of them as odd but friendly creatures, fashioned from foam rubber, their movement controlled by steel rods.

"I am from Hungary," I replied.

"Say what?"

"That is where I am from. People there all talk like me, therefore, when in Hungary, *you* would be the one talking funny."

"Where's Hungry?" he asked, sincere curiosity on his face.

"Hun*gary* is in Eastern Europe."

"Is it anywhere near Norway?"

Are these youngsters no longer taught geography? "No. Norway is far north, and Hungary is more to the south and the east. But Finland is right there by Norway, and the people of that country speak with a similar accent."

"I'm Hungary." A sly smile spread across his face.

"Hungarian? I think not." Of East African descent, most likely.

"Yeah, sure am." The boy giggled loudly. "I'm Hungarian for some ice cream."

Had there been a place open, I would have stopped and bought the boy ice cream, but alas, there was no such place. Shortly thereafter, we arrived at the destination, and as the boy unbuckled his seatbelt, I could see a change in him, as if whatever flame burned inside his soul, which hungered for food and thirsted for knowledge, suddenly choked from lack of air.

"Thanks, mister." The boy mustered a brave smile as he got out of the cab and walked toward the dark house. I watched him pound on the door and wait too long before his mother opened the door, then turned around and walked away. The boy waved before disappearing into the darkness behind the closed door.

****

As the week wore on, my distraction decreased, the job successfully providing ample need for mental focus. What Kern had said about March traditionally being an excellent cab-driving month finally proved accurate. Earlier in the month, the girls' basketball and boys' wrestling championships had provided such bounty that the Cab Gods were able to take a short respite from their ever-important duties.

And this weekend was the best event of all, the boy's state basketball championship. Kern said this was always the best tournament because of the large volume of visitors and because, for some reason, there was always a blizzard that weekend.

Every single motel in the entire city was full, and, true to Kern's prophecy, it did snow, thus offering further encouragement for these geographically confused visitors to take cabs instead of attempting to navigate a bewildering morass of snow-covered streets.

Overall, I earned about $500 in that one week, while still remembering to take my weekly sustenance, which, of course, proved even easier than usual with the influx of largely befuddled people.

After five extremely hectic nights, it seemed I had earned my rest when Sunday finally arrived. I had planned on rising well after sunset, relaxing with a good book and some music. It even seemed like a good time to very carefully inspect Nicole's volume of Suetonius, though it would be prudent to let the tome remain secured within its steel box. Tacitus was back on the shelf, but *Candide* struck me as appropriate, for it seemed a good time to wax philosophical.

But alas, those best-laid plans were dashed when a loud rapping at the door smashed through my slumber, the digital clock reading three p.m. I ignored the rapping, but it continued, growing more insistent until I threw the covers aside and answered the door.

It was Nicole.

"I had hoped you would call first," I said groggily. "I have your book here for you, but you have awoken me from my slumber." Which, of course, was not a pretty sight. Without another word, I plodded toward the bookcase where I had placed her father's book.

She slammed the door shut. "Forget the damn book," she said sharply.

"I didn't come here about the goddamned book."

"Why did you come?"

She stood, arms akimbo. "I'm here 'cause I wanna know just what the fuck is going on, Al."

"I am afraid my mind does not function optimally before sunset. What in the name of Hades are you talking about?"

Nicole craned her neck, glanced at the ceiling and exhaled loudly through her mouth. "We had the annual membership meeting yesterday. Your absence was slightly conspicuous."

"I had no idea attendance was mandatory."

"It isn't." She paced back and forth, arms wrapped tightly about her chest. "You know a driver named Frank Nelson?"

So much for the virtue of inaction. "Just in passing, as it were."

"Well, he seems to know a lot about you, Al. He asked for the floor, then stood up and told everyone you're some kind of monster, some kind of vampire."

Silence was my reply.

"One of you is either lying or crazy," she said. "Or maybe it's both. Which one is it, Al?"

Chapter 9

DIARY OF A MAD CABBIE

Y ou are partially correct," I answered.

"Which part?" she snapped.

"Your mere presence here should provide the answer. One of us *is* insane, but neither I nor Frank are failing to tell the truth."

Nicole glanced at the door, seeming ready to abandon this entire escapade, but thought better of it. "Look, I want to believe you...."

"I can assure you, I am neither a liar, nor am I insane."

She studied me a moment. "If you're not lying, if you're not crazy—but what you tried to tell me, that *was* crazy."

I shrugged. "In a secular, materialistic world, yes, what I had attempted to tell you was crazy, was unbelievable, but tell me, Nicole, given a choice as to who you would believe is insane, who would it be? Me or Frank Nelson?"

"I don't know." Her voice cut like rapiers. "Christ, for all I know, this is just some joke between the two of you."

"I can assure you, we are not in league. More than likely, this fellow does wish to see me come to harm." A thought passed across my consciousness, and it made me laugh; amusing how the thought of hospitality could have come to me at such a time. But at least I knew that she was not likely to betray me. Otherwise, she would not have visited me at my abode. "Please forgive me. I have been remiss as a host. Would you like something to drink? You must be parched."

"Yeah. Sure." My civility seemed to smooth her tone.

"What exactly did Frank say at the membership meeting?" I disappeared into the kitchen. Nicole followed, probably to make sure that her drink would not be laced with something she would rather not ingest. I opened the refrigerator, but found it empty.

"Tap water is fine." She looked over my shoulder, inspecting the refrigerator, most likely curious as to the complete lack of contents. "It was toward the end of the meeting. The time when anyone who wants to speak about anything can. Frank stands up and says he's gotta warn us about this menace that would suck the life from all of us. He starts telling us about how a few months ago, this strange creature started bugging him. It came to him in his dreams, and it even started coming to his window at night. Then finally, the thing stopped bothering him, until recently. But he said he outsmarted it, tricked it into revealing its true form to him, but the thing doesn't know it did—"

"Until now," I interrupted, handing her a glass full of cold water.

"Whatever. Anyway, he says it's you. That this strange creature is a vampire, and it's you, and it's come for him and for everybody, but he'll get it first. He even showed us pictures."

"Pictures?"

She took a long sip of water. "Yeah, but by that time, he'd been pretty much shouted down. He tried to show people these pictures, but no one was listening anymore."

"Did you see these pictures? What did they look like?"

Nicole drained her glass. I refilled it and handed it back to her, then motioned for her to have a seat at the folding table covered with two week's worth of *The Wall Street Journal*.

"Thanks," she said, taking a seat.

"You were a bit overwrought. I trust you feel better now." I took a seat, but made a point of not sitting too close.

"Yes." She smiled as if she did not really want to. "Anyway, Frank's pictures didn't look like much. All they showed was some guy with a woman, but you can't really see the guy, just pants and a black leather jacket standing up by themselves."

I arose and retrieved my leather jacket from the closet. "Did it look something like this?"

"A zillion leathers look like that."

Having hung up the jacket, I returned to my seat. "I can assure you that there is no deception in my words, Nicole. I *am* a vampire."

She rolled her eyes. "I mean, that's nuts." She shook her head. "Jeez, you don't seem crazy, but Christ! You *are* talking crazy. C'mon, Al. How the hell can you expect me to believe that?"

I shook my head sadly. "Secular materialism. There is a whole universe out there you people refuse to acknowledge."

"Nice words, Al, but they're only words."

Her bravado was commendable. She dared me to prove to her what I really was without knowing if indeed such a revelation would be dangerous. Of course, if I were lying, the danger would be relatively minimal. Being not much smaller than I, she most likely believed she could fight her way out of my apartment largely intact. Under *normal* circumstances, that would most likely be true.

"I want you to watch very carefully." I lifted my upper lip and showed her my teeth. "They look like yours, do they not?"

"Yeah." She studied me closely. "You pretty much look like anybody else. You're just very pale, but so's a lot of people. Hell, Jack Williams, he drives only late night shifts, never gets up before six. He's paler than you."

I opened my senses, casting adrift the sensory filter that is usually present to keep me from a constant state of hunger. Quickly, her scent washed over me, not her perfume, but the very smell of her flesh, the very bouquet of her being. Her beating heart pounded loudly inside my skull.

Long, pointed fangs slid from their housings. I struggled not to look into her eyes, not to fall into the vortex of all that blood coursing through her body.

I could feel my own blood pumping through me, my head pulsating. My breathing labored, grew louder. Just a moment more, just as long as my discipline could stand this test before I might drown in an ocean of her scent and her hot, steaming blood.

"Oh my fucking God," she gasped, her voice sounding shaky and distant.

I took a long, deep breath. My heart slowed. Fangs retracted into their housings.

Nicole stared at me, shock and fear registering on her face. Her heart beat rapidly, her sweat grew acrid, and her body tensed, as if she might bolt toward the door.

"Do not worry," I reassured her. "I will not harm you."

"After what I just saw, I can't say I believe you."

"All you saw was a clear illustration that Plato presents a more sophisticated and real view of the world than Aristotle."

She laughed dryly, then grabbed her glass, went into the kitchen for more water then quickly returned to her seat, her eyes only leaving me when the kitchen wall separated the two of us. "Christ, this is so fucking unbelievable." Her breath having finally returned, she sounded much more calm. "I felt like I was starting to get to know you, so it was difficult to swallow what you were saying, but—and you really aren't going to hurt me?"

"No. That is the last thing I want to do."

She nodded, apparently believing me. "So, what does this have to do with Frank?"

"Upon arriving here in Madison, Frank was the one who picked me up at the airport. When we reached our destination, he was so kind to provide sustenance."

Nicole's eyes opened wide. "You attacked him? Sucked his blood? You sucked his blood and he survived? He didn't turn into a vampire?"

"Hollywood." I spat the word from my mouth like a substantial gob of phlegm. "I am not a killer, and my bite does not transform one into a vampire. I merely try to sustain myself while causing as little pain and anguish as possible to those who act as my donors."

"Without consent," she added sharply.

"No, but with a mere meeting of the eyes, I can, in effect, hypnotize a person so they never know what happened to them, and I only take a very small amount. Not even a pint."

"If you hypnotize your victims, how do you explain Frank?"

"On very rare occasions, the effect will not be permanent." I related the incident in the bathroom, which had apparently triggered his recall.

Nicole glanced thoughtfully at the ceiling. "So what are you going to do about it?"

"I will *do* nothing."

"Al, you gotta do something. Isn't this situation dangerous?"

"Potentially, but what would you have me do?"

"I don't know. Something. Anything."

"Action will only exacerbate the situation. No one will believe him.

Eventually, he will probably cease to believe it himself."

"It'd be nice to think so, but you weren't at that membership meeting. He seemed pretty convinced." She paused, studying her long, graceful fingers. "What if you 'hypnotized' him again? Maybe you might push it right out of his head."

I shook my head. "Ill-advised. Such action would bring undo attention to the situation. Besides, if he is as convinced as you say, even I would find it difficult to control Frank's mind. He would fight me and most likely win."

Nicole rose. I wondered how the shock had affected her. Though she seemed reasonably comfortable with this revelation, it would take her some time to truly come to grips with it.

"Look," she said calmly, "I'm just trying to help. But it looks like you don't want any help, so I'm just going to leave you alone." Quickly, she was out the door, but this time she did not slam it behind her.

As she left, I started to open my mouth to speak, but she was gone before I could tell her that she should take her father's book.

****

My two days off passed as I pondered the circumstances, still unwilling to take action. Nicole had offered reasonable arguments, but certainly she did not have the benefit of a thousand years of experience, nor could such a young person understand that rash action will generally result in undesired results.

Upon arriving for my next scheduled shift, I found a waybill envelope with my name on it tacked upon the bulletin board next to the time clock. Inside was a set of plastic vampire fangs made for children to wear on All Hallows' Eve and a note that read, "You can't hide. I know what you are."

I folded the note, then secreted it and the fangs within the pocket of my leather jacket and stepped inside the dispatch office to receive a cab.

"Got a nice sled for you, Al," Maggie said. Nicole's auburn-haired Celtic friend was answering phones. "Eighty-eight, waiting just for you. Nicest cab in the fleet. A real thoroughbred."

"Excellent," I replied. "Have we been busy today?"

"Not bad. No snow coming this week, but the weather's still crappy. Good for business."

"I am anxiously awaiting." I took the key and turned to leave.

"Just a second, Al. Maureen wants to see you. She's upstairs."

"Thank you," I said, leaving and climbing the stairs, hiding my displeasure at this summons. I did not need any more trouble than I already possessed. What errors in judgment had I possibly made? Had one of my passengers been upset by an action or lack thereof on my part?

Maureen sat behind her desk, which was clear except for one manila folder. When I crossed her threshold, she rose, bearing not the casual appearance I had seen before. She wore a ruffled, high-necked blouse and a navy blue skirt. A matching blazer hung on a rack behind her.

"Al. Come in." She motioned toward a chair in front of her desk, then looked herself up and down. "Yeah, had a meeting with the Wisconsin Taxi Association today. A bunch of living stereotypes, all fat guys smoking big cigars. They don't take me very seriously, being a woman, but they seem to like the work I've been doing setting up an insurance mutual that'll save us from those bloodsuckers who've been overcharging for our liability insurance for so many years. Please, have a seat. And close the door." She paused until we were sealed within her office. "You weren't at the membership meeting this Saturday."

A statement of fact that sounded like an accusation. I did not know attendance was mandatory, but I did know it does not take the wisdom of Solomon to determine who really holds the reins of power at this alleged cooperative. "I had no idea attendance was mandatory," I replied.

"It's not," the general manager replied. "It's good to have as many people at a membership meeting as possible, but no one *has* to be there." She dropped her forearms on the desk and leaned forward. "There's something very serious I need to talk to discuss with you."

So, this is when the cooperative mask is removed, revealing the true face, the true nature of the creature's state of being. Everyone is equal, but some are more equal than others. And this woman, who has the power of life and death, who holds my fate in her hands, was about to demonstrate just that because I was not being a good enough cooperative member.

"Al, I want you to know that as long as I'm general manager, no form of harassment will be tolerated."

Suddenly, I found myself confused. I squeezed the fangs in my pocket and nodded, simply answering "Uh-huh," as the Americans do.

Maureen held up the manila folder. It bore the name Frank Nelson. "You know about the statement Frank Nelson made at the membership meeting, don't you?"

"Yes."

"He's getting a four-point letter for that, but I'm talking to you now because I want to know if he has in any way harassed you personally. Have there been any incidents between you and him?"

My mind raced. The fingers in my pocket tore the fangs into two mangled pieces. Perhaps, I should just handle this situation myself and not get anyone else involved in order to avoid calling too much attention to myself. However, if Maureen chose to intervene, maybe it would be best to simply let her do as she wished.

Maureen leaned forward and her voice softened. "Look, Al, you don't have to be afraid of him. If there's been other problems, I'll write a twelve-point letter. Maybe the letter might get overturned by the Appeals Committee, but as far as I'm concerned, you say the word, and he's gone."

I suddenly felt myself genuinely touched by her concern. How ridiculous that I had believed she was about to issue me a letter of discipline. No, she really wanted to help. I must really learn to be less judgmental.

She held her peace. It occurred to me that she knew there had to have been some kind of incident between Nelson and myself, and if I denied that such an occurrence had taken place, that would call more attention to the situation than would be prudent. Finally, I related the incident in the bathroom and showed her the note and the fangs—or, rather, their mangled remains.

Maureen shook her head sadly at the story's completion. "Okay, Al. He's gone." She leaned back in her chair and tipped her head up toward the ceiling. "I never like firing anybody, and I was really hoping Frank was going to work out, but he's sick, and he needs professional help."

"I am afraid I have no idea of what it is you are talking about."

The general manager laid a hand on the folder. "I'm not really supposed to tell you this because it's a confidential, personnel matter, but this does involve you, and besides, you could hear about it from several other people. Hell, Kern was there when it happened."

"When what happened?"

"A few months ago, Frank totally went off his nut. We don't really know exactly what happened, but one night in late November, he fell through a second-story window. He was okay, just cut up a bit, but when Kern found him, he was babbling about some glowing creature coming to him through his windows. Kern was nearby because Frank had called the dispatch office asking if a cab could come by and check if someone was messing around outside his window.

"Well, Frank spent some time at Mendota Mental Hospital. They let him out a month ago. He said he was okay and needed a job. Hell, we were glad to hire him back and help him if we could. I guess he needs more help than we can give. I hope he gets it."

"Yes, and so do I." Indeed, but what kind of help? Those Dr. Frankensteins, who consider themselves so damned qualified to manipulate the human mind, could not comprehend the giant worm that had planted itself inside Frank's head. Their alleged help would do nothing but exacerbate his agitated state. I rose from my chair and thanked Maureen for her attention.

Descending the stairs, thoughts rushed through me. Was it truly time to take action? If so, what would be the best manner in which handle this situation?

Clearly, more information was needed. If only I was not scheduled to work the next five days; some intelligence gathering would be useful if the time was available.

Kern appeared at the bottom of the stairs bearing his usual smiling countenance, though his expression was softer than usual, and there was a certain peculiarity in the way he gazed at me. Clearly, he looked concerned.

"Hey, Al," he said. Al, not Count. He *was* concerned. "How's it going?"

"Well, I just met with the boss," I replied with a sardonic grin, "and I have survived."

"You're the boss, Al," Kern countered. "We're a co-op. Maureen works for us."

"Indeed. And an excellent job she does."

"She met with you about Frank. He's history, isn't he?"

I nodded. "Frank has been discharged."

"I knew something happened between the two of you. Must've been pretty nasty."

"Sufficiently nasty."

Kern shook his head sadly. "Well, he's pretty loony-tunes. He can go be crazy someplace else."

"Maureen said you know something about it."

Kern repeated the story pretty much as Maureen had told it, except his version seemed a bit more vivid, down to a detailed description of the cuts covering Frank's face and arms and how the blood squirted rhythmically from sliced arteries.

"Just a little heads-up," Kern said, stepping out of my way. "Frank's on his way here. He's scheduled to work tonight, but I guess he won't be doing his shift. You probably don't wanna be here when he gets here."

"No. Thank you for the warning."

His grin spread fully across his face. "Glad to help. And if you need anything, let me know. Don't worry, it's gonna be all right."

Indeed. I yearned to share Kern's confidence, but he most likely would not be quite so optimistic if he knew all there was to know.

****

At shift's end, Nicole found me in the parking lot as I walked to my car, ready to depart after a fair but uneventful shift. "I'm meeting you at your apartment," she said.

I voiced protest, but she would hear none of it.

"I have information," she answered.

"What information?"

She reached into her rucksack and pulled out a spiral notebook. "It's Frank's diary."

"Where did you get that?" My voice sounded a bit frantic and for good reason; this form of theft could be just the thing to push Frank over the edge, as if his firing might not be sufficient .

"His motel. He's staying at this really sleazy place. God, you should see it. A fucking pigsty. Trash and used food containers everywhere. The place stank of cigarettes, stale beer and his dirty laundry. Gross! But what was real creepy was there were all these flowers made out of plastic beads set up on the dresser, all arranged in neat, symmetrical rows. Oh, and I got these too." She handed me a pair of dark, grainy photographs. "That *is* you, isn't it? Your pants, your leather jacket?"

"Yes."

"Who's the woman?" She pointed at the plump blonde holding one of the jacket's arms.

"A prostitute."

"Great!" Her reply sounded irritated. "Look, I don't wanna bother with that now—"

"You should not have done this, Nicole. He was fired today. Surely, he will notice that these items have been pilfered. How did you get in there anyway?"

"I told the desk clerk I was Frank's sister. And I gave him five bucks." She paused. "Look, it's too late to worry about this now. You gotta read this diary."

She was right. "You know where I live. I will see you there shortly."

****

"This guy's really sick, Al," Nicole said, sipping the Russian Caravan tea I had brewed. After her last visit, it seemed reasonable to keep some refreshments around the apartment. "You gotta check this out."

I sat and she pushed the diary across the table.

"It's hard to tell when he wrote these entries," she said, "but it seems they cover the time after you attacked him and before he went to Mendota. After that, there's a little bit of his time inside and then almost up to the present."

I nodded and opened to the first entry, dated November 29, just a week after my arrival.

Have to say it was simply a case of being in the right place at the right time. Got lucky and hooked an out-of-towner toward the end of a twelve-hour hack shift. Janesville. Forty miles of highway, a buck-twenty per mile of easy money. Good old cab 66. Always did bring me luck.

On the way back, bumfuck nowhere, pitch dark except the reflected glow of my headlights, nothing but road stretching out in front, grassy median and oncoming lanes to my left and forest all over the place. All alone, not even any truckers for company.

That's when I saw it. Just a flash, a quick glimpse of something out there, running or jumping in the median. Something doing something, that's all I can say. It was there, then it wasn't.

The thing had two legs and two arms and a head, kinda like a teenage kid, just smooth without any real features and sorta glowing, but not exactly, like maybe you wouldn't want to try to read by it.

I just can't stop thinking about it. The sight of this creature has become an obsession very quickly. It sounds crazy, but I know I saw it. I wish I knew what the hell it was.

I thought about asking some of my friends, the ones I was pretty sure wouldn't laugh. Only problem was I wasn't sure who'd laugh and who wouldn't. The next night, I was sitting by myself at the bar, stewing about this whole thing, feeling frustrated about not having anyone to talk to about this. Then I saw Greta. She'd believe me. Hell, she's a Born Again Pagan, or at least that's what that button of hers says.

So I told her the whole story, about how I was unsure on the one hand, but knew I'd see something, maybe even a quick glimpse across dimensions, or something like that.

Greta lit a cigarette and took a deep drag. She nodded thoughtfully in what looked like agreement. Then she told me about the time when she was a teenager, and her parents were gone for the weekend, and she walked into their bedroom around dusk and saw something standing in the room. She said she knows it was really there, but could never be certain, because she was so frightened she sprinted out of the house to a neighbor's as fast as she could.

I really like Greta and felt really grateful until I realized she was talking way too loud, and that asshole Jon overheard and came over by us to give us a bunch of shit.

Jon told Greta her eyes were just playing tricks. Greta responded by blowing smoke in his face. Jon, in an exaggerated motion, waved the smoke away from his face and called her a flake. Greta called Jon arrogant and pig-headed. Then Jack, another friend who'd been shooting stick with Jon, stepped between the two. He grabbed a smoke from Greta's pack that was sitting on the bar, lit it and glared at me through a cloud of smoke, thanking me for sharing my experience with them so the thing will come after all of us and not just me. His voice dripped with sarcasm. Everyone laughed, even Greta.

I hesitated, then joined the laughter. Embarrassed, yes. I shut up, let the conversation meander elsewhere, let the subject drop and just pretended to forget about the whole thing.

Just pretended, but I just couldn't stop thinking about that creature. I thought about it until bar time. I thought about it on the way home. Thought about it while watching a little TV before bed.

Then I dreamed about it. Dreamt I was driving back from Janesville in old 66. Dead of night, real dark—pitch black, clear, crisp, chilly night, bare sliver of a moon and a sky full of stars. I was driving 66 down the highway. Miles and miles, and there were no other cars around. Just me. Then I saw a shimmering in the distance. I punched the gas and closed in on the shimmering, which began taking shape.

Then I was right behind the thing. Well, not exactly right behind it. I was in the left lane, and there it was, right there in the median, running, its two legs a yellow blur. I sped up and pulled within twenty feet of the thing so it was actually in my headlights. I could see it had a head like a bowling ball sitting atop an otherwise slender body. And it was human-shaped, like some guy in a rubber suit.

But I only saw its back. I tried speeding up, but 66 just couldn't seem to go any faster, just couldn't get close enough to see more than the creature's backside. Then I woke up. This is really weird.

"Pretty fucking bizarre," Nicole said, having seen that I had finished the first entry. "Amazing how obsessed the guy got. Did you actually do this to him, or was he just a ticking, nutty-nut time-bomb waiting to explode?"

"Perhaps a little of both."

"Hmm." She finished her tea and took the diary. "Do you have any more? This is real nice."

"Certainly." I took her cup and went to the kitchen to make more tea.

"Hey, listen to this," she shouted. "Fuckin' weird. He keeps dreaming about this stupid thing, but never gets a good look until this one night: 'Then I floored it and was actually able to pull even with the thing. Hell, there it was, running right alongside the cab. I could see it did look like a guy in a yellow rubber suit, but there was no bulge between its legs. And its head *was* shaped just like a bowling ball, but smooth with no nose or mouth and only round bits of coal for eyes, like some really abominable snow-dude.

"'Weird thing though, I drove alongside the thing for a couple miles, and it just ignored me. I stared at it—hell, admired it, the way its skinny legs were a blur of motion, like Wile E. Coyote when he stumbles off a cliff and tries to run back to terra firma.

"'But I didn't want to be ignored! I tapped the horn. Leaned on the mother. For what felt like forever.

"'It turned, and I saw what I'd thought was an expressionless face, but it wasn't. Those black button eyes seemed to stare through me, vaguely transmitting a feeling of being pissed off.

"'Suddenly, I was wide awake, sitting bolt upright in bed, my stomach muscles so tight they hurt. Something tells me this is a little abnormal, but I know it's real. I just wish there was a way to find out.'"

I leaned against the refrigerator waiting for the water to boil, wondering about the creature he described, hoping it was not what it seemed it might be.

"How long did he have those dreams?" I shouted.

"For awhile, then they come true," Nicole answered. "Apparently, the cab company had retired Sixty-six. Good riddance. That thing was a death-trap. Anyway, he was able to buy it when the old cabs were auctioned off. Then he went out searching for the thing, just like in his dream. Geez, this guy can wax poetic. Listen to this. 'With the night off and it being black as pitch even in the city, with just a bare sliver of a moon and the black sky pierced everywhere by millions of pinholes of light, I decided it would be a good night to go hunting for the creature.

"'When I maneuvered Sixty-six out of the city, the sky opened to absolute crystal clarity, and the stars layered themselves so thickly that the constellations themselves were obscured. The night itself was like tar, sucking—hell, devouring—the paltry glow of my headlights, as if it were laughing at me for trying to light up the road ten feet in front of me.

"'It felt just like the dream. Somewhere around Edgerton, I was thinking it strange that I hadn't seen another vehicle for several miles. Then I saw something shimmer a bit at the end of the horizon. I punched the accelerator and watched the gas gauge and speedometer needles lurch in opposite directions.

"At first, the shimmer seemed to stay at the edge of my sight, but as Sixty-six lumbered forward faster and faster, the shimmer finally seemed to get closer.

"'Up ahead, I watched the shimmer disappear over a steep rise. Sixty-six followed, struggling up the summit, then hurtling down the other side. The road leveled, and Sixty-six steadied at a cool 80 miles per, shaking a bit, creaking like the bulkheads in those shipwreck movies, but hugging the road tight.

"And there it was, just a few hundred yards ahead, running on the wide, grassy median. I let up on the gas slightly and moved into the left lane for a closer look.

"'The creature's luminescence made it visible, plain as day, revealing to me uniform yellow-white skin, covering a smooth, symmetrical body with that perfect, bowling-ball head.

"'I punched the gas, pulled even with the thing and drove alongside for awhile, but the creature would speed up, and Sixty-six, not to let some alien kick her ass, matched its speed. Yeah, maybe the creature could run like nothing on earth, but Sixty-six packs a vee-eight, three-sixty with a four-barrel carb. And a Smith and Wesson sure as shit beats four aces.

"'We played this game of chase, while the creature also played a game of pretending I wasn't there, until it finally turned its head toward me, showing me eyes, but no real face—no nose and only wrinkles converging where a mouth would be.

"'But those eyes, those blank, black coal eyes spoke clearly to me, saying *yes, I'm pissed off.*

"'It stared, and I stared back, feeling its message but unable to turn away.

"'And almost not noticing the sharp curve in the road. Sixty-six almost flew into a ditch. I swerved into the far right lane and cut the wheel barely in time. When I finally straightened the car, the creature was gone.'"

I handed Nicole the cup of tea, and she took a tentative sip, her throat obviously parched after her recitation.

"Here, let me have a look at that," I said.

"Sure. That thing gives me the creeps, and your *light and airy* look here doesn't help make me any less creeped out."

Indeed! Whether the creature was real or merely a product of Frank's imagination, either alternative was frightening, especially to the uninitiated. I started reading where Nicole had stopped:

Well, if there was any doubt about what I saw that first night on the way back from Janesville, it was gone. This time, it was there plain as day. But now, it was gone, and 66 was rushing us to the next exit. Nothing to do but go home, hit the hay and think of what to do next. Maybe mount a camera on 66, take pix of the thing, show Mister Empiricist Jon, sell them to the supermarket tabloids for big bucks.

My mind was reeling with infinite possibilities when, with about two miles between us and the next exit, I saw a distant shimmering up ahead. Then not so distant and not shimmering, but a glowing blob, glowing and growing, getting bigger and bigger as 66 gobbled up the road in front of me.

I eased up on the gas. Watched the blob rush toward me, take definition. Sprout one, two legs. Arms. A head. Coal eyes growing larger, larger, until the road, the night disappeared, and nothing but glowing yellow and huge black circles filled the windshield.

I slammed on the brakes, felt the back end fishtail. An inhuman squeal filled the air. Was it me or the screeching tires?

And the entire car was engulfed by glowing yellow. A chill like dry ice passed over me so quickly I hardly felt it, but a memory of it stuck, like the way dry ice peels skin off bones.

Then nothing. Just me and old 66 sitting stationary out there alone in the blackness, no sound except 66's steady chug-chugging and my pounding heart.

Treat a good cab like a lady and she'll always get you home. Like any good cab, double-six kept her head, found the next exit, turned us around and took us back toward town at a nice, safe sixty miles per hour.

In defensive driving, they train you to check the rear view mirror a couple times per minute, even when there's no other vehicles on the road, even all alone on a nice, private little highway, nothing but me and good old 66.

And some glowing creature out there someplace.

I checked the rear view mirror. Nothing. I stared at the road ahead.

Nothing. Well, road and darkness and trees mostly bare, almost all their leaves torn off by a sharp December wind.

Headlights from behind sparkled in the rear view mirror. I glanced up. Not headlights! A single, Cyclopean eye sparkling in the distance!

The shimmering mass grew as I watched. I punched the gas, checked the mirror, studied the shimmer.

Floored it. I felt 66 shudder, then roar! She obeyed, responded to my will, propelling me forward as I watched the shimmer in the mirror shrink. Then grow! First, the same size as before, then bigger, just a little bigger, still not big enough for me to tell what the hell it was.

With that Police Interceptor engine opened full throttle, we were flying, 66 guiding us forward while I watched our backs, waiting for the shimmering to make its move.

Light flashed in front of me. The shimmer was just a diversion. A pair of shimmers in front. Bright red eyes glowering at me. Eyes!

No! Taillights. Impact coming!

I cut the wheel sharply to the left. Swerved, passed and flew onto the left shoulder. Barely enough time to brake and turn right to keep from flying off the road. The trucker honked as I eased to a stop. I glanced over in time to see him flip me off.

There was this screaming inside my head. I looked toward the lights of a town. The stars were invisible, washed away by the lights of civilization. And the rear-view mirror—well it was dark, the shimmer gone. But was it still there and hidden—or was it just hiding for now? Was it scared of civilization—our civilization—or did it use civilization as camouflage?

I drove home slowly. It was three-thirty in the morning when I finally parked good ol' 66. The adrenaline finally gone, I was worn out. What do I do now? Well, there wasn't anything to do until morning, and I was beat, so I stripped, hit the lights and crawled under the covers, fidgeting and shifting, trying to find the warm spot in the bed while waiting for the electric blanket to kick in.

Almost asleep—then a chill washed over me. I hunched my shoulders up to my ears. I curled into a tighter ball, pulled the covers tighter about me. Then I felt the chill again.

A chill and something telling me to look toward the window. I tried to ignore it, but the chill began settling into my bones, turning into a dull ache. And my head was buzzing with a voice that wasn't mine, telling me, telling me to look, look, look toward the window.

I turned, opened my eyes and looked toward the window.

And there it was, glowing and glaring, that bowling-ball head and those coal eyes staring at me.

I pushed myself away from it, pulling the covers up to my chest, until my back struck the wall. My breath left me like I'd been punched in the stomach. I opened my mouth to scream, but nothing came out.

I finally sat up, leaped off the bed, sprinted across my little efficiency, scooped up the phone, dived into the bathroom and slammed the door.

There's no windows in the bathroom.

Damn near hyperventilating, I called the cab company. My hand was shaking so much, it took several tries to get the right number. Finally, I heard the Dexter's voice on the other end. Reality! I settled a bit.

I was glad it was Dexter. He's one of the more sane and competent of our dispatchers.

I tried to sound calm, but I could hear my voice shaking. I told him I thought there was something outside my window and asked him if he could send a cab over to take a quick look. He said sure and put me on hold.

I just said 10-4 and fought the urge to tell him to hurry. Instead, I just held the phone, squeezed it in my hand just to feel the hard plastic dig into my flesh, while I sat on the toilet seat, pressing the phone to my ear, listening to the silence, my eyes darting from side to side.

I was real happy when I'd found this place. Got it for a song, and I was especially happy about how light and airy it was.

All those windows.

Windows on three of the four sides of the efficiency. Three on one side. Two on the other two. Windows everywhere.

I listened to the silence and stared at the cold ceramic tiles between my bare feet.

Nothing there, Dexter said after what felt like forever. He'd sent Kern who was less than a mile away. Kern gave it a good, close look but didn't see anything.

I thanked Dexter. He asked if I needed the cops. I thanked him again and hung up.

I wanted to laugh at myself, but there wasn't as much as a giggle inside. Fine, just leave the bathroom. Can't stay there all night. If I didn't leave right then, I'd never leave. I'd have to live in my bathroom. Have meals delivered there. Buy a computer and have it installed right on top of the toilet tank. I'd work out of my home, right in the bathroom. I'd never leave cuz I'd have everything I'd need literally right at my fingertips.

I laughed at that image and kept laughing as I threw open the bathroom door and quickly scanned the windows. Nothing there. Still, I wasn't going to take any chances. Dug extra blankets from my closet and tacked them up over the windows. If I can't see it, it's not there, right?

Wrong-o!

I flicked off the lights and crawled back into bed, rearranged the blankets and shifted until I found the warm spot. Nice and warm. Toasty. Then, a chill.

Damn, damn, damn. My eyes snapped open, and I stared at the blanket that covered the shades that covered the windows. Opaque nothingness, but my friend was there. There underneath all the layers. Invisible, but I could feel its presence.

Damn! I bolted into the bathroom and sat on the toilet seat staring at the tiles, wondering how much money I could make doing computer work at home. In my bathroom.

I figured there'd be a way to figure this out tomorrow, but for now I had to survive the night. But how? Then ... inspiration.

I couldn't live with my guest. Couldn't run from it. But maybe I could enable myself to ignore the bastard, at least temporarily. I remembered the bottle of rum left over from a Halloween party. I carefully opened the bathroom door, stared at the windowless wall and moved toward the pantry where I'd last seen the bottle.

Salvation! The bottle was still half full!

I gripped the bottle tightly and walked backward toward the bathroom, carefully staring at a dirt spot on the windowless wall. Before I knew it, I was sitting on the toilet seat, wringing the dead soldier's skinny neck, my head spinning. The rum burned at first, but got smoother with each swig until there was none left, and I even craved just a little bit more, just to make things feel a little smoother.

I kicked the bathroom door open, then stood and stumbled over the threshold. I straightened and felt the whole room spin. Took a careful step, then another. I felt fine, I thought, and took a couple less careful steps, tripped over a boot and tumbled forward, falling face-first right beneath the window, the big one directly across from my bed. I reached a hand forward and gripped the molding below the window, pulled myself up to my knees, my nose inches away from the blanket.

Couldn't see anything, but damn, I felt cold, colder than I'd ever felt in my whole life. Cold, then hot, as drunken anger washed over me. I grabbed the blanket and tore it away from the window frame, leaving me face to face with a familiar shape, plainly visible through the shade.

I stared at the bastard. I swear I could see those terrible eyes staring back at me. Staring at me!

What do you want from me? I shouted. Why are you doing this? What did I ever do to you?

A shrieking exploded inside my head. Stomach muscles contracted, then convulsed. I fell backward. After that, I don't know. All I remember was waking up lying on my back, my legs bent underneath me, dizzy, head pounding like a motherfucker. I reached back, touched the back of my head and winced with pain. Vomit was everywhere. On the window, the molding, all over me.

And through the vomit-splattered window, I could still see the bowling-ball head, the coal eyes staring at me.

I struggled to stand on wobbly legs and stared right back at the creature. What the hell did I ever do to you? I shouted. Before the creature could respond, I charged, my arms outstretched, hands reaching right for its throat.

I crashed through the window, felt fangs of glass bite into my arms. But I was going to get that thing. I was going to get that thing. My hands inches away from the creature's throat, right there, right there....

And that's all I remember. They say Kern found me on the front lawn. Covered with blood and vomit, a few broken bones, but otherwise none too worse for wear.

No, I didn't feel the impact, only the shrieking inside my head, the constant echo of the creature's reply:

You invaded my privacy, so I invade yours.

And that was that. Now, I sleep in a room with no windows, but I still see the creature. See it in my dreams, but this time it's different. I don't find the creature in my dreams, it finds me. Comes to me in my dreams and just stares at me.

Dreams are windows, I guess. I guess I'm just kind of screwed.

I rubbed my eyes after completing that long entry. *Is it scared of civilization or does it use civilization as camouflage?* When my eyes focused, Nicole was staring at me.

"This mean anything, Al?"

"Nothing, just ramblings."

"Don't give me that bullshit." She played with her empty tea cup. "You're like, totally engrossed. What's it all about?"

"I cannot be certain."

"But there's something, isn't there?"

The woman certainly was perceptive. I was not sure whether I wanted to share it with her, but it seemed she would not allow any option other than total disclosure.

"Mortals," I began, "see their world as an aggregation of three-dimensional objects and fail to see anything outside of that limited spatial concept. They see not a fourth dimension. For them, time is a strictly linear construct, hopelessly rooted in the present, where past and future exist merely as states relative to the present."

"Uh-huh," Nicole said. "I presume this has something to do with the topic at hand?"

I nodded. "Yes. You see, mortals fail to see the dimensions between dimensions, the three-dimensional worlds not very different from their own that exist quite literally right in front of their eyes."

"And that's what Frank saw?" Nicole walked into the kitchen. "Go on, I'm listening. If I drink any more tea, I'll float away, but I wanna hear this, and I think I'm gonna need some more caffeine. Besides, I don't think I'm gonna want to sleep tonight. So, what does this have to do with Frank?"

"Frank's 'creature' *was* real. It exists in the realities of many civilizations all over the world and has been called many names. Perhaps Western civilization would call it a gremlin, which, oddly, in your lexicon, is defined as a 'mythical creature' simply because this industrialized, technology-based society is too mired in empirical thought to believe what the eyes do not always see."

"Gremlins? Jesus Christ, you gotta be kidding. How did he get to see one of those?"

"A moment of shared consciousness—"

"Shared consciousness? You're talking about when you bit him. Is that what happens? People go off their nut?"

"No. I feel what they feel, and they feel what I feel. It goes both ways, but the effect is short-lived, and normally they do not remember any of it."

"But Frank did."

"My senses are more acute than yours, Nicole. I see things you cannot. Frank got a glimpse of this creature as a direct by-product of my actions. Mere remote coincidence let Frank be in the right place at the right time to glimpse a creature that is really quite harmless. They just tend to be a bit puckish sometimes."

The sound of boiling water emanated from the kitchen. Nicole, empty cup in hand, looked at me from across the threshold, eyebrows scrunched downward. "Not harmless, Al. Obviously, not harmless. Don't think for a second that it was harmless."

"The creature itself *is* harmless—"

"Bullshit, just look at—"

"Please listen and try to control the histrionics. Frank only glimpsed the creature briefly, but imagine it like this: You are in a dark room with a closed door separating you from the bright light on the other side. The door is opened a mere crack, allowing the tiniest sliver of light to pass the threshold. But imagine how bright that tiny sliver of light would seem from within that dark room. Yet, it is still a mere sliver of reality, folded as it were, but you unfold it, and there is an entire dimension. Frank only saw a tiny sliver of the creature's being, but it was enough to crash through his perceptual limitations."

Nicole gasped, almost dropping the cup, not even noticing the whistling of the teapot. "Christ, that'd be enough to make a person crazy."

"Indeed. It would."

"It'd be like dropping acid without knowing it. Everything looks different, but you don't know why. You just think you've lost your mind. Christ, how would anyone deal with it?" She poured herself another cup of tea. "Shit, oughta make a whole pot. I really don't think I want to sleep tonight."

"Under the circumstances, I would not blame you."

She returned to the table. "Christ, the therapists tried to help him, but there wasn't a damn thing they could do for him."

"No, not while operating under such a materialistic paradigm."

"But he needs help, Al. Maybe you could talk to him. Help him."

"If he's not so far gone that he wouldn't accept help."

"You gotta do something. This *is* your fault. You do know that, don't you?"

"Yes, I understand."

"You better understand." Nicole picked up the diary and fondled it between sips of tea. "He resisted the therapy at first, thought he might fool them by cooperating with their efforts. Even willingly took part in occupational therapy. That's where the flowers come in. Finally, they convinced him he'd only been having delusions. Probably, by then, the dreams had stopped. Your creature must've gotten bored. They let him out of Mendota, and he came back to work at Co-op Cab. He was fine until he saw you again. He talks about some altercation between you and him in the bathroom where he saw you in the mirror, but didn't really see you. From the way he rambles after that, it seems that incident started to push him over the edge, but he still wasn't sure. He talks about not really believing what he'd seen, that it wasn't real. They'd told him that he was creating alternative realities to act out an unwillingness to take responsibility for his own failings. He almost believed it, but then the dreams came back. Listen to this entry. It's dated March fifteenth, not even two weeks ago:

"'Goddamned asshole psychotherapists!

"'They said I was having delusions. They said I had to let go of these delusions, and then the dreams would stop. Well, the dreams stopped, but that creature is still out there, only it's taken a different form. Fucking psychotherapists. Don't know shit.

"'I know this because the truth came in a dream.

"'I'm sitting in my cab, in the cab stand at the east-side Greyhound depot, waiting for the call that'll give me the late-shift clean sweep. I'd drawn a four-o'clock end-time, as opposed to knocking off at two—bar-time. But I've got experience. I'd been in the right cab stand for the guy who goes from the near south-side to the Hill Farms Office Building, which set me up for the woman from the deep southwest-side to the state office building off the Square. Then I slide a few blocks east to post up at the Skinny Dog for Cletus. He'll get in the cab and say work and nothing more. The meter'll run nine bucks, he'll hand me a ten, and I can call it night.

"'It's deadly quiet, as if a neutron bomb exploded.

"'Out of the corner of my eye, a yellow blur flashes past. I ignore it. It's late, and my imagination is getting the better of me. The creature has left me alone. It no longer invades my dreams.

"'There's a rap at the window. I feel a jolt from the base of my spine to the top of my head. I turn and see a face. It's familiar, a fellow driver. It's that guy, fucking Euro-faggot named Al. Has this real stupid accent.'"

Nicole laughed loudly. "Just like Maggie said. You sure you're not gay?"

I frowned. "Please continue."

"'What's he doing here? It's three-fucking-thirty in the goddamned morning. He's not driving. Why isn't he home asleep?

"'I roll down the window. His face glows bright yellow in the halogen lights outside the bus depot. He asks if I have any money for a cash advance. Sure, no problem, I say. We do that all the time.

"'I reach for a charge slip to record the advance. I face him again. He's smiling, showing lots of teeth. I see a pair of sharp fangs. I see two black eyes staring at me. Then, nothing but black. There's a sharp sting against my neck, a pair of sharp stings piecing my flesh. I hear a soft sucking sound. I feel my strength draining from me. I feel my life draining—

"'Just a dream? No way. No fuckin' way.

"'I've been haunted by faces staring through clear panes of glass: An alien face, bright yellow, round like a bowling ball, with round lumps of coal for eyes, no nose and no mouth; and a human face that's not human, whose skin is too white, whose teeth are too sharp, whose image cannot be seen in a mirror.

"'Mirror! Glass!

"'Windows! Illusion!

"'The faces aren't important. One is a true form. One is a clever disguise that so carelessly reveals its true nature.

"'Glass, that's what's important—the window between the implied and the inferred. It can be shattered!

"'They all said I was crazy, but I'll show them. Just have to get the evidence. I've got a special camera, with special film and special infra-red gadgets, gizmos, thingamabobs and thingeegiggees.

"'I was the hunter, then became the hunted. Now, the hunted will become the hunter once again.'"

Nicole shut the diary and slid it across the table. "There's one more entry. It's real short. He must've written it after the membership meeting. He's raving at that point, about how we're all fools not to heed his warning, but he would show us all."

"This is all my fault."

"Damn right—"

There was a loud thud just outside my apartment door, which literally jolted Nicole out of her chair.

Then an insistent rapping at the door.

Chapter 10

THE RESPONSIBILITY OF DISHONOR

I leaped across the room, knocked Nicole to the floor, just as the door flew open.

A white-hot dagger seared through my chest cavity. The room swirled before my eyes momentarily before coming into focus. Frank stood above me, a burlap sack slung over one shoulder, corneas a spider web lattice-work of crimson, pupils dilated, breath hot and fetid, heart pounding like hammer blows struck by a yeoman blacksmith. He dropped the sack and reached downward toward the stake protruding from my chest, which pierced flesh, but had been mercifully stopped by sturdy breast bone.

I scurried out of the range of his grasp. Nicole jumped to her feet and gave Frank a shove. Staggered only slightly, he steadied and threw a punch, connecting loudly with her jaw, more a slap then a crack. Nicole landed hard on the floor.

Frank laughed loudly, then grabbed the sack, held it upside down and let the contents fall. It was the black boy who had ridden in my cab a mere few days before. He was stripped of his clothes, stripped of his life, his flesh more gray than chocolate, face bruised, abrasions and contusions livid on his chest, stomach and legs, one arm bent at a cockeyed angle. Crusts of dried blood delineated a pair of puncture marks on his neck.

Rising to my knees, I tore the stake from my chest. Jagged shards of pain ripped through my being, quickly replaced by a sharp tingling as tissue knitted itself back together.

In the momentary haziness, as my body repaired itself, Frank kicked hard at the wound in my chest. An angry red wave washed over me. I toppled to the floor, then rolled over to see Frank grabbing Nicole under both arms, effortlessly lifting her in the air, then flinging her toward the boy. His strength was unfathomable, surely augmented by adrenalin and madness.

"Look at that!" he shouted, as he moved to her side, bits of spittle splattering her face. He pointed at the boy. "Look at that! I warned you. All of you! He's a monster, but you wouldn't believe me and now look what he's done!"

Nicole's face twisted into a dark scowl as she kicked him in the groin. I jumped to my feet, pulled him away from Nicole and backhanded him across the face, sending him sprawling across the apartment. "You're the monster," she yelled. "Al's been with me all night."

Frank's mad, grinning countenance remained unchanged. I stepped between him and Nicole. He pointed an accusing finger at the boy.

"I showed them," he said. "Showed them all just what kind of blood-sucking monster you are."

"*You* killed him!" I shouted. "It was *you*. *You* killed him. *You* took his blood. *His* blood! What have you done with his blood?"

Frank laughed, then reached for a rucksack that lay next to the empty sack. He lifted a large jar full of blood from the rucksack. "Oh, you weren't very hungry, so you only drank a little bit, then drained the rest and put it in a jar. The police'll find this in your fridge."

"Idiot! If I only needed a little bit, why kill? Why? Tell me why! Tell me!"

I stepped toward him. Frank stood his ground, then reached for a silver crucifix and held it before my eyes. His laughter turned hysterical. I slapped the crucifix from his hands. The cross struck the wall loudly. "Fool," I said. "You have watched too many Hollywood movies."

"His mind!" Nicole shouted. "Try touching his mind!"

Frank stood motionless, his face a hardened mask except for rapidly shifting eyes. I focused on the movement, let my consciousness adjust to the movement until it slowed to almost a complete stop, allowing me entrance through the dark openings...

—Only to be staggered by an impact against solid granite. My consciousness reeled, then pulled back and focused upon a curving stone wall. I followed the wall as it curved in one direction, then another, then back again as the line of stone seemed to fall back into infinity, curving back and forth—

—Before finally opening to a dark, dense forest surrounded by swamp.

My consciousness began tramping through the swamp toward the forest. The muck grew thicker, holding tighter. Each step took a greater and greater effort while the forest seemed to grow no closer—

—Until no more steps were possible, the muck enclosing around my legs, holding me fast as—

—The forest turned to fire, foliage burned away in an instant, all the trees stripped to mere glowing posts, collapsing, falling toward me—

—Flying toward me. Thousands of burning stakes flying toward me, striking my consciousness, ripping, tearing until something pulled me away from the dying embers of the burnt forest, away from the stagnant pools of fetid water, back and forth along the curving granite wall—

—Frank's grinning personage filled my sight, his hands wrapped around a stake, its sharp point impaling the flesh covering my heart. Hands on my shoulders pulled desperately from behind, preventing the stake from finding its mark.

In full focus, ignoring the pain, I grabbed the stake with both hands, pushed against the opposing force until it came free, then twisted it out of Frank's grasp, turned and swung the blunt end at his head. He crumpled to the floor, but quickly rose, blood dribbling from his ear, the grin wider still, the sound of his pounding heart almost deafening.

In the long, swollen moment that followed, numerous images from the past flew across my sight: the Grand Inquisitor passing sentence on myself and Julianne; the burgermeister listening so attentively to brigands who had tried to rob me, then accused me of consorting with the devil; and all those Nazis, those who I killed and those who I imagined as they murdered my dear Anya.

All the faces of those true believers—different faces, yet always the expression never changed and was just the same as the countenance which charged at me with no weapon save his bare hands.

No more battering. No more pain. I let him charge at me, at the last moment opening my arms for him to fall within my embrace.

"No!" I heard Nicole scream.

Our flesh collided, and though the force was great, Frank moved me not a whit as I reached for his chin, twisted sharply until a loud crack filled the room, and Frank crumpled to the floor.

I turned toward Nicole. She stood against the wall, palms pressed against the paneling as if to brace herself from falling. Her face was flushed, eyes darting back and forth, from one corpse to another.

"Nicole?"

No response for a moment, then her gaze met mine. "You killed him," she said dryly, almost matter-of-fact.

Yes, a mortal was dead at my hand—and a boy was dead because of me as well. My fault, my responsibility. Her tone was dry, and it seemed I wanted to hear anger, wanted to hear accusation, blame. See her point a sharp finger at me like a stiletto of truth stabbing at the lies and deception that punctuates every day spent among mortals. Yes, I had killed Frank, and maybe it could be called self-defense, or in the language of their judicial system, justifiable homicide, but since when had their laws applied to me? Usually their wrath superseded their own laws, affording me none of their protection.

Regardless, two mortals lay dead in my apartment because of my vanity.

"Yes, I killed him." That was all I could say, not even allowing myself the luxury of verbalizing the fact that there was little else that could be done, not when a maniac lunges at your throat with nothing short of murderous fury. Or rationalizing that this was not so much a killing as an act of mercy, for it seemed doubtful that Frank truly desired to be the monster he had become.

Nicole pushed away from the wall. She ran her fingers vigorously through her hair, almost as if she wanted to tear the fine strands out by their fragile roots.

"I'm leaving," she said, her voice bland, but steady. I made no move to stop her as she shuffled slowly toward the door. She gripped the doorknob, turned and faced me, eyes glistening brightly. "This is too much, Al. I thought you were cute, nice. I just thought it'd be cool having you as a boyfriend."

Without another word, she was gone.

I stared at the closed door, listening to her footsteps as they retreated into nothingness, the grainy wood spiraling before my eyes until the present asserted itself from someplace far away.

There were two corpses in my apartment, and they had to be disposed of before a dawn, which would come all too soon.

I buried Frank in a wooded area just south of Madison, in a place where he certainly would not be found.

However, other considerations prevented me from disposing of the boy in the same manner. One of the peculiarities I had noticed since returning to America was the preponderance of missing children, their faces ubiquitously posted on milk cartons that pleaded for any information and even offered rewards. The parents of a missing child from Minnesota offered a million dollars for the return of their son.

Surely these children were dead, but these people somehow maintained their faith. To me, these parents seemed tragically deluded, and it seemed cruel to subject this poor boy's mother to the same ordeal. Thus, I left his body where it could easily be found. At least his mother would know her boy was dead, if she cared. Also, I resolved to set up a trust fund for the boy's siblings and their descendants from one percent of my future earnings, in perpetuity.

I readied for flight in case the neighbors had heard sounds of struggle from within my apartment, or if anyone had spotted a shadowy figure hauling an oddly shaped canvas sack over his shoulder, or if anyone had filed a missing person's report over Frank, or if the authorities suspected any connection between the boy's murder and his nightly cab rides between the homes of his aunt and mother.

Two days later, the boy's murder was front-page news. I read with interest as the police said they had no suspects, but were tracking down every possible lead. Details of the killing were sketchy. Officially, the police refused to comment on the condition of the boy's body, though rumors were rampant, and his mother went on record as saying her son's killer was a very sick person.

And she was right.

For one week, this was Madison's top story, attracting voluminous coverage in the newspapers and on television, but as leads dried up, the media seemed to lose interest.

Then, one week later, a twenty-year-old technical-school coed was found: naked, mutilated, her body rumored to have been drained of blood.

Chapter 11

THE INEVITABILITY OF HUNGER

I feel like you're jerking my chain about these blood-drained bodies lying around. What was it? Two women? I feel like you're gonna tell me vampires did it. Did you start to wonder that?

No, sir, I did not. Even killer vampires fear exposure and do not leave bodies lying about, not when it is so easy to dispose of corpses. Serial killers, however: *they* prefer leaving their victims where they can be found, their way of sending a message to the rest of humanity that they are superior.

So? Didn't you wanna do something about this, regardless of who was doing the killing?

Again, no. This was an affair for the local constabulary.

A bit cold, Farkas.

No, just pragmatic. My main concern was what it always is: that hunger comes.

Hunger comes? Whaddaya mean by that?

You wanted to know what there was to do in the wake of this sad episode, what there was to do with an entire city tensed and on guard. Hunger comes, that is all I can say.

Nothing is more sure, more certain. The hunger comes with the inevitability of the rising sun, its spidery tendrils climbing up and down my spine, plucking a symphony on my nerve endings.

A thousand years ago, the hunger would come daily. Now, one fairly small feeding each week is adequate. It's a weekly event, something to be planned for, but nothing of any great consequence; the act itself takes maybe a minute, while the planning, in a highly public, well-populated city, merely consists of deciding which end of State Street to search for sustenance. Certainly, my existence is not comparable to that of, say, a shark, which constantly searches for food. However, these two murders in close succession changed the casual nature of my feeding.

My night off usually meant an excursion to State Street, but on a fairly warm night in early-April, I found this artery silent, the usual coursing corpuscles absent from the street, evidently somewhere they perceived as more safe.

Of course, the street was not completely devoid of people, but they traveled in packs, seeking protection in their numbers. Several pairs of police officers paced the sidewalks on foot. Other constables drove up and down in their cruisers.

For the first time since arriving in Madison, my solitary presence on State Street felt conspicuous. A tingle made my whole body shudder, not that the hunger had really asserted itself, just a suggestion that it might if there was no one to be found walking without a companion.

A bold newspaper headline caught my attention from the inside of a vending box:

"Madison Mangler Makes More Malevolent Mayhem."

I dropped coins into the slot and removed the newspaper—the last one actually, the display copy—and began reading. There was a maniac on the loose, the newspaper asserted, even though the authorities strongly stated their unwillingness to link those two killings with each other, let alone with the similar killing a few months before. The authorities called it a "copy-cat crime," saying they had no evidence whatsoever that these crimes were related. Still, it seemed the media had chosen to vociferously insist otherwise. These nameless, faceless maniacs known as serial killers seemed all the rage in America, and Madison's media acted almost as if Wisconsin's capitol needed its own homicidal maniac just to put their city on the map.

As I stood reading, a rather undistinguished student passed, stopped and attempted to read the headline over my shoulder. I turned, and our eyes met for a mere instant before he continued walking, a decided alacrity to his step. As I watched his gait, a police car moved closer, slowed to nearly a complete stop, the officer behind the wheel scrutinizing me closely. I tucked the newspaper under my arm and moved with my own high degree of alacrity.

Hunger comes.

I drove my car into the Frances Street parking ramp, ducked down and waited for nearly an hour until distant footsteps drew my attention. At the far end of my row, a rather mercantile-looking fellow in a gray pin-stripe suit unlocked a large black sedan. Quickly, I dematerialized, then rematerialized in the front passenger seat just as he opened the car door. Astonishment flashed across his face for a moment before my gaze met his.

In less than five minutes, I was in my car, leaving the ramp, having satisfied my hunger, but felt dismay over the clumsiness of the action.

For obvious reasons, I followed the stories closely, but found it increasingly difficult to find an available newspaper in the usual newspaper boxes. Thus, it became a ritual to buy the first morning paper from a dispenser immediately following shift's end instead of waiting until the next day when there would be none available. Sometimes I would lie in wait, watching for the distribution person to refill the box. Then I would take my newspaper and read in the moonlight.

The killings became an obsession for all of Madison and quickly provided a bonanza for all of Madison's cab drivers. And, as if the heightened demand were not sufficient, cab business increased further when the University of Wisconsin started providing free cab rides for students after dark.

Publicly, the university was able to use the "U-Ride" program as a means to provide positive publicity for itself due to its quick response to a dire situation.

However, we cabbies knew better. Negotiations had commenced weeks before the first absurdly alliterated headline appeared in the newspaper. Having cut funding to a volunteer-based night-ride program for women, the university realized it had to provide a replacement, and this gave them the incentive to bring that notion to fruition.

Despite this monetary boon, I was ready for flight at first provocation. As it turned out, supreme good fortune was mine. Frank's disappearance interested no one; not a single constable visited Co-op Cab with questions as to his whereabouts. The only observed comment was placed anonymously on the sign bearing Frank's name under the heading "No charges, no advances." Next to his name, someone wrote, "abducted by aliens."

But what of the boy?

A few days after the news of the boy hit the papers, there was a call at the Silver Dollar, yet another of the many saloons off the Capitol Square. Dexter had said it was for a driver. Actually, it was three drivers. Shortly after pulling alongside the bar's picture window, Paul Davis, Jane Peronowski and Ken Singleton emerged.

I knew the trio somewhat. They all drove Friday nights and were members of the infamous "Saturday Morning Beer Drinking Committee," an aggregation of late-night drivers who, after shift's end, would drink beer in the driver's room and discuss cooperative politics, posting their unusually creative proclamations on "Democracy Wall" before departing. They often urged me to join their committee, but of course, I do not drink beer, and their meetings would usually last until well after dawn.

"Oh, no!" Ken shouted when he climbed into the front seat. "It's the Count! It's Count Farkas!"

"Run for your lives!" Jane shrieked. Paul screamed loudly. The other two joined him, their throaty shouts filling my cab with their beer-and-whiskey-tainted breath.

Finally, they stopped screaming, their shrieks replaced by near-hysterical laughter.

"Where may I take you?" I asked, simply acting indifferent to their rude behavior.

Jane was the first to regain some semblance of composure, reporting that they were going to the Club DeWash.

"Careful," Ken said. "It's the Count. Who knows where he'll take us or what he'll do to us."

"Yeah," Paul added, "he got that kid. Count, man, you shouldn't be leaving your leftovers lying around."

Hide in plain sight?

"Shut up, you assholes," Jane rebuked. "C'mon. Let's leave Al alone so we can get moving. We've already missed the opening bands. I don't want to miss any of Killdozer."

"No big deal," Paul said, "missing Art Paul Schlosser."

"But if we miss just one note of one Killdozer song," Jane said, "I'm gonna cut your brake lines."

"Won't matter after the Count's done with us," Ken said.

Without a word, I turned the cab around and proceeded toward the Club DeWash. By then, Paul and Jane were finally quiet. Ken began singing in a deep, gravely voice:

He was nothing but a whining cur,
The asswipe called my bitch a whore,
So we made the him a her,
And now the puppy is no more, no more.

"Was that Killdozer?" I asked.

"Yeah," Paul said. "A song called, 'The Puppy,' about a real murder case, happened here a few years ago. Real losers. They were bikers, but didn't have motorcycles. And in court, they kept referring to the victim as 'the puppy.' Fuckin' creepy."

"This isn't the way to the Club DeWash!" Ken shrieked. Paul and Jane joined in. I had just turned onto West Washington, which led straight to their destination. "Where are you taking us? What are you going to do us?"

"Please don't hurt us," Paul pleaded. "Please have mercy on our wretched souls."

The trio again broke into hysterics. Jane patted me gently on the shoulder. "Sorry," she said. "We're just being assholes."

"Being an asshole ain't against the law," Ken said.

"But neither is being a vampire," I replied.

"It sure is when you break our laws." Paul's voice rang falsely earnest.

"The laws of you pathetic mortals apply not to one such as myself." It was my turn to laugh. And loudly, as I felt my lips form a vulpine smile. "This being the case, you would be wise to show proper respect and pay the proper tribute."

None of the four of us stopped laughing until we arrived at the Club DeWash. They paid the fare and included quite a generous tip.

****

My thoughts should have been exclusively centered upon survival, yet images of Nicole would not stop flashing across my consciousness—no longer Nicole superimposing herself upon Anya. I did see her at the cab company occasionally, gaining a furtive glimpse, which raised my spirits slightly, even if we avoided each other. On those instances, she always bore a queer expression, not so much of fear, but confusion. I simply felt sad, but certainly understood that what she had experienced would overwhelm anyone.

Oddly, even though we had not had much opportunity to get to know one another, she had indeed awakened something that lay dormant inside me, a very special hunger far more profound than mere blood.

What was to be done?

I shuddered while second-guessing myself over the entire Frank Nelson affair, especially the encounter with the prostitute. At the time, I thought I had been discreet. It seemed my actions had been relatively prudent, but in retrospect, my perceptions had been clouded by my own personal vanity.

Hunger is danger. Existence is risk.

All I had wanted was to taste the prostitute's orgasm, to taste that which is the sweet metaphor of life, even more sublime than the hot, steaming river which courses through the veins of all those mortals.

She gave me nothing but the essence of sheer nothingness, not even death.

My hunger remained.

At least there was work and much money to be made, even if those infernal U-Rides had come to dominate our business. Yes, all calls are good calls, but most U-Rides were short, and the students very seldom tipped. Generally, those calls took longer to load, and each one generated additional paperwork.

Thus, when a U-Ride took me east of the Capitol, I did not hesitate to bid when Dexter called an east-side intersection that was a little farther from my destination than most drivers preferred to travel. The intersection was east of U-Ride's zone of operation. Hopefully, it would be a cash call and not some other account where there was no tip.

"Count, four-forty-four Kedzie," Dexter said, adding, "Cash."

"Excellent," I replied, happy to get a call with at least a chance of a tip as well as the opportunity to see some different scenery. The streets were finally clear of snow, but the trees were still completely bare, thus allowing the concrete, steel, and plastic of civilization to dominate the landscape.

My mood was not even altered by the fact that it took a phone call from Dexter to get her out of her house. Sometimes the passengers watch; sometimes they do not. It *is* preferable when they do watch, time, after all, being money.

A young woman emerged, dressed in a loose-fitting sweatshirt and sweatpants, a large bag slung over her shoulder. Long flaxen hair cascaded down her shoulders. Even in the dimness of night, she looked rather plain.

"Where may I take you?" I asked once she was securely inside.

"The Rising Sun," she replied. Instantly, I felt regret, for making her say that she was going to that massage parlor of ill repute just off the Capitol Square. She was a regular customer, and even if she had never been in my cab, I was fairly certain the Rising Sun was to be her destination. Still, I had to ask.

"You guys busy?" Her tone was chipper.

"Yes. With the publicity regarding those killings, it seems everyone wants to take cab rides rather than walk."

She sighed in agreement. "I hope we'll be busy tonight. I only had two programs in six hours last night."

Her frankness was shocking. I certainly had no intention of asking about her work, and if she had told me her destination was 117 W. Main, I would have taken her to the Rising Sun without mentioning the name of the establishment. However, it seemed admirable that she could be honest about her vocation, though many would treat her with disdain. Indeed, the woman was quite genuine; the ride progressed pleasantly as we simply chatted jovially about this and that until we arrived.

"That will be five dollars," I said, feeling myself smile, having enjoyed this little interlude between U-Rides.

"Well, here you go." She handed me a five and two ones, the notes folded twice upon themselves. "If you're working late, you might get me going home. I'm Jasmine."

I turned and faced her. She smiled and looked directly into my eyes. "My name is Al."

"Nice to meet you, Al." She extended her arm and shook my hand firmly.

A week later, I got another call for Jasmine, but this time it was a delivery.

"Count," Dexter said, "go to the Walgreen's at the East Side Shop. Pick up a pint of Ben and Jerry's Chunky Monkey ice cream and four dozen non-lubricated condoms. Turn your meter on with the time on when you pull up to the Walgreen's. Take the stuff up to Jasmine at the Rising Sun. Charge her the meter, plus a dollar-fifty handling charge, plus the cost of the goods."

Motherless spawn of Satan! What in the name of the four winds of Hades was Chunky Monkey ice cream? And four dozen condoms? In my short tenure, I had delivered food, cigarettes and, one snowy night, a newspaper, but ice cream and condoms? How bewildering.

Upon climbing the stairs up to the Rising Sun, Jasmine was waiting for me just inside the half door at the establishment's entrance. But this was not the same plain woman who had ridden in my cab.

Glamour was at work here. Glamour in the classic sense, which tricks the eyes and bewitches the heart. Jasmine wore a faux silk Chinese dress, her breasts pressing hard against the blue fabric, the color identical to that of the evening sky when the last remnants of sunlight have passed beyond the horizon. Her hair was pulled back just enough to accentuate what was really a noble set of cheekbones. She had done up her face to the point where her skin appeared smooth and flawless without giving her the appearance of being "painted."

"Hi, Al," Jasmine said upon seeing me, seeming pleased with herself that she had remembered my name.

I handed her the bag, and she promptly examined the contents. "You did say non-lubricated condoms, did you not?"

She lifted the ice cream container from the bag and rolled it in her palms while licking her lips. "Yeah," she said, nodding her head, smiling at me. "I prefer K-Y jelly."

Vampires do not blush, which was good, for I certainly would have turned quite crimson at that very moment. Instead, I just took her money, which included a five-dollar tip and descended to my cab to get my next call.

A lightning bolt of inspiration struck me later that night.

On my very next night off, I climbed the steps up to the Rising Sun to have an appointment with Jasmine. What had she called it? A program?

It seemed insane, yet something compelled me to do this, for in a world of imprudent choices, this might be the least of all possible evils. Certainly, it represented a compromise between the street-whore and Nicole. Jasmine seemed a reasonable and professional sort, and regardless of how much ease there could be finding sustenance on State Street or anywhere else in this town, a certain other hunger remained, a certain need had to be satisfied.

Also, considering the mood of fear and hysteria permeating the city, in which even the smallest mistake could be magnified tenfold, it might prove useful to have an associate with which to make certain rather special arrangements if circumstances so dictated.

The burly fellow at the door told me Jasmine would be available shortly. He took my money and instructed me to have a seat in the waiting room, which lay just inside the door. The room was stark and shabby with imitation walnut paneling covering the walls. I sat in a bright red wing chair, upholstered with cheap vinyl that squeaked with each movement. A matching chair and sofa surrounded a coffee table covered with pornographic magazines of varying degrees of distaste. A television sat where it would in anybody's living room. A VCR sat atop of the TV, surely for the viewing of pornographic videos.

The fellow at the door—not so much of a pimp, Jasmine would tell me, but more of a bodyguard—had collected fifty dollars from me, and I would tip Jasmine another fifty. Though extravagant, this expense was not unreasonable considering my lack of expenses for food and drink.

Jasmine appeared shortly. "Oh, hi, Al," she said, smiling broadly with recognition. "I guess turnabout is fair play."

"Yes. It is."

Jasmine led me to the room where she plied her trade. As I followed, white, rounded flesh from underneath her short, matte-black skirt revealed itself ever so slightly with the rising and falling of her steps.

"What'll it be?" She closed the door and faced me, her breasts bobbing up and down under the clingy fabric of her nearly see-through gauzy top. The room was stark with white walls, the only furniture a black, vinyl couch sitting against one wall and a padded massage table in the center of the room. A shower lay in an adjacent alcove.

I dropped a fifty-dollar bill on the massage table. "I just want to talk."

"Okay," she said, scooping up the fifty. "I'm all ears."

"I know you work outside this place." My voice was little more than a whisper.

Jasmine nodded. "I think all you cabbies know that."

"Indeed. We are often privy to many secrets that we do not divulge. May I expect the same discretion from you?"

The woman smiled warmly. "Sure, Al. Hey, everybody's got a secret. You, me, everybody. What's yours? Thrill me."

I paused, taking a moment to consider whether this was not the most moronic action of my long, protracted existence. "My secret will likely shock you. You probably will not even believe it."

"Go ahead, flatter yourself." She laughed loudly and took a seat on the message table, crossing her legs, showing ample amounts of muscular flesh. "You guys always think your little secrets are so damn shocking. Hell, you wouldn't believe some of the things I've heard, some of the things guys wanted me to do. Guys want me to strap on a dildo and fuck *them* up the ass. Guys want me to fuck their dog while they watch. So, if you can really shock me, I'd be pretty damn impressed."

"I can appreciate your unique position to observe the wide variety of human deviance." A momentary pause allowed me to carefully choose my words. "There is much that is strange in this world we live in."

Jasmine slapped her thigh and nodded her head vigorously, then pulled at the chain around her neck, lifting a piece of rose quartz from between her breasts. She fondled the crystal between her fingers. "Tell me about it. I just moved outta my apartment. Place was haunted."

"Really?" I felt myself smile. "You believe in the unseen, the unexplained?"

"Yeah." Her voice was hushed, as if she did not want anyone to hear her denounce the doctrine of scientific secularism.

"What if I were to tell you that I am not what I appear to be?"

"And what are you really?" She leaned forward, her expression earnest despite the sarcasm dripping from her words.

"I am a creature of the shadows, rising with the sunset, subsisting on the blood of the living."

Jasmine laughed loudly. "And I suppose you vant to suck my blood."

"Yes," I answered, "as a matter of fact, that is exactly what I desire."

Jasmine stood and backed quickly toward the door. "I scream, and you're flying down the stairs faster than you can say Bela Lugosi."

I quickly rebuked myself, having foolishly taken for granted that even Jasmine would be affected by this wave of fear and suspicion sweeping across the city. Quickly, I sought to ease her misgivings. "Please, Jasmine. Fear not. If I am indeed that monster of your streets, your so-called Madison Mangler, I would not tell you I am anything unusual."

Jasmine exhaled loudly and stepped away from the door, regaining her perch atop the message table, arms crossed about her chest. "Then you're just crazy. Crazy is okay, but it'll cost you extra."

"Please," I said. "Please listen to what I have to say. I *am* a vampire. I have been for a thousand years."

"Oh yeah sure!" Jasmine snorted. "If you're a vampire, prove it."

Ah, skeptical, but somewhat open-minded. Applying concentration, I commanded my fangs to come forth from their retracted hiding place, then lifted my upper lip.

"Big deal," she said. "I used to know a guy with teeth like that. Big guy, worked in the trees, had pet wolves. You gonna tell me he was a werewolf?"

"I do not presume to insult your intelligence."

"I should hope not. Got any other tricks, Drac?"

A chuckle escaped my lips. She would certainly laugh at my next attempt. "Look into my eyes."

She did not laugh. Her eyes met mine, and momentarily, she was taking off her dress, turning it inside out, then putting it back on.

"So, you're a hypnotist," she said, studying her clothing when released from this gentle spell. "Doesn't prove anything."

If there had been a mirror in the room, perhaps that might have been a way to prove my point. Instead, another tactic would have to suffice. "I want you to watch me very carefully," I said finally.

"Whatever you do won't prove anything," she said. "How will I know you didn't just hypnotize me again?"

"Do not look into my eyes. Then, you will know you have not been hypnotized once again." I shut my eyes, willed the cells in my body to move farther and farther apart until I disappeared in a cloud of mist, then rematerialized behind her and tapped her on the shoulder. Jasmine turned, a loud gasp escaping her throat. She shook noticeably

"I will not hurt you." I held up both hands palms outward and took a couple steps backward. "Please do not worry. My requirements call for only a very tiny amount of blood."

She crossed her arms in front of her. Slowly, the fear dissolved from her face. "Okay, so it won't kill me when you take my blood, but if you bite me, will I turn into a vampire?"

"Certainly not." I felt myself smile.

Jasmine acquiesced in response to my gaze. "What do you want me to do?"

****

"Please enter," I said, responding to the knock on the door. Jasmine crossed the threshold of the cheap motel room. She wore a short white dress with a halter top divided into two sections like the wing-covers of a beetle. Alabaster cleavage pushed through the slit between the two segments of the halter. A silver comb held her flaxen hair away from one side of her face, the hair carefully swept forward on the other side.

"Hi, Al," Jasmine said with an easy smile, closing the door behind her. She noticed the hundred-dollar bill sitting on the dresser, scooped it up and put it in her purse, then glanced in the mirror and only saw a stiff set of clothes sitting atop the bed. For a short moment, there was a visible chink in her calm veneer.

"Thank you for coming, Jasmine," I said, rooted to my spot, watching her every move, listening carefully to her heart race; she was nervous.

Without a word, Jasmine turned and faced me, then reached around to the back of her neck, unhooked the clasp and let the twin halter segments fall to her waist, revealing large, pale breasts. "Do you like what you see, Al?"

In fact, I did. Her breasts were well rounded, firm, though they sagged a bit, but pleasantly so, like a teardrop, as opposed to those infernal implants that leave women's breasts the consistency of concrete. The nipples were erect; she had probably rubbed them just before entering. Still, despite this intellectual deconstruction, the sight of her was most certainly pleasing.

She smiled at my response. "You were a bit vague when you told me what you expected. What do you want me to do?"

"Take off your dress."

Jasmine nodded. She slipped her dress over her hips, let it fall to the floor and stood before me in nothing but thin panties. There was a slight roll around her abdomen, and her legs were not model-thin, but she looked fit and well toned, certainly more healthy than these cadaverous American women.

She studied my reaction then smiled, stepping out of her remaining undergarments. "You want more for your money than just staring at a naked body, don't you?"

"I want you to seek the source of your feminine mystique. You will entice it, cajole it."

"Got a pretty strange way of putting things, Al. Translation, you want me to whack myself off?"

I nodded silently. "I want you to seek and find your own pleasure."

The woman laughed. "You want me to whack off until I come? That's when you bite me, right?"

"Precisely, my dear. I'll take some blood, but only a little bit, hardly enough to even render you light-headed."

Jasmine shook her head. "You know, Al, I know the customer is always right, but I have an idea that might make this more fun for you. More fun for both of us."

"I am listening."

Jasmine leaned against the dresser, the flesh of her ample, but well rounded backside spreading behind her as she spread her legs ever so slightly. "As you put it, I *am* a professional, and I'll do whatever the client wants and is willing to pay for, within reason, of course. But I want you to know, under almost all circumstances, I don't come with Johns. It's too personal. But this situation is kinda a unique."

"Kinda unique is perhaps a bit of an understatement."

"Hell, I might scream like bloody fuckin' murder, 'I'm coming, I'm coming, I'm coming', but it's all part of the show. This is very, very different."

"I understand. You do not have to do this if it makes you feel uncomfortable."

"No. I want to do it, but—"

"But perhaps you are proposing some sort of trade, some sort of quid pro quo?"

"Romans were a kinky bunch, but yeah."

"Surely, Jasmine, I hope you will find me not an unreasonable person."

She shook her head. "You're pretty old, right, Al?"

"Yes. Quite old, really."

"Know a lot of tricks?"

"If you mean sexually, I suppose that might stand to reason. I have had many liaisons over the centuries. Not as many as you might think, but I have experienced sexual relations with a wide variety of people from a wide variety of cultures."

"With a wide variety of techniques?"

"Of course."

Jasmine smiled broadly and licked her lips in an almost vulgar manner. "You got a deal, Drac. I'll do what you want, but you gotta help."

"I can agree to those terms." Jasmine moved to the bed and sat beside me. My hands began to slowly caress her all over, gently pressing and kneading her breasts, back, stomach, inner thighs. After a long time caressing every inch of her body, my hands finally probed between her legs.

"You are already wet," I said.

"It's because of the way you do me," Jasmine replied.

"Ha!" I snorted. "You probably say that to all your clients."

The woman laughed. "I *do* say that to all my clients, but you're not like any of my other clients. To tell the truth, I can't help but find this whole thing pretty damn exciting."

My fingers worked insistently, but gently, enticing, not forcing. Jasmine threw her head back, her arms wrapped around my shoulders, pulling me close to her. I held my other hand on her stomach, lightly caressing her soft skin, feeling, monitoring, waiting, hoping she was indeed full of life and not an empty vessel masquerading at being alive.

"Stick your fingers in me," Jasmine said, pushing my hand away from her clitoris.

I probed and caressed the sensitive skin, searching, knowing the very special spot I would find. My eyes closed, my fingers probed, and there it was. Her stomach tightened, then contracted violently, her legs closing tightly around my hand. A loud, guttural shriek passed her lips.

I turned and reached for her, firmly gripping her shoulders as she twitched violently. Fangs plunged into her throat, breaking flesh. Hot blood shot into my mouth. The room disappeared, replaced by a blinding flash, my entire being pierced by a wall of glass shards glowing like molten gold.

Then, blackness. Jasmine quaked beneath me. Another wave of glowing arrows pierced my being, slightly smaller than the first. Then, blackness again. Another golden explosion, then blackness, again and again, until the sensation receded into reality.

We found ourselves wrapped tightly in each other's arms. After a bit, we parted and smiled at each other, both slightly embarrassed.

"Wow!" Jasmine said, still breathing hard.

"Ahh," I replied, smiling, "you probably say that to all your clients."

Jasmine slapped me playfully on the arm. "I do, but this is different. Christ, I should be paying you."

She rose abruptly, almost forgetting herself, then remembered and steadied against a rush of dizziness that never came. Jasmine picked up her dress and pulled it over her head. "You really didn't take much blood."

I watched her as she dressed, savoring the sway of her breasts as she tucked them back in their halter. "My sweet," I said wistfully, "you have provided something much greater than mere blood."

****

A certain irony struck me about this encounter with Jasmine. Had business not been so good, she would have been an unattainable extravagance. Yet the reason for the increased business was the same as that which had caused me to seek her out. Regardless, after that first session, I sincerely hoped future encounters would be affordable, within the earnings of a hard-working cab driver. She did indeed satisfy my hunger. Also, I found her most likeable.

However, as April progressed and Mother Nature loosened her fist, the days warmed, buds formed on the trees, and the fear seemed to wear off somewhat as the lack of further developments kept the story out of the newspapers. No killings followed, no clues materialized and the coming of spring reduced the student populace to absolute giddiness. A high temperature of a mere forty degrees and students sashayed around town in shorts! Mostly the Scandinavians, of course, with their flowing Nordic blonde hair and long sinewy legs, but soon everyone followed their example.

Then came that one-week vacation from classes known as spring break, and Madison was a ghost town, leaving me tormented by Tacitus, which I was again attempting to read, feeling in a mood for self-flagellation. Thankfully, a call at Buck's Madison Square Garden spared me the tedium.

And thankfully, the gentleman was actually watching from inside the bar and promptly emerged after I had pulled up, for once disproving the image of this particular establishment as represented by Dexter, who frequently would refer to the place as "Buck's Madison Square No-Load."

It was a good call as well, going all the way to the far north side of town. This call could be a cornerstone of my shift, a good run on the meter, with a good tip, except I found myself wordless, my mind rendered into a stupor by that infernally dull Tacitus.

Unfortunately, my passenger filled in the blanks left by my silence, babbling drunkenly the entire trip. The thought entered my mind to bite him, or at least take momentary control of his consciousness, just to get him to hold his peace, but alas, the man sat in the backseat, well out of my reach.

To compound matters, he wanted to pay with a check. "I am sorry, sir," I was forced to say. "We do not accept checks."

"What do you mean, you don't take checks?"

"Just what I said, sir. We do not accept checks. If the check is returned for insufficient funds, I am held personally responsible."

"There is nothing wrong with my check."

"Perhaps there is not, but I have no way of knowing that."

"Hey, I know your owner. We play golf together. If he were here, he'd tell you there's nothing wrong with my check."

Dale's words during orientation echoed through my skull. "We are a cooperative," I replied, more sharply than I would have expected, surprised to be defending the serfs for once. "We are all owners. We are owned by no one but ourselves."

"Yeah, that's what you think." The man slapped the top of the front seat loudly. "You must be pretty new if you don't know my friend. We go back a long way. Wake up and smell the coffee. My friend, he's the one who really owns you guys. You might not know him now, but you'll get to meet him someday—when you fuck up and he tells you to hit the bricks."

It seemed obvious that Kern would say this guy was using the oldest line in the book. Much to my surprise, I found myself getting angry that he was attacking our cooperative. *My* cooperative!

After a moment's consideration, I replied, "Right on the outside of the cab it says, 'worker owned and operated.' We are a cooperative, all owning an equal part, as per very specific guidelines from state law. Sir, it seems apparent that you are living in a fantasy world."

"Jesus fucking Christ, what planet are *you* living on?"

"Obviously, not the same as you are, sir."

The man said not another word, loudly tearing free a check, tossing it over the front seat and exiting the cab. I considered chasing him, but after studying the check, it seemed best to just leave it be. He had paid the whole fare, plus a two-dollar tip. The check was numbered in the 6000s, and this neighborhood was fairly affluent. If the check did in fact bounce, I would hunt this man down and collect my pound of flesh.

I left the man to his folly, drove back uptown and found a free cab stand where I languished with only Tacitus for company. Out of boredom, I closed the book and turned on the radio. The FM band offered only infernal rock 'n' roll or that pathetic country music. Desperate, I switched to the AM band, hoping to find some classical music or maybe some jazz. Instead, my ears were the recipients of a nearly overwhelming aural assault:

"Molly steps back in." The high-pitched voice was a bit haggard, a bit tense, but chipper. "Two strikes. Two outs. Here's the pitch. To left and deep! Heeeeey! Get up! GET UP! GET OUTTA HERE! GONE! A grand salami! Molly's done it! He's hit a grand salami! The Brewers win! THE BREWERS WIN!"

Silence. Had the poor man suffered an aneurysm and suddenly found himself lying face down, his skull full of blood, death taking him very quickly?

No, the voice returned, but—motherless spawn of Satan, what in the name of the blistering winds of Hades was that? Curious, I continued to listen.

It was a baseball game. All that commotion over a bunch of illiterate grown men chasing a little ball while thousands of beer-swilling members of what Mencken called "the booboisie" watched in rapture—all of these people, players and spectators alike, too daft to comprehend a *real* game, like cricket.

Still, the passion was admirable. Apparently, the Brewers of Milwaukee, playing at their home arena, were trailing by three scores when a fellow named Paul Molitor attempted to hit. The announcer had called him Molly—Americans and their nicknames. Molly, with one fierce strike, allowed his team to overcome their deficit and replace defeat with victory.

I found myself amazed by the seriousness with which these mortals placed upon these games. There might be murder, mayhem or high property taxes, but these people seemed more interested in discussing the latest exploits of their Brewers, Badgers or Packers. Extraordinary.

Further proof of this American preoccupation with sporting events came at shift's end when I found Kern and another night driver, Henry, discussing the baseball contest as they completed their paperwork. Supremely overweight, with a shaggy beard and wild, greasy hair restrained by a soiled baseball cap, Henry was about as jocular as a tall glass of vinegar, but apparently he truly loved his sports; this evening's baseball match was the only topic of conversation where I had ever witnessed any joy or animation on Henry's part.

"Man, oh, man," Henry squealed, "what a game! What a game!"

"That was an exciting conclusion to that contest," I interjected, settling down before an adding machine at the table next to theirs. They turned and stared. When in Rome, I suppose.

"I didn't know you were a baseball fan, Count," Kern said.

"Figured you more for soccer," Henry added, then turned back to Kern. "Europeans dig soccer because they're so used to long, protracted land wars. That's why Americans can't get into it."

"Actually," I countered, "it was an accident that I managed to hear the conclusion of the contest. I was searching for something palatable to listen to when I heard the game-winning stroke."

"A great call," Henry said. "I love it when Uecker calls a home run. 'Get up! Get up! Get outta here! Goooooooooooooooooone!'"

"I love the tips I get when outta-towners hear Bob, and I tell 'em it's Bob Uecker, and he belongs to us." Kern laughed loudly. "They're used to the buffoon on the Miller Lite commercials, but they don't know he's a Milwaukee boy, born and bred."

"I must say, I found him quite evocative," I replied. "Baseball is not a game of which I have ever paid much consideration, but certainly the man's passion for the event was quite compelling."

"Ever been to a baseball game?" Kern asked.

"It has never been high on my list of priorities."

Kern slapped himself loudly on an ample thigh. "Well, it's high time you shifted your priorities. A group of us are going to the Muskies game Monday. Wanna come with?"

"Muskies?" What on Earth was a Muskie? Was that not a senator from the state of Maine?

Henry answered my apparent consternation. "That's the Madison Muskies. The A's single A club."

"I am afraid I still do not understand." Motherless spawn of Satan. When will the Americans ever learn to speak English?

Kern shoved the adding machine aside, tucked his waybill into the envelope and sealed it with the attached string. "The Brewers play in the major leagues. That's the highest level of baseball in the country."

"Whole fucking world!" Henry interjected.

"The Japanese might disagree," Kern countered, "but anyway, there's twenty-six major league teams. Each major league team has several minor league teams where they develop their younger players. The highest level in the minor leagues is triple A. All the major league franchises have one of those teams, plus two double A teams, two single A teams and then one instructional league team where the youngest players start out."

"Single A is a very low level?" I asked.

"You got it, Count," Henry replied.

"These Muskies must not be a very good team."

"Well, it's not major-league quality," Kern said, "but it's right here in Madison, it's really cheap and it's lots of fun."

"And beer's only a buck a can," Henry said, licking his lips.

"Yeah, so how 'bout coming with?" Kern asked. "We're meeting at the Crystal Corner about six thirty. Game time's seven thirty. It'll be fun."

Count Farkas going to a baseball game! The notion seemed laughable, yet how else might I spend my night free from the shackles of indentured servitude? Tacitus was growing increasingly tedious. Also, I had been discovering a burgeoning erosion of my resistance to developing friendships with my fellow drivers. Though they had seemed so young, uncultured and uncivilized, I discovered that many were of a decent sort. Hardworking, honest, sometimes even witty and sharp of intellect. Much to my surprise, not only had the cooperative's appeal become apparent, but I had begun to find that I liked many of these people. Besides, letting them get to know me and see me as a normal person had to be a help in my efforts toward camouflage.

The game would be played in at least partial sunlight. Yet, even though the mid-April sun would not quite be settled beyond the horizon by six-thirty or seven-thirty, the rays would be weak enough to cause a bare minimum of discomfort.

"I will join you fellows at your baseball contest," I said finally, still wondering what, in the name of the hundred false promises of heaven, was a Muskie?

Kern smiled. Henry laughed heartily, holding his jiggling belly. "You sure got a funny way of putting things, Count," Kern said.

I merely nodded. "Who else will be attending this contest?"

"Well," Henry answered, "you, me, Kern—"

"And Nicole," Kern said, grinning broadly. "You know Nicole, right?"

The smile dropped from my face. "Yes, I do."

Chapter 12

TAKE ME OUT TO THE BALLGAME

You certainly may scoff at the notion of Count Farkas attending a baseball contest, but much to my surprise, I found it an intriguing experience. However, the issue of Nicole's presence presented quite the awkward scenario.

Over the past month, we had exchanged a rare glance and a few conversational pleasantries, but our mutual discomfort was quite apparent. Doubtless, my presence at the baseball game would make her uneasy.

Canceling this engagement might seem suspicious. I did want to attend the contest. And yes, I did want to see Nicole, talk to her, and bathe in her scent.

Providence. Shortly after the invitation, misgivings piling upon misgivings, I spotted Nicole at the petrol pump. My naturally surreptitious approach startled her. She turned toward me with a start.

"Please," I said, holding a hand up, "beg my pardon."

"Christ," she said in a whisper, "it's almost like you materialized out of the darkness."

Silence was my answer. "I hope your shift was profitable."

Nicole leaned against the hood of her cab. "Yeah. It was. What do you want?"

I nodded at her directness. "Of course, after nary a word the past month, it would seem odd for me to approach you merely to make small-talk."

"Damn right." She crossed her arms in front of her chest. The pump clicked off loudly. Nicole reached for the nozzle to top off her gas tank.

"It is nothing, really." Both hands held up now, palms facing her, no steps taken closer. "Kern has invited me to attend that baseball contest next week—"

Loud laughter interrupted my explanation. "Is that what this is about?" Her arms dropped to her sides as she continued to laugh. "Hell, I thought this was about something serious."

"Considering the events of a month ago, it seemed my presence might disturb you. If so, please let me know, and I will tell Kern I have to decline his kind invitation."

Nicole laughed again. "Somehow, I'm having a hard time picturing you at a baseball game."

"As do I."

Nicole laughed so hard she was nearly doubled over. "This isn't happening." She covered her face with her hands until her laughter subsided, then she stared at me with a look that almost stripped me naked. "This whole thing is unbelievable. You kill somebody right in front of me, then a month later you ask if it would bother me if you went to a baseball game with me, Kern and Henry."

"I never had any intention of exposing you to any of that."

"No you didn't," she replied, her voice forgiving. "No, it's really very kind of you to ask, very considerate. Christ, that's a lot more consideration than I got from my last five boyfriends. Combined! Al, you're a real gentleman. A gentleman who happens to drink human blood and kill people every once in awhile."

"I only kill when all other options have been exhausted." My voice was barely audible.

Nicole nodded. "Can't say I blame you much for whacking Frank. After what he did to that kid, I probably would've done the same. Just a few questions."

"You may proceed."

"What'd you do with Frank's body?"

"He is buried in a deep grave, ten miles outside of town. No one will ever find him."

"Of course. Why'd you leave the boy's body where it could be found?"

"Regardless of how horrible his fate, the boy's family deserved to know their boy was dead. The futile hope held by these parents of missing children sickens me. If their child is dead, they deserve to know."

She nodded. "Fair enough. Of course, you realize that whoever killed that woman a week after they found the boy probably did it because he figured the cops would pin it on whoever killed the boy."

My shoulders shrugged as I turned away from the accusation. My voice sounded too dry when I replied, "Regrettable, but there is only so much hand-wringing I can do and still manage to survive in this world."

"Nice philosophy." Her voice sounded accusing, then her tone shifted. "Those two women, *you* didn't kill them, did you?"

"No."

"You don't kill when you feed."

I laughed lightly. "That is Hollywood. No, I do not kill when I feed because it is not necessary. What amounts to little more than a trickle satisfies me. And my bite does not produce vampirism. That is also Hollywood."

Our mutual silence hung awkwardly in the air. "Okay," she said finally, clapping her hands together, hanging the nozzle and replacing the gas cap. "It's not great baseball, but it's right here in our town. Look forward to seeing you."

Astonishment. "I have only just heard my first baseball game tonight. I know nothing of this game's nuances."

"That's okay." She smiled and slapped my shoulder. "I'll be glad to tell you all about it."

****

Monday came, and, with excitement, I braved the last rays of sun to meet Nicole and the others at the Crystal Corner Bar, on Madison's near east side. Upon plunging into dark depths of the saloon, I was grateful to remove my sunglasses, fighting against the overstimulating aural assault of the jukebox punctuated by the crack of pool balls, the click-clatter of pinball machines, the thwack of darts striking their targets, the numerous conversations blending into one, the countless heartbeats. Even though the bar was not crowded, the scent of sweat, skin, perfume and all those distilled and fermented beverages made my nose crinkle.

Yet the gentle fluorescent light proved a comfort, making all in the saloon, warmed by the unnatural glow of ionized inert gases, appear the pallor of chalk—excellent camouflage.

The tall, slender fellow with the cowboy hat smiled at me from behind the long, oval bar, his well-muscled arms crossed in front of his chest as he surveyed the room, seeming happy that all was orderly.

Kern stood out from the back of the bar, his height and long, thinning hair making him quite distinctive. My trainer quickly spied me and waved vigorously. Nicole and Henry flanked him, both swathed in black leather. Underneath her jacket, Nicole wore a thick sweater, a long scarf hanging loosely around her neck.

"A couple four-way splits at the air, a couple five-bangers at the Badger Bus," Kern said as I approached. Apparently, they were, talking shop. Have they nothing else to discuss? "Christ, what a bounty," he said. "Yeah, like I was saying, I remember one time getting a six-way out of the Badger."

"A six-way?" Nicole wondered. "Isn't that illegal? The most we can take is five, or four, if the cab's got front bucket seats, right?"

"Capitol Cab'll load up seven or eight," Henry said.

"I didn't mean to take that many." Kern downed the rest of his bottle of beer, the bright red and blue label identifying the brand as Point. "They were swarming at me, like *Night of the Living Dead.* Anyway, I dropped off one, then another, then looked in the back, saw four people crammed back there and said, 'Jesus, where did you come from?'"

The trio laughed, then turned and saw me standing at their side. "Hey, Count," Kern said. "Glad to see you could make it."

Nicole smiled warmly and said hello. Henry grunted as he took a long sip of his cocktail. I turned and saw the bartender with the cowboy hat staring at us, both hands pressed against the black plastic railing circling the entire inside edge of the bar. The stance made his biceps flex into hard, round clumps of muscle.

"Hey, Todd," Kern said, turning to the bartender, "this is the Count."

"A Bloody Mary for you tonight, Count?" Todd smiled graciously.

"Thank you, no," I replied, laughing lightly, "but Kern, I do believe I owe you a drink, do I not?"

"That's right, that four-way I set you up with." Kern lifted the empty bottle to his lips and sucked at the remaining foam residue at the bottom. "Can't say no to a free beer. Thanks, Count. Another Point, Todd."

Todd reached into the cooler behind him, grabbed a bottle of Point by the neck, and in one fluid motion, flipped the bottle, caught it at the bottom, drew a bottle opener from his belt and popped the cap. He handed the beer to Kern and quickly replaced the opener as a movement caught his attention. In what seemed a continuation of the previous motion, the bartender pulled a cigarette lighter from the pocket of his black denim trousers, loudly flipped open the cover, struck the flint and lit the cigarette that Henry had just drawn from a pack that sat on the bar.

"That's one-fifty, Count," Todd said.

"Keep the change," I said, handing him three dollars. Such panache deserves ample reward.

"Does anyone else desire refreshment?" Todd asked.

Nicole looked down at her half-full glass of beer and shook her head. Henry downed what remained of his drink, ice clinking against his teeth. He handed the wide-mouthed, cut-glass tumbler to the bartender. "Stoli and cranberry," he said.

"A man of impeccable taste." Todd grabbed the glass and took his leave to pour a fresh drink.

"Yeah, Count," Kern said, "we were just talking about the goodies from the Cab Gods out there last night."

"Ah, the end of Spring Break," I replied. "All those college students returning from their vacations, tanned and refreshed."

"It was so nice and quiet while they were gone," Nicole said.

"But their absence was a detriment to business," I replied. "I do not know how I managed to survive the boredom last week. The tedium was so excruciating that even the great joy of the printed word could not save me."

"You need something more interesting to read, something you can sink your teeth into," Nicole replied, taking a small sip of her beer. "Like Suetonius, maybe."

"I concur completely," I replied blandly, ignoring her clumsy double entendre.

"Too damn busy to read," Henry said, taking a large gulp of the cocktail Todd had just handed him. "Hell, whoever killed those women, we oughta give the fucker a goddamned medal."

"Especially with the students back," Kern said. "Anybody can make money with it that busy, even the Count here."

"Thanks to the expert training I received," I said.

"And don't you forget it," Kern said, taking a long drink from his beer. In a few gulps, the bottle was nearly empty.

"You want another beer, do you not?" I said.

"Beggar!" Nicole mocked.

"The successful cab driver has no shame," Kern replied. "You can call this job, 'anything for a dollar.' The time I picked up this little old lady at Sentry Hilldale and she says, 'Would you like to earn an extra dollar?' I said, 'Sure. What do I have to do?'"

"What *did* you have to do?" Henry asked.

"And was it as good for you as it was for her?" Nicole added.

Kern laughed heartily, shaking his head and waving the bottle of beer at Todd to get his attention. I put a couple dollars on the bar and shoved them toward Kern.

"What the hell," Kern said. "Got about another fifteen minutes before we head to the ballpark. So, Count, how'd you happen to hear Uke's home run call? You must've been pretty bored to cruise the AM dial."

"Yes. And I was so bored driving Friday and Saturday night that I listened to the games played on those nights as well. That Uecker *is* a very funny fellow. During one game, he and the other announcer had a rather earnest conversation about the most ideal ways to toast bread."

Henry nodded. "I remember one time hearing Bob talk about winning a cow-milking contest when he played in the minor leagues. He said the cow wouldn't leave him alone after the contest, that she followed him around for days and that she was a pretty good date."

Nicole laughed, then coughed loudly, nearly spitting out the sip of beer she had just taken. She calmed and took another sip. "Kern," she asked, "do I have time for another beer?"

"Sure," he replied. "I haven't heard my songs on the jukebox yet."

Apparently, Todd overheard. "Kern, if you play 'Mountain Jam' again, I'm rejecting it. I'll give you a drink chip, but I don't wanna hear that song anymore tonight."

"Better give me my chip now," Kern replied.

Todd shot Kern a mildly angry look and tossed a red disk onto the bar. When it stopped bouncing, I picked it up and studied it. The chip bore the name of the bar on one side and on the other said, "good for one free large drink."

"That's pretty underhanded," Nicole said in a hushed whisper. "You didn't have time to listen to that song before the game anyway."

"A card laid is a card played," Kern said, shoving the chip into his pocket. "You want I should give back a free drink chip?"

"You're such a mercenary bastard," Henry said, emptying his drink and putting it down on the bar where it was easily visible to Todd. The bartender promptly picked up the glass and refilled it.

"Hey, that's what makes me such a good cab driver."

It was not until after seven when the three cab drivers managed to finish their drinks at the same time and we were able to commence our journey to the ballpark. But who would drive? Henry volunteered, but was quickly vetoed.

"You're way too fucked up to drive," Kern protested.

"I will gladly drive," I said. "We can all fit in my Toyota. The Muskies play at Warner Park, right? At Sherman and Northport?"

"Right, Count," Kern said, "and thanks. Now, who's willing to volunteer to explain the action to our good friend here who barely knows baseball from cricket?"

"I'll do it," Nicole said enthusiastically. "You can sit next to me and ask me any questions you want. Before the game's over, you'll know everything there is to know about baseball." She patted me gently on the shoulder, her hand lingering for just a moment.

Well, at least I was going to find out what a Muskie was.

****

It is rather queer how Americans swear allegiance to these professional sporting franchises, more queer still how so many of the teams have heroic names: The New York Yankees, commemorating that great mercantile tradition that helped build their country; the Dallas Cowboys, commemorating the so-called rugged individualism of the Wild West; and just a general sense of warlike fierceness embodied by Giants, Warriors, Falcons, Hawks and Raiders. However, it does seem these Americans, in their occasional confusion, seem to also honor malapropisms, what with the Los Angeles Lakers and the Utah Jazz.

This Madison baseball team must not have been very good, having taken their name from a fish. How silly of me not to have realized that this was the diminutive term for the muskellunge, that large, muscular, rather truculent member of the pike family, a great prize for sport anglers, sometimes known to attack ducks and other waterfowl with their sharp teeth, and even, on occasion, to bite humans.

Signs in the parking lot at Warner Park, at the ticket booth and all around the entrance read, "Go Fish." At the main gate, someone wearing a costume of bright green nylon with glowing white teeth, crimson eyes and a spiny cobalt dorsal fin greeted fans, shaking hands and accepting warm pats on the back. The giant muskie posed for photographs with children who squealed with delight, and, in general, was on the receiving end of a great deal of genuinely warm adoration.

It was oddly gratifying to discover that these good Christians were indeed pagans. They worshiped fish! And why not? Lakes cover this glacier-scoured state of Wisconsin. Fish, the bounty of these sparkling bodies of water, provides sustenance for these good Christians, who, in tribute, make a Friday night tradition of attending fish-eating orgies and make their pilgrimage to Warner Park to pay homage to their Madison Muskies.

Ritual seemed a large aspect of what people do at the ballpark—ballpark being an apt term. Wembley Stadium is indeed a stadium, whereas this is a park, with a short chain-link fence ringing the field, except for the outfield, which was circumscribed by a ten-foot wall of plywood bearing various advertisements for assorted goods and services, ranging from telephones to tobacco, automobiles to automatic garage-door openers. Where Wembley had actual seats, this park merely offered long steel benches. However, Warner Park more than compensated for its lack of majesty with the way it allowed one to commune with nature; the grass was neatly groomed and quite lovely, and from the elevated vantage point of the bleachers there was a nice view of a modest forest, beyond which twinkled Lake Mendota, the last rays of sun sparkling off the lake's surface.

Shortly after we had selected our seats, a chipper voice boomed from the public address system, ordering us to stand for the national anthem. Little surprise that sports and patriotism should go hand in hand; few sports are not analogs of war, and a powerful nation must always have a populace ready, willing and able to go to war, regardless of the relative stupidity of said war.

Following everyone's example, I stood as the announcer screeched the song, joined by the several hundred fans, each in their own key. A loud cheer followed the song's completion, surpassed only by the great expression of joy in our section when a barrel-chested young man appeared, hefting a large plastic cooler.

"Beer man!" Kern shouted. The vendor nodded in acknowledgment of Kern's hail and quickly climbed to where we sat.

"I'll have one," Nicole said.

"Me too," said Henry.

Kern tapped me on the shoulder, pointing at the beer vendor. I shook my head. "Our designated driver," he said, smiling and patting me gently on the back. Nicole handed me a dollar, which I passed to Kern, who passed it to Henry along with a dollar of his own. The beer man removed three cans of beer from the cooler, opened them and poured the contents into plastic cups. My fellow drivers had their ballpark beers, presumably satisfying yet another ballpark ritual.

"Hey, there's Leon," Henry said, pointing a few rows down toward a swarthy fellow with long, unkempt black hair, a thick mustache and a rather sharply hooked nose. He wore a Muskies cap, which bore the image of a muskellunge wearing a baseball cap and holding a baseball bat with one of its fins.

"Who, may I ask, is Leon?" I inquired.

"He's sort of an unofficial cheerleader for the Muskies," Nicole replied. "He's pretty well known. He works for the state as a computer programmer, but about ten years ago, he was vice president of the University of Wisconsin Student Association."

"He looks a bit old to have been a student, even ten years ago," I commented. Indeed, the fellow looked over forty years of age.

"I think he used to take just one class," Nicole answered, "or maybe he was a grad student. I'm not sure. Anyway, he and this guy, Jim Mallon, they were tired of the same-old-same-old stupid shit with student govern-ment, so they formed their own party—the Pail and Shovel Party—and got voted into office. They ran the student association for two years."

I momentarily played the devil's advocate. "Is there not an old adage that people get the kind of government they deserve?"

Nicole did not respond, merely continuing her historical digest. "Leon used to wear a clown suit to senate meetings." She laughed loudly. "They did some pretty wacko stuff. Like covering Bascom Hill with pink fla-mingos. They commissioned a papier mache bust of Lady Liberty right on the ice on Lake Mendota."

Action on the field drew my attention to where another ritual seemed to be taking place—the ceremonial throwing out of the first pitch. This night's honoree was a corpulent commercial developer, more than likely responsible for helping create Madison's burgeoning state of urban sprawl.

After the fellow shook hands with anyone within arm's reach, the umpire handed him the ball. His throw bounced ten feet in front of the plate and barely managed to roll to the catcher. The fans applauded wildly.

The Muskie players took their positions throughout the field, and the crowd hushed. The umpire pointed at the opposing batter, then yelled from deep within his gut, "Play ball!"

Leon rose from his seat, a grin suddenly appearing, giving him an almost cartoon-like animation. "Let's Go Fish! Let's Go Fish!" he shouted, clapping his hands together, not in the usual horizontal manner, but vertically, with his arms fully extended.

Immediately, the whole crowd was chanting, "Let's Go Fish. Let's Go Fish," and clapping in that queer manner.

"What in the name of heaven are they doing?" I asked Nicole, pointing at the crowd. Henry and Kern were doing it too.

"It's the fish clap," she replied.

"Fish clap?" There must be too much mercury in the fish these people consume.

"Yeah, the fish clap." Nicole started doing it too. "Let's Go Fish!"

I watched her do the fish clap, then it dawned on me: those clapping hands were intended to emulate the snapping maw of a vicious muskie.

If baseball is considered America's pastime, America is indeed a strange place.

Scrutinizing the fans, I missed the first pitch, merely hearing the loud "pat" as the ball struck the catcher's glove and the deep, guttural, "Hu-huh!" of the umpire. The fans cheered louder.

"What happened?"

"Strike one," Nicole said. My expression must have betrayed confusion. "Lesson one, right now. The pitcher throws the ball, and the batter tries to hit it. A pitched ball may be a ball or a strike, depending on whether or not the pitcher throws it in the strike zone, which is in line with home plate, above the knees and below the shoulders. If the batter doesn't swing at three pitches thrown in the strike zone, he's out, what's called a 'strike-out'. If the pitcher throws four pitches out of the strike zone, the batter is awarded first base. That's a 'walk' or a 'base on balls.'"

I nodded and turned back toward the action—or the inaction; the pitcher had not yet thrown another pitch. He bent over and stared toward the batter, shaking his head, shaking his head, shaking his head, before nodding, straightening and throwing. "Pop." "Hu-huh!"

"Strike two?" I asked.

"Very good, Al," Nicole said.

"See," Kern chimed in, "I said he was a fast learner."

"The object of the contest is to actually hit the ball, is it not?"

"Yeah," Nicole answered. "Put it in play, meaning between the two lines that run all the way from home plate to the outfield. If the batter swings at a pitch, strike or ball, and misses, it's a strike. If he hits the ball, but not within the white lines, it's a foul ball, which counts as a strike."

The pitcher threw, and the batter swung, barely tipping the ball, sending it flying against the fence behind him. "Like that?" I said.

"And watch out for flying baseballs," Henry added. "We're pretty close to the action. A line drive might come screaming in here, so heads up."

The pitcher leaned forward. Shook his head once, then again.

"Why does the pitcher keep shaking his head like that?"

"Pitchers are arms with no brains," Nicole said. "The catcher is signaling to the pitcher what kind of pitch to throw. If the pitcher shakes his head, he doesn't like the call. When he nods his head, that means he's in agreement with the catcher, but I'll tell you, most of the time, it's the catcher who decides what to throw and where to throw it."

The pitcher finally nodded.

"See how the catcher is sitting toward the outside of the plate?" Nicole said. "He's called for a pitch away from the hitter as opposed to inside."

"Heater," Kern said.

"Naw," Henry countered. "Bender."

The batter swung and missed. A loud roar rose from the crowd.

"HEEEEEEE struck him out!" Henry shouted in such a manner as to tear away the first two layers of skin from the inside of his throat.

Head bowed, the batter shuffled away from the plate, the crowd chanting, "Left, right, left, right, left, right," until he reached his team's shelter. Then, "Step, step, step," and finally, "Siddown, ya bum!"

More rituals. "May I presume they do this every time an opposing batter strikes out?"

"Sure," Nicole said, "it's one of the most fun things about going to a Muskies game. Madison is known throughout the Midwest League for this."

Leon sat after leading the cheer, punching left, right, left, right fists in the air. The fans sitting directly adjacent all took turns shaking his hand, all just wanting to touch him as if he were Jesus Christ, or, rather, Jesus Christ wearing a propeller beanie.

I turned to Henry and Kern. "What are heaters and benders?"

"Different types of pitches," Kern said. Henry was too busy drinking his beer to reply.

Nicole touched me lightly on the shoulder as the next batter stepped into the batter's box. "A heater is a fastball. A bender is a type of a breaking ball—a slider. A hook is a curve. There's also knuckleballs, split-finger fastballs, sinkers and palm balls."

"Don't forget spit balls," Henry said, stifling a burp under his breath.

"They're illegal," Kern said.

"Pitchers spit on the baseball?" I asked, wondering where the vulgarity of these Americans ended.

"They're not supposed to," Nicole said, "but some guys not long ago made a living at it."

"Gaylord Perry," Kern added.

"But what possible effect might spitting on a baseball have?"

"A lot," Nicole said. "Maybe it's spit, maybe it's Vaseline, maybe it's God knows what. You get something embedded in the seams of the ball and it affects the air resistance. The ball'll do funny things, making it much harder to hit."

"Ah ha," I said, feeling a sudden burst of realization. "Friction is constantly at work here. Pitchers can achieve certain effects depending on how the ball spins. Correct?"

"Or depending on how it doesn't spin," Kern added. "A knuckleball ain't supposed to spin. That's what makes it break one way, then the other."

"Surface, you idiot," Henry snorted. "Don't you know dick about physics? If a knuckleball doesn't spin at all, it won't break. It'll just be a sitting duck. Ideally, a knuckleball will spin exactly one rotation between the pitcher's mound and the plate. Because the rotation's so slow, it'll break one way, *then* break back the other way."

A loud crack rang through the night, and the crowd groaned loudly. The batter had just gotten a hit and was now standing on first base. The pitcher stood straight this time, shook his head, glanced toward first base, glanced back toward the plate, shook his head again, then turned and threw to first base.

"He's trying to hold the runner," Nicole said, "to keep him from stealing second." She anticipated my next question. "Any time someone gets on base, they can attempt to reach the next base without the aid of a batted ball. The runner'll take off when the pitcher throws to the plate. If he makes it to the next base before getting tagged by whoever takes the catcher's throw, he's safe. That's what it means to steal a base."

Shake, glance, throw. Shake, glance, throw. A few minutes passed, and all that had happened was that the pitcher had still not agreed with the catcher on a pitch and had thrown to first base several times.

"Amazing that you Americans think soccer so boring." I did not intend to be overly provocative, but this game of throw-and-catch grew quickly tedious. At least in soccer, the ball always moves. Here, these ruffians seemed to be spending most of their time scratching their privates. "There seems to be nothing happening."

"And there never seems to be anything happening in a Jane Austen novel," Nicole said, "unless you read between the lines."

"I believe I have just been victimized by a vicious punster," I said, contemplating the white lines that formed the border of the playing area. "As you Americans say, I will bite. Tell me what it is I am missing. I am all ears."

"There's a lot of options here," Nicole began. "The guy on first is fast. He's very fast. With his speed, he's a big threat to steal or take an extra base on a hit. So, the pitcher tries to keep him close by throwing to first repeatedly."

Nicole explained how a speedy base runner provides greater options for the batting team in its effort to move him closer to the eventual goal. She spoke of "bunts" and "steals" and something called "the hit-and-run." Somehow, it sounded dangerous, as well as a problem for the opposing team.

"Now, the defense is fully aware of all of this," Nicole continued. "They might call for a pitch-out. That's when the pitcher throws intentionally out of the strike zone where the batter can't hit it. The catcher can get to it and make a good, strong throw to second base, hopefully if the runner is running."

"Ah," I said, fighting a losing battle against confusion. "But the offense is aware of this preoccupation and may not let the runner run for fear of an oncoming pitch-out. Correct?"

"Yeah," Nicole replied, "but they also know the defense knows that the offense is well aware of the defense's awareness."

"I am certain that goes without saying."

"Sometimes, what can happen," Kern added, "is that a pitch-out gets called, but the runner isn't going. So, figuring they're not going to call two pitch-outs in a row, they'll send the runner on the very next pitch."

"But the defense is thinking this way as well," I offered, "so they order another pitch-out."

"But," Nicole added, "the offense might be one step ahead of the defense and not give the runner the green light, and suddenly the batter is ahead in the count two balls and no strikes."

"Then it gets real complicated," Kern said.

"You guys are making me fucking dizzy," Henry snorted. "Beer man!"

The pitcher finally threw toward the plate, but there was no pitch-out.

Apparently the hit-and-run had been summoned forth, but it proved disastrous as the batter hit a line drive right at the second baseman who threw back to first base to record an out against the runner. After a lengthy explanation, Nicole said this was a double play.

Perhaps it might be time to reread the works of Miss Austen.

After an uneventful first inning, where more was happening than would appear to the uninitiated, the Muskies drew first blood, scoring on a home run hit high into the darkening Madison sky.

"Must've hurt his hands," Kern said, pulling his leather closer to his body. He gripped the material of my shirt between his thumb and forefinger. "Aren't you cold?"

Unlike my companions who were well bundled or the other fans who wrapped themselves in blankets as the night's cold settled in, I wore merely a button-down shirt under my leather jacket. It had been warm that afternoon, and I had no need to put on heavier clothing. Now, my attire appeared suspicious.

"I am quite comfortable," I replied. "I am well accustomed to the cold."

The Muskies added another couple of runs, but saw their undaunted opponent match their tally and exceed it as the game reached the halfway point, the milestone marked by a team of fit young men and women who, amidst cheers, sprinted onto the infield and smoothed the earth with thick, weighted canvas sheets which they dragged behind them. Once their task was completed, the groomers turned toward the bleachers and bowed before running off the field.

More ritual: Before resuming play, the voice from above announced it was time for something called "the bat race."

"Check this out," Nicole said laughing.

Two portly men stood near the home team's shelter, each holding a bat upright against the grass. When the signal was given, the men ran in tight, rapid circles around the bats they still held.

"Kern, didn't you do this once?" Nicole asked.

"I got hosed," Kern replied. "I played it smart, going around the bat slow enough not to get too dizzy, and there I was, clear-headed, running for the gold, but they made me go back and run one more circle. I made ten circles, I know I did, but they said it was only nine, the fuckers."

"We'll put it on your fucking headstone," Henry said. "'It was ten circles, not nine. I got hosed.'"

One gentleman completed his ten circles, dropped the bat and was ready to run ahead to the goal to win the contest. He took one step, stumbled and fell to the turf. *Carpe diem*! The other man speeded up, dropped the bat and prepared to rush forward as though to grab the Holy Grail. He stumbled, fought hard to steady himself, then wobbled sideways and fell into the shelter. The first man finally rose and trotted gingerly to the finish line to win his prize.

The hundreds of fans laughed loudly. Leon rose and gestured broadly with his arms, beckoning the fans to give this valiant duo a standing ovation. Before the game resumed, the announcer offered a few veiled, but choice, words about safety. "Parents, watch your children. Everyone, use the buddy system. And do not go into the parking lot by yourself after the game."

Only a couple of families had brought their offspring, most likely because the children had to get up for school the next day. The youths had been climbing all over the steel bleachers until the announcement. Parents then pulled their children close.

"Christ," Henry said, rising, "I'm hungry."

"Brat run?" Kern asked.

"Yeah, you guys want anything?"

Nicole reached across me to hand Henry a five-dollar note, her breasts gently brushing against my arm. "Can you get me a brat with sauerkraut and mustard?"

"Ditto for me," Kern added, "but make it two. And I want ketchup also."

Henry took the bills and made a sour face. "Ketchup? Ketchup? What kind of maniac puts ketchup on a brat?"

Kern sneered at his fellow driver. "Bud Selig puts ketchup on his hot dogs. If it's good enough for the owner of the Brewers, it's good enough for me."

Henry snorted loudly and left to run his errand without another word. The next half-inning had expired before he returned with his fleshy bounty and a fresh cup of beer.

Kern took a bite of his bratwurst and smiled broadly. "Nothing like a brat at the ballpark." He shoved the sausage in my face. "Want a bite, Count? It's real good."

I said no thank you, suddenly feeling nauseous. My well-practiced mental discipline had allowed me to filter out the sensory overload of this tightly packed mass of humanity, but suddenly it all came crashing inward. The sickening stench of charred animal flesh clashed violently with the sweet scent of sweat and living skin. And my eardrums seemed on the verge of rupturing from the suddenly intolerable symphony of clapping thunder as the thump, thump, thumping of several hundred hearts, loudly pumping sweet nectar through all those bodies, all beat as one.

I caught Nicole looking at me. "You look flushed," she whispered.

I nodded and excused myself, departing to get some air. Loitering in the spacious area behind the bleachers, between a concession stand and the water closets, I listened to my own labored breathing in an effort to regain my composure.

Soon, my breathing slowed, allowing me to relax, then the thumping echoed inside my skull once again, not the hammering of all those singing hearts, but instead the distinct beating of two hearts from within the men's water closet a mere few feet away.

I stepped inside and stood in front of a urinal, two urinals away from a man who was fortunately too oblivious to notice what I was not doing.

"Hey, Sven," the man said over his shoulder, zipping his trousers and stepping away from the urinal. "You pinch off that loaf yet?"

The man answered with the rapid staccato of violently passed gas. "In a fuckin' minute," he replied.

"I'm leaving," the first man said. "You better hurry up if you want a buddy. You heard the man. Don't go anywhere alone."

The fellow inside the stall laughed loudly between more passed gas. "Whatever. Catch you back out there."

The other man laughed, then departed. More loud passed gas, silence, then the fellow inside the stall groaned loudly. A large plop followed, as if an heavy object had just fallen into the toilet bowl.

Just the two of us. No other heartbeats nearby.

Suddenly, the fellow was looking up from his seat, trousers down at his ankles. Before he knew what was happening, he knew nothing at all, as if he had fallen into a waking dream, not knowing, not even wondering what was making that queer sucking sound.

"Feeling better?" Nicole asked when I had returned to my seat.

"Yes. I just needed some air."

"Well, you look better." She smiled and moved a bit closer to me, her breath hot against my face. She whispered in my ear. "Your cheeks look nice and rosy, and I'll bet the farm it's not from this brisk early spring weather."

I simply nodded, savoring the warmth of her body, finding her ear with my mouth, the soft scent of her long hair washing into my nostrils. "A kind fellow I met in the lavatory," I whispered. "Kind and charitable. With no pain, no fear and no knowledge. And not even a pint short."

Nicole snuggled closer, not saying a single word.

More ritual: By the seventh inning, the visiting team had opened their lead to four scores, but the announcer was undaunted as he enthusiastically announced that it was time for "the seventh inning stretch."

The fans rose in unison and stretched. Leon turned and shouted, "Sing!" as he exhorted the crowd, waving his arms to and fro, just as a drunken conductor might. A recorded voice sang over the loudspeaker, and the crowd happily joined in:

"Take me out to the ball game / Take me out with the crowd / Buy me some peanuts and Crackerjack / I don't care if I never come back / So, it's root, root, root for the Muskies / If they don't win it's a shame / 'Cause it's one, two, three strikes yer out / At the old ball game."

The fans applauded wildly after shouting and punching fists into the air—one, two, three, then remained standing and sang another song, one I knew—"Roll Out The Barrel." Perhaps they sing "Take Me Out to the Ball Game" at every park in the country, but "Roll Out The Barrel" had to be peculiar to Wisconsin. And why not? All these Germans, all that beer and bratwurst. The only thing missing was a polka band, and here they were, nearly everyone paired up, dancing the polka right in the stands.

When the Muskies' last chance arrived in the bottom of the ninth, they had cut the four-run deficit in half and had put runners at every base, but after a strike-out and a short fly ball caught within the infield, they were truly down to their last chance.

The situation seemed bleak, but these good Christian pagans held steadfast to their faith in their Muskies. Taking Leon's example, everyone rose to their feet and chanted in lockstep rhythm, "Let's go fish! Let's go fish!" Hundreds of hands clapped together, emulating the vicious muskie maw, calling forth the spirit of their team's patron totem.

"C'mon," Kern said. "Baby needs a new pair of shoes. Baby needs a new pair of shoes!"

"Little bingo here," Nicole said. "Little bingo."

I turned toward my instructor. "Bingo? What is that?"

She looked at me blankly. Suddenly, a loud crack rang out, followed by a gasp throughout the crowd. My head turned toward the sound, seeing several fans duck as the hard line drive flew at us, directly at Nicole's head.

At the last moment, I reached out and grabbed the ball in mid-flight, the impact sharp and ringing, but the ball's momentum halted, the small spheroid held safely within my tightly closed fingers. I casually handed the ball to Nicole.

"Thanks," she said, a high degree of astonishment in her voice. "Doesn't your hand hurt? That was a real screamer."

I shook my head. Kern and Henry patted me on the back. Leon stared directly at me, his expression shocked, then dissolving into a smile as he flashed a thumbs-up at me.

"Okay, it's three balls and two strikes," Nicole said a few pitches later. She rolled the ball nervously in her hands. "Unless the batter fouls the ball off, the game ends right here. A hit'll score three runs for sure because we've got faster runners on base, and they'll be moving with the pitch."

"Let's go fish! Let's go fish! Let's go fish!"

Crack! A line drive to the left side of the infield. The third baseman leaped, missing the ball by inches. The shortstop lunged, stretched out as far as his limbs could reach, but barely missed the ball. The fellow in the outfield charged forward.

One run. Two runs.

The fellow on first had nearly reached second when the ball was hit. He steamed toward third. The surrogate leader standing behind third base made a wide windmill motion with his arm. The runner spun around the base without hesitation.

The outfielder scooped up the ball and hurled it toward home plate with all his might.

A few strides from home, the runner leaped hands first, arms fully outstretched and slid in the dirt toward the plate.

The throw bounced once. The catcher, standing in front of the plate, clearly in the runner's path, caught the ball cleanly four feet in the air, then thrust his glove down hard onto the runner's back.

The crowd hushed, waited. For a long, pregnant moment, the umpire stared at the tangle of bodies, seeming to wait for the dust to clear.

The umpire crossed his arms in front of his chest, then thrust them sharply apart.

The crowd roared. Henry and Kern jumped up and down. Leon faced the crowd, arms raised in the air, fists pumping. Nicole wrapped her arms around my neck, jumping up and down.

It took a moment to realize that this was victory. Victory! Let the British keep their cricket! Their game has not the passion or drama of this moment.

****

The ride back to the Crystal Corner was quiet; my fellow cabbies were happy, but emotionally drained.

"Coming in?" Kern asked when we arrived at the bar.

"No," I replied, having had more than enough humanity for one night. "I think I shall just go home and quietly savor this stunning victory."

"Well, thanks for driving, Count," Henry said.

Kern and Henry departed, but Nicole lingered. "You enjoyed yourself, Al?"

"Yes, I did. Surprisingly so. Thanks for describing what was happening. I do not think the contest would have made sense without your illuminating narrative."

She laughed lightly. "You sure do have a funny way of phrasing things." Nicole paused a moment, looking down at her hands which still held the baseball as if it were a fine jewel. "You sure your hand's okay?"

I held out my hand for her inspection. No tell-tale signs betrayed the collision. "Immortality," I said, "means near-instant tissue regeneration.

Had the ball struck your hand, or Kern's, or even Henry's ample paw, or any mortal at the ballpark, a visit to the hospital would have been necessary to repair crushed bones and smashed blood vessels."

Nicole gazed at me thoughtfully. "You are *completely* invulnerable?"

"No." I shook my head. "The heart. That is one area where Hollywood is not dealing in complete fantasy. A sharpened wooden stake, though crude, would, as you Americans say, do the job, as would a bullet or a knife."

"The heart." She bit her lip. "A vulnerable heart. Can a vampire's heart be broken?"

"Yes."

After a short, awkward silence, she took my hand, surreptitiously stroking it with a finger. "You know, this was fun. I mean, considering all that happened, it was nice to just have a nice, normal time. And—" She paused demurely. "And, if we *could* have nice, normal times, well, I'd like to see you again. What do you think?"

What do you think?

Are there four more imposing words in this infernal language?

Chapter 13
A LOAF OF BREAD, A BOTTLE OF WINE AND THOU

Christ, you're such a schmuck. You got this babe who's got the hots for you, and you didn't know what to do?

Sir, you are quite the vulgarian. Do not scoff. You talk so loosely, as if you would have known exactly what you would have done if you were I, but you cannot even imagine what it is like to be me.

Fine. Whatever. So what did you do?

I sought the counsel of a professional, who did put things into a perspective far wider than I would have imagined.

"Maybe you might think about actually taking off your clothes." That was Jasmine's ultimate response to my question regarding the situation with Nicole.

Walls. She spoke of walls surrounding me, behind which she said I hid.

"My rules are different," was my reply. Self-preservation is imperative. Those walls Jasmine spoke of are a human construct, irrelevant to one such as myself.

Jasmine shook her head vigorously, her soft flesh pressed close to me. An expert at reading people, she saw through my facade, but hell's damnation, do not walls have their use? Why in the name of all the false gods of heaven would I risk existence for a few fleeting moments of mundane pleasure?

Why indeed.

"Maybe you might think about actually taking off your clothes," Jasmine repeated, toying with the top button of my shirt. She undid the first then second button, rolled on top of me and rubbed her breasts against my smooth, hairless chest until her nipples came erect. "You're hiding behind your clothes, and you're hiding behind lame excuses."

"I beg your pardon."

"You heard me. Like you've never had a human lover in all these years you've been alive? Like you've never been intimate with a human woman? C'mon, maybe you can fool that little girl, but you're not fooling me." She rose to her knees, straddled my midsection, reached down and undid the remaining buttons. "She's not gonna wait forever for you to make up your mind."

I smiled at her. "Perhaps it is foolish to ask questions when the answers are already known."

Jasmine reached for my belt buckle. "I wish you luck with your little girl. I'm gonna miss you, Al. You want me, you know where to find me."

"Your sentiment is greatly appreciated."

She grinded her pelvis against my loins. "Just remember, some jobs *are* best left to professionals."

****

Her father's book was still in my possession, which offered a pretense for inviting her to my little apartment a second time. Why not offer her dinner as well?

It was no surprise when she accepted my offer, enthusiasm clear in her voice.

Dinner was veal Parmesan, with pasta and zucchini and a nice Chianti. Nicole ate with great relish, and when she was done, we moved to the futon where we continued our conversation as she sipped her wine, the fruity bouquet pleasantly tickling my nostrils.

"I do remember my grandmother's stories," Nicole said. "She would talk about vampires, but I never believed her. I'd pretend I did 'cause I loved hearing her stories."

"What kinds of tales did she tell?"

"She'd tell stories about creatures rising in the night, appearing in a cloud of mist, feeding off the blood of the living. My favorite was about how when she was just a little girl, she was in the woods, gathering wild berries. She lost track of the time, and before she knew it, the sun had set. It was dark, and she was lost, and she was really scared. Then she saw this cloud of mist suddenly appear in front of her. In the mist, a face formed, white as a full moon. Then, it was a man standing before her, but she knew it wasn't a man. He smiled, and she saw his fangs, but he extended his hand and told her not to be scared. She took his hand, and it was ice cold. He walked her through the woods, quickly guiding her home. When my grandmother's house was in sight, the man disappeared in a cloud of mist."

The tale brought a smile to my face. "That is certainly a plausible story. We, like you, are equally capable of good and evil."

She shook her head, smiling. "This all seems so unbelievable. At first, I thought you were crazy. I didn't want to think so, but I really didn't have any choice. But there's no doubting what I've seen." Nicole reached into her purse, drew a mirror, turned her back and looked at the reflection over her shoulder. She shook her head again, shuddering ever so slightly.

"I am not really real, not in the sense that you normally think of within your accustomed context."

"But I see you. I can touch you."

"My natural state is more like mist than corporal matter. What you see is, in a sense, an illusion."

"An effective one, I'd say." Nicole replaced the mirror and turned toward me. "So, that story about that woman—Anya—that was on the level?"

"Yes. We had the misfortune of being in Prague when the Germans invaded. Before we could escape, the Nazis broke into our garret. They raped and killed Anya while I lay helpless within a crate."

Shock registered on her face. "Helpless! While they killed the woman you loved?"

I studied the swirling grain of the stained oak paneling. "It was just about the most hideous experience in all the years of my existence. The coming dawn finds me near comatose, too weak to even move. When the Nazis broke in, the sun had just risen. All I could do was listen. I had not even the strength to lift my arms."

A hand rose to her mouth. "Ohmygod. What did you do?"

"Nothing." The word passed my lips like a spike driven into damp earth. "When I was finally strong enough to rise, I buried Anya, then killed every German soldier I could find."

Nicole reached for my hand. "Oh, Al, I'm really sorry. Christ, that's years ago, but for somebody as old as you, it must just seem like yesterday."

Her fingers felt smooth as she squeezed my hand. "Ay, there's the rub. You are correct. I may be a thousand years old, but I still see Anya standing right before my eyes as if it were yesterday."

"A thousand years." Nicole seemed to speak to the air floating above us. "Were you—were you human? Once upon a time?"

"That last moment of mortality remains with me, always remains with me, like some hideous painting, perhaps like a combination of Van Gogh and Munch at their most macabre.

"When I gaze upon that painting, it is as if I am on the outside looking in. I see myself lying on my bed, an expression of abject horror on my face. To my side lies my wife, her skin gray and bloodless, her throat ripped open, her blood all over the sheets. Straddled over me is a vampire, mouth open, poised to strike, blood and saliva dripping from his fangs, his face contorted in manic, animalistic fury.

"He sank his fangs into my neck and drank deeply until I no longer could feel my body. It felt like I was flying. The room before me disappeared. Blinding, white light appeared ahead of me, and all I wanted was to fly toward the light, feeling the peace within its embrace, knowing that my wife waited for me there.

"But then, there was a salty taste in my mouth. The light faded and disappeared, and I was back in the shabby little hovel that had been my home, our home, the vampire sitting on my waist, his wrist pressed to my lips.

"Rage filled my entire being. Almost home, but then he pulled me back to a place that no longer held any meaning for me! I could not have known exactly what his blood would do to me, but somehow I understood and fought to keep my mouth shut, but the blood spurted down my throat. As soon as I swallowed those first drops, lust for more of this grand blood supplanted my rage. Not believing my own eyes, I actually held his wrist tightly with both hands. It took a greater-than-human effort for the vampire to wrest his arm free of my grip when I had taken all he was willing to give.

"I can never forget his words. 'You are like me, a hunter of the night. You feed by drinking of the blood of the living. You travel in the night, and you must stay far from the light.'

"Somehow, I understood. I *did* become a hunter of the night, marveling in my strength and stamina, which enabled me to run a hundred miles a night. Those first years, I must have traversed central and eastern Europe many times, feeding upon whatever creatures I would find, occasionally coming upon a populated village."

Nicole gasped loudly. I turned and gripped both her shoulders gently. "Yes, my dear, I was not always the same creature you know now. I would descend upon these villages, ripping, tearing and wantonly killing with the same fervor as the creature who had murdered my wife. Nothing mattered anymore. I had died! And I had welcomed death, only to have it taken away from me, replaced by a soulless, faithless hell."

"How did you change?" Her voice shook.

"One night, I arose from the earthen forest floor and sped off, running, just as I had for I knew not how long. By this time, my humanity was completely stripped away. I ran naked, my body caked with grime, my hair a matted, tangled mess. A strong, gamey scent washed into my nostrils, and I ran toward the smell, but suddenly found myself sitting on the forest floor, having struck some sort of invisible wall.

"A rather dandified gentleman stood above me, grinning in an annoyingly bemused manner. I immediately demanded that the fellow identify himself, but he just laughed and replied, 'Ah, the creature has a tongue,' much sarcasm dripping from his words. I rose and charged the fellow, but collided with a tree. He somehow had disappeared even though he had just stood before me."

"He turned to mist, just like my grandmother's vampire. Can you do that?"

"Yes, but I had no such talent at that time, nor did I even realize that such abilities existed. I attempted to charge again, but once again, he disappeared. Suddenly, I felt a great crushing weight against my larynx. The fellow had an arm wrapped tightly around my neck. I struggled, but he was too strong.

"'Killers like you are far too dangerous to be allowed to exist,' he said, his voice an angry whisper.

"I was no brainless creature, even though I had become a remorseless killer. My mind worked quickly. 'Maybe there is another path which you might show me,' I answered.

"His laughter nearly broke my eardrums. 'Are you even worth the trouble, creature-with-a-tongue?' he replied.

"'You will not know if you make not the effort,'" I argued.

"You convinced him?" Nicole asked.

"Yes. At that moment, he could have easily snapped my neck, and my existence would have ended. But he did not, and he never, ever explained why."

"I'm glad he changed his mind."

"As am I. François was his name. He took me to a monastery where they cleaned me, clothed me and gave me a well-rounded education. François himself made a concerted effort to mold me, teaching the importance of possessing some form of morality, some sort of respect for the mortals who provide our sustenance. I owe my survival to François. You see, he had a profound understanding of the path humanity was taking or would eventually take. François was quite prophetic in his prediction that humanity would eventually reject superstition in favor of science, and then our kind would be more likely accepted at face value."

"What happened to François?"

"He still exists. That I know though we have not seen each other in almost two centuries. As time passed, I moved west, and he moved east. The last word I had from him, he was in Tibet."

Nicole hugged herself tightly. "Fuck. I don't know whether to envy you for being able to live forever or feel sorry for you for all the terrible things that've probably happened to you over all those years."

"Ah, but imagine seeing Mozart perform. Imagine meeting DeVinci. Imagine being in Paris during the French Revolution."

"Cool!" Nicole rose dart-straight in her chair.

"Well...." Images of coarse commoners cheering at a public guillotining passed before my eyes. "Not so, as you say, 'cool.' I was lucky to escape the guillotine myself. The Committee of Public Safety took none too kindly to any members of the aristocracy, French or otherwise."

She raised both eyebrows. "Of course!" She laughed loudly. "Count Farkas. You really are a count, aren't you?"

"Technically, yes. Centuries ago, I was able to purchase a title from an unfortunate Hungarian nobleman, but that was long ago, and now I am a lord with no manor."

"I wondered about that. Why are you working? I'd think someone would have to be a total idiot to not be filthy rich after a thousand years."

I smiled uncomfortably. "One *would* have to be an idiot to not be wealthy after all that time. I was wealthy, but your nation's stock market crash last autumn took care of that. My perception was clouded by greed, and I had not properly hedged my portfolio. An incompetent financial manager prevented any semblance of a recovery. There was still some money left, but he embezzled nearly all that remained."

"But I'd think there must be plenty of ways to get money without having to work."

"Perhaps I truly desire to work."

"You can't really mean that."

"Why can I not?"

"Well, I wouldn't work if I didn't have to."

"Ah, but that is precisely my point. I do not actually have to work."

"But you don't have any money."

"I could live in the woods and subsist like an animal."

Her laughter echoed loudly. "Oh, pu-leeze. I think you like us humans too much to hang out in the woods with all those dumb animals."

"True." I gazed at her, admiring the way the flickering candlelight made her raven tresses shimmer. "But if I were not to work, what would you have me do?"

"You could use your powers and hypnotize people into giving you their money."

"Simple thievery? How dishonorable. How … common."

"Maybe you might turn yourself into mist and rematerialize inside a bank. You could take a buncha money and be set and not have to work."

"That is still thievery, my dear."

"Well, what if you just *borrowed* the money?"

I shook my head, perhaps feeling a certain disdain at what seemed a bit of amorality on her part, but the moment passed quickly. "This is penance for my poor judgment, for being lazy. I am striving to relearn how to fend for myself. Besides, I would not want to abuse my abilities for monetary gain. I have made my peace with mortals—"

"Sounds a bit haughty there, Count, almost like you meant to say, 'mere mortals.'"

I lightly patted her hand. "There are exceptions, but generally, I do not consider myself superior, just different. I need your species, and I learned long ago that it is best not to kill the goose that lays the proverbial golden eggs. My outlook has certainly changed over the centuries, but certainly the Judeo-Christian notion of loving thy neighbor as thyself is still well ingrained within my being."

She grinned broadly, shaking her head. "This is so *fucking* unbelievable. I mean, this is great. A real vampire! And here I am just chatting with him, just like he was anybody else."

"Quite a curiosity, is it not?"

"Quite! So many questions. I don't know where to begin."

"Understandable. You grow up hearing stories at your grandmother's knee, but most of your perception is based on books and movies."

Nicole pulled her knees to her chest. "I hear when the Hiring Committee asked you who would play you in a movie, you said Frank Langella because of the 'sensitive sensuality' he brought to the role of Dracula. Do you actually watch vampire movies?"

"I find them amusing. And I've read many vampire books as well. Most of the movies are ridiculous, but I liked Langella because he did capture the sheer sexuality of the role. Bram Stoker's book really had little to do with vampirism. Actually, it was more a metaphor of Victorian sexuality."

"Yeah." Nicole's head bobbed up and down. "I would agree with that. So, Hollywood's done a pretty abysmal job portraying your kind?"

"Well, *Love At First Bite* was not bad."

"*Love At First Bite*?! You're kidding me, aren't you?"

"Well, the film does make a mockery of the Dracula legend, but in terms of what real life is like for a vampire, it is not too far off the mark."

"Ever read Anne Rice?"

"Of course. I find her writing quite enjoyable, especially *The Vampire Lestat*. The story was touching, and the prose was lush and passionate."

"But what about Lestat himself?"

I shook my head vociferously. "A most engaging character, but he is too foolhardy. Other vampires would have destroyed him without a thought. Creatures like that are simply too dangerous to be allowed to exist. Actually, Chelsea Quinn Yarbro's Saint Germain rings truer than any other fictional vampire I can think of."

Nicole sighed. "He is wonderful, isn't he?"

"Perhaps a little too wonderful."

"Jealous?"

"No. It is just that Saint Germain is too perfect. He always does the right thing. He always makes the right decision. His virtue never comes in question. How would you feel if you had to live up to that kind of unattainable perfection?"

"Well, I wouldn't like it, and I don't like it," she answered, her tone oddly harsh. "Hell, women face those kinds of comparisons all the time. Men want us to look like supermodels, movie stars and centerfolds. I'm sorry. I'm not anorexic, and I'm not getting a boob job. You'll have to accept me just the way I am."

"Which is perfect—perfectly wonderful."

Nicole immediately softened. "Ahhww, shucks." She took one of my hands, wrapped it within her warm, soft fingers. Her eyes met mine. "So, Count Farkas, what do we do now?"

I squeezed her hand gently. "That is up to you. I do not want to rush you into something you are not prepared for."

Her smile widened as moist lips parted. "This futon opens into a bed, doesn't it?"

I nodded.

"Wait," she said, as if she suddenly remembered something she should have. "How do you, well, you know—"

"Lovemaking with a vampire is not that much different from what you are accustomed. That is, if that was your question."

She smiled shyly, almost coquettishly. "But you'll bite me, right? But only just take a little bit of blood?"

"Yes, just a little. At the time of the climax of your pleasure. That allows me to taste your pleasure through the shared consciousness that occurs at that moment."

"Shared consciousness?" She sounded excited. "Does that mean I'll be able to feel you feeling my orgasm?"

"Hopefully."

Nicole practically jumped from the futon. She grabbed a handful of fabric and pulled it from the wall, nearly knocking me over in the process. "Let's get to it." Then, she paused. "Just another couple questions. I won't turn into a vampire when you bite me, will I?"

"No."

"Yeah, I thought so." She spread the futon as I gathered the pillows, sheet and blanket. "What about AIDS? I mean, you don't screen your victims. It might not affect you, or maybe it does. But how will it affect me?"

"That is a very good question." We sat together on the newly made bed, Nicole leaning into my open arms, her hands running over my back. "When I first heard of the virus, I did some experiments. I can assure you that neither of us has anything to worry about. Perhaps, if I were to bite someone with the virus, then shortly thereafter bite someone else while the previous person's blood still coated my fangs—that might be a problem. But the virus simply cannot live, let alone propagate, within my body. First, my body temperature is too cold. Second, whatever it is in my blood that makes me what I am, that is death to the AIDS virus."

"Maybe they could use your blood as a cure for AIDS."

"Then there would be all these formerly HIV-positive people turning into vampires—but maybe someday one of us will figure how to isolate the vampiric part."

"Someday, but not today." Nicole wrapped her arms around the back of my neck and pulled me closer to her. Our lips met. Hers, moist, soft like rose petals, kissing me with passion and fervor, her tongue passing my lips, meeting my tongue, caressing my teeth, searching for the two very sharp, very pointy, very special ones.

Our mouths remained locked together, arms clamped around each other as we slowly peeled off each other's garments, slowly, ever so slowly revealing each other's secrets. Her hands unclasping each button, lingering upon the flesh underneath. Mine feeling the softness of her round breasts, the delicate lace of her brassiere lightly tickling my fingers.

Then, all secrets were stripped away, and we momentarily parted just to gain greater perspective in order to gaze upon the truth before us. And the truth was accepted, and it was beautiful, and we joined together again, hands again touching, kneading, probing, and soon lips and tongues did what hands had done.

"God, your skin is so cold."

"Vampires do have a much lower body temperature."

"Mmmmm. That'll be nice when it gets really hot."

Nicole moved between my legs, taking what had been my mortal manhood in her mouth. The pleasure of her tongue caressing what was still sensitive skin distracted me from something I should have told her. After a bit, she stopped and looked up at me.

"Al, is there something wrong?" She held the limp organ, her expression most mournful.

I sat up and tenderly caressed her hair. "Nothing is wrong, my dear. I am sorry, I should have told you. That is the one thing I cannot do."

"You can't get it up?" She let the organ drop through her fingers.

"A reproductive organ in a creature that does not reproduce through sexual intercourse is as useful as a mortal's appendix. I hope you are not disappointed."

She moved her body upward, resting her head against my beating heart. "No. It's okay." Nicole faced me, a sweet smile on her face. "*That* I can get from any Biff, Chip, Dick or Harry, but this should be something special, something unique. I just worry that it might not be as good for you."

I laughed heartily at that. "Do not worry about that, my sweet. What I will experience far surpasses the vulgarity of a grunting, slavering male's ejaculation."

And then we resumed, our bodies merging as one through the touching of skin against skin, the exploration of fingers, lips and tongues, and when my fingers reached downward to her cleft of mystery, she was wet, her voice suddenly speaking like it was the wind urging me onward, telling me, "Yes, yes, yes."

I moved between her legs, exploring this mysterious land with my tongue, reveling in her scent, her taste, which was clean and salty-sweet, so very, very sweet, like the taste of sweet, sweet blood.

Then, the time had just about arrived, and I removed my mouth from where it was, leaving my fingers in its stead, urging her forward to the inevitable conclusion, my lips kissing her soft neck, tongue licking her flesh, mouth opening, fangs finding their spot, pressing against the skin, lovingly caressing the spot where we would join.

She gasped loudly, her body shuddered, then fangs pierced flesh. Hot blood shot into my mouth. The room disappeared into blackness. Whiteness pulsated in the distance, pulsated like a beating heart, growing, moving closer, more and more quickly.

Growing, growing. Moving closer.

Exploding.

A mammoth chrysanthemum exploded from bud to fully bloomed white blossom with plump petals, this flower obscuring all sight, all sense, all everything before wilting and fading, something distant pulling it away, then replacing it with another pulsating speck of white light. A speck, a dot, a sphere, again moving closer, growing. And exploding, another white chrysanthemum, with such plump, juicy petals.

Again and again, for an indeterminable period of time, until finally the flowers began to get smaller, their explosions blossoming with less fury until they would bloom no more.

"Flowers," Nicole said, her breathy voice again like the wind.

"Yes, flowers." I kissed her softly on the lips, enveloping her in my arms. We lay intertwined together for a long time, silent, with no words needed, for our bodies had spoken, as had our souls.

Finally, Nicole's laughter broke the silence. "My boyfriend, the vampire." More laughter. "I like the sound of that."

Chapter 14

THE VAMPIRE CABBIE FALLS IN LOVE

Nearly a month had passed, a month of sheer bliss as spring truly arrived, with love blossoming just as the parade of flowers had gone from mere buds to full bloom. Flowers! It was a marvel to witness those amazing creatures as they grew fleshy appendages, stretching, reaching for life-giving sun. And there could have been no better way to observe the spectacle than from the vantage point of a moving taxi, all those blossoms clearly visible to my eyes, even in the deepest darkness.

First, the magnolias, their fat white blossoms tinged with pink, looking like overgrown tulips, then the cherries and crabapples, building canopies of white, pink and deep, dark purple.

And when the peonies dotted the city, round and fat, white and magenta, I knew that one can never be too old or too damaged to fall in love again. Everywhere I drove, the fragrance of those flowers washed over me, and no matter where I was, what I was doing, her scent was with me, sometimes because it still stuck to my skin, other times because it was imprinted within the very core of my being. Even while driving cab with maximum effort, it took little to bring her scent to the forefront.

Ah yes, you laugh, you scoff at these musings. Call them ridiculous? Retrospect might find your observation correct, but how dare you cast a pall over even a moment's joy with your biased assumptions. I have unique needs, yes, but I still possess certain emotions which, like all these exploding blossoms, will whither and die when needs and wants remain unfulfilled.

"Simmons, party of one, at the Geisha House," Dexter said, interrupting my musing, "comes up."

I subdued my recollections of the previous night's glorious lovemaking and acknowledged the call, and shortly was guiding the cab between the two twenty-foot steel posts supporting the sign that read "Geisha Bath House" in lurid, quasi-oriental letters. A fat, balding man in his mid-forties sat on the front steps. He looked up as the cab's headlights struck him in the face and stared blankly into the twin beams before slowly rising and waddling to the cab.

Kern had explained that Madison had formally been known as the Athens of the Midwest, attracting businessmen not for the opportunity for education, but for the depravity. Decadence, Kern said, had taken a back seat to commerce, but apparently this fellow was from the old school, having sought the halcyon atmosphere of yesterday's Madison. Surely, he had enjoyed a night at Visions, Madison's lone remaining house of burlesque, reached a critical mass of excitement and walked across the street to the Geisha to relieve his tension. And on a Tuesday night!

Layered smells emanated from the gentleman, washing into my nostrils, and he was not yet within the confines of my cab. Porcine perspiration. Cheap whisky. A potpourri of sex, cheap perfume and baby oil.

And blood.

Damn this pathetic mortal for obscuring Nicole's sweet scent. He opened the front door and wiggled into the cab. I flared my nostrils, trying to recall the sweet scent of my love, only to have the man's aroma wash over me, alcohol-tainted blood overwhelming all the other smells. The man's heart thundered inside my skull, pumping blood through clogged arteries. He had a strong heart, but high blood pressure—a massive coronary awaited, but tonight the organ was working just fine.

"Where may I take you, sir?" I asked.

The man closed the door and paused a moment until his eyes focused. "Ish thish Madishun?" he asked.

My head cocked to one side. "Excuse me?"

"I said … Ish! Thish! Madishun!"

"Yessir, it is. This is the east side of Madison, but only a few miles from our beautiful downtown. Where may I take you?"

"Inn!"

"Which one? Madison? University? Badger?"

"Thass the one."

"Wh—" I stopped myself. "The Badger Inn?" The man shook his head.

"The Madison Inn?" He shook his head again. "The University Inn?"

"Yeah, i's that one."

"I will take you there." As Dexter was so fond of saying, our drivers are totally fluent in drunk. Certainly, I had mastered that skill with relative quickness, as exhibited by my handling of the four drunk Norwegians who I had been assigned to pick up at Visions one evening. I was told they were going from Madison's only strip club to the Concourse Hotel, but when they got into my cab, they seemed to have a different plan.

"Ya," the man sitting in the front seat said. "Squveezers. You take us to Squveezers."

Laughter came from the back seat. "Squveezers. Ya, we go to Squveezers."

"Where?" I asked, knowing no such establishment existed, either called Squveezes or Squeezers. Though a mere rookie, I knew this with utmost certainty.

"Squveezers! Ya, You take us to Squveezers."

I considered asking the dispatcher for help, but knew the response would more than likely be, "Count, are you not fluent in drunk?" I was determined, by Satan's beard, that I would solve this mystery on my own. I carefully turned around in the parking lot, stalling for time, really, and gave the matter consideration. Context, I thought. Context is everything. I picked them up at a strip club. Where would they want to go if they were not going back to their hotel?

"Massage parlor!" I blurted out. "You want to go to a massage parlor?"

"Ya! Squveezers! Squveezers! You take us to Squveezers!"

I sighed deeply and took them to the Rising Sun. I hoped Jasmine would be grateful.

Being fluent in drunk is a skill that does come in handy. Hastily, I turned the cab around, eased out of the parking lot, activated the meter and carefully merged onto East Wash.

"Have you had yourself an enjoyable evening, sir?" I asked.

"Yeah, you betsha. Saw some bitches with great tits. Got laid. Besht goddamned night of my fucking life."

My smile was perfunctory as my thoughts drifted back to Nicole. But it was no use; my body had already begun to tingle, that unmistakable feeling that every single nerve ending was being plucked all at once by invisible fingers, all with the aplomb of a world class harpist.

As the Americans say, especially those provincials who drive tractor-trailers, I put the hammer down, watching the Capitol dome grow closer and closer, nodding politely as the man babbled incoherently about rubbing "snatches" while shoving ten-dollar bills down g-strings.

At First Street, we topped a rise that afforded an unobstructed view of the Capitol. It was a quiet night; there was not a single car between First and the Square. Where were the drag-racing, hormone-addled adolescents? A quick check of the rear-view mirror showed that no cars approached from behind. When the light turned green, I feathered the accelerator.

"Like I wush saying," the man continued, "there's beaver, and there's beaver, and there's—"

"Sir!" Vulgar bastard! How could he reduce something so sublime to a mere, inanimate piece of meat?

"W'ya faggot or something?" He turned, his expression angry. Our eyes met, then his face went slack, eyes turned blood red, the echo of his beating heart growing louder and louder within my skull.

Ahead, behind, no other cars. As the cab sped forward, I grabbed the man by the back of the neck, pulled him to my chest and chomped down on his throat without even lifting my foot from the gas pedal. Yes, I had sworn not to take blood from passengers, but as the Americans say, there is a first time for everything.

He *did* suffer from hypertension. Hot blood, fouled only slightly by what the man had drunk, gushed down my throat. Fortunately, his taste was not as bad as his smell. After taking about a pint, I gently eased him to his side of the front compartment and enjoyed the peace and quiet.

The cab remained centered within the proper white lines. I licked the blood off my lips and wiped my mouth with a handkerchief, then dabbed the blood off my passenger's neck.

The fellow's loud snoring brought a smile to my face; he would not awaken until we reached his motel, allowing me to peacefully listen to the radio and, with luck, get dispatched to another call before arriving at the destination. Additionally, my musing could resume, my favorite smell could return to the forefront and my favorite image could dance before my mind's eye.

Ah, Tuesday night, the one night when Nicole and I both worked, which meant we could go home together at shift's end. I worked Tuesday through Friday, and she worked Sunday to Tuesday, allowing the rest of the week for schoolwork. I had dropped Saturdays to allow more time together. As for the other nights, we could rendezvous if she managed to stay awake until my shift had concluded, or if she felt like seeing me at the conclusion of her shift.

"West near West Towne. Near the West Side Depot. Crystal Corner."

I hit the bid button, lifted the microphone from its cradle, held a thumb poised over the talk button and patiently waited for Dexter to call my number.

"Eighty-four." Pause. "Sixty-eight." Pause. "Ninety-seven." Pause. "Sixty-seven." Pause. "Sixty-three."

"Pinckney and Gorham to the University Inn," I answered.

"Stand by, Sixty-three and Ninety-seven. The call's at the Wash Hot. You're both dead even. I'll get back to you both soon."

I glanced at the passenger. Still asleep. He would wake up woozy; but then again, he was already woozy. I pressed the accelerator to the floor, crossed Wisconsin Avenue under a yellow light and sped toward State Street. Ahead, a green light grew quickly stale. A couple of drunken women stumbled into the intersection, but saw my cab and scurried back to the corner.

"Where now, Ninety-seven?" the dispatcher asked. Pause.

"Where now, Sixty-three?"

The cab flew around the curve where Gorham becomes University, jostling my passenger, but he remained asleep. The light at Frances was green. I turned right onto Frances just as the light turned yellow, then keyed the mike and spoke.

"Frances and U to the University Inn. I am clear of the light."

"Sixty-three, get the Wash Hot. One Lisa on U-Ride number fifteen. Goes to Frances Court."

My acknowledgment was chipper, but I groaned inwardly. It would surely take far less time to drive the three blocks to the destination than load the passenger from the Wash Hot—cab slang for the Washington

Hotel, a large, once venerable hotel which housed a late-night restaurant, a rock 'n' roll club, a bar known for fancy drinks, a gay discotheque and a gay bar frequented by men in black leather.

I smiled sardonically as the cab came to a stop in front of the motel. All calls are good calls, but apparently, some are better than others. I reached over and gently roused the passenger.

"Where?" the man said.

"Your motel."

The man looked up, looked outside toward the motel's entrance and looked at me, his expression disoriented.

"That is ten fifty."

The man fumbled through his pockets: front, back, hip, breast, chest, until he found his wallet. He finally handed me a ten and a five. "Keef the change and gimme a receipt," the businessman said. With surprising aplomb, he took the receipt, opened the door and climbed out of the cab.

He was about to close the door when he reached toward the wound on his throat, rubbing it with his fingers. "Jeshus Chrisht! Wha the hell!?"

I smiled sheepishly.

"Ya got some pretty big fuckin' moskeetoes around here."

"With all the rain we have been having," I replied, "they have been growing to the size of small dogs. They have been known to fly off with young children."

The man stared incredulously at me for a moment, then shut the door and stumbled off.

I tucked the bills into my shirt pocket, watched the man enter the building, then proceeded to my next call.

Apparently, all calls *are* good calls.

****

Nicole's face fascinated me. She never seemed to mind my staring at her, though she would shake her head, this embarrassed expression on her face, but how could I not stare? Those dark, almond eyes. Those long, shiny, raven tresses. Those long, graceful jaw bones that came together at her chin to form her lovely angular face. All those womanly curves, unlike these other American women who looked as though they never ate. Looking at Nicole was almost like looking at a woman from the old country, and as good fortune had allowed, at shift's end, Kern had vacated the seat directly across from where Nicole sat struggling with her paperwork. Apparently, she had too many charge slips for a spring night. Ah, but it was a Tuesday night, the one night we both worked. As soon as we both completed our paperwork, we could enjoy each other's company for the few hours before sunrise.

"How was your night, Count?" Kern said, interrupting my meditation.

"Adequate," I replied.

Nicole looked up from her paperwork and smiled warmly at me. She held up a fistful of charge slips. "U-Ride hell for me."

Kern snorted loudly. "Too much trouble, not enough tips. Dealing with the university is like dealing with the fucking devil."

Truck burst into the driver's room and slammed his seat-pad along with the rest of his cab-driving paraphernalia loudly on one of the table tops. His clipboard clattered on the floor, where he let it lie.

About to leave, Kern had been holding his cushion, clipboard and a book under his arm. He put his materials on a table, reached for a cigarette and lit it.

"How was your night, Truck?" Kern perched himself atop the table and took a deep drag from his Marlboro.

"U-Ride hell," Truck replied. "U-Ride hell, pure and simple." This burly bear of a man paused, obviously noting that everyone in the room was staring at him in rapt attention.

"I tell you, it's bad enough we have to give those damn university brats free cab rides to hell and back—"

"The program *is* projected to gross almost a half-million dollars of annual revenue," I interrupted.

"Yeah," Truck countered, "but out of forty rides tonight, why did I have to run ten of them? And not a goddamn tip from any of 'em."

"Gotta play the airport more," Kern interjected.

Truck paused again. He took off his horn-rimmed glasses, rubbed his eyes and scratched his beard. "But you know what? I got to throw one of those little fuckers out of my cab tonight."

"No way."

"Is that so?"

"Way to go."

"Yeah. Bastard gets in the cab, him and some girl. Man, she was fucked up. All glassy-eyed. I ask for his student ID, he says, 'Just drive.' I tell the peckerwood frat boy he's gotta show me his student ID because the university says so. He says, 'Fuck you.' Well, then I tell him he's gotta change his attitude right now. He says, 'This is U-Ride. You have to take me. You're just a fucking cab driver.' So, I get out of the cab, go to his side, open the door and say, 'you have one of two choices. Either get out now or be carried out. You have 'til three to decide. Two!'"

Truck stood frozen a moment, body rigid, head craned forward, eyes glaring like Rasputin's. Laughter filled the room.

"Way to go, Truck," Kern said. "Man! I would've loved to have been there."

Truck relaxed and smiled at Kern. "It was fuckin' beautiful, man. It was retribution, not just for me, but for all my brother and sister cabbies."

"How was your night, Al?" Nicole asked.

I picked up a handful of charge slips, all reading "U-Ride" on the "charge to" line. "A bit of U-Ride Hades for me, too. But I did have one cash passenger who tipped pretty well."

"How well?" Nicole asked.

"Well, what is it I can say? Some tips are like snacks and some tips are like meals."

Nicole smiled broadly. And with apparent understanding.

****

We spent the last couple hours before sunrise on the north shore of Lake Monona, wrapped in a blanket, staring up at the stars. It was a clear, mild night, warm for early May. A waxing quarter-moon cast a long reflection off the lake, pointing arrow-like at the State Capitol, which loomed brilliant white, surrounded by traffic lights blinking yellow and red. All was quiet. Within earshot, a few ducks quacked.

"Dinner?" Nicole inquired, pointing toward the ducks.

"I am well-sated. They may quack in peace."

Above, the constellations lay in stark contrast to their black background, their ancient light old enough to make even a thousand-year-old vampire feel not quite so old, nor quite so wise.

Nicole took my hand. "I think I'd like to live forever." Her voice had a certain far-off, musing quality.

"Eternity is a long time," I replied. "And immortality is a double-edged sword. On the positive, there is what I have seen. And, on the negative, there is also what I have seen."

"Riddles." She pressed closer to me, trying to shield herself against the chill of the coming dawn. Even wrapped in a blanket, I could feel her begin to shiver a bit.

"You are cold," I observed. "Perhaps we should leave."

Ebony had begun to yield to royal blue. It was time to depart. Dawn would not come yet, but we would want some time at my apartment before the sun's first rays sapped all my strength from me. As we approached my car, a broadside posted on a telephone pole attracted my attention.

The posting bore a full-color photo of a young woman, blonde and angelic. Under her picture, in large, bold letters, lay the word, "Missing."

"She's probably already dead," Nicole said bitterly.

The poster offered a $500 reward for information leading to her safe return. Apparently, Dawn Stevens of the Delta Gamma sorority, a sophomore at the university, had been missing since April 5. I remembered reading a short item about her in one of the Madison dailies. Her sorority sisters had gone out that night. She had stayed home. When her sisters returned, she was gone and had not been seen since.

"Violence is tearing your nation apart," I said, suddenly feeling an urge to rant and rave pedantically. "Your inner cities full of violence, with teens bringing guns to school, so many young faces plastered on milk cartons and posters like this. And all those serial killers. Centuries ago, before people routinely traveled the world, it was not like that. Their communities were their world. People felt responsible to their community, and if they did not, the community was swift in its punishment. Now, with all this freedom of movement, that responsibility is gone, and these killers feel free to indulge the whims of their rampant id."

"Well, that's pretty prosaic, Al," Nicole replied sharply. "But what gets lost in your world-according-to-Al is that this fucker is doing this to women, and that's something that's always been an accepted part of patriarchal society. Even in your precious communities of yesterday."

I shook my head, but held my peace. Though I did not completely agree with her assessment, it somehow seemed best to be conciliatory; our time so short, so precious; why squander it? "Where do these monsters come from?"

"Monsters?" Nicole answered quickly. "Hell, you oughta know something about that. Do you believe any of those rumors about the bodies of those women being drained of blood?"

"No." We climbed into my Toyota. I started the engine and commenced the short drive to my apartment.

"Think it could be a vampire?" Nicole asked.

"I seriously doubt that. One of my own would have to be quite foolish to leave blood-drained corpses lying about."

"But what would you do if it was a vampire committing these crimes?"

"Stop him." My terse reply was followed by a tense silence that fortunately lasted only a short interim, ending when Nicole laughed and pointed out a store just a few blocks from my apartment called "Gifts of the Magi Occult Shoppe." Strange that I had never noticed it before.

My laughter echoed hers, our mood returning to a certain modicum of lightness.

"Do they sell Aleister Crowley greeting cards?" Nicole asked, between laughs.

"I do not know, but it does make me wonder. There is such a thing as social science, yet something that once upon a time employed totally legitimate scientific methodology gets scoffed at and dismissed as occult. It seems absurd."

"Yes, Al, quite. Quite absurd."

****

As the students say, "Friday night in Madison is party central." Despite the presence of a roving killer, that year-round carnival known as State Street was in full revel, so giddy they were with the blossoms of spring. Strolling crowds filled the sidewalks, spilling out into the street, crowding around the jugglers and the various troubadours, young people, older people, white, yellow, brown and black, wearing standard western garb or traditional clothing from their home countries, speaking in at least a dozen languages other than English.

I searched State Street for flags, wondering if it was indeed not Mardi Gras or Rio. It was near bar time, but there was a lull in the board business. Being the ever-enterprising cab driver, I sought the business wherever it might happen to manifest itself.

Technically, I should not have been cruising State; cabs are only allowed on this mall when picking up or dropping off passengers and are supposed to enter and exit on the same block. Driving at a snail's pace, I rehearsed my excuse speech.

"Sorry, officer," I would say. "I had a call here, but when I arrived, they were already gone."

In front of Pic-A-Book, which marked the lower end of State nearest the campus, where most of the action was situated, Catfish sat on a bench, playing some Robert Johnson with his Bayou slide guitar, wearing his trademark straw cowboy hat and bushy Fu Manchu. A small crowd gathered, watching Catfish and tonight's guests, a skinny kid playing upright bass and a big, burly, bearded man who hauntingly stroked a violin.

I rode the brake in front of The Pub. No takers; the people in the window seemed content to remain there, displaying their cards numbered one to ten, held up to assess the relative aesthetic qualities of those passersby.

Ahead, Art Paul, tall, lanky and bug-eyed, sang to his loyal fans, strumming a battered guitar, a kazoo mounted to his neck with a wire coat hanger. His off-key rendition of Bob Dylan seemed oddly appropriate.

From within Monday's Tavern, a petite blonde emerged sans jacket, despite the evening chill. She darted across the street, waving and yelling. I drew the cab to a stop. The woman opened the left rear door and climbed inside.

"Thanks for stopping," she said. The woman reeked of beer, schnapps, sweat, smoke and perfume. Her heart beat rapidly, but slowed quickly.

"Where may I take you tonight?"

"Just over to Langdon. One-oh-three. Sorry it's not farther."

"That is okay." I eased the cab forward, waiting for the slow-moving pedestrians to yield to the greater power of my cab. "So, how are you tonight?"

"Drunk and tired. I just wanna go home."

"Well, I will get you there quickly."

The woman leaned back in her seat. Moments later, we were in front of her house at the corner of Langdon and Carroll.

"That is two-fifty."

"Just a second," she said, digging into her pocket, pulling out four separately wadded-up ones and handing them to me. "Keep it."

"Thank you very much." As I watched her open the door, my gaze drifted toward her building. Above the door were two Greek letters, Delta and Gamma.

"You are a Delta Gamma?" I asked.

The woman answered enthusiastically. "Yeah, I am."

"I wish to express my sorrow over Dawn Stevens."

The woman's tone sobered. "Thanks. You know, we're doing all we can. Putting up posters all over town, talking to parents, Dee Gee alumni, trying to raise more money for the reward. We're not giving up hope."

"I wish you luck."

"Thanks." The woman paused a moment. "I just can't figure out why anyone would want to hurt Dawn. She's just the sweetest girl. Nice to everyone. And shy, too. Hell, she's only had one boyfriend since she's been here. And what sucks is she'd just met some guy she really liked. At a frat party! Can you believe that?"

I shook my head. "At which fraternity did she meet this gentleman?"

"Smegma Chi."

"Excuse me?"

The woman laughed. "Sorry, I mean Sigma Chi. That's just a joke. They're good guys, but they get hammered at those parties and become real jerks, calling us Dick Grabbers. A girl's really gotta watch herself."

"Why do you go to these parties, if your hosts behave so disgracefully?"

"Well, the parties *are* fun, there's free beer, plus no one's checking IDs. Besides, Smegma's been throwing the best parties this semester. Once a month, on the night of the full moon, they go all out. That's where Dawn met that guy, at the March full-moon party."

"When is the next full moon?"

"Let's see, they threw their April party a couple weeks ago, so I guess in another couple weeks. And it's the last full moon of the semester. And I'm pretty sure it'll be a Saturday night! It'll be the best party of the whole school year. I bet you'll probably be taking lots of people there."

"And taking them home too?"

"Maybe, maybe not." The woman winked, then walked toward the sorority house. I watched her until the door closed behind her, then waited a little while longer, just to be sure, silently wishing her health and safety.

****

It was indeed a good shift; my mood was that of satisfied exhilaration as I refueled my cab, especially because Nicole was refueling at the same time. She had worked for her roommate, Maggie. Nicole had said she needed the money because her quickly approaching final examinations would cause her to miss work. Regardless of the reason, it pleased me that she had worked this night, for it provided more mutual free time for us.

"Got us a vid," Nicole said, waving a video cassette in the air, overhead halogen light reflecting off the plastic case. "By the way, you ever figure out how to program your VCR?"

I smiled shyly. A thousand years old, an accomplished biologist, biochemist and a few other things, yet this contemporary technology was beyond my comprehension. "That contraption is the work of sheer devilment," I replied.

"Don't feel bad." She smiled saucily, almost tauntingly. "A million VCR owners can't program their own machines."

"Ah, such security in the company of such competent minions. It is quite reassuring. So, what will we be viewing tonight?"

The saucy smile turned downright devilish. "H.P. Lovecraft's *Re-Animator*. I've heard it's supposed to be pretty good." Her gas pump clicked off loudly. Nicole coaxed a bit more fuel into her tank, then hung the nozzle.

"Ah, Lovecraft," I replied, "the father of modern horror. Of Modernist horror. No longer evil, but otherness. A writer far ahead of his time."

"A sexist pig actually, and a racist too," Nicole corrected.

"Once again, you have chosen horror. Why are we always watching films literally dripping with red-dyed corn syrup? Would there be anything wrong with a nice comedy, or perhaps a romance?"

Nicole laughed loudly, her expression that of feigned nausea. "Guilty pleasure, I guess. They're fun. Fake horror is a good way to forget about the horrors of the real world. It's therapy." She climbed inside her cab, tires squealing as she searched to find the last available parking space, leaving me to have to move my car in order to park my cab.

Moving with alacrity, I managed to reach the dispatch office at roughly the same time as Nicole, only to find Dexter sitting in the dispatch chair, a puzzling scene. By the blisters of Satan, what was he doing there on a Friday night? Was this not his weekend? Where was the other dispatcher?

He handed us our call slips, hands shaking, face ashen. His Adam's apple bobbed rapidly up and down, but there was no joy in his face, which was the expression that normally accompanied the excited movement in his throat.

"What are you doing here, Dexter?" I asked.

He looked at me, eyes glazed. "Howard was too upset. He split." He swallowed hard, took a deep breath, his Adam's apple bobbing with increasing rapidity. "The police called a little while ago. They asked us not to say anything over the radio."

"What's wrong?" Nicole asked. I felt her hand reach for me, fingers clamping hard against my waist.

"Truck's dead." Dexter ran his hands roughly through the little hair that remained on his head. "The cops called an hour ago. They just found his body. He's been murdered. Somebody cut him up real bad and just dumped him at the side of the road. Over near the bonezone. Just left him there to die."

Without a thought, I laid a hand on the dispatcher's shoulder and let it linger there. Even though the night was cool, his shirt was soaked with sweat. "Murdered? How? Why?"

"The cops don't know anything, but they probably figure it's their buddy who they don't know dick about. They'll round up the usual list of suspects. Jeez, it was Truck's...." His voice trailed off for a moment. "It was his night off, so it wasn't like some psycho he'd picked up decided to slice and dice him." Another deep breath. "There'll be a funeral in a few days. If you're working, you should go. Even if you're not working, you should come here and grab a cab. We owe it to Truck, to give him a big cabbie send-off."

"I will be there. You have my word on that."

Dexter was silent for a few moments. I withdrew my hand. "Jesus, Mary and Joseph, I don't understand this. Everybody liked Truck. And that motorcycle club, they're just a bunch of guys into Harleys. It's not like they're a gang or anything like that. Who could've done something like this?"

I shook my head. Indeed. Who *could* have done something like this?

Then, it struck me. There was no familiar scent wafting over my olfactory. Nicole was gone.

An engine revved loudly. I ran from the building in time to see Nicole's car disappear into the night.

Chapter 15

FUNERAL FOR A CAB DRIVER

Nicole was gone. Gone without a word. Gone without even having done her paperwork, which surely would prompt a summons from the waybill office. Gone before I even noticed her leaving, nothing but a pair of glowing, scarlet taillights shrinking into the night.

I completed my own paperwork, confusion and anger alternating as supreme emotions, battling each other as numbers violated their own cold, constant mathematical rules, one plus one somehow equaling something other than two.

Why had Nicole fled? A reaction, yes, but this from the same woman who had stood by my side under far more gruesome circumstances?

And, motherless spawn of Satan, who in the name of the four winds of Hades would murder Truck? He, truly, had been a kindly fellow. This I knew well, having experienced firsthand the generosity of his concern.

Inside the dispatch office, Dexter stared at the computer screen, silently rubbing his chin. Upon seeing me drop my waybill envelope into the safe, a flood of words flew from his lips, all at once angry and confused, bitter and hopeless.

But the words seemed to bounce off me, just sounds, just emotionally charged tones.

"Another one for the Madison Mangler," Dexter said.

Ears pricked to attention.

"That's what they'll say in the papers," he continued. "Another one for the Madison Mangler." He shook his head slowly, then held his peace and resumed his steely, unfocused gaze upon the green-glowing computer screen. With a soft goodbye, I slipped into the night.

Another one for the Madison Mangler.

Questions consumed me, which took my mind off Nicole's abrupt departure. Why Truck? How could someone inflict that kind of damage on one so imposing as Truck? This fellow, with bulging lumps of muscle well visible even under rolls upon rolls of fat, was no timid little coed, about as able to defend herself as a doe blinded by the headlights of an oncoming car. Truck had served in the military, had been a member of one of those tribal motorcycle clubs where they can and will take care of problems easily and swiftly *by themselves*. Kern once told me someone tried to rob Truck and spent a month in the hospital.

Questions, questions, questions. Had not Dexter said that Truck's remains had been taken to the University Hospital morgue?

What if it was a vampire? What would you do?

Stop him.

Questions posed themselves. Questions demanded answers.

Guilt ate at me. I should have investigated when that first body was found in the snow. Too late for recriminations, I told myself as I drove to the University Hospital. Still sitting within my Toyota, parked a discreet distance from an inconspicuous rear entrance, I became mist and let the force of my will guide me into the hospital, down to the basement and into the morgue. When sensing myself alone, I rematerialized.

All senses on alert. No one around, my search commenced. The morgue was quiet and stark, with steel tables and dingy, white walls. Florescent lights bathed the room in a sickly glow. Ahead, a set of double doors loomed, the stench of disinfectant from within swimming up my nostrils, making my skin crawl.

Beyond the double-doors was a narrow room with stacks of drawers on either side. Finding the correct drawer was easy; only three drawers were labeled, all right next to each other reading, "Slinsky, David—A," "Slinsky, David—B," and "Slinsky, David—C." I hastily pulled open drawer A.

"Motherless spawn of Satan," I spat, staring at the headless corpse, my whisper echoing against sterile walls. Truck's flesh was pale and chalky, rips and tears covering his thorax and abdomen—and most notably and grotesquely—from his groin. Apparently, the police did indeed find a body drained of blood, tapped from all those numerous cuts, including the jagged stump of what was left of Truck's penis.

Within drawer B was a familiar face, an expression of anguish clearly visible through the plastic wrapping. I compared the scraps of skin hanging from what remained of the neck in the first drawer with the bottom of the severed head. There had been a fair degree of gnawing, and the remaining neck vertebrae were twisted far from their normal alignment.

Even if it was obvious that Truck's penis lay inside drawer C, I made myself to open the drawer and inspect the organ wrapped in transparent plastic, forcing myself not to shut my eyes in disgust.

No human possessed the strength to inflict this kind of carnage. That was clear. My eyes slammed shut as the picture formed in my mind—a vampire, saliva-dripping fangs glowing in the moonlight, ripping Truck open one tear at a time, savoring his victim's fear, prolonging life merely to taste the terror.

Images from the past flooded my vision. A wife, her throat torn open. A vampire hovering above, face mad with feral ferocity, poised to strike, but waiting and relishing the wait. Death, then a new kind of life that finds sustenance only from the lives of others, lives taken with the brutality of one without faith or hope, a mere empty shell, mindlessly seeking fulfillment.

Until another path was found.

My fists clenched tightly as I slammed the drawers shut, caring not if anyone would hear. No one deserved to die like this. This monster had to be stopped.

****

It would have been wisest to proceed immediately to my cramped abode, but despite a lightening sky, anger clouded my thoughts, as did concern for one still living. The road ahead seemed to veer, diverting my southward path.

And then my car was parked outside Nicole's house.

No lights burned inside the split-level Georgian. No matter. Within moments, my body rematerialized inside Nicole's bedroom. Posters of Emma Goldman, Che Guevara and a young, slatternly couple captioned "Sid and Nancy" guarded her sleeping form from their spots above the triple-layered bookshelves that lined opposite walls.

Nicole lay tucked in a tight ball, her quilt pulled tightly around her, leaving patches of the mattress as well as her calves bare. She groaned loudly, tossed and pulled the quilt with her as she turned to the other side of the bed.

I spoke her name softly. No reaction but for a groan followed by a vigorous toss and turn as if she wrestled with a demon from her dreams.

The darkness that painted the walls lightened, transforming into swirling shadows. It was time to leave. Nicole groaned loudly again, and then my cells spread apart, my eyes still transfixed on her sleeping form, the image of her nearly rolling off the bed splintering in my sight.

****

Just before the funeral, the mortuary parking lot was full of cabs, but Nicole was nowhere to be seen. I had left for work two hours prior to my eight o'clock start time, at the first moment the sun was low enough in the sky for the pain to be tolerable, the rays stinging, but not burning, not searing flesh from bone white to charred black. My Muskies cap, sunglasses, a bandanna around my neck, long slacks and a long-sleeved shirt provided ample protection, though no amount of covering, not even sunscreen, could provide complete protection. Not even François could fully explain this, except that it is the mere presence of the sun that burns our kind, more in a metaphysical than real sense.

I scanned the crowd for Nicole, opened my nostrils, searching for that familiar, sweet scent. I searched for others as well, others come not to mourn, but to gloat, to drink the sadness and anger of those assembled. Truck's killer would no doubt find such a taste as sweet as the blood of the most innocent of virgins.

The attendees clustered themselves in factions defined by their relationship to Truck. A quartet of large-boned, heavy-set women sat in silence, huddled on a couch next to the chapel entrance, their faces puffy, eyes bloodshot, their expressions stunned, eerily similar to the fear-grimace frozen upon Truck's face.

A trio of bikers flanked the chapel entrance. One could have been Truck's brother, except his long hair and shaggy beard were blond. He wore a green polyester blazer and stood next to a tall, skinny fellow, his ribs nearly visible underneath a too-tight jacket, his Adam's apple bobbing violently as he listened intently to a rather short, muscular gentleman dressed in leather and a denim vest bearing their club's emblem. His raven hair was pulled back tightly, accentuating high cheekbones and prominent scars.

"We ride tonight," the short one said, his voice a hissing whisper. "Tonight. Every night."

"Until we find the fucker who did this," the fat one said. He patted his chest where something bulged underneath his blazer. The short one nodded, eyes narrowed to vicious slits.

"We'll get that fucking bastard," the tall one said.

Someone tapped my shoulder. It was Kern, along with Maureen, the general manager, and the operations manager, Kevin. Maureen wore a rather conservative beige dress, Kevin a navy blue suit, his tie hopelessly askew. Kern's appearance was sloppy as always, but his grin was conspicuously absent.

"Hey, Al," Kern said.

I greeted my fellow cooperative members. Maureen shook my hand firmly. Her flesh felt cold and clammy. Underneath the scent of her lilac perfume lurked the astringent aroma of perspiration.

"Thanks for coming, Al," Maureen said.

"It is important." These were all the words I could muster forth. How to put this into words! It seemed a prudent thing to do, to attend Truck's funeral, but with more and more consideration, it became obvious that I wanted to be there as much as anybody else to share my outrage and grief.

"I hate funerals," Maureen said. Kern nodded. Kevin twitched and shifted his feet back and forth. "I hate having to bury the people that helped make the co-op into something."

"Yeah," Kevin said, pulling at his tie. "Like Benny."

"Like Benny," Maureen repeated, her astringent scent suddenly becoming more prominent. I could almost feel each individual bead of sweat pierce her skin. "Benny—" She shook her head. "Hell, the whole cooperative was his idea. If it weren't for him, we'd all be at somebody else's cab company, slaving for dirt wages."

Kevin laughed dryly. "Hard to believe. Hell, I knew Benny way back at Yellow Cab. Seems like forever."

"It was," Maureen added, a wistful smile on her face. "That must've been twenty years ago."

"Yeah," Kevin said, "and Benny was just a fuckhead of a college dropout."

"Just like you," Kern added, the grin finally returning for just a moment.

Silence. A quick glance throughout the lobby. No sign of Nicole. No stranger cowering from the sun's beams, feeding off the emotions of those in attendance. The circle of bikers grew, their whispers still angry, their bodies pressed closer together. The short biker broke from the circle and approached Truck's female relatives. "Anything I can do," he told them, "anything at all, don't be afraid to ask."

"Fucking sucks," Kern said finally, fists clenched at his side. Kevin nodded. Maureen sighed, then greeted a couple rookies whom I did not know.

More stunned silence for a few long moments. "At least people like Truck and Benny leave us with significance," I said finally. "The memory of what they did, who they were, it lives on in those who remain, for as long as they remain."

"I hate funerals," Maureen said bitterly, her lilac perfume completely obscured by the scent of her own perspiration.

"Well, at least Truck had the pleasure of throwing out a U-Ride passenger at least once," Kern said.

Kevin twitched even harder. Maureen glared at Kern. "I never heard about that," the general manager said.

"Good," Kern replied. "It means the little fucker never called to complain. Probably 'cause he was too busy cleaning up his underpants."

"What the hell happened?" Maureen asked.

Kern retold the story, which drew laughter at its conclusion, even from Maureen, who commented that, off the record, Truck should have gotten a medal for putting that young man in his place.

I laughed with the others, visualizing Truck entering the driver's room, slamming his things on a table, responding to our prodding, then giving a dramatic elocution as he told how he had thrown that "little fucker" out of his cab.

Then, it occurred to me that perhaps that "little fucker" was indeed the Madison Mangler. No possibility could be ignored. But to find a vampire, even in a small city, that was a most daunting task.

Finally, we were ushered into the chapel for the funeral. I scanned the crowd. The chapel quickly overflowed with a diverse collection of people, but no one who looked out of place and particularly distinctive.

And there was no sign of Nicole.

A minister, tall and fleshy, took the pulpit and began speaking of "David's" faith, his long-fingered hands gripping the edge of the dais so hard that his knuckles glowed white. David. The name conjures up such delicate images of a ruddy-faced, muscular young man of singular beauty, making it difficult to think of Truck as "David," though indeed, he was perhaps truly a king among men. The minister described how he had known Truck since he was a child, that even well into adulthood, he still attended services on a semi-regular basis, and on a regular basis, he worked with children at the church.

"David was a very gentle soul," the minister said. "He didn't always let people see that. It is a difficult world, and David knew that and wore his gruff exterior as an armor of protection. But his generosity was very real, as was his great faith, a faith in the inherent goodness of people."

A familiar scent washed over me. Scanning the crowd, I saw Nicole standing at the rear of the chapel, her expression blank.

The minister concluded, and the short, muscular biker took his place at the pulpit. The fellow began by reading a poem Truck had written about cab driving, about how it is important to know where it is you are going.

The biker related how Truck published poetry in numerous journals across the country. How he was an accomplished trumpet player, having graduated from the Julliard School of Music, and though he disdained playing professionally, Truck had given music lessons to children, free of charge.

The biker said Truck, like his fellow bikers, sometimes got into fights, but that he only fought when it became necessary to come to the aid of a fellow biker.

"One of those times," the biker said, "Truck got a guy out of a jam, then turned around and punched him in the mouth because the guy was wrong."

When the funeral was complete, it was time to commence the procession to the cemetery, which would take us from the north side of Madison to the graveyard at the near west side. The graveyard was actually one of three cemeteries sprawled together, bordered by a triangle of streets, forming an area known in cab lexicon as the "bonezone." Ironically, Truck was to be buried a mere stone's throw from where his body had been found.

By the time my cab joined the line, the front of the procession was further ahead than I could see. And many cabs still remained in the parking lot, waiting to join the queue.

If my existence continues for another thousand years, I doubt that I will be able to forget the sight of that procession. As the line moved down the avenue, neither the front nor the rear of the line of vehicles was visible from my vantage point.

When my cab reached State Street, large crowds of pedestrians clumped at each corner, unable to pass until the final vehicle in the procession had cleared the intersection. Astonishment was clearly visible on the faces of many of those pedestrians, as was burgeoning impatience, if not anger, in annoyance that a funeral procession was keeping them waiting so long.

There was no parking lot at the cemetery. All these vehicles, all these cabs had to park on the narrow driveways that wound through the grave-yard, transforming those arteries of asphalt into a immense yellow snake.

The graveside ceremony seemed almost anti-climactic after this pro-cession. It was short, and then it was done, and Truck was gone, but not forgotten. Then, it was time for those working to start running the calls that surely had mounted during this interim.

When it was over, Nicole approached, her expression still blank.

"Are you all right?" I asked gently.

She shrugged her shoulders, her fingers toying with the key to her cab. "Okay, I guess," she replied in a flat tone.

"You disappeared the other night. I was worried."

Another shrug of the shoulders. "I just needed to be alone. That's all."

I touched her lightly on the shoulder. She trembled slightly at my touch. "If you need to talk—"

"No." Her voice rose, then fell. "No. That's okay. I'm fine. Really." Animation returned to her face. "We're on for Saturday?"

"If you so desire."

She nodded vigorously and smiled, much as she usually did, but her expression was just the slightest bit crooked, a tiny fissure shattering her veneer, revealing that something—something undeterminable—lurked underneath.

We parted, then quickly I was assigned a call at the Glenway Golf Course, a mere stone's throw from the cemetery. The man in unmatched plaid, with golf shoes slung over his shoulder, was a perspiring mess of impatience.

"What the hell took you so long? I've been waiting for forty-five minutes."

"I was at a funeral." And that was all I said. No apologies, no explanations. And not anything resembling a pleasant tone in my voice.

****

"I want to watch you feed." Those were Nicole's first words when I had arrived to pick her up Saturday. None of the normal platitudes or greetings, just this strange request, a slight agitation tainting her enthusiasm.

"You cannot be serious." But it seemed quite apparent by the sly smile on her face that she was, and it also seemed quite obvious that resistance would be futile; I simply could refuse her nothing, and surely she knew this.

Nicole took my hand and squeezed it as we walked to my car. Saturday night and we had not yet decided how to spend our evening. Would it be a movie? Or a long walk? Anything of her deciding would be satisfactory to me.

"I'm serious, Al," Nicole said. "I want to know more about you. I want to watch you feed."

We leaned against my Toyota, the steel skin cool and damp from the condensation of this warm May evening. The stench of rank, decaying aquatic vegetation hung in the air, wafting from Lake Mendota across the street.

"But you have seen me feed."

She slapped me lightly on the arm. "Yeah, but that's not the same. I've seen Al Farkas, vampire lover, but I want to see Al Farkas, heartless, vicious, savage predator. I want to see you as you really are, not the guise you wear when you pretend to be human."

Her hyperbole drew laughter from me. "What I am is many things, sometimes savage, sometimes sublime."

"But always humble." She slapped my arm again, then gently rubbed my shoulder and kissed my cheek. "Please. You're not getting all the food you need from me. I know you're feeding somewhere else. Let me watch."

I groaned inwardly. My taking of sustenance is a deeply personal matter. Even though my trust for her ran quite strongly, even though she had done much to earn my trust, the request simply felt remarkably bizarre. However, it seemed there was little choice in this particular matter, despite my protests that this was dangerous, especially considering the heightened tension all over the city, which had only become worse since Truck's murder. People did indeed leave their abodes, but not alone or even in pairs. All over the downtown and campus areas, the citizenry seemed to travel in packs.

Instead of discussing the matter further, I walked around to the passenger side, opened the door and ushered her inside. "State Street on a Saturday night is always a fertile hunting ground." Better to get this over with, it seemed, or else I would never hear the end of it.

"I'll bet." Nicole smiled broadly as we drove uptown.

We parked on Frances Street, right off University Avenue, around the corner from the 602 Club. Together, we cut through the alley between the two bars.

"This is the 604 Club," Nicole said.

"Excuse me."

She laughed quietly. "An informal annex of the 602. As Tate, the bartender puts it, this is where people go to smoke 'them left-handed cigarettes.'"

"Marijuana?" I whispered.

She nodded as the alley opened to a small, wooded lot, with the back door of Genna's Lounge on one side and the loading dock for Pizza Pit on the other. Beyond the lot, lay a sidewalk running from University Avenue to State Street, between two parking ramps.

"Wait here," I said, pointing toward the interior of the Frances Street Ramp. "Stay out of sight. This will take none but a moment."

Nicole grabbed my arm. "Let me help." She pushed me back, then proceeded down the alley toward State Street.

"Nicole," I called after her. "Stop. This is dangerous."

She kept walking, leaving me to watch as she reached State and stood at the mouth of the alley, figures passing in front of her in both directions.

A tall, muscular young man stopped. She spoke with animation, arms flailing in the air. He nodded. They both turned and moved back up the alley. I quickly secreted myself around a corner and waited until hearing their footsteps, smelling her scent and his, able to hear their conversation thanks to my highly attuned senses—she had told him she could not start her car and had asked if he could lend assistance.

When they reached me, she was holding his hand. Nicole spun away as I pulled him toward me, sank my fangs into his neck and drank the usual amount, careful to maintain my mental screens, for I had no desire to see this fellow's disgusting mental image of copulation with my love. It was over so quickly that it made me wonder if she wanted me to do it again so she could get a better view.

The fellow wobbled a bit, but by the time he had reached State, he appeared steady. I was certain he was still slightly dazed and unsure how he had spent the last few moments.

"That was incredible," she said finally, once words were able to form on her lips. "So fast. No hesitation. No remorse. Savage and sublime at the same time. It was beautiful."

"Perhaps you are over-romanticizing. It is just the way I feed. If I did not do it in the manner I do, survival would not be possible."

"Yeah, I can see that, but it really was fantastic."

"Ah, but what of the spider, or the shark, or the lion? This is really no different."

"They pale in comparison." She laughed loudly. We emerged from the alley, passersby looking at us, giggling, obviously suspecting us of some form of lascivious behavior.

"What shall we do now?" I asked, desperate to change the subject.

"How 'bout the Cardinal Bar? I wanna go dancing. Maggie's gonna be there."

Dancing. Suddenly, images of swirling women in white wigs and hoop dresses came to mind. "I am not certain I would know how to dance as today's youth does."

"Don't worry, Al. It's not a question of knowing the ordered steps of a particular dance. It's all in *feeling* the music and letting your body move by itself. Besides, maybe there'll be vampires there at the Cardinal."

"There are no other vampires in Madison," I snapped. The words rang too sharply—a lie, a blatant, bold-faced lie, but if Nicole knew the truth, she would want to help, surely placing herself in danger far worse than what she had previously experienced.

Nicole ran a hand vigorously through my hair. "I meant it figuratively. Not real vampires. They just dye their hair black, wear black clothing and don't go out in the sun hardly at all. And they kind of sit back there at the fringes, being above it all."

"How charming." I opened Nicole's door, then my own. "The Cardinal it is."

This old and venerable bar, just off the east side of the Capitol Square, was certainly lovely. Diamond-shaped tiles of black and white marble made up the floor. Carved mahogany molding circumscribed multi-colored, leaded glass windows. More mahogany made up the bar, which had a very nice cut-glass mirror behind it. Of course, we walked past the mirror quickly, though it has been my experience that bar patrons usually tend not to notice the lack of reflection in such a mirror.

The back room where people danced, however, had none of the charm of the main barroom. It was an absolute assault on the senses, with brightly colored lights flashing and strobing and the recorded music—if one could call it that—played at an excruciating volume.

Nicole bounced onto the dance floor, hips gyrating, shoulders twisting, arms flailing like a whirling dervish. She quickly found Maggie and gave her a violent hug. I followed, attempting to "feel" the music—but by Satan's blisters, was *this* music?

Nicole tried to tell me something. Her lips moved, but I could not discern her words. "What!?" I shouted.

She placed her lips right on my ear. "It's called 'House' or 'Industrial' or sometimes 'Progressive Industrial Noise.'"

Indeed. "Industrial Noise" certainly seemed apt. The cacophony of screeches, scrapes, scratches and crashes, all woven atop the pounding rhythm section, which maintained a steady beat more like a rapidly beating heart, was anything but melodic, but did provide a fascinating challenge just to maintain movement within its frenetic temporal framework.

Song segued into song. Subtle changes in the music led to subtle changes in our movement. My body began to improvise as my thoughts drifted into the ether.

The crowd on the dance floor grew. As Nicole had promised, youths in black lined the walls, their eyes lined in black, their hair black, their expressions dull as if boredom were fashionable. On the dance floor, a couple of women in shorts and tie-dyed shirts flailed their bodies, bouncing off the tightly packed, sweaty crowd, their long, straight hair flying to and fro. Other women danced with other women. Men danced with men, with women. A short, gray-haired Asian fellow danced with three women simultaneously. A tall, sinewy fellow with not the slightest amount of body fat danced by himself, merely jumping up and down in the same spot, arms pinned to his sides. Apparently, this energetic fellow was rather famous and was simply known as Marco Pogo. And, in the middle of it all, an exotic Latin American woman in high heels and a white dress, its neckline plunging deeply, danced a tango with a middle-aged black man in a polyester suit with no tie, the collar of his jacket tucked underneath his shirt collar.

The beat pounded. The dancers' hearts pounded in many small voices, circling around this great monolith, until one by one these small hearts joined lock step behind their bigger counterpart. Just as the room filled with a single, unified booming heart, Nicole grabbed me by the arm and dragged me toward the small bar at one side of the room, Maggie following.

"Yer wearing me out there, Count." She smiled, her brow covered with little pearls of perspiration. "Vodka cranberry," she said to the bartender who promptly handed her the bright pink concoction in a plastic glass with a little red straw.

I felt myself smile, even at the "vampires" who sipped their drinks, their hair lacquered into points at the top of their heads, ears pierced, noses pierced, probably various other body parts pierced and covered with tattoos.

"Having fun, Al?"

"Yes." I kissed Nicole on the cheek, wrapped an arm around her shoulders and squeezed lightly. "Yes, this is fun. This sound is not music, but I do not care. The passion it ignites in this unordered way. The energy it takes to dance. It takes me back. It reminds me of those nights—long ago."

"I hoped you might like it. I wasn't sure, but I'm glad you do."

"I'm going for some air," Maggie said. Her face was bright red, and her cotton T-shirt clung to her. Nicole downed her drink, and the two of us followed her friend.

The night air felt cool against my heated skin, which was moistened with perspiration, though not as much as my two lovely companions.

Nicole stood almost as soon as she sat on the curb in front of the bar. She smiled casually. "What the hell? Guess you don't buy vodka, you only rent it. Be right back."

Maggie punched my shoulder lightly after Nicole departed. Perspiration pasted curly strands of darkened hair to her broad forehead. "You know, Al," she said, "I gotta say, I really like you."

"Oh?" I replied, wondering if this was, as the Americans say, a come-on. Or a set-up for one of those bits of lasciviousness for which Americans have a reputation.

She slapped my thigh, seeming to read my mind. "No, I mean I think you're a good guy, and I'm really glad Nicole's going out with you."

"Thank you," I replied. "That is most kind of you."

"Yeah, well, usually Nicole's got a real knack for picking 'em." She shook her head. "Christ, her last boyfriend was a real creep, and I thought she'd really dug up the scum of the earth before."

"Indeed." What else was there to say.

"Just be good to her, okay? She's been through a lot, and she's not really herself right now, so be careful, okay?"

"Well, I know it must have been difficult for her, with her father—"

"Her father!" Maggie's voice rose a couple of octaves. "Did you know her father—"

"Hey, whaddaya guys talking about?" Nicole chimed in, having returned quickly from the WC—too quickly, for I wanted to know what Maggie had meant when she said that her friend was not truly herself.

Maggie surreptitiously squeezed my knee, fingernails digging deeply into muscle. "Al was just telling me about a split-load at the airport he had last night."

"Ah, yes, it was exceptional. Radisson. West Towne Suites. Quality Inn West Towne. And the Holiday Day Inn West. A Holy Grail indeed."

"Hot damn!" Nicole said. "Must've been good for about forty on the side."

"Nearly fifty," I replied. "They tipped well because I am such a brilliant conversationalist."

We returned to the back room, almost reaching the dance floor before a commotion drew our attention.

Even above the volume, the sound was easily apparent. A loud slap of flesh against flesh. A splash. A trio of young men stood before a woman, her hair drenched, her blouse soaked, shock, anger and embarrassment reflected on her face. One of the men held an empty beer pitcher. All three laughed loudly.

It was hard to tell under this queer lighting, but something about the trio looked strange. Their faces almost seemed to glow—bright white like bone. I took a couple quick steps toward them, then felt my arm pulled sharply.

"Al," Nicole said, shouting over the din, "leave it alone. Let the bar take care of it."

I tried to break away, but Nicole pulled harder.

"C'mon, Al. This isn't any of our business. Just leave it alone. Let's get outta here."

"Yeah, let's get the fuck outta here," Maggie shouted. "Goddamned frat boys. Fuckers ruin everything."

Before I knew it, we were standing on the sidewalk just outside the bar. "Dumb ass frat boys," Nicole spat.

"Frat boys?" I asked. "How could you tell?"

"Easy." Nicole's voice shook slightly with anger. "Their perfect hair. Perfect teeth. Designer clothes scuffed up to look like they got 'em at some second-hand store."

"Eugenics gone bad," Maggie said. "Breeding. Christ, men from so-called good families searching other so-called good families for pretty cows to use as breeding stock just to make sure their kids are good-looking, which to them means their faces have no distinguishing features."

"Hell, yeah," Nicole said. "Just look at them, the whole way they were acting, like they think they can do anything they want 'cause daddy's so fucking rich."

"Damn right," Maggie said. "Largest number of sexual assaults in Madison? Langdon Street. Christ! One of those motherfuckers probably asked her for a blowjob, and when she told them to fuck off, she got a pitcher of beer dumped on her head."

"I hate frat boys," Nicole spat. "Nuke Langdon Street, and the world won't be any worse off. Probably be better."

"We can go someplace else," I interjected.

"Please," Nicole replied. "Anywhere."

"That is satisfactory to me. Where would you like to go?"

"How 'bout the Crystal Corner?" Nicole said. "No frat boys there. Bikers scare 'em off."

"We are there. I rather like the Crystal. Maggie, do you care to join us?"

She shook her head. "Naw. Enough excitement for this girl. I think I'll just go home." She drew her keys and quickly found her car, which was parked within a hundred meters of the Cardinal Bar.

The Crystal was fairly crowded, but still provided a much more relaxed atmosphere than the Cardinal, a welcome change indeed. The music was not so loud—and much more melodic, even if it was that infernally simplistic rock-and-roll. The patrons did not dance, instead merely stood or sat with their drinks, conversing calmly with compatriots. The only flurry of movement came from the two bartenders, who rushed to and fro in an attempt to assuage the thirsty throngs crowded along the long, oval-shaped bar.

"Good crowd tonight," Nicole said.

We squeezed our way to the bar, just as Todd saw us and moved our way. "Evening, Count," the cowboy-hat-clad bartender said. "What is your pleasure?"

"Just vodka cranberry for the lady," I said, glancing at Nicole, pleased that the fellow had remembered me. She nodded. Ahead, through the arch that separates the two sides of the bar, Kern stood next to one of the pool tables, applying chalk to the shooting end of his stick. He saw us and waved.

"Ah, there is Kern," I said.

"Let's go say hello," Nicole replied. I paid for her drink, then she took the cocktail from Todd and followed me through the crowd.

"Wanna shoot some stick, Count?" Kern asked. He picked up another pool cue and started to hand it to me.

"You mean billiards?" I stared questioningly at the scuffed felt covering the table.

"Billiards, stick, pool, snooker, it's all the same to me." Kern flashed his goofy grin. "Whaddaya say? Just a friendly little game?"

I looked at Nicole.

"Sure, Al. Feel free."

"You sure it's okay, Nicole?"

"Fine by me. I'm not the Count's keeper."

I smiled at her. "Do not worry, this match shall not last long."

Kern snorted loudly. "Sez you."

"No, do not misunderstand me, Kern. I have not played this game in quite some time. I am sure you will make short work of my most inadequate skills."

"Yeah, right." Kern began gathering the balls at one end of the table. "You're talking like a hustler. How do you feel about a friendly little wager?"

I pointed to the sign on the wall behind the pool tables that clearly said "no gambling."

"Well, how 'bout we just play for a drink then?"

"But I do not drink."

"Yeah, that's right. I always forget." Kern placed the balls within the rack and arranged them to his liking. "Gotta give you credit for coming into bars and not having a problem not drinking."

"One day at a time," I replied, parroting the cliche I had overheard passengers use who were being transported to an in-patient substance-abuse facility. "I have an idea. I *will* play for a drink. For Nicole."

"Sounds good to me, Al," Nicole said.

Kern nodded and rolled the cue ball toward me. "You break."

"How magnanimous of you." My stick struck the cue ball with authority, scattering the balls all over the table. None, however, dropped into any of the pockets. It had been a long time since I had last played this game.

Kern raised an eyebrow, then took his first shot. He slammed the ball hard into the pocket, an obvious psychological ploy that proved a tactical blunder; the shot had been lined up perfectly, with little distance separating the cue ball and his target. He could have easily made the shot without hitting it so hard, thus leaving himself in a better position to take his next shot, which he missed.

It *had* been a long time. That previous occasion, the billiard table was much more opulent—longer, wider, the felt covering immaculate, the table itself made of ornately carved solid teak, with brass fittings at each pocket. However, there seemed little doubt that the blue-blooded aristocrats playing on the Baron's magnificent table would find themselves humbled by these unwashed plebeians holding court on the Crystal's dilapidated pool tables, in a small way demonstrating how capitalism brought the aristocracy to its knees. Ability, after all, does indeed supersede breeding.

I paused over the next shot; the geometry seemed a bit skewed on this smaller playing surface. Many viable shots presented themselves, but billiards is a game of sequences, not single shots, and it was taking a bit of time for the geometry to present itself.

Kern cleared his throat loudly and impatiently. "The shots aren't gonna get any easier there, Count."

I simply nodded and took my shot. Then, another and another. And one more before yielding the table to my worthy opponent.

"I *am* being hustled." He was still smiling, a good deal of astonishment on his face.

"Just luck," I replied. In four turns, Kern had knocked in two balls while I had only the eight ball remaining. But to Kern's credit, he did an excellent job of defense, prolonging the inevitable, almost making a miraculous comeback, shooting in all but two of his balls before the contest ended with my victory.

"How 'bout another?" Kern asked. He handed Nicole her cocktail. I looked at her.

"Okay by me, Al." She nodded. "I'll just mingle."

I watched her move toward the back of the bar as Kern racked the balls. He was unable to put up as much of a fight as during our first contest; much of the rust had been scraped clean from my game, and Kern's spirit seemed slightly broken. He still had five balls on the table when the eight ball fell into the pocket, ending our match. He stepped toward the bar, but I stopped him.

"No, Kern," I said, smiling broadly, "I can buy Nicole's drink."

"You're a hell of a boyfriend, Count. And trusting too." Kern pointed toward the back of the bar where Nicole stood conversing with a rather slender fellow, his hair long, straight and jet black. He wore a black T-shirt and black denim trousers, his face twisted into a scowl as if that was its natural state.

"Without trust, there is no such thing as love."

"I couldn't agree more." Kern grabbed his beer and migrated as far from the pool tables as possible.

I had noticed that Nicole's tumbler was nearly empty, but it proved a most difficult task to find a bartender to fetch her next cocktail. The bartenders were inaccessible from behind the arch, so I moved toward the front of the bar where a gap opened next to a pair of women who sat conversing. One was a rather Rubenesque blonde, which perhaps in today's vernacular translates as overweight, but she looked a full figure of delightful womanhood, a true beauty as much as any women I have ever seen; in fact, something about her face and the way she wore her hair made me almost think she was French.

The other woman was black and also quite lovely, though in a less classical manner. Though thick and muscular of torso, her eyes sparkled, and she laughed easily. On a finger, I noticed she wore a gold ring bearing Hebrew lettering. The woman noticed me staring at her ring.

"Can I help you?" she said. Her voice bristled.

"That is Hebrew, is it not?"

"Yes, it is," she replied, smiling broadly, revealing a gap between her two front teeth. "My father's mother was Jewish," she said. "That makes me part Jewish. My mother made sure I had the chance to learn what it means to be a Jew. It was something she considered important."

"She was very perceptive."

The woman nodded. "I have a daughter, and I'm making sure to give her the chance to learn about her heritage. I'm not forcing it on her, but if she wants to learn, she'll get the opportunity."

"What a good mother!" the blonde said.

"The best," the black woman said. Both women laughed heartily. "I'm Carol, and this is Jenifer." The blonde smiled and waved.

"I am pleased to make the acquaintance of both of you."

Jenifer looked at me. "I know you. You drive for Co-op, right?"

I nodded.

"I drive for Kapitol Kab. I've seen you at the airport."

Carol downed the rest of her cocktail. As if coming from nowhere, Todd appeared to refill her glass. I took the opportunity to order Nicole's cocktail, while looking at Carol's drink quizzically. The liquid within her tumbler was the oddest shade of brown.

"Long Island Iced Tea," she said. "Todd's specialty."

Todd returned with Nicole's drink. I paid him, bade my farewells to my new acquaintances and went in search of Nicole. She still spoke with the man in black. Up close, I noticed that rings encrusted with a gaudy rainbow of semi-precious stones adorned most of his long-nailed fingers. An ankh hung from his neck. The scowl remained, looking somewhat forced. It seemed perhaps that this fellow spent much time looking at his reflection in a mirror, making sure his expression bore the proper combination of disdain and disinterest with all that surrounded him. Though it is rather impolite to make hasty judgments regarding another's character, something about this fellow struck me as contrived, as if he was trying to appear more than his years, which were scarcely out of childhood.

"You're back," Nicole said, taking the cocktail.

"Yes," I replied. "It took little effort to vanquish Kern a second time, but there was quite a crowd at the bar."

Nicole's conversation partner turned to leave, but Nicole grabbed his shoulder. He stopped. "Al, this is Charles."

I extended a hand, as the Americans do. He seemed reticent, clasping my hand lightly. His eyes sang of pure disgust, and I realized that there is nothing wrong with a hasty judgment—if it is correct.

"Nice to see you again, Charles," Nicole said, her voice warm and sincere. He said nothing, merely nodding his head as he walked away.

"A friend of yours?" I asked.

Nicole took a sip of her drink, her eyes darting back and forth between me and the direction Charles had gone. "Not really," she answered, picking lint from her sweater. "Just somebody I know."

****

When we arrived at my apartment, Nicole's passions were swollen, if not inflamed; as soon as I had pulled the futon from the wall and spread it on the floor, she was upon me, shoving me to the mattress's soft embrace, climbing atop me, nearly sending my buttons flying as she opened my shirt, running her hands over my chest. She lowered her mouth to my neck, kissing, licking and biting my flesh. Biting with a great deal of force, almost as if she wanted to break the skin open.

"Take care, my love," I said, moving my neck away from her mouth. "You would not want to break the skin and drink of *my* blood."

"Would that make me like you?" Vodka slurred her words.

I nodded.

"Maybe that's what I want. To be a hunter, preying on the life surrounding me, having you at my side. Forever."

The image of the vampire, of my wife, superimposed itself over the present for a fleeting moment as a blinding light filled my sight, the light growing as it came closer. I let myself fly toward the light. My wife was there in the light. I could feel it. That molten gold was warmth, was love.

But just as the light touched my fingertips, it flew away from me, shrinking until there was nothing but darkness in my sight, cold against my flesh and a vampire telling me that I was a creature of the darkness, forever banished from the light.

"You cannot really mean that," I said finally.

Nicole lifted her head as she straddled my hips. "Tell me you love me, Al."

I laughed. "Of course I love you. You know that."

"I wanna hear you say it. I love it when you say it."

"I love you, my dear. I love you with the ferocity of a lioness with her cubs. I love you with the sureness of the sun rising in the east each morning."

"Is it really true? Could you make me into a vampire?"

I felt my expression grow serious. The logic of lovers is quite the dangerous game. "Yes, it is true. If you were to drink of my blood, you would die, but rise again as one who must hunt in the night."

"Make me like you. I want to be like you."

"No. Absolutely not, Nicole. Ask me anything, anything at all, anything but that. I will not do that."

Her smile faded away. "You said you love me. Wouldn't you do this for someone you love? I love you, Al. I want to be your lover forever."

"My love for you is precisely why I would not do this. If I were to make you into a vampire, I would not be giving you something. I would be taking something precious away from you."

"You mean my life?" She shook her head vigorously. "My *life*? My life's a fucking joke. It's all pain and sickness, growing old and then dying. Hell, *you* get to live forever."

"Nicole, my love, what happened to me is something that never should have happened. My wife and I should have grown old together, taken care of each other when we were sick. We should have died together. Should have been buried together. Do you know what it is you ask of me?"

"But we could be lovers forever."

I cupped my hand against her cheek, but she pushed it away. "If you became a vampire, you would lose interest in me."

She grabbed my hand and pressed it against her soft breast. "No, I wouldn't, Al. No way."

I nodded sadly. "Vampires have no need for reproductive organs. Like me, you would lose your ability to have an orgasm. And like me, you would hunger for the sweet taste of human pleasure. You would seek human men, perhaps human women, in order to taste their orgasm the way I taste yours."

She appeared to pout silently; I had hoped she would not be one to pout. That has always seemed mere manipulation performed by those of an inferior level of maturity.

"What is wrong, Nicole?"

Her eyes glistened slightly, but she did not cry. "I'm sorry, Al. Vodka makes me get kinda mushy, kinda silly sometimes. It's just—I'm scared to die."

I sat up and hugged her tightly. "There is nothing at all wrong with being frightened of dying. To fear death is simply to be human. All I can say is that it is normal to fear the unknown, and that is exactly what death is, the unknowable unknown. I myself died, but remain bound to this Earth by that which courses through my veins. As to what awaits all of us, I do not know, though I can say it is not anything of which to be frightened."

She somehow did not seem to fully comprehend my words.

"But if I was a vampire, I wouldn't have to be scared anymore."

"Vampires constantly face destruction. We have to walk around in fear all the time, fearing the suspicion and hatred from the humans who inadvertently allow us to maintain our existence. Do you know what immortality really means? It means an eternity of watching others die, being doomed to an eternity of loneliness with mere interludes of friendship. Vampires so often shy from intimacy with humans because the mere wink of an eye for us is a lifetime for a mortal."

Nicole stared ahead pensively before collapsing onto the bed. "I'm sorry, Al. I'm just being silly."

I kissed her on the forehead. "It is perfectly okay for you to be silly every once in awhile. I will love you anyway."

She smiled and yawned. "God, I'm suddenly tired. Is it okay if we don't make love tonight?"

"Of course, my sweet."

She stripped off her clothing and crawled underneath the covers. And she spoke not another word before lapsing into slumber.

I reached for her, but Nicole eased herself to the far side of the bed, a chasm separating us, cold as a grave.

Chapter 16

VAMPIRE CABBIES IN LOVE

L*emme guess. Sounds like a one-way ticket to dump city. So the bitch dumped you for the guy in the bar?*

Sir! By the torments of Hades, you will not speak of Nicole in such a manner. And you will cease these interruptions. They are most impolite—and please do not jump ahead of the story. If you were to call me a fool, you would be absolutely correct. I was a fool, fooled by love, my vision clouded by the giddiness of the emotions of the immature.

Nicole quickly became incommunicado. Looking forward to our usual Tuesday tryst, disappointment greeted me as Dexter told me that she had called in sick. A half-dozen messages left on her answering machine brought no reply. Saturday night—our night—came and went, with me stalking State Street alone, half-heartedly searching for Madison's other vampire, but it was not unlike perusing a haystack for a mere needle.

By the next week, the peonies began to bloom fully, making it easy to forget about how drab the city had been just weeks before, when the streets were covered with the slush of the melting snows. Still, slush-covered asphalt was all that filled my inner sight, so heavy was my heart.

Finally, a phone call to Nicole's house brought an answer. It was Maggie. "I'm not here," a muffled voice said from the background.

"She's not here, Al," Maggie said after a brief pause.

"Tell her I am sorry to hear that." With not another word, I dropped the handset onto its cradle, shaking my head, laughing bitterly at myself.

You know, after a thousand years, it is not difficult to be philosophical about those things that happen to us in our intercourse with others. I tried to focus on the sheer bliss of the previous month, but the task proved difficult, so I attempted to seek solace in the fact that good or bad, at least she had made me feel something.

The next night, parked at the Concourse taxi stand, Maggie joined me in my cab. I quickly turned off the dome light, which makes my flesh look quite unwholesome, then put away *Candide* and prepared to entertain my guest.

"Sorry about the other night," Maggie began immediately. "I lied to you. Nicole was right there when you called. You deserve better than having me lie to you. If she doesn't want to see you anymore, she should have the decency to tell you herself."

"Apparently, we cannot always expect people to behave with the maturity their age might indicate is the accepted norm." Momentarily, Maggie appeared a bit bewildered at my syntax.

"Whatever. Anyway, for whatever it's worth, I told her I'm not lying for her anymore."

"Your sentiment is greatly appreciated. But I would like to at least know, why is she behaving in such a manner?"

Maggie pulled at the straps of her tank top and ran a hand agitatedly through her thick red hair, an obvious gesture of discomfort over the illumination of some unsavory information. "Look, I tried to tell you she's not really in a good way." My guest paused a moment, her gaze dropping downward. "She's seeing someone else."

My spine tingled with momentary anger, then I felt amused at the sensation. Jealousy? How absurd.

And this intellectualism of my feelings was dishonest. Knowing that Nicole was no one's property could not prevent me from imagining the torments I might inflect upon he who had stolen her from me.

"It's a guy she used to go out with," Maggie said, answering my silence. "She hadn't seen the guy since he dumped her. But when she ran into him recently, she realized she still felt something for him."

"Slender fellow? Black hair? Dresses in black?"

"Yeah, that's the guy. His name's Charles." Maggie reached over and lightly touched my shoulder. "I'm really sorry, Al."

I turned, and her hand fell from my shoulder. "Please, Maggie. Do not worry about me. I will be okay."

Maggie paused for a second, biting her lip. "I tried to tell her the way she was handling this was bullshit. Now, she's not talking to me either."

"Do not worry," I replied, smiling bravely. "You have been friends since childhood. This will all blow over. Her anger will pass."

Maggie nodded pensively. "Yeah, I know, but I miss her, Al. And I'm worried about her, but she won't let me help her. That's why I'm here. I just don't know what to do. Can you help her?"

My laughter filled the cab, my reaction stronger than desired.

Maggie paused, crossing her arms in front of her. "Look, Al, I know you're feeling hurt, but she didn't mean for it to happen like this. She's not really herself right now."

"If not herself, then who?"

A horse-drawn carriage passed the cab. Inside, a young couple snuggled close together. Maggie glanced at the pair, then returned her gaze back to me. "Love is illusion, isn't it?" she asked rhetorically, as if she spoke not to me or anyone in particular.

We watched silently for a moment as the carriage disappeared into the night, the hoofbeats fading into inaudibility. "Look, Al, you can't just all of a sudden not care about her, can you? No matter what she does?"

"No, Maggie," I replied. "I do care, but it seems quite apparent that she does not want me in her life. She does not desire my help and would view such overtures as an unwelcome intrusion." Indeed. With a killer vampire running amok, why should the petty problems of a confused child be worthy of my trouble?

Maggie's reply seemed non-sequitur. "Did you know Maggie's father killed himself?"

My back straightened. "She most certainly did not tell me that. She merely told me that he was dead, but did not tell me how he had died."

"Nicole was fourteen. She came home from school one day and found him. He'd blown his head clean off his shoulders. The paramedics had to pry his fingers off the shotgun."

"How horrible!"

"She's never been the same since that day. Most of the time, she's fine, but every once in a while, she'll go through a suicidal episode. Something triggers it, and all of a sudden, she becomes really self-destructive, if not suicidal. Over the years, she's slit her wrists, taken pills, tried to jump into the Wisconsin River. I stopped her that time."

"Suicide can be like a contagious disease sometimes," I said. "When life is considered so precious, it is a shock to see someone voluntarily snuff it out."

"I think Truck's murder did it this time."

Of course. Her erratic behavior did indeed coincide with his death, and such a senseless death! These mortals find death disturbing enough as it is, but when it is as senseless as that, where there is no reason and not even an identifiable killer, they become paralyzed.

"And that fucker Charles—" The words flew excitedly from her mouth. "He's bad news, Al. Bad news. He's into Satan worship, and I think he's getting Nicole into it too. I'm worried. I think something real bad is going to happen. She said he offered her immortality. Do you have any idea what the fuck that means?"

Infernal words echoed inside me. *Make me like you. I want to be like you. I don't want to die. I want to live forever.*

Alarms rang. Actions and motives, all crystal clear. Her words had said she was afraid to die; her silence had said that if I would not give her what she wanted, she would find someone who would. Surely, Nicole would not be so foolish to be taken in by a charlatan like Charles, but as Maggie was relating, she was not entirely herself.

A cultivated, icy calm coated my exterior despite what I was feeling inside. "I cannot make any promises, but I think I would be willing to have a talk with this Charles."

"The hell with talking, Al. Kick his skinny little ass."

"Oh, I have something far better in mind."

****

Taking Maggie at face value would have been foolish. It did seem best to seek answers from Nicole herself.

Passing the Crystal Corner in my cab, Nicole and Charles were clearly visible through the glass front door of the bar, thus quickly ending my search. I parked my cab, entered the bar and walked to her side. Nicole said not a word as she turned and faced me, her expression quite blasé. Shortly, she turned her attention back to the new object of her affection. Charles turned not his head, his expression still that forced combination of boredom and scorn, his thin lips pressed tightly together.

"We do have to talk, Nicole," I said quietly. No reply. I stood my ground, noticing Todd hovering nearby, keeping a close watch. Our eyes met for a short moment. He gave me a sympathetic shrug, then departed to fill a patron's drink order.

"Nicole, we *do* have to talk. Nicole—"

She turned, fire in her eyes. Charles continued to stare straight ahead. "Talk? There's not a damn thing to talk about." Nicole again turned her back to me, but I was not leaving without satisfaction.

"Nicole," I said after a few silent moments, "it is very important that we talk."

"Fine!" She jumped off her stool. "You wanna talk? Talk then. Talk 'til you're fucking blue in the face."

"Outside."

She glanced at Charles. He nodded, the movement nearly imperceptible.

"What the fuck do you want from me, Al?" Nicole asked as the door slid shut behind us. She rubbed her arms; covered merely by a long-sleeved T-shirt, Nicole shivered against the chill of this mid-spring night, having left her jacket draped over her bar stool. Her nipples asserted themselves against the fabric, and I caught myself staring at them, a stinging pang of longing searing deep into my being.

"You here to talk or stare?"

Her remark lay unacknowledged. "Nicole, I just want to say, you are free to do whatever you want—"

"Damn right!" Her eyes burned white hot. Of her many moods and her various modes of anger, none seemed so intense. "You don't own me."

"I never said I did." My words rolled softly over my tongue. This was not intended to be an argument. "I would have appreciated a little more consideration—"

"After everything I gave you? After everything you took?" She slapped the side of her neck for emphasis. "What else do you want?"

"Nothing, Nicole, nothing." By the earth of my homeland, there would be no provoking me, for that certainly had nothing to do with my motivations at this point. "I merely am concerned. Maggie sought me out. We had a conversation."

"Ha!" Her dry laughter echoed against the brick wall next to the door. Two men across the street turned and stared at us. "Why don't you ask *her* out and leave me the fuck alone. That stupid bitch thinks you're the best thing since sliced bread."

"You should not be talking such about your friend. She is concerned about you."

"Let her mind her own damn business." Nicole made a move for the door. I grabbed her arm. She twisted away and slapped my forearm hard. "Don't fucking touch me!"

"You said you were willing to listen to what I had to say." My tone shifted from soft to commanding. "I will talk, and you will listen. If you choose to burn in a hell of your own doing, so be it. I will not stop you, but do not say I did not point it out as the hell that it is. Maggie is a good friend, and she is worried about you. She told me how your father—"

"Don't talk to me about my father, you goddamned bloodsucking freak!" Nicole slapped me hard in the face. A hint of something putrid tickled my nostrils. I grabbed her wrist and shoved the sleeve up to her elbow, revealing the jagged outline of a pentagram, the tattoo so fresh that it bubbled with plasma and pus, the flesh around it red and puffy.

The design bore not the style nor artistry of a tattoo done by a professional. The pentagram was obviously homemade, and each of the five points was punctuated by circles of reddened and blackened flesh, the crusting skin oozing more pus.

"He is a danger, a menace." My voice was a near-shriek. "Maggie is right about him. You should listen to your friend. Please, Nicole, please. You must end this insanity. This fellow will be your ruin."

"You had your fucking chance, Al. I wanted something, and you wouldn't give it to me. Charles can. And will. And he really loves me. And he can make love to me like a real man, unlike some people I know."

Laughter drew my attention. A pair of pool players—the tall, muscular, rather masculine woman with the professional-caliber game and the immense fellow with the long beard, cowboy hat and rattlesnake-skin case for his pool cue—tittered their way toward the door. My grip loosened around Nicole's wrist. She calmly let her arm fall to her side, pushed down her sleeve and returned to Charles.

From outside, I watched her kiss him hard on the lips with great ardor. Upon breaking from her embrace, Charles turned and looked at me through the glass door. For the first time, he smiled.

****

There can be little doubt that jealousy provided at least a modicum of motivation for my following course of action, even if this Charles fellow was clearly a menace and had to be stopped. However, that did not mean I could not enjoy myself in the process.

Finding and stalking Charles proved to be of little difficulty; for such a would-be creature-of-the-shadows, he maintained a reasonably high profile, his presence ubiquitous all over Madison's near east side, easily recognizable, always wearing the same black shirt and trousers. Did he not possess any other garments?

On a night when Nicole worked, I decided to take action, following him home from the Crystal Corner to his apartment on Johnson Street above Mildred's Sandwich Shop, a small restaurant quite popular with my fellow drivers.

From across the street, I watched electric lights snap on one by one, then off one by one as candlelight illuminated his apartment. Through the open window, his head and shoulders were visible in the flickering amber light as he sat, his chanting audible to my ears.

Listening to whatever psuedo-occult gibberish he was chanting, I dematerialized, then rematerialized inside his apartment, next to a crude altar fashioned from a wooden crate and strips of unvarnished pine before which Charles knelt. Cloying incense hung thickly in the air, unsuccessfully masking the stench of pestilence.

Charles gasped loudly. He lunged for a bloody dagger that lay on the altar next to a gutted hamster and jumped to his feet. Holding the dagger with both hands, he stepped back a couple paces. "Stay back, Al," he said, his voice wavering.

"Shocked to have actually succeeded in summoning forth a demon, Charles?" I grinned broadly at him and took a step forward. Despite my anger, I fought to maintain a most sardonic tone of voice.

He took another step back, then stopped, his face twisting with irritation. "She's mine. You can't have her." He edged toward me, anger dissolving his fear, giving him resolve.

"Pathetic fool," I replied. "Nicole is her own person, not for you, I or anyone to possess."

Charles lunged at me. I turned away from his thrust, grabbed his wrist and squeezed until his grip loosened. The dagger slid easily through his fingers. I shoved him until he was pinned against the wall, then took a pensive moment to study the dagger. It was lovely—high-carbon steel with a pewter hilt of three intertwining vipers. And sharp, too. With a short thrust along the top of his arm, a line of blood came to the surface. I licked the blood off his quivering flesh, then flung the knife at the poster of Aleister Crowley that hung on the opposite wall beneath a jagged pentagram of dried blood. The knife struck the number 666 in the middle of the magi's forehead. Laughter escaped my lips as a recollection of meeting Crowley crossed my mind. The fellow, so revered by bewildered youths like Charles, had been little better than a snake-oil-selling flimflam man.

"Beer and whiskey," I said, releasing him, spitting the blood onto the carpeted floor, amidst the collection of dried stains and splotches. "You had best be careful, Charles. Summoning demons while intoxicated is a dangerous endeavor. If they appear, it is only because they know they can take advantage of your altered state." I backed away from him and took a seat in the wing chair next to the altar. A sharp kick to the apparatus scattered plywood splinters all over the room.

"What the hell do you want?" He glared at me, his anger an expression of false bravado.

"I am merely here to tell you to stay away from Nicole."

"It's a free country. She wants to be with me, that's none of your business. Read my fucking lips. She wants me, not you."

"Read *my* lips and heed what I tell you."

"Funny, she never told me you were the jealous type."

"You were misinformed." I smiled inwardly; he talked so bravely while backing himself against the wall.

"Actually, she said you were kind of a wuss."

"Again, Charles, there is a great deal of difference between reality and another person's perception. Be that as it may, you will stay away from

Nicole."

His bravado exploded. "Hey, get off my fucking hoof!" Charles sprinted toward the poster of Aleister Crowley on the other side of the room, an arm reaching upward toward the dagger.

Great hoofed one indeed! Enough of this pathetic, Satan-embracing child! I leaped to my feet, dematerialized, then instantly rematerialized in his path, too abruptly for him to stop. He collided with me full force and would have tumbled to the floor had I not grabbed his shoulders. Quickly, I spun him around, wrapped a hand around his throat and slammed him against the wall.

Pressing hard against his larynx, I lifted him in the air until the top of his head touched the knife blade. When I pushed upward against his chin, he winced as the knife slit open his scalp, then his eyes opened wide as his dark hair soaked up the blood from the wound, quickly reaching saturation. A single thread of crimson slowly dribbled down his forehead.

My nostrils opened, letting the aroma of the blood waft inside. My mouth opened. Fangs dropped from their hiding place, saliva dripping from their sharp tips.

I licked the blood from his face in long, slow strokes, then pulled my face away so he could look at me, mouth open, fangs dripping with his blood, but hungry for more, eyes open wide, glazed and wild with animalistic passion.

"*Child*! You will listen to me. It is of no concern to me what you do, but I will not allow your poison to infect Nicole. Do not give me cause to have to visit you again."

For a moment, I held him there, staring into his face, relishing his utter terror. The odor of fresh urine wafted into my nostrils, indicating that the message had finally been fully grasped, thus allowing me to dematerialize, knowing he would crash to the floor once my grip had ceased.

****

There is a problem with such petty, negative emotions like jealousy. One can seek wickedness as a diversion, but the effect does not last. Thus, after only momentary satisfaction, it seemed time to resume my purpose and concentrate on making money.

It was time to go fishing.

Kern had said playing the airport is like fishing; in order to catch the big fish, one must be patient. Indeed. The following Tuesday, I sat at the airport, last of six cabs, knowing three planes would land within the next twenty minutes. Perhaps the big fish would be a lucrative fare going to the far west side, or perhaps the Cab Gods might be so kind as to provide a four-way split, the biggest of the big fish.

Nicole pulled behind me. She got out and marched to my taxi, raw anger registering quite clearly on her face.

"Who the fuck do you think you are?" she shouted, arms flailing in front of her.

"I beg your pardon?" I replied, as calmly and blandly as possible.

"Don't give me that Old World shit! You know damn well what I'm talking about. You went and talked to Charles, didn't you?"

"Yes."

"Well, he's gone. He split town and didn't even say good bye." She stood arms akimbo, chest heaving. I gave no reply. Tense silence hung in the warm night air for a few long moments. "What right did you have to interfere? What was it? Jealous? Jealous that I found a real man, a man who could actually get it up?"

She launched her words like slaps to my face. They stung, but I would not react, would not let myself yield to the very human emotions she obviously was trying to provoke.

"People like Charles are dangerous," I said finally. "I cannot even begin to tell you how many times I have seen people—people like yourself— harmed by people like Charles who so foolishly flirt with dark forces they do not understand. Regardless of what has happened between us, I still care, and that is why I acted as I did."

"Fuck you!" She ran to her cab and fled the cab stand, tires screeching loudly.

Following her departure, I loaded a four-way. It was unfortunate that she had left; Kern pulled up behind me minutes after her departure, and he too loaded a four-way.

Does this sound callous? Yes, I suppose it does, but what else was a vampire cabbie to do? What else would there be for anyone to do? Even if our relationship was over, I did still care. For anyone in a situation like that, the best, the only course of action would be just to continue to exist and do the best that they can.

I just hoped she could do the same.

****

"Sixty-six," Dexter's voice said. "Sixty-six, are you out there?"

I had just unloaded the last passenger from my split-load and was driving back from the far west side. All the calls were downtown, but there was no reason to despair. That four-way had been good for $20 in side money, in addition to what was on the meter.

"Nicole," Dexter said, "are you out there?"

A harsh feeling of dread washed over me. Cab 66. No coincidence that she drove that vehicle; well, perhaps a slight one, for it was one of the newest cabs in the fleet. But why was she not responding to the dispatcher's hail? Perhaps because she was angry. Perhaps, she had decided to go calm down someplace and had forgotten to ask for a break.

"Nicole. Sixty-six." Dexter's voice began to sound annoyed after about ten minutes spent trying to raise her. "Six-six. If you do not respond within sixty seconds, I'm gonna have the cops out looking for you."

"Attention all units," Dexter said finally. "If anybody sees cab sixty-six, please let me know. And a reminder. After dark, I like to keep track of all units, so if you get out of your cab for more than a few minutes, please let me know."

An unauthorized break. Surely that was all it was.

Suddenly, a loud rattling, grinding hum filled my ears. Dread washed over my entire being, a consuming, overwhelming dread that made it difficult to maintain the cab's position between the white lines. Promptly, I turned onto an access road leading to a yet-to-be constructed industrial park, then hit the 10-7 button, barely waiting for Dexter to respond before getting out of the cab. The world spun before me, the subsequent vertigo making it difficult to even stand. Rather than fight, I surrendered, slowly rotating 360 degrees before discovering that the source came from the northwest.

My eyes closed. The hum grew louder and more distinct, clearly revealing itself to be tires revolving against a gravel pavement. An image congealed before my eyes—darkness surrendering ever so slightly to dim light.

No, not dim light, but bright beams—twin beams—simply overwhelmed by the vastness of the oncoming darkness. Yes, oncoming darkness, black night and—

—And swirling ribbons of road, not approaching, but being approached, at a steadily increasing velocity.

The road disappeared, replaced by a jumble of images: a steel bridge above a black river, its currents and eddies visible in the bright moonlight; the 200-foot sheer cliff marking the far shore; and a patch of sandy gravel just before the bridge, leading to an abruptly dropping precipice.

My legs wobbled. I let myself drop to the soft, dewy grass, sat cross-legged, closed my eyes and brought the image of Nicole's face to the forefront of this dark consciousness, knowing that I had to help her, that I had to go to her side to stop her from doing what I feared she was about to do.

How far away could she be? These images were not in Madison, but how far? Ten miles? Twenty? Thirty?

The humming grew louder. Inhale. Exhale. Inhale. Exhale. I commanded myself to relax, to not think about the danger of this task. Past experience proved one mile to be within the realm of possibility. Therefore, five miles could be possible. But what were the limits? How long could my concentration be maintained? If concentration lapsed, would my very cells lose their cohesion and be spread as if blown by the four winds of Hades?

No thought, no doubt. I owed it to Nicole. To Anya. To all mortals who had shared their blood willingly, and unwillingly.

Inhale, exhale. Focus on the target, let the feelings—Nicole's feelings—direct me to their source.

I opened my eyes and watched my vision dissolve. The darkness swirled, the street lights and traffic lights spread and dripped all over the canvas of my sight before disappearing completely.

The weight of reality seemed lighter; the substance of my own clothing grew less significant until there seemed to be no more feeling against my skin, no itch of fabric, no prickle of humidity, no tickle of cool breeze.

Bridge, river, cliff, shore, ledge. The images beckoned, and I followed, using them as a beacon, imagining the jumble as bright, glowing pieces, forming a brilliant light, flashing on and off, the hum modulating with the light's flashing rhythm. Fly toward the light!

The light dimmed ever so slightly. The flashing slowed, the humming quieted.

The beacon seemed to move further away. How could that be? Impossible. Moving toward it, it seemed to move further away. Was it not a fixed spot?

My grip was loosening. I weakened, simply unable to hold much more. My consciousness had reached the apex of its capabilities and was coming crashing down as my entire being was indeed losing its cohesion.

Nicole? My mind struggled to even remember her name, to even remember what it was that was being attempted. To remember why. Struggling ceased. My individuality yielded to the all-encompassing air. No longer me. Just air. Just everything. Just euphoria.

A voice screamed.

Al!

Al. Keep it together. Dammit, you're so close.

Keep

It

Together

Blinding light seared, flashing so rapidly as to be constantly light and dark. The hum grew louder and louder until it appeared as grains in front of my eyes, forming a tapestry, painting a pointillist portrait of forest, a bridge and sheer ledges above a rushing river. And twin beams of light.

Suddenly, the grinding filled my ears with sound. A yellow cab bore down upon me. Brakes squealed, and the cab came to a shaking stop, the bumper coming to rest mere inches from my shins.

Nicole jumped out of the cab and slammed the door shut with all the force she could muster. Kicking bits of gravel, she bounded toward me and slapped me hard across the face.

"What the fuck are you doing?" she shrieked.

I let out a sigh of relief. "Just what I felt necessary." That was my only reply; no other words seemed necessary.

Nicole slapped me again, then turned back toward the cab.

"Could you at least give me a ride back to town?"

She spun toward me. Even in the moonlight, her face was luridly red. "Fly back. You seemed to get here with little trouble."

"Please, Nicole. This trip has pushed me to the absolute limits of my ability. I can scarcely stand, let alone attempt to return."

She threw her arms up in the air and returned to her cab. The gesture seemed to indicate a resigned willingness to provide me transportation back to civilization.

No words were exchanged during the return trip. Nicole seemed too angry to speak, and I simply was content to let her be angry, to let her be angry at me. At least that way she would be safe from herself for the time being. Anger, though a powerful emotion, is relatively sane compared to the tangle of confused and contradictory emotions that had led her to this place.

"Well," she spat when we had returned to my cab, "your stupid debt of honor is paid, so you can leave me the fuck alone."

"I will comply with your wishes." With that, I departed, fully satisfied to let her think whatever she wanted, whatever might help keep her alive, knowing full well that the debt had not been paid. Yes, I had saved her life, but at the same time, she had saved mine.

****

Two nights later, I found a sealed envelope outside my apartment door. It was a letter from Nicole.

> Dear Al:
>
> First, I just have to say, I'm sorry about how I treated you. You really are a special person, or whatever, and you deserved better than the kind of shit I gave you.
>
> Second, I really have to say thanks. I've cooled off a bit, and I now realize that you saved my life, even if I didn't want it saved. I'm sorry, but you just have to understand that I'm really kind of fucked in the head, and sometimes I do things to hurt myself. Unfortunately, sometimes good people like you and

Maggie get caught in the crossfire.

I'm leaving town for awhile. I just need to get my head together. I have an aunt who lives in Vermont. It's pretty boring at her place, but I think I've had a little too much excitement for awhile.

This is goodbye for now, but hey, who knows about the future? For what it's worth, I'll treasure the good times we had. I love you and won't ever forget you.

Love,

Nicole

I gently replaced the letter within the envelope and tucked it into the back pocket of my blue denim trousers, then went to work because it was simply the thing to do. Bills had to be paid, money had to be saved, and, as the say, that was that. Also a killer vampire had to be found; this had not been forgotten, and obviously, a cab certainly seemed a useful tool in the search.

Co-op cabbies: remember, we're professionals with a job to do.

That is what Dexter had announced over the radio the night of Truck's funeral. And it was those words that echoed inside my head after the completion of this affair. Despite all that had happened, despite my pain, there was a mission and a goal. There was indeed a job to do.

However, the job was becoming less pleasant as the weather warmed. Despite it only being mid-May, this night was hot and muggy, one of those nights where it actually feels more oppressive after the sun sets, even for one such as myself. Extreme temperatures do not cause us much discomfort, though heat is somewhat less comfortable than cold. But the discomfort was greater in my weakened state, the effects of the long-distance teleport from two nights earlier still felt. Still, the shift would not have been altogether unpleasant had I not been chasing my tail, circling block after block, racing for calls only to lose to another driver. My mood, already sour, only worsened as the night wore on, and the disposition of my passengers certainly did little to make life more pleasant. These things shall pass, yes, but there was no comfort in philosophy, not in the short term and certainly not on this particular night.

Finally, a call at the University Inn. Mine, but a traffic light kept me waiting, as thick, dripping haze froze the light forever red. The opposite light finally turned yellow, but a group of college students decided to make a run for it. They ambled ahead, slowed as if expended, then lumbered the rest of the way against the green. I turned the air conditioning up a notch, wanting my next passengers to be comfortable.

As soon as I arrived at the motel, a trio of businessmen jogged to the cab and hastily climbed in.

"Hello," I said. "Where can I take you tonight?"

"Spectators," one said.

A soft groan passed my lips. Why could they not walk a mere quarter mile? "Right away, sirs," I said with a smile, hearing an annoying falsetto remind me, "All calls are good calls."

"Jee-suz Chrawst!" one said. "How'd it get this danged hot. I thought I'd left the heat back in South Carolina."

"It was that front that came in, sir," I replied. "It pushed away the nice weather we had been having. They say it will be hot and humid for the next few days."

"Well, that's just fucking great," the passenger said, his friends silent. "I didn't come here for the heat."

"No, you came here for the poontang," another passenger said.

Mercy made the ride short.

"That'll be one-seventy-five."

"Pay the man," the passenger on the far left said, getting out of the cab. The man in the middle climbed out and turned to the third man who remained rooted to his seat.

"Aren't you coming?"

"Naw. Think I'll just stay in this nice, cool cab."

"C'mon, Jasper."

"I do have to get on with the rest of my evening, sir," I gently added.

"Here," Jasper said gruffly, as he finally slid out of the cab. "Keep the change." The man slammed the door. A single crumpled, sweaty dollar bill and a dollar-off coupon lay in my palm.

"Lake and U," Dexter's voice crackled.

I quickly punched the bid button, shifted into gear and raced toward the only call on the board.

"It's yours, Count," Dexter informed moments later. "U-Ride voucher twenty-five. Mad Hatters for three to Langdon. Pick up on Lake Street at the U-Square pee-oh."

Almost five minutes after arriving at the pick-up point, seconds before a two-dollar no-load fee could have been charged to the university, three men, one tall and slender, another short and stocky, the third scrawny and of medium height, along with a petite Asian woman, turned the corner and strode toward the cab. The short, stocky one opened the front door on the passenger side.

"U-Ride?" he asked.

"Yes. You are going to Langdon Street?"

"That's us." The short, stocky man slid into the front seat. The two other men climbed in the back. The woman sat between them.

"There are four of you."

"You got a problem with that?" said a voice from the back.

"It violates the rules. Only parties of three or less may call for a U-Ride."

"Hey, be a dude," said the guy in front. "Just pretend there's three."

"I am sorry. I do not make up the rules. When you call for a U-Ride, you can at most be a party of three. However, if one or more wants to stay behind and call again, we can send another cab quickly."

Silence. I glanced furtively at them, sensing something strange, but was not quite able to grasp it. The tall, slender passenger opened his door, yanked the woman's arm, pulled her across his lap and flung her from the cab.

"I guess we're three now," the gentleman behind me said.

"Oh, man," said the student in front. "What'd you do that for?"

"Hey, we'll find another. There's plenty more where that came from."

I paused and glanced toward the woman, watching her crawl on the sidewalk, then slowly rise to her feet. She took a step, stumbled, steadied then stared at the cab. Her lips moved, but only the sounds of the remaining passengers were audible—their laughter, soon obscured by the sound of three hearts beating, pumping blood through three bodies, only to be covered by the loud, steady thump, thump of my own pounding heart.

"Enough!" I shouted. "I have had enough. You will all get out of my cab. Right now! This ride is over."

"Hey, man," the guy in front said. "We're just kidding around. What's the matter? Can't take a joke?"

"This is U-Ride," said the fellow behind me. "You're just a fucking cab driver. You have to take us."

I jumped out, quickly circled the cab, opening all the doors. "Out! Right now! All of you. Get out or I will call the police."

One by one, the passengers climbed out of the cab, each slamming their doors loudly. Two walked away. The tall slender one remained by the cab and glared at me. "That was stupid," he said, dropping his voice a couple of octaves. "You might just regret something like this."

They walked slowly to the corner where they stood staring at me, their pale flesh glowing brightly in the moonlight. Suspicion filled me. Did their flesh perhaps glow too brightly? Why would their flesh be so pale when these Americans prefer to sear their skin in the sun until cooked a golden brown?

The woman fell again, scrabbling on hands and knees. Damn these fellows! This woman needed help, and that was my top priority. Paying the students no further mind, I opened the front door and helped her inside. "Come. We must get out of here. I will take you wherever you want to go." I punched the accelerator and squealed the tires, driving without destination, simply trying to put as much distance possible between the cab and the three students. I did not even turn on the meter.

After a few blocks, I slowed to a stop. "Is there someplace I can take you?"

"Huh?" she said quietly. The woman stared straight ahead. I flared my nostrils and let her aroma wash over me: sweat, a trace of soap, that trendy perfume popular with the sorority girls that smells like insect repellent. And something else, something very faint, so faint only a vampire would notice. Sweet, like lilies, but with a slight bitterness. Something I had not smelled in a long time.

"Datura," I said aloud. Known as jimson weed in North America and found in various forms all over the world. *And sometimes used during unsavory religious rituals.*

I flicked on the dome light and studied my passenger. Her skin was pale, she was perspiring, and her breathing was labored. Turning the light off and on revealed the woman's pupils to be dilated. The dosage was substantial and fairly concentrated. She needed prompt medical attention. Fortunately, the Madison General Hospital emergency room was very close.

"Stop the cab," the woman said. "I'm gonna be sick."

I stopped, and the woman jumped out just in time.

"Oh, god," she said, crying, holding her stomach. "I don't feel so good. Can you get me to a hospital?"

"Right away, ma'am."

****

On the way home from the office following shift's end, the faintest hint of flickering light caught my attention. In the rear view mirror, a quarter-mile behind, a pair of headlights pulled from the curb.

The car followed my turn onto East Washington, then followed my zig-zag to John Nolan Drive. Though the speed limit was 35, I let up on the accelerator and slowed to 25. The other car maintained its quarter-mile following distance.

A right turn, another right, then an immediate left. After the third turn, I glanced at the rear view mirror.

Twin white dots glowed in the mirror.

Chapter 17
RETRIBUTION

Right turn, left turn, left turn, right turn. With each respective turn, the headlights reappeared in the rear-view mirror, the distance constant, yet discreet.

My mind quickly sifted through recollections and possibilities as my foot pressed against the gas pedal, maintaining a velocity of exactly five miles-per-hour below the speed limit.

Merely a few hours ago, three men had threatened me when it was they who had been in violation of the rules; their companion had been dosed with datura, a somewhat exotic drug. While they themselves possessed the arrogance of many affluent college students, their threats had seemed real; though the opportunity had not been there for full scrutiny, their appearance did seem strange—they were pale! Yes, quite pale when compared with all these students, who upon returning from their Florida vacations at the conclusion of spring break bore bronzed skin, their flesh intentionally charred by the sub-tropical sun—

—*This is U-Ride. You have to take us. You're just a fucking cab driver.*

Truck had been murdered by something not human, and he had had a similar encounter with a college student who belligerently refused to obey U-Ride regulations. Hypothesis: Truck had been murdered by vampires because he had offended their sense of entitlement, and now the same vampires wanted their vengeance over me for exactly the same reason.

It was time to test this hypothesis. I accelerated, parked at the far end of the block, willed myself into discorporation and rematerialized, straddling a high branch of a densely leafed oak tree across the street.

It was time to be a hunter once again.

The white sedan squealed to a stop alongside my Toyota. A trio of young men got out, leaving the motor running, serenading the block with the engine's soft, muscular purr. One fellow was tall and lithe, another scrawny, the third a bit stout.

No doubt remained; they were indeed the same trio as before.

This is U-Ride. You have to take us. You're just a fucking cab driver.

One reached for the driver's door, only to find it locked, only to find the car empty. He kicked a tire, then threw a single punch at the driver's side window. A muffled crash broke through the silence of night.

The other two leaped atop the car, one on the trunk, the other on the hood, both jumping up and down, causing my poor Toyota to rock violently. The first fellow ran to the passenger side, threw two quick punches at the quaking vehicle. Two more crashes echoed up and down the block.

The gentleman jumping on the hood leaped high in the air and landed on the edge, causing the fellow on the trunk to fly upward. As the fellow in the rear descended, he thrust his leg out to smash the back window, then leaped to the pavement.

The gentleman on the hood spun upward, jumped hard onto the center of the hood, then spun again, kicking hard at the windshield, which shattered like ice. With a backflip, he joined his comrades who surveyed the damage, their laughter an obvious indicator that they had enjoyed this vandalism and were impressed with their ability to cause this much destruction.

They made no attempt to scan the nearby terrain for any sign of their apparently-human prey, not even making use of their enhanced senses. Doubled over with laughter, the trio returned to their car and disappeared into the night. After a bit, I dropped from the tree to survey the damage done to my trusty steed.

"I am so very sorry, my sweet mount," I said, stroking the steel skin of my Toyota's roof, momentarily disappointed that such a reliable car had to be sacrificed to gather intelligence about these brigands.

But much evidence presented itself. The windows were completely shattered. The back window bore a massive, jagged hole in the center, spiderweb cracks covering those chunks of glass that remained around the edges.

As for the windshield, astonishingly, it was simply no more. Jagged shards of glass lay all over the front and back seats, forming only a slightly broken pattern where they lay, indicating a clean break as the thick wind-shield yielded to a radiated tremor of force that sliced the glass from the inside out. I picked up a triangular piece of glass. The edges were smooth, very sharp and nearly straight.

Anger suddenly boiled inside me. If they had gotten this much enjoy-ment out of wrecking my car, how much glee did they feel when they murdered Truck? Surely they had fed off his fear as much as they had his blood. Had I been human, they would have killed me with the same rel-ish. With the same relish as when they had murdered their other victims.

But *who* were they?

And where had they gotten datura with which to dose that woman?

And what had they planned to do to her?

More recollections washed over me. The sorority girl who had disap-peared. The trio Nicole and Maggie had identified as fraternity brothers, who had slapped the woman at the Cardinal Bar and dumped a pitcher of beer over her head.

"I will see that you receive the best of care," I said to my car, as I attempted to brush the glass from the driver's seat. Under close inspec-tion, some of the shards were dappled with droplets of blood. The trio had not seemed to care; more blood would always be readily available, always there for the taking.

Having cleared the driver's seat, I drove off, a hidden piece of glass stabbing my thigh. I did not care about spilling a little of my blood either, for there would be more for *my* taking.

A sharp breeze ripped through my car as I drove homeward. As expected, they had revealed themselves, and it would be a simple matter of sifting through the night's call slips to find their address. Without that information, it was best to wait on the oncoming morrow to commence the hunt, after seeing to repairs of my trusty Toyota. For the time being, there was nothing to do but tolerate the rushing air, this wind a beast of a thousand teeth, a thousand pairs of unsheathed fangs, a thousand hungry, merciless—

—vampires!

Not merely vampires, but sadistic, evil little trolls who also happened to be vampires, possessing all that raw power while totally lacking any sense of ethics and morals, let alone respect for the mortals who so kindly provide sustenance. And completely lacking responsibility toward their fellow vampires.

Much to my disgust, I could empathize, knowing full well what it was like to feel Earthbound and soulless, with all faith ripped away.

Through the smashed windshield, the moon glowed brightly above Lake Monona, plump, pregnant, almost full.

The moon would be full tomorrow night. And had not the woman from Dawn Stevens's sorority said that Sigma Chi throws a party the weekend of each full moon?

More coincidences.

Had not Dawn Stevens disappeared shortly after attending a Sigma Chi full-moon party? What was the address of that fraternity? Whatever the address, intuition said it would be the same as that on my call slip.

A hypothesis is like a bridge. It begins with a theory and a conclusion, but needs evidence to connect the two extremities. Indeed, a visit to the waybill office would be the next step, and once receiving confirmation of certain theories, I would attend that Sigma Chi party, even though no one had seen fit to send me an invitation.

As they say, this party was a must-go.

****

When the telephone rang at six the next evening, I had already arisen, was dressed and ready to report to work, two hours early. In fact, I had only just returned from the body shop where they had assured me that my Toyota would be "good as new" by Tuesday.

It was Maggie calling from the cab company, wanting me to come in early. She said they had a gross preponderance of time calls and needed some extra help. She also said she had received a cordial but somewhat distant postcard from Nicole. Apparently, her friend was bored, but doing satisfactorily.

Little did she know that their need for drivers was consistent with my plans. I told her my vehicle was being repaired and asked her to send me a cab as quickly as possible.

****

By the time I had arrived at the cab office, there were twenty calls on the board, all downtown, thus allowing no opportunity to visit the waybill office, leaving no alternative but to get my cab ready for the night's shift. When just about to leave the lot, Maggie came running out to my cab.

"Hey, Al! Wait!"

"What is it, Maggie?"

"You're in luck. We need you to run to Janesville, pick up a rail crew and bring them back to the Wisconsin Calumet Depot."

This was in contradiction with my plans. Maggie managed to sense my silent consternation.

"Hey, you'll be back in no time." She patted me on the shoulder. "I know those rail guys never tip, but it's easy money."

I forced myself to smile at her. "Thank you very much for this bountiful call. I shall return quickly to help you service all those downtown calls."

Maggie returned my smile, then left me to my bounty.

I lifted a spare tire into the trunk of my cab and tossed in a jack—both items required when we go out of town. Fortunately, this would be a short run. Likely, my prey had yet to rise, and they would most likely not commit any nefarious deeds until midnight, "the witching hour." Besides, the fare would run about $75 for doing nothing more than driving for an hour-and-a-half.

****

Upon returning to Madison, the call volume had reduced to a mere trickle, affording the opportunity to drop off the tire and jack. I went inside to wash the tire grime off my hands, then stepped into the dispatch office. Sharon, the dispatcher, was doodling on blank call slips. Maggie leaned back in her chair, smoking a cigarette, staring at a phone that just didn't want to ring.

"It has gotten very quiet," I said.

"Just the lull before the storm," Sharon replied.

"What was all the excitement about?" I asked.

Maggie extinguished her cigarette. "Some frat party, I think."

"Was it at Sigma Chi?" I asked.

"Beats me," Sharon said.

"Whatever's at two-twenty-one Langdon," Maggie said. "Had a bunch of U-Rides going there. Langdon Street, lakeshore dorms. All of 'em Buffys and Muffys."

A quick scan of the phone book confirmed the address of Sigma Chi as 221 Langdon.

"I saw the lights were on in the Waybill Office," I said. "Is anybody up there?"

Sharon glanced up from her doodling. "Dale's up there working on payroll. What's up?"

"I just remembered something. I need to check out something from a waybill about a week or two ago. If it gets busy, I will be up in the waybill office."

"Don't get lost up there," Sharon said. "Could get busy again soon."

With Dale's help, I first scanned the U-Ride call slips for my assignment from the previous night finding: U-Ride number 25. Origin, U-Square P.O. Destination, 221 Langdon.

I never had the opportunity to check on the woman. The nurses at the emergency room thanked me and said they would take care of her.

She appeared drunk, perhaps even suffering from alcohol poisoning. The fraternity boys acted drunk as well as stupid and truculent, just like normal college students—typical on the surface, but somehow I knew better.

I began sifting through waybills, struggling to remember the exact date when Truck had told the story about throwing a U-Ride passenger out of his cab, his words echoing inside my skull as he told the tale of the ill-tempered fellow accompanied by a woman he had described as "fucked up and glassy-eyed."

Without the exact date, the task proved difficult. It was time-consuming to find Truck's waybill and then his call slips, but eventually there was enough cross-referenced information to allow me to find the proper slip from the U-Ride bundles.

I found confirmation. *Destination: 221 Langdon.*

The sorority girl *had* said that drunk frat boys could be jerks, especially "Smegma Boys," even if they were good, decent people most of the rest of the time.

She said they could be "animals."

Maybe they were.

****

As they say, take the bull by the horns.

I drove uptown quickly, pulled up to the curb right in front of the fraternity house, then got out and walked up the front steps.

A UW football player stood blocking the door, an undersized Bucky Badger T-shirt stretched tightly across his bulging chest. He was built like an oak tree. He crossed his arms in front of his chest and stared at me.

I smiled meekly. "Did someone here call for a cab?"

"I don't know of nobody calling for no cab." The gentleman flexed his ample biceps and frowned.

"Maybe someone inside called." I took a step closer to the door.

"You ain't invited, you ain't going in."

I stepped back as the fellow flashed a draconian smile. A short, skinny fraternity fellow poked his head from behind the bouncer.

"Yeah, we didn't invite you, so you can just fuck off."

I smiled at the pair, then took a couple of steps back, flared my nostrils, opened my senses, but felt nothing unusual. I turned and returned to the cab, planning another route of access into the house. Suddenly, a scream sliced through the inside of my skull. A blood-curdling scream, not heard with my highly sensitive ears, but felt with my entire being, a genuine scream, full of real terror.

A blood-red swath obscured my sight. Then, I was mist, my consciousness following the resonating echo, the smell of blood, the hint of datura. I do not even remember first parking in a cab stand two blocks away and hitting the 10-7 button.

I rematerialized in darkness, thumping music pounding like heartbeats above my head. Corridors sliced through sticky darkness, thick with spiderwebs and dust which choked my nostrils. A door appeared just ahead, the bitter stench of datura hanging thickly in the air.

The door was locked. But by the blisters of Satan, no lock, no barricade, not even all the guardians of Hades would keep me out. With a swift kick, the thick door flew open, revealing the sight of the three fraternity brothers standing in a circle above their prey, none seeming to move or react to the intrusion.

They stood naked before an immense pentagram of blood painted on the mildewed wall, their voices merged in a single chant. Between them, a naked woman lay spread-eagled on the floor, manacles biting into her wrists and ankles, scratches and slices covering her chest, stomach and hips, her blood splattered all over her flesh, all over their bodies. An oversized ceramic phallus stood between her legs, mottled with blood.

This was not Dawn Stevens, just another random victim, glazed eyes staring at the ceiling. Another senseless killing—

—The woman blinked. Pricking my ears, I heard a faint heartbeat. A roar filled the basement room, a roar which came from my mouth, originating deep within my being. Their oblivion finally broken, the fraternity brothers finally turned, shocked at the violation of their sanctity. But only for a moment.

The tall, slender fellow charged. The others followed.

Back arched, hands clenched, flexing razor sharp claws, I growled, standing my ground as they struck, hurling me into a concrete wall, the sound of a half-dozen cracking ribs filling my ears.

With an irritating tingling, the ribs knitted themselves almost instantly. Before their next salvo, I threw myself at the tall, slender fellow.

My momentum flung us against the wall on the other side, the other fellow absorbing most of the impact. Ribs crackled like kindling. He fell stunned to the floor. I turned and faced his two companions.

"Hey, he can't fuck with us," the plump one shouted. "Bobo! You said we have the Gift of the Magi. You said no one can fuck with the Gift of the Magi. You said that."

Bobo responded not, but I did, leaping at the plump one. The scrawny gentleman stood paralyzed, unable to move as his brother got fucked with, as the Americans say, by some interloper who sank a grinning mouth into a jowly neck, jerked his head back and spat out half of a throat, letting the twitching body fall to the floor, blood squirting rhythmically from where the throat had been torn.

The short, scrawny fellow whimpered as he stumbled backward away from me. With relish, I matched each slow step, until something hit me from behind, sending me flying into the prey before me, the two of us crashing into a wall.

Icy droplets struck my neck. Twin pinpricks pressed against my throat. I reached back and blindly slapped at the space behind my head, boxing a pair of ears.

Bobo shrieked. I spun around and slashed his face, ripping off about half of one cheek. He yowled until a backhanded fist sent him spinning to the floor, silent for the moment.

I turned to find the scrawny one shaking his head, seeking to return to awareness. While he slapped weakly at my face and shoulders, I lifted him high in the air, slammed him to the floor next to Bobo, then took a high step and brought a heel down hard upon his neck.

The loud crackling of shattered vertebrae provoked a whimper from Bobo as he snapped back to awareness. Like a beached crustacean, he scuttled backward on his rear, until his back struck the opposite wall. Quickly, I dematerialized, then rematerialized, crouched on the floor, an arm wrapped tightly around his throat.

Full circle, a symmetry of existence. A thousand years ago, the fraternity brother was me, and I was Francçis, staring with contempt as an immature vampire begged for his life.

"Please," he whimpered.

"Monster!" I spat. My voice sounded low and gravelly, but as deeply buried as my consciousness was at that very moment, I knew that François had chosen to let me live because he knew most creatures are not inherently good or evil. Through instruction, the more primal urges can be sufficiently tempered.

"Why should I not destroy you?"

His eyes opened wide. "Money! I can get you money. Lots of money! My father's filthy rich! He can send you a check tomorrow. You're that cab driver. Say the word, and you won't have to drive a cab ever again."

Without a word, I pressed both hands against the sides of his head and slowly twisted, ignoring his screams, kneeling hard against his abdomen to keep his body still, twisting until bones crackled, snapped and flesh tore. The body slipped to the floor with a muffled thud, agitating dust into the air. A severed head sat in my hands, its lifeless eyes staring at me blankly, accusingly.

Three dead bodies littered the floor. Three more people dead at my hands. A shriek passed my lips as the events of the past few months passed kaleidoscope-like before my eyes.

Because death courses through my body, must death follow me every-where I travel? Must these hands take life when they could just as easily create rather than destroy?

The woman moaned, interrupting my musing. Quickly, I rushed to her side, finding her jugular with my fingers, searching for a pulse. Her heart continued to beat, weak but steady. Had she enough blood to live?

A single drop of blood struck my hand, falling from a small cut where Bobo had tried to rip open my neck. Blood. Life for the living. Life of a different variety, but life nonetheless. If I so chose, her existence could continue.

I made quick study of the woman, ripping open the manacles on her wrists and ankles. She reacted not. Dilated eyes stared at the ceiling, blinking rapidly, her breathing shallow.

Her blood-spattered flesh was pale, but her wounds were all superficial; no arteries were severed, and the punctures had all knit with coagulation.

They had tasted her, but had not yet taken her life's blood. She *would* live, but needed immediate medical attention. Before departing to notify the authorities, I surveyed the carnage left behind. Perhaps, François would have chosen this course of action. Or perhaps not. Perhaps, the opportunity will someday present itself where I can ask François what he would have done.

However, these concerns were quickly supplanted by some unfinished business. One question remained: Where *does* one buy powdered essence of datura at midnight in Madison?

****

You are indeed correct; the plump fellow had made reference to the "Gifts of the Magi," and yes, there was a store by that name a mere two blocks from my abode. The irony of this situation was hauntingly apparent: that I had scoured the entire city for vampires, only to find the source just under my nose at the Gifts of the Magi Occult Shoppe. Suddenly, it no longer seemed odd that the store was never open during the daylight—at least according to the sign in the front window.

At exactly midnight the next night, I paid a visit to the store, circumventing the front door and instead materializing in the rear, the stench of mildew nearly making me sneeze. I studied the books as I moved toward the front counter. They were mostly hardcovers with Latin titles.

The man at the sales desk looked up only when I stood in front of him. He was short and slight with long, thin, scraggly hair, a patchy beard and little round glasses. An ankh hung over his chest. The man looked about forty, but certainly this was unlikely.

"I want to buy some powdered essence of datura," I spat, staring malevolently at the shopkeeper.

He smiled, showing me the sharp points of his fangs; there was no need for deception at this point. "So you're the one who murdered my children," he said, his accent British, specifically from western England. "I've been expecting you."

"Murder, you say? I think not. It is certainly not murder to destroy rabid beasts."

"And I suppose you've come to destroy me as well?" He laughed heartily. "Perhaps you will find me a bit more formidable."

"I came to talk. To talk about responsibility—"

"I think you mean slavery. Responsibility? To who? Humans?"

"Did you not think it irresponsible to give such power to such vain, arrogant, immature creatures? They were a danger to us all."

His face pinched in disgust. "My children were glorious! True hunters in the way we were meant to be."

"Murderers!"

"Hunters, not murderers," the shopkeeper countered. "You, my good fellow, are pathetic. You're decadent. Are you forgetting what you are? We *are* superior. The humans should worship us. As in the old days."

"Humans have advanced far beyond that. They have evolved, while we merely fight extinction." François, after all, had predicted the Age of Reason centuries before it came to be —and was correct to foresee that it would provide a better world than the ignorant, superstitious one left behind.

"You just don't know what it's like being worshipped. A hundred and fifty years ago, *I* was worshipped. You can't know—"

Something within my mind clicked. "You're Cornish, aren't you?"

He nodded. "And you're Hungarian, just like Bela Lugosi. Quite the cliché, aren't you?"

A loud laugh exploded from deep within my gut. "The Cornish lead miners who settled Wisconsin, it was they who worshipped you, was it not? You are the original Bucky Badger! Were your ceremonial robes cardinal-red?"

Anger seethed from his pores at the mention of the ridiculously anthropomorphized weasel who functions as mascot for the University of Wisconsin athletic teams and is the emblem for the entire state of Wisconsin.

"They feared me, all right!" he roared, then calmed and shook his head condescendingly once again. "I can't believe what a pathetic excuse for a vampire you are." He shook his head in a contrived gesture of sadness. "Is this what the modern world has come to? Good God, man, you've got the noble blood of Isis and Osiris coursing through your body, yet you slink through the shadows, relying on rats and other vermin to satisfy your hunger. You're a coward, that's what you are. A coward!"

Why does my kind so often fall prey to the popular mythos of our origins? The truth is that not one of us has any idea how we came to be, though some like to invent such noble origins.

Without tensing, he raised his hands up to the counter, pushed down and leaped at me.

Bending my knees, I twisted away from the shopkeeper's lunge and shoved him hard as he passed. He crashed into a wall. I spun and slammed the back of my fist against the man's jaw. He kicked upward blindly, connecting squarely with my chest, staggering me. A breath brought a sliver of pain. The kick had caused a hairline fracture of my breastbone, which might split in two pieces if he connected again before the bone repaired itself.

The shopkeeper leaped to his feet, feinted with an elbow to the head, then came underneath. A fist pounded my sternum. A foot struck the back of one of my heels. I toppled backward, pain slivers transformed to razor-sharp shards. The shopkeeper jumped on top of me, pressing against my torso with all his weight. An edge of my sternum pressed against my lungs. My mouth filled with the salty taste of my own blood.

Razor-sharp fangs lowered toward my jugular, eyes glowing obsidian, surprisingly strong arms pinning my shoulders and arms to the floor.

A shock of realization washed over me. One thousand years of existence would end here because overwhelming pain obscured my ability to muster enough concentration to turn to mist and escape his grasp. Given just a short interim, the injury would heal enough for me to escape, but time was a luxury; the shopkeeper bent down for the kill.

No! The mind can think. The mind can reason. The mind can sift for possibilities, even when none seem apparent. Despite the fire burning in my chest, despite the utterly hideous sensation of bone knitting back together, an idea came to mind. For a very short moment, I pushed futilely against his grasp with all my might, then relaxed, giving up any semblance of struggle.

With a harsh cough, a bubble of blood formed on my lips. I allowed my face to contort into a look of fear, conceding defeat, showing him resignation, hoping he would take the opportunity to savor his victory.

My attacker's smile broadened. His descent stopped. Yes, he was enjoying my defeat, tasting my apparent fear, savoring this unique moment, obviously knowing that the longer he waited, the sweeter my blood would be.

Twin droplets of icy saliva struck my neck. A whimper passed my lips. I shut my eyes. From somewhere far away, he laughed.

Shards dulled to splinters as fangs pressed against my throat. I took a deep breath, imagined myself standing straight and erect—

—and rematerialized standing above the shopkeeper who lay on his stomach kissing the floor. I kicked him square in the face, reached down, lifted him by the shoulders and flung him at the sales desk.

I watched the man crash, then lunged at him, grabbed his collar, lifted him to his feet and smashed his face against the counter-top. The thick glass cracked internally, spider-web fractures spreading instantly across the pane.

My fangs sank into the man's throat. Almost immediately, I felt revitalized. I drank deeply of his hot, angry blood, stopping just before another gulp would completely drain him. I lifted him upward, then dropped him to the floor, smiling, savoring the rare taste of vampire blood; it provided extra sustenance for me, but the shopkeeper would be helpless without an immediate infusion of our special nectar. He lay motionless, staring up at me, glassy eyes full of fear.

I pointed toward the front windows. "Eastern exposure? The sunrise must be stunning through these windows."

Sluggish eyes snapped wide open. I walked around to the back of the sales desk and shoved it until it toppled over him. Shards of broken glass spread across the floor. I raised the window shades, flipped the open/closed sign to closed, locked the front door and flicked off the lights.

"You know," I said, "as vampires get older, they are better able to tolerate sunlight. But the dawn's first light is always the most dangerous."

The shopkeeper stared up at me, hopelessly pinned, too weak to even reply with word or thought. I walked back toward the rear of the store, then turned as if I had forgotten something.

"They say," I added, almost as an afterthought, "that a vampire who survives the first two hundred years will probably live forever."

****

The parade of spring flowers eventually ended. A canopy of emerald enveloped the city only to be replaced by crimson and umber as trees drooped from the weight of all their fruit, which finally fell to the ground, summoned by the gravity of eventuality.

The gravity of eventuality. I attempted to comfort myself with this notion of what will be, what will transpire. The humans have this queer notion of "normal," but what is normal for me is certainly far from normal for humans. It seemed that perhaps the gravity of eventuality is a law of nature, meaning that normal events will happen to those who are normal, and abnormal events will thus happen to those who are not normal in the sense that normal people are normal. One must understand and accept this in order to find the inner peace necessary to be able to adapt and adjust to an ever-changing world.

Utterly simplistic, you say? Yes, but what else was there to do but seek solace in philosophy? To adapt and adjust may sound simple, but to do so is actually quite a difficult task.

And how did I adapt and adjust? Perhaps I did neither. Perhaps the greatest solace came as the Cab Gods looked out for me, providing enough bounty even during the summer to allow me to save at least $500 per month.

Shortly, the strange case of the Madison Mangler was closed. That last victim did indeed survive. Apparently, the tale she told the authorities of her abduction and rescue satisfied them enough for them to believe that the Madison Mangler would take no more victims, though the mystery as to who had come to her aid and killed her tormentors would remain. A week later, they found the body of Dawn Stevens, mutilated, drained of blood and dead, for several weeks. After that, no more bodies were found, nor were there any more reports of missing persons that would cause them to reopen the case.

Days later, the Sigma Chi house was burned to the ground.

My first anniversary at Co-op Cab approached. The leaves had once again been ripped from the trees by the angry November winds, puffed up in pride over their victory in the annual battle of climatic supremacy against summer. All life began that process of curling up and dying. Still, comfort and inspiration came to me at this time.

One night while sitting at the Concourse stand, reading the *Wall Street Journal*, trying to decide upon a good mutual fund in which to invest my first full year's patronage dividend check, I reflected upon a call that had come up earlier at the U-Square PO. Immediately following my arrival, three men and a woman had approached the cab.

"Damn," I said under my breath. This ironic déjà vu was certainly not lost upon me. They opened the doors and climbed inside.

"I am sorry," I said, "but U-Rides are allowed only for parties of three or less. Some of you may ride. Those who remain are welcome to call U-Ride for another cab, but I cannot take all four of you at once."

There was a moment of silence. Finally, the men climbed out of the cab.

"Hey, that's okay," one said. "Take her home. We'll just walk."

"You sure that's okay?" the woman said.

"No problem," another man said. "You take the ride. We can walk."

The men began walking away from the cab. One broke from the group and approached me.

"You make sure she gets home safe," he said through the open window.

"That is what we do," I replied with a smile. The man smiled back. A cool breeze gusted through the cab.

"Seventy," Dexter's voice crackled, interrupting my contemplation. "There's a telegram waiting for you at your office. Just arrived."

"A telegram?" I answered, wondering who might send me a telegram. "Do you know from whom this telegram is?"

"Yeah," Dexter replied. "Some guy named Bob Johnson."

That could mean only one thing. In his last letter, my former aide-de-camp had said he had actually found some promising leads regarding the whereabouts of a certain Jenkins fellow. The previous memory immediately faded, replaced by images of restored fortunes and sweet, sweet revenge.

Chapter 18
FULL CIRCLE

Jenkins found. See the Bruja, Catemaco, Mexico.

The terse message quickly obscured all other concerns, etching its way into my memory, the telegram read and read again until the paper, through excessive handling, grew to resemble parchment.

Suddenly, the sparseness of my drab abode became all too apparent. No longer could its shortcomings be obscured through a conscious lapse of attention to these details.

But no longer!

My bed would be the most exquisite carved mahogany, the mattress like clouds, the sheets the finest Chinese silk money could buy. The splendor of my new abode would be such as to dazzle even the most jaded of aristocrats.

After departing work, I returned to this temporary home, listened to a scratchy recording of Rossini and studied the atlas, closing my eyes, imagining where next I would call home.

I *would* have my revenge. After retrieving my fortune, Jenkins would watch in horror as his skin was peeled off his quivering skeleton, his chest ever so slowly torn open, his heart ripped from his chest, his lifeblood squeezed into my mouth from a heart beating its last.

I located Catemaco in my atlas as the Italian maestro reached a stunning crescendo. Yes, this tiny pueblo on the Gulf of Mexico, just south of Vera Cruz, seemed perhaps a good place to lose oneself; Jenkins would never suspect what visitor he was about to entertain.

It seemed an easy task, thanks to the typically excellent and thorough job by my former aide-de-camp, Bob Johnson. Simply travel to this quaint little pueblo and seek out the local witch doctor, who would direct me to my quarry. Travel expenses would eat up much of my savings, but this seemed quite a clever investment. Quite clever indeed.

****

I had been too long away from the tropics, too long exiled in the deadly silent, lifeless wasteland called Wisconsin. Strolling through the jungle surrounding Catemaco, jolts of electricity coursed through my body, the sweet scent of enormous flowers wafting into my nostrils, along with the musk of all that hidden life. A jaguar screeched, monkeys shrieked, macaws squawked, toads croaked and a thousand insects clicked, chirped and whistled. This symphony of life filled me with the indescribable vitality of all of that impending essence out there just for the taking.

With my first step inside Catemaco, my boot sank into the mud of what was considered a street, a waterlogged quagmire in a place that apparently possessed no knowledge of cement, asphalt or even gravel. Six blocks was the total extent of the village. Above, a lone electrical cable snaked from one end of the pueblo to the other, satisfying Catemaco's modest desires for power, a strong contrast to the insatiable hunger back in the United States. There, high tension wires connect the vast gulfs separating communities, mounted upon those ubiquitous steel structures so much like those used to execute the poor souls crucified in ancient Rome. This procession, leading from community to community, has always reminded me of the accounts of how the Romans had lined the entire Appian Way with crucified followers of Spartacus.

Darkness had descended prior to my arrival. Most of the inhabitants seemed to have retreated into their modest *casas,* built from sun-hardened mud or sod, roofed with tin or palm thatching, the occasional corrugated-steel abode a sign of wealth and status.

A loud crash drew my attention to a nearby *cantina*. Silence, then a shouted exchange: one low, gravelly voice, *"Pindejo!"* and a high-pitched reply, *"Chinga tu madre,"* then a cacophony of smashing furniture and broken glass, which would undoubtedly lead to the spilling of blood.

Blood *would* be spilled tonight, but not only that of these peasants, fighting over insignificant insults that would surely be forgotten on the morrow. Blood would be spilled because of this insult to me: that someone in my employ could take my fortune, rob me of my livelihood and force me to serve others like a common mortal.

The sounds of the fight inside the *cantina* faded from my hearing as I focused on the sounds from the jungle creatures rising in the night, fighting their ongoing battle to survive, killing merely because it is what they do.

Ahead stood the Catemaco's only church, its spire majestically piercing the blackness of night. The Catholic church was my marker, for so often the *bruja* lives next to the church, being a religious as well as a medical leader in any given community.

Even without seeing the church, the bitter scent of datura along with the smell of garlic and a dozen powerful herbs said the lovely *hacienda* next to the church was the place I sought. An immense shrub bearing several brilliant white-trumpeted flowers of datura sat before the abode. I smiled ironically at how beautiful the flowers were, yet how badly the drug had been misused by those unfortunate miscreants. Surely they would exist today had they been instructed by this *bruja* instead of that dangerously deluded vampire whom they had called father.

This was not a rich person's *hacienda,* but with its stucco sides, corrugated steel roof and the shiny propane stove in front, it looked like the home of one well-off.

The town *bruja* would be well off. Her skills would be appreciated by the community. Her wisdom would bring gifts of gratitude. I carried a pocketful of coins, which I hoped would be sufficient compensation for the information she would provide.

I walked through the open doorway and crossed the threshold of her home as the pleasing aroma of all those herbs entered my nostrils. I looked up at the ceiling and was amazed by the collection: cloves of garlic, fresh cinnamon, parsley, basil, oleander, more datura, sacks of rice, sacks of beans and large bunches of bananas.

The room was dark, except for a lone kerosene lamp and three candles. I took a few steps toward a figure sitting motionless in a tall wicker chair in the deepest corner of the room, but was intercepted by a plump woman wearing a lovely embroidered dress, her long black hair coiled in a bun, bright red lipstick and blue eye shadow clearly visible in the flickering candlelight.

Just short of an arm's length away, the woman stopped, her expression shifting from astonished to frightened, the steadiness and relative grace of her bearing transformed to twitchy nervousness.

"*Diablo!*" the woman exclaimed. "*Ay! Maria, está aqui un hombre del Diablo!*"

"*Claro,*" replied a serene voice from the darkness. "*Nos vemos mañana, Leta.*"

The plump woman crossed herself and quickly left the *hacienda*. A bony shape, draped in fabric, rose from the chair, using a cane for aid. Once standing, she stood tall and straight, the candlelight illuminating a face deeply creased and craggy. She was very old, yet the long hair hanging loosely about her shoulders was black, marred not by even a single gray hair. She wore a light green dress, covered with many kinds of birds embroidered in bright red, blue and yellow thread. A pair of large gold hoops dangled from her ear lobes, and a thick silver crucifix hung from her neck. Like her assistant, she wore bright red lipstick and blue eyeshadow.

I stood motionless as she moved toward me, her eyes studying me, peering into me, her expression that of earnest curiosity.

"*¿Diablo?*" she asked calmly.

I shook my head.

"Not human," she replied in Spanish.

"Certainly not. But not a threat."

She continued to meet my eyes with a steely gaze. "That I can see. Not a threat, but exceptional. You honor me with your presence. Why have you come?"

"Information. I am looking for a man."

"Does a man really matter to you? *Can* a man matter to you?"

"This one does."

"You seek the gringo who lives on the other side of Vulcan San Martin, do you not?"

"I seek an American, but I do not know his exact whereabouts. How is it you know whom I seek?"

She smiled broadly, showing perfect white teeth. "All of you from el Norte, you are only concerned with yourselves. We concern you not at all. When the gringo arrived seeking solitude, I knew another would follow, seeking him."

"Will you tell me how to find him?"

With a nod, she took my arm and led me toward the door. The *bruja* pointed upward with her cane. Ahead, under a nearly full moon, loomed the silhouette of a small volcano.

"Directly on the other side, on the beach, nearly on the ocean. That is where the man you seek lives. That is where he seeks death."

"*¿Que?*"

"You seek retribution, but he seeks death. They bring him mezcal every day, and he finishes all that they bring." Her voice raised a decibel. "They laugh and bring more than the day before. He pays gladly and drinks all that they bring."

"I merely seek satisfaction, *señora*." Satisfaction indeed! Hopefully, he had not squandered my entire fortune on cheap liquor.

"I wish you good luck in finding it." She turned away then faced me again, a certain sadness in her eyes. I reached into my pockets for the coins within, hoping the offer would not be insulting. Seeing what I was doing, she shook a hand in protest. "*Por favor, señor.*"

"But I wish to give you something."

She shook her head. "Come and honor me with your presence again. There is likely much I could learn from one such as you."

I left knowing the same was true about her.

✳✳✳✳

With a shrieking snarl, the jaguar leaped from the darkness. Splintered moonlight flickered off protruding claws and bared fangs, at the last moment betraying the cat's attack, which had been so cleverly masked by the shifting wind. The hunted had become the hunter.

The cat struck me hard in the chest, knocking me to the earth. Claws ripped fabric. Flesh tore. A paw raised, poised to finish me off with a hard strike to my throat, but a quickly-thrust forearm deflected the cat's blow.

Taking advantage of the jaguar's momentary loss of balance and summoning all my strength, I flipped the cat onto its back, plunged fangs into its muscular neck and drank of its blood, not stopping until my stomach was full, and the jaguar lay on the jungle floor, now food for the local carrion beasts.

By the time I reached Jenkins's home at the beach, my wounds had healed, the flesh underneath the torn fabric completely unmarred.

The house was the lone structure on the beach, its deplorable condition a blight on the beauty of this place. Had Jenkins no shame? Refuse surrounded the modest house, its clapboard sides patched with crates, pieces of driftwood, and strips of cardboard. A pile of debris sat alongside the building, waiting to be used to repair the many remaining holes.

Jenkins sat before the ramshackle structure in a weathered wooden chair, staring at the crests of moonlight-dappled waves as they rose and broke at the shore, the salty mist blown inland by a soft breeze. A semicircle of empty liquor bottles surrounded him.

Long moments passed as I watched this corpulent, pathetic lump of flesh. Even from a distance, he reeked of cheap mezcal, tobacco and sweat, fresh and stale. Though Jenkins's heartbeat echoed loudly inside my skull, my observation remained unnoticed. Despite my recent meal, hunger welled inside me, but I willed my fangs to stay within their enamel housings—for now.

He took a swig directly from a bottle, burped then finally turned toward me. "Mister Farkas," he said, his tone flat but his enunciation surprisingly clear, "I knew someone'd find me. Didn't think it'd be you, doing your own dirty work."

I moved toward him, anger welling inside me at the utter flippancy of his manner. Standing over him, blocking his view of the crashing waves, I peered inside the small structure. The floor was dirt, and there was no furniture save a soiled mattress and a square enamel table standing valiantly on three legs. "My money, Jenkins. I have come for that which you stole from me."

He laughed. "And I thought you were here to kill me."

It was my turn to laugh. "Do not worry. I shall not disappoint you. But first, my money."

Jenkins shrugged his shoulders, his lips forming an innocent smile. "Sorry. Money's gone."

"What do you mean, gone!?" Angry red lightning flashed before my eyes, then I was straddling his knees, lifting Jenkins to his feet, my mouth wide open, fangs dropping into place. He stared at me, his eyes still barely slits.

"What kind of creature are you?" he asked, his tone surprisingly bland.

"As you Americans are so fond of saying, I am your worst bad dream."

He laughed again, flooding me with his foul breath. "I think you mean to say, 'I'm your worst nightmare.'" His laughter resumed and would not stop.

"Silence," I commanded. "You will cease that infernal laughter and tell me where my money is."

"What's the matter, Al? You pissed 'cause I'm not scared enough? Sorry to disappoint you. I'm probably too drunk to be very scared."

"I simply want my money."

"I don't have your goddamned money." He paused, studying my features closely, his expression that of curiosity, not fear. "Seen 'lotta strange things since coming down here. My old boss being a vampire don't really surprise me."

The fingers gripping his collar loosened, and Jenkins dropped back into his seat, his bulk causing the wood to creak, buckle and nearly break. I stared down at him, feeling my eyes burning into his. "Then, it should not surprise you that I am a creature capable of flaying you alive. Ever so slowly and painfully peeling flesh from bone. Opening your chest and ripping out your still-beating heart. So I ask you again: where is my money?"

His laughter resumed, and it took great discipline not to tear open his throat right then and there.

"Go ahead, Farkas," Jenkins said blandly. "Kill me. I don't care anymore. A visit from a killer. Fine by me. I don't wanna live anymore."

"I am not a killer," I replied, still straddling his knees.

"That so?" Jenkins smiled broadly, studying my face for some kind of reaction. "I thought vampires were killers. Ain't that how you eat?"

"Too much Hollywood. Some vampires are killers. I am not."

"But you're gonna kill me. Kinda makes *you* a killer, don't it?"

He was distracting me. "My money, Jenkins!" I slapped him hard across the face. "Where is my money?"

Jenkins flinched not at all. He must have been very drunk. "How do you rationalize that kind of thinking, Farkas? Saying you're not a killer when you're here to kill me. Makes you a killer, doesn't it." This time, not a question at all, but an accusation.

I took one short step backward. "The issue here is not sophistry, Jenkins. The issue is my money and where it is and how you will return it to me."

"Tell you what. Show me yours, and I'll show you mine. Answer my question, and I'll tell you about your money."

This was getting most tiresome, but patience was necessary because Jenkins could provide no answers after I had killed him. "Very well, Jenkins. Ask me your question."

He grinned, almost childishly. "You say you're not a killer, but don't you kill when you eat?"

"No. I take what I need and no more. Those I take from are left relatively unharmed."

He rubbed his chin and stared thoughtfully toward the beach. "You're here to kill me, but you claim you're not a killer. Kill anybody else recently?"

Blood spilled across the canvas of my inner sight. Frank Nelson, Bobo, his brothers, their father. Motherless spawn of Satan! These hands had killed *five* beings in the past year? *Five?* The necessity to kill had not made itself apparent for forty years and now—

"Yes," was my only reply.

"But you're not a killer."

"They deserved to die. One was—"

"Deserved?"

"Do not interrupt. One was self-defense—a mortal—the other four were vampires whom I killed to keep them from killing mortals."

"Hmmm," Jenkins replied. "Justifiable, I'll give you that, but what gives you the right to make that kind of decision?"

"Jenkins, confusing the issue with sophistry merely serves to prolong your pathetic existence."

"Yeah, okay, maybe. But you're here to kill me, and that's just for revenge, no other reason. How can you kill me and not be a killer?"

"I kill only when necessary. Killers kill indiscriminately."

He smiled, and I realized that he had backed me into an untenable position in this debate. "You don't have to kill me. Killing me don't mean anything one way or the other."

An inhuman growl escaped my throat. Jenkins cowered visibly. "I have answered your question to the best of my ability. Now, where is my money?"

"Like I been trying to tell you, your money's gone. Like, poof! Gone." He threw his hands up in the air, seeming to take strength from this cavalier gesture.

My mouth opened in a feral smile. Fingers clenched, fangs wanting satisfaction. Blood filled my sight. Jenkins's beating heart pounded loudly. To Hades with the money! I wanted his blood, wanted to rip into his flesh, imagined his heart warm and still beating, could see the steam as hot blood struck my cold tongue, could feel his blood gushing down my throat.

I exhaled loudly through my mouth, fighting for control. Only through patience and discipline would my money be returned. "Please, Mister Jenkins," I said, with almost no animation, "tell me exactly what happened."

He paused a moment, well aware that his life would continue for at least a little while longer, knowing it had almost ended just then. He smiled. "You never should have hired me, Farkas. I'm a pretty lousy financier. I did as bad a job on my own portfolio as yours. Got too greedy. Didn't feel like I could ever have enough money. Made some really stupid investments. Managed to piss away most of what I stole, and that was only the half of it."

"Yes."

"Well, I tell you, it's pretty hard to embezzle a lotta of money. Every monetary transfer caught someone's attention. There was always somebody wanting a cut. And, on top of that, being on the run, always having to look over my shoulder 'cause I knew you'd be after me, well, people can sense that. Everywhere I went, there was always somebody with a hand out. I'm sicka running. I've got about a hundred thou left, so here I am, last stop, end of the line. Since the day I got here, I knew I would die right on this beach. Today's as good a day as any."

He lit a cigarette, took a long sip from the nearest bottle and stared wistfully at the surf. Waiting for me to kill him, undoubtedly. Our eyes met, and his dull, bloodshot orbs did not flinch at my gaze. Then, they disappeared, replaced by golden, feral eyes with a bloated oval moon of black. Those eyes slowly glazed over, the bloated oval closing to a mere sliver, as if forced shut by a blinding light as darkness descended.

I had killed the jaguar. Killed it! How could I have killed that magnificent predator? How could I have shown it such contempt when it served no purpose to do so? And this wretch, this swine, this bloated mass of decaying flesh was absolutely correct. How could I kill him out of revenge and not be a killer? Had I not long evolved from that to a state able to kill when only absolutely necessary?

My gaze broke away from his, but from the corner of my eye, I could see that he continued to stare forward, as if my eyes still fixed upon his. "Have you no interest," I said, facing him once again, "in hearing how I managed without a fortune?"

Jenkins laughed and took another sip from his bottle. "Sure, what the hell. Had to get a job, right?"

"Precisely, I moved to Madison, Wisconsin and secured employment with a worker-owned-and-operated taxi company."

Jenkins howled with laughter. "Al Farkas, vampire cabbie. Hauling students?" He interrupted himself with his own laughter.

"It really was not such a horrible thing."

"Why should it? Hell, nothing wrong with working for a living. Most people do it, you know. 'Sides, Madison's a great town."

"There is certainly nothing wrong with working. Maybe I had forgotten, but now I know it for sure."

"Tell me all about it." Jenkins leaned forward, opened another bottle and lit fresh cigarette.

"I shall spare your pitiful life. In exchange, you may be my audience, my confessor even." I took a seat on the sand in front of Jenkins, pausing to listen to the crashing waves, to enjoy the salty scent of sea breeze. It seemed amazing that this had begun only a year ago. In an existence where a century feels like yesterday, where a decade feels like a mere moment, what is one year?

"Well," I began, "I might tell you that the story begins in Paris. Or maybe it might be more accurate to say the story really begins in the Black Forest of Germany. Or maybe the story begins simultaneously in both places."

www.ingramcontent.com/pod-product-compliance
Lightning Source LLC
Chambersburg PA
CBHW050559260626
47157CB00002B/625